THE LEGEND BEGINS

Copyright © 2012 by Charles & Irene Nickerson.

Library of Congress Control Number: 2012917539
ISBN: Hardcover   978-1-4797-2035-4
                Softcover   978-1-4797-2034-7
                Ebook   978-1-4797-2036-1

All rights reserved. No part of this book may be reproduced or transmitted in any form or by any means, electronic or mechanical, including photocopying, recording, or by any information storage and retrieval system, without permission in writing from the copyright owner.

This is a work of fiction. Names, characters, places and incidents either are the product of the author's imagination or are used fictitiously, and any resemblance to any actual persons, living or dead, events, or locales is entirely coincidental.

This book was printed in the United States of America.

To order additional copies of this book, contact:
Xlibris Corporation
1-888-795-4274
www.Xlibris.com
Orders@Xlibris.com
121830

Contents

Acknowledgments 7
Prologue 9

Chapter 1	New Beginnings, Old Secrets	11
Chapter 2	The Story of the Ghost Revealed	21
Chapter 3	Into the Mix	30
Chapter 4	Carnise Asteroid Drift	35
Chapter 5	Hit and Run Like Hell Gunfight at Carnise Drift	47
Chapter 6	Destroyer vs. Destroyer	54
Chapter 7	The next move	64
Chapter 8	Carnise Drift and Beyond	72
Chapter 9	Dead Ships, Ghosts, and Projects	80
Chapter 10	Reports, Doubts, and Long Hours	87
Chapter 11	Calls Home, Calls for Help	96
Chapter 12	Dryden the Forest Moon	105
Chapter 13	Long nights, Hard Flights	126
Chapter 14	Into The Belly of the Beast	142
Chapter 15	A Few Day of Rest and Relaxation	150
Chapter 16	The Calm before the Storm	172
Charter 17	Storm Warnings	189
Chapter 18	First strike	196
Chapter 19	A Moment of Peace	211
Chapter 20	Storm Clouds Gathering	226
Chapter 21	The Storm Hits!	264
Chapter 22	Home Comings	300
Chapter 23	Epilogue	346

Main Characters 349
Terms 357

Acknowledgments

First I want to thank my daughter who helped write important parts of this story or helped clarify ideas.

The cover art is by Sammy Montgomery a talented young artist.

My mother, Wife, Amy and Rosie Balvanz, and Hope Navin who helped review this book.

Most importantly the Creator of the Universe and his son Jesus with whom all things are possible.

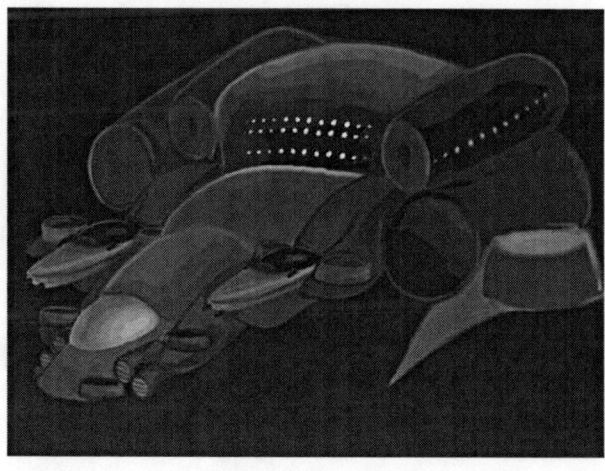

Charles L. Nickerson

Prologue

Our story begins in a star cluster in the Milky Way Galaxy. It is at the junction of three groups, the Bearilian Federation, the Antillean Confederation, and the Arcrilian Star System.

The Antilleans and the Bearilians have fought a losing battle against the Arcrilians who conquer planetary systems and then use their Hive ships to strip them of their natural resources leaving barren and scarred planets, just as locust do on earth.

Over the last 1000 years the Bearilians have evacuated the planets being attacked and retreated or abandoned the systems the Arcrilians attacked. One system that was affected was the Vandar system and the planet Andreas Prime, which was the home of the Ursa Maxmimus clans.

The Ursa Maxmimus resemble the ancient giant ground sloths of Earth. When Andreas Prime was attacked its Clans evacuated. Out of 120 Clans only 40 survived. The only Survivor of the Royal Family was Princes Maria Caesar. Her rescue pod was picked up by other survivors of the ambushed evacuation fleet.

Other Bearilians resemble other Bears of Earth. The Bearilian Federation consists of 15 Star Systems located in the same spiral arm as the Earth and its Solar System but closer to the Center of the Milky Way Galaxy.

Chapter 1

New Beginnings, Old Secrets

 Beary looked around at the other Bearilian Astrofleet Cadets in his group, all were first year cadets and represented a cross section of the Bearilian race. Beary and one other were of the Ursa Maxmimus race that resembled giant ground sloths on Earth. The other eight were; three Kodacians, with their massive paws and four Sunnarians and a Polarian. The young Polarian stood out with his white fur and his blood red uniform of a Bearilian Marine officer candidate. The Sunnarians were smaller than the other cadets but were known for their quick analytical minds and language skills. Some of the best communication officers and navigators in the fleet were Sunnarians.

 Beary's attention turned back to the other cadet of his race. Though he seemed familiar Beary wasn't sure. He didn't recognize the family crest the other cadet wore on his wrist. There were maybe 40 families left of their race. Not that the families were small and some families had split recently to form new lines. Still he hoped to talk to the other cadet.

 Beary's eyes soon diverted to the ship they were approaching it was a new fast destroyer The *BAF Saber Claw*. Her design was built around her newly conceived VALLEN/ MAXUMUS CX engines. Beary quietly smiled to himself and prayed he wouldn't be put in engineering. A first year cadet isn't supposed to understand the delicate working of a high speed warp engine especially one that was first tested just three years before. But Dr. Vallen had insisted on adding Beary's name to the engine he had helped design.

Beary thought about his application to the Academy he hadn't lied, he had just failed to mention that he already had two PhD's by the age of 15 one in Astrophysics and the other in Warp Engineering. Besides, he was pursuing a new degree at the Academy. The fact that for the last three years he had been part of an elite Marine unit as a corporal didn't need to come up because it had been highly classified so at 18 he was just another cadet. He figured that his secrets were safe. After all, what could go wrong? Over the next few weeks he was going to find out just how quickly secrets can become known.

The shuttle finally docked with the Saber Claw. The 10 cadets disembarked from the shuttle and were met by the First Officer Commander Jax Centaures. The First Officer was an Ursa Euarctos; while he was smaller than five of the cadets he addressed. Beary could see the power in his shoulders and realized that the Commander was a powerful warrior. He greeted them and then started giving out their assignments. The Polarian Marine was assigned to security. The Sunnarians were split between communications and navigation. The three Kodacians were assigned to weapons control. The other Ursa Maxmimus, whom Beary learned was named Caesar Vantanus, was assigned to the medical section. Beary wondered why the name seemed familiar.

Then Commander Centaures looked at Beary's name, "Cadet Maxumus you will be assigned to engineering." He looked at Beary very closely, and then shrugged his shoulders. He then told them to report to the ship's gymnasium. Beary shook his head. This was not good.

When they arrived at the gymnasium Beary's heart sank standing at the other end of the room was Master Chief

Gunnery Sergeant Grizlarge. The Chief quickly explained that these young cadets were being sent to him to learn how to defend themselves and this ship. After he was done he told them to report to their berthing assignments and to get squared away.

As they were filing out the Chief said "Cadet Maxumus would you stay for a moment." In a quiet voice he asked "Cub, what by the Moons of Bantine are you doing here?" Beary explained the situation and then asked "Gunny please don't say anything. I just want to be another cadet."

"What assignment did they give you, Cub?" the Gunny asked.

Beary lowered his head and said, "Engineering in the engine room"

The Gunny roared with laughter, "Well, at least if they mess-up the engine you can fix it." Then the Gunny got serious "Cub you need to know your secret won't survive this cruise. We are going on patrol and your skills may be needed. I will tell the Captain and the First only if it is necessary. But don't worry the Captain is as fair as they come and a good leader. You had better go to your quarters and get some rest. Tomorrow it all begins. Cub may The Creator go with you."

With that, Beary saluted his friend and started for his assigned quarters.

When he arrived at his quarters, Caesar Vantanus greeted him. "Hail, Beary son of Octavious by Angelina."

Beary looked at him, "How do you know my family?"

Caesar laughed, "My family name is Vantorious. My father is Servitous and my mother is Candas. We have not seen each other for several years."

Beary said, "I know your family. But you go by Vantanus?"

"As you know, I am the Seventh Son of twelve my father asked me to start a new line. It is a great honor." Caesar said. "Your mother, Angelina, helped me get through medical school and your father got me an appointment to the Academy." Beary was listening when he noticed another Bearilian in the room.

The Young Polarian Marine cadet looked at him and asked, "You are Beary Maxumus son of Senator Octavious Maxumus?"

Beary looked at him and nodded his head.

At that the young Marine leaped down from his bunk pulled his dagger and landed on one knee in front of Beary. He held the hilt of his dagger up to Berry and lowered his head.

"What are you doing?" Beary asked.

The young Polarian lowered his head more. "Master, I owe you my life and I pledge myself to you."

Beary shook his head. "What are you talking about? I am no one's master! I am just another cadet."

The Polarian raised his head. "Sire, I am Ben Maritinus. I am the brother of Captain Dontanus Maritinus. You saved him on Pratis V. You also destroyed the Arcrilian outpost on the planet."

Beary said, "My friend please, I was just one lowly marine. It was Chief Gunny Sergeant Grizlarge that led the rescue. So you see it was the unit not me that rescued your brother and his men." Beary lifted him up off his knee and looked into his eyes. "Please, if you will just offer me your paw in friendship and no more. Except, please, you both know secrets that I have tried to maintain." Caesar and Ben both looked at him. Beary sat down. "Don't you see I never told anyone who my father is? I haven't told anyone about being in the Marines, or about the fact I designed the engine that drives this starship. If they knew, I would be treated differently. All I want is to be a regular cadet. Can you understand?"

Caesar spoke first, "Beary, I understand. But you cannot hide from who you are. Already, three bears on this ship know who you are. I will keep your secret because we are connected through our families. Yet, I do not see your secrets surviving." He thought for a moment and laughed, "How are you, going to stand there and listen to someone telling you, about your engine with a straight face. If something goes wrong are you going to be able to stand by and do nothing? I think not! You are a Maxumus; your family has never been able just to standby. Yet I will abide by your wishes."

Ben spoke next, "I do not understand? You are a hero to my clan for what you did, yet you ask for nothing but my friendship.

I also will keep your secret. I agree though with Vantanus. You cannot hope to escape yourself. Secrets will not last once thing go south. Where we are going on this cruise they will."

Beary and Caesar stared at him. "Where are we going?"

"Did you not hear? We are going to the Tarsus' system. Some Freighters have disappeared there. We are being sent to investigate." Ben told them.

After a few moments, the three quietly squared away their room. After a few words they turned in. The next morning they awoke early dressed and reported to their duty assignments.

Beary reported to engineering. There he met Chief Engineer Jovious Tantous.

The Chief Engineer glanced at Beary. "Cadet Maxumus, you will spend the next few days familiarizing yourself with this ship's procedure. Under no circumstances are you to touch any part of this engine without proper supervision."

"Yes, Lt. Commander." Beary responded.

"Cadet," Lt. Commander Tantous asked "are you related to the co—designer of this engine?"

Beary pondered the question. Technically he was not related to himself. "No, Sir, I am not related to its designer."

With that the Chief Engineer told everyone to begin preparing for engine start-up.

Beary was taking it all in going over the startup procedure in his mind and trying to stay out of the way as he had been ordered to do. That's when he noticed a Moonarian technician go into the plasma injector control space. As he watched the Moonarian took the C3A plasma control circuit out and as he did, he seemed to shimmer and briefly turn green.

Beary tried to get Lt. Commander Tantous attention but he was waved off. He thought very quickly and hit the red button on his watch and sent a message to Chief Gunnery Sergeant Grizlarge. "Possible intruder in Engineering, I believe it is a Chameleon."

The Chief read the message, grabbed a weapons belt, and headed for engineering. Along the way he told two security personnel to follow him.

The Intruder started to move toward the exit but found his way blocked by other technicians realizing that avenue of escape was no longer available; in the time left he started moving in the direction of the cargo transporter at the rear of engineering.

Beary, realizing his intent moved to block his way.

The Chameleon realized he had been discovered and reached into his pocket for a neutronic grenade.

Sensing what was happening; Beary pulled his dagger and threw it in one fluid motion. The blade struck the Chameleon in the throat severing its spinal cord between the third and fourth vertebrae. Upon dying the Chameleon changed into his true lizard form.

It was then that the warning bells started going off. Technicians scrambled to check their boards to try and figure out what was going on. Beary saw that the Ch3 Control panel was unoccupied. He jumped up to it entered his own command code isolated the C3A Plasma injector and dumped the built-up plasma out the emergency plasma ports and started a controlled shut down of the engine.

While this was going on, Chief Grizlarge arrived and saw the grenade still in the hand of the now dead Chameleon. He drew his own dagger, severed the hand that held the grenade, raced to the transporter, and beamed both hand and grenade into space. When they rematerialized the grenade separated from the severed hand and exploded harmlessly in space.

Lt. Commander Tantous looked around. The engine was shutting down and there was a dead lizard lying on his engine room floor. He looked around again and there was cadet Maxumus standing next to a control panel. "What by the moons of Bantine is going on here?" he roared.

Chief Grizlarge walked over to him. "Sir we had an intruder, a Chameleon posing as a Moonarian technician. Cadet Maxumus noted that he entered an area where he should not be during start-up. He noticed him faze when he messed with the plasma injector circuit. He tried to notify you sir but you were occupied so he contacted me. I am assuming for whatever reason the intruder was trying to reach the transporter. Cadet Maxumus blocked his escape. The intruder pulled a grenade and Cadet Maxumus eliminated the threat with his dagger. I arrived and transported the grenade off the ship." The Chief reported.

"Chief, where was Cadet Maxumus standing, when he made that throw?" the Chief Engineer demanded.

The Chief looked, "In front of the transporter."

"That is a throw of 15 SMU! You expect me to believe he knew he could make that throw?" The Chief Engineer growled.

The Chief stepped closer to Lt. Commander Tantous and lowered his voice, "Sir, I am telling you that Cadet Maxumus could have made the same throw with the same accuracy at twice that distance. Also Sir, if he hadn't, you, and your staff would all be dead."

Lt. Commander Tantous blinked, "How do you know that?"

The Chief smiled, "Neither I, nor Cadet Maxumus are at liberty to discuss that with you, Sir."

At that the Lt. Commander demanded, "What happened with the engine?"

The Chief just shrugged. "Sir you are going to have to ask Cadet Maxumus."

The Lt. Commander strode over to Beary, "Cadet Maxumus, Would you please explain what is going on?"

Beary looked at him, "Yes, Sir. I realized the control circuit had been inverted causing a plasma back-up in the C3A plasma injector. The Ch3 control panel was open, so I used it and ran emergency checklist 36C. I isolated the injector and vented the plasma through the emergency exterior vents. Then I started a controlled shut down in accordance with checklist 36D."

The Chief Engineer blinked. "Those are the proper procedures Cadet, but you cannot do that from that station!"

"That is incorrect, Sir. By inputting the proper command codes any console can be used. That is part of the design to insure command and control if engineering is damaged." Beary concluded.

Lt. Commander Tantous growled "These consoles are programmed to respond only to three command codes. Mine, the First Engineer, and the Second Engineer. No one has access to those codes. So there is no way you could have done what you said you did."

Beary thought "That's correct, Sir, your codes are not available. However, two other codes are hard wired into these engines: Dr. Vallen's and the designer's."

"I asked you if you were related to the designer. You told me you were not Cadet!" the Lt. Commander roared.

Beary looked at him, "That is correct Sir. I do not believe I am related to myself."

Lt. Commander Tantous looked incredulously at Beary; "This engine was designed by Dr. Beary Maxumus. You are what, 18? How could you have designed this engine?"

Beary shook his head. "Sir, do you wish to verify I am who I claim to be?"

"Yes!" was all the Lt. Commander said.

Beary walked over to the command console "Sir if you would type in 6795cab7."

The Lt. Commander typed in the code. A picture of Beary came up along with a complete biography. As he read the biography, the Lt. Commander became very angry. He turned toward Chief Gunnery Sergeant Grizlarge. "Chief, I want you to remove that body from my engine room. I also want Cadet Maxumus placed under arrest and escorted out of here now." the Chief Engineer ranted.

The Chief looked at him and shook his head, "No Sir. Major Basil, the head of security will need to complete his investigation and sweep the engine room before the body can be moved. Also, Sir you have no grounds to press charges against Cadet Maxumus. He saved your engine and he saved you and your crew's lives. I will escort him out of engineering and I will make a complete report to the Captain."

"Cub," Chief Grizlarge began as they were walking down the corridor, "you have made an enemy in the Chief Engineer. Without trying, in his mind you made him look bad in his own engine room. What you did was necessary and you saved the ship. However, there can be no more secrets at least with the Captain. If you are to make this deployment we will have to tell the Captain everything. Do you understand Cub? I will have to tell him everything."

Beary looked at his mentor, "Chief, I didn't mean to cause this trouble for you. Perhaps it would be better if I did leave the Saber Claw. The Chief Engineer will not be happy with you defending me. You should have arrested me as he ordered. At least then you would not be in trouble."

Chief Grizlarge stopped and looked at Beary. He shook his massive head and let out a roaring laugh. "Beary," He said, "I am not worried about the Chief Engineer. I work directly for the Captain and truly answer only to him. I need you on this deployment and worked very hard to maneuver you to get this assignment. So you will not be leaving. I have some very fine young Marines on this Destroyer but I have no one with your unique skills and training. You proved today that you haven't lost your edge. Where we are going, I will need the Ghost."

Chapter 2

The Story of the Ghost Revealed

They arrived outside of the Captain Darius Atilus' office.

The Gunny looked at Beary and said, "Wait here while I talk to the Captain." Beary took a seat and prepared to wait. He felt like he had been sent to the principal's office. That's when he heard his name. He immediately snapped to attention.

"Commander Centaures," Beary stammered, "Sir I . . . ."

"At ease, Cadet Maxumus," Commander Centaures smiled, "When you decide to make an impression you go all out. So you designed the VMCX engine?"

Beary looked at the Commander. "Sir, I was working on my Doctorate in Warp Engineering at the Vallen Institute. Dr. Vallen asked me to work on the design with him. He is a brilliant engineer and scientist. Together we designed the CX engine and its control systems. But I was just the student learning at the master's feet."

"That isn't how Dr. Vallen tells it." Commander Centaures said. "He claims you were the most brilliant 14 year old Cub he had ever met. You wrote all the technical manuals for the engine and designed several key components. I do not believe he is known to overstate his assessments. You see, Cadet, it seemed strange to me that you and the engine designer had the same name. So I called Dr. Vallen. I didn't care about your secret, as long as I knew the truth. Yet there seems to be more to the story. I suspect that is why we are both here now and the Chief is in with the Captain."

"Sir," Beary began, "I only wanted a chance to be a normal cadet. I graduated collage at ten, received my first PHD at 13 in Astrophysics. At 14 my father got me an appointment with Dr. Vallen. After graduating from the Vallen Institute I fell in with a group of shady characters lead by a Captain Valorous and a Gunny Sergeant Grizlarge."

"How did you fall in with such a group of cutthroats?" The Commander asked.

Beary smiled. "My father is Senator Octavious Maxumus. He was appointed to be a special Ambassador to the Doorgan VI negotiations. MSU6 was assigned as my protective unit while I traveled with my father. Being young, I asked them to train me. I turned out to be very good at what they trained me to do. So I quietly joined the Marine Reserves and became part of the Unit secretively. Not even my Father knows what I did for the last three years." Beary thought for a moment. "Sir, I don't know how much I am allowed to tell you. Except that I hold the rank of Corporal in the Marine Reserves Special Unit Command and have received a special deferment to attend the Academy."

"Why, didn't you enter as a Marine Cadet?" The Commander asked. Then continued, "I have to believe the Marines would have preferred if you would have."

Beary nodded. "Yes, Commander, they would have preferred it. I am good at what I do. But in the Marines I would never be able to fly fighters or command a ship like the Saber Claw. These are my dreams, Sir. Is it wrong to pursue my dreams?"

Commander Centaures blinked. He had never heard the question asked so abruptly yet so earnestly. "That depends, Cadet on two things. First, is what is in your heart? If you are doing it for selfish reasons, seeking glory for yourself or power then your dreams will be empty. They have no place in the service. Second, are you willing to have those dreams changed by the will of the Creator, or are you stiff necked?"

Beary listened to his words, then spoke quietly, "Sir, please believe me I don't seek glory or power. All I want is to serve my bears and my Creator. I just want to fly fighters. I am already qualified in jump ships and most shuttle crafts. The BAF doesn't allow Marines to fly fighters or command Starships. So this is the path I am following."

"It seems, Cadet Maxumus there is more to this story than even my sources have been able to uncover. Ah, it seems the Captain is ready to see us. Cadet, the Captain is a good leader. I would lay down my life for him in a heartbeat and consider it a repayment of only a small debt. Do you understand?" The Commander looked at him.

Beary understood that the Commander and the Captain had been together a long time and shared what to Beary's bears was considered a blood bond. Such a bond was second only to the bond that you had to your family. Beary said, "Yes, Sir I understand. I am ready and I will follow you in. Sir, Thank You."

The Commander smiled opened the door. "It's time."

While Beary was talking to the first officer the Chief was reporting to the Saber Claw's, Captain Darius Atilus. The Captain had become a legend during the evacuation of civilians off of Pratis V during the Arcrilian invasion. While in command of the old destroyer BAF Dagger Claw, He held off three Arcrilian Battle Cruisers for three days. In the end, he was forced to withdraw leaving a small marine detachment behind that was later captured.

In the fight one Arcrilian Cruiser was destroyed and one was badly damaged. The Dagger Claw had also been badly mauled and was retired from service. He and his crew's reward were being assigned to the first VMX Destroyer.

The Captain looked at Chief Gunnery Sergeant Grizlarge and waved him in. "All right, Major Basil, do your sweep and let me know what you find" The Captain hung up and turned to the Chief.

"Well?" was all he asked as he leaned back in his chair.

The Chief began his report; "Cadet Maxumus was in engineering he noticed an intruder . . ." after a few moments the Chief concluded his report."

The Captain nodded. "Chief is it normal for a first year Cadet to be able to recognize an intruder and have a direct link to the Chief of the Ship? Also, is there a new training protocol at the Academy that teaches cadets combat skills their first year? My last question is he just happened to have top secret codes that allowed him access to the engine that he just couldn't have is that correct?"

The Chief looked at the Captain pulled a small data card from his pocket and handed it to the Captain, "No, Sir. This will explain it all."

The Captain looked at it. It was marked UTS. He inserted it into his computed immediately the screen flashed purple then the words "Ultra Top Secret" appeared on the screen along with the words, "eyes-only". The Captain looked up, "What does this mean Chief? Who is Cadet Maxumus?"

"Sir, what it means may be up to you. As to whom that is a little more complicated. He is Dr. Beary Maxumus, the co—designer of the engine that powers this ship. He designed it at age 14. At 15 he accompanied his father, Senator Octavious Maxumus, to Doorgan VI where MSU6 was assigned to protect him." The Chief paused for a moment. "We were expecting a spoiled politicians Cub. He surprised us."

"Chief," Captain Atilus said, "You've explained the engine. I already knew that Cadet Maxumus was Dr. Maxumus. The First officer told me this morning. I didn't know that you knew. Why didn't you tell me?"

Chief Grizlarge looked at the Captain and pointed to the computer, "Sir, I was under orders not to give you Corporal Maxumus file unless it was necessary. Since the Saber Claw was attacked before we even left spaceport I felt it was time."

"Whose orders Chief, a Senator's? What do you mean, Corporal?" The Captain demanded.

"General Augustus Zantoran, Commander Fleet Marines gave the order, Sir." The Chief continued, "Captain, Cadet Maxumus joined the Marines without his Father's approval or knowledge. For the past three years he has been a valuable member of MSU6. What you have is his file I request that you read it."

The Captain opened the file, and read the list of decorations. One caught his eye the order of the Bearilian Star and the Silver fang for operations on Pratis V. the Captain clicked on the citation. He continued to read on after, 15 standard time units, he looked up, "Is half of this for real?"

Grizlarge said, "Sir, I was there everything in his file is 100% accurate. However there is a complication that even Cadet Maxumus doesn't know about all cadets are required to take a class in Astrophysics. He took the class and passed it what he didn't know was that some of his essays were used in the book. He has a Ph. D. in Astrophysics. It could be considered an ethics problem. I know it was not done intentionally."

"You may not be such a good judge of his ethics. I also need to know if your loyalty is to this one cadet or to this crew and this ship." The Captains eyes flared at the Chief with a look that had made others melt. The Chief just smiled and came to attention.

"Sir, I am Command Chief Gunnery Sergeant in the Fleet Marines. While I serve on this ship at your pleasure my orders come directly from General Zantoran. We can work together, you can try and have me relieved, or you can ask the real question that's bothering you." The Chief concluded.

The Captain blinked. No one had ever talked to him like this, and since the Chief had the Captain realized he could. "Okay, Chief, I don't like secrets on my ship, especially if those secrets put my crew or my ship in danger. Did his presence cause the attack on this ship? Also why do the Arcrilians call him the Ghost?"

The Chief softened his tone. He had almost gone too far. Now was the time to retreat a little. "Sir, I would not do anything to risk this ship or its crew and I believe it was providential that Corporal Maxumus was in Engineering. Who else could have done what he did? As far as why he is called the Ghost that will require a demonstration."

The Captain said "Alright chief, let's call them in."

Commander Centaures entered first and moved over toward the right side of the Captain's desk. Beary entered the room, standing about ten paces behind the Chief he came to attention and saluted. Just then the Chief spun around and threw his dagger into the center of Beary's chest. The Commander and the Captain both came to their feet.

Beary continued to hold his salute and said "Cadet Maxumus reporting as requested Captain Atilus."

The Captain returned his Salute and stared.

Beary asked, "Sir, may I have permission to return Chief Grizlarge Dagger to him.

"Permission granted Cadet." was all, the Captain said.

With that Beary pulled the bent dagger from his uniform he shook his head. "Here Chief, I see you used one from the armory, this time not one of your own."

The Chief smiled. "Had to be done, send the uniform to me and I'll get it repaired."

"Sir," Beary began to explain, "As you know, my race evolved a little different, from the rest of the Bearilian races in fact

Our original home world was Andreas Prime, which became uninhabitable during the first Arcrilian incursion. All, my race have a layer of bone between our first and second layers of skin.

One out of every 100,000 has a mutation of that layer of bones that seem to take on almost a metallic quality, which protects them from blade weapons. In rare cases this condition extends to the hair follicles, giving some protection from energy weapons. It seems I have this condition."

The Captain waited a moment, and then spoke. "Cadet Maxumus we seem to have a major problem here. While it could be argued that you did not technically lie to get into the Academy, you did fail to give all pertinent information whether they asked for it or not. You took a class that you could have taught and the text book contained an article you wrote. That could be considered a code of conduct violation. Then you come on My Ship and disrupt its operations and embarrass my Chief Engineer in His engine room. Do you think that because you are some whiz bang senators kid that you can do whatever you want?"

Beary stood at attention and did not waver. "Sir, if any of my actions, calls for a Code of Conduct Board then I am ready to be call before such a board and except their decision. As to my actions on this ship I acted as my training dictated for the protection of this ship and its crew. If my actions in any way violated this ship's procedures or your rules then I will accept whatever punishment you deem appropriate."

The Captain looked at Beary and at the folder in front of him "Cadet, step out till we decide your fate."

Beary saluted and walked out.

After Beary stepped out, Chief Grizlarge was the first to speak. "Captain Atilus, I don't understand how you could have threatened him like that. He is a highly decorated Marine and he saved this Ship!"

"That will be enough, Chief!" The Captain said with just a slight edge to his voice, "Your, to close to this Cadet. Also I have to question if you did not orchestrate some of this situation or were ordered to make these revelations known."

The Chief lowered his head and reached into his tunic and handed the Captain a sealed envelope. "I was to give you this after we left spaceport but events overtook this message. I was not trying to betray your trust, Sir, but I had my orders."

The Captain looked at the envelope. It was marked "Top-secret Eyes only". He set it down and looked at his first officer.

Commander Centaures looked at his commander as he twirled the bent knife in his paws. "I like the young cub. He never used his father's influence to get into the academy. He won his appointment based on his service, besides your irritation at the young cadet is probably misplaced. That envelope contains orders explaining that a group of Admirals and Marine Generals have discovered the problem and have reestablished the ensign 3rd class program. Our young Cadet is considered to be too valuable to lose over a minor technicality."

Both The Captain and the Chief asked "How do you know what is in this letter."

The Commander smiled, "I have my sources. After all, I am also the intelligence officer on this ship. May I suggest, though, that the Cadet never know about the contents of that letter? Let it be our decision."

The Captain opened the letter, and sure enough it said exactly what the Commander said. Captain Atilus just shook his head. "Okay, so we were all set up including the Cadet to a point. Let's call him in let me handle this."

"Cadet Maxumus come in." The Chief said.

The Captain looked at Beary; the young cadet was standing as straight as a statue; no emotion, no fear, just professionalism.

"Cadet, I can break you down to a Marine Private and send you back to the fleet. Do you, understand that?"

Beary just replied, "Yes Sir."

"However, you did save my ship and you have served the fleet well. So instead of punishing you we are going to put you in to a program called the Ensign 3rd program. You will be doing a Master's program in command and your training starts on this ship under the tutelage of the Commander and the Chief." Captain Atilus said.

Beary blinked, and then regained his composure. "Sir, are other cadets being placed in this program?"

"Why are you asking Cadet?" the Captain asked.

"Sir, Cadet Vantanus has completed all his medical training except fleet medical . . ." Captain Atilus cut him off.

"Cadet Maxumus, do you think that the fleet would do something just for your benefit?" Captain Atilus continued. "We are reviewing all cadet records."

The Chief and the First Officer smiled at each other. Without knowing it, now Ensign 3rd Maxumus had just opened a can of worms. They also knew that at least on this ship, records would be reviewed.

"Cadet Maxumus you're dismissed. I want you to go with the First Officer. Commander you will personally take over his training. Chief you will stay." Captain Atilus pointed toward the door.

"Chief Grizlarge, you caused this mess. You are going to help me fix it. Get the files. I want Cadet Vantanus file first." Then the Captain picked up the phone.

Chapter 3

Into the Mix

Doctor Wu Fang, a Pandarian, was sitting in his office reviewing the file of Doctor Vantanus. The letters from colleagues he had known for years all praised the young Cadet. Then he came to the last letter:

> To: Doctor Wu Fang Chief Medical Officer BAF SABERCLAW
>
> Doctor Fang, greetings. Young Caesar Vantanus is The best young Doctor I have ever trained.
>
> Give my love to your family. I hope we may get together soon.
>
> Affectionately
> *Angelina Maxumus*
> Dr. Angelina Maxumus

Dr. Fang shook his massive head. She didn't write in flowery language as others had, yet it was her letter that carried the most weight.

As he was putting the file down the phone rang. "Commander Fang", he answered. "Yes Captain, I have been reviewing his file. Dr. Vantanus is a very good Doctor by all accounts." Dr. Fang listened a few moments. "Sir, It would be my recommendation to at least put him in the Ensign 3rd program. In my opinion, he should be given the rank of Medical officer 1st."

Captain Atilus put down the phone. "Chief, Cadet Vantanus is to be placed in the program. Notify him immediately."

The Chief put down the files, saluted, and left the room.

As he reached the berth of the three cadets he heard two voices asking questions. He raped on the door. Cadet Maritinus opened the door and came to attention. "Master Chief," he stammered "how may I serve you."

"At ease, Cadet, is Cadet Vantanus here?" The Chief asked.

"Here, Master Chief." Vantanus replied.

"Dr. Vantanus you are being advanced to a new program and will be promoted to the rank of Ensign 3rd. Please report to supply and draw new uniforms." the Chief said.

"Chief, I don't understand." Vantanus responded.

"Dr. Vantanus, you have completed your medical training. You are a licensed physician. All you need is to learn fleet procedures. That will be a Master's program for you. Do you understand? If not Ensign 3rd Maxumus can explain it." The Chief said looking at Beary. With that he left the room and smiled.

Ben Maritinus looked at his roommates. "I guess I will have to move to a new room. You both have been promoted."

Beary looked at him and shook his head, "Ben, we would not wish to have anyone else share this room."

The young Polarian smiled.

It had been a long day and all three hit their bunks.

Beary was the first to fall asleep, but it was a fitful sleep. He found himself back on Pratis V. He could see the Arcrilian encampment below. The plan was simple he was to draw out as many of the enemy as possible while the rest of the team, rescued the Marines that had been captured after the evacuation of the planets population. But in his dream everything went wrong. His team and the captured marines were slaughtered before his eyes. He woke up in a hard sweat looked around and tried to go back to sleep.

Caesar was the next to fall asleep in his dream he was standing in an ER surrounded by bleeding bears all begging him to help them. All he could do was cry. He woke up with tears streaming down his face. He slowly got up and dressed and went for a walk.

Ben was the last to fall asleep his dream took him back to the cold waters of his home he was swimming in the great cold sea hunting carnacs—a large under water animal similar to a cross between a shark and an alligator. He swam after it armed with his spear and his knife. With one quick throw of his spear and a finishing slash of his knife he killed the great creature. Ben rolled over and smiled.

The next morning Ben was up and moving singing a tribal song of his clan. The other two slowly rose and put on their uniforms.

Ben was the first to speak, "We have our training assignments. Ensign Maxumus you are to report to Commander Centaures. Dr. Vantanus you are to report to the Chief Medical Officer Dr. Fang. I get to report to Master Chief Grizlarge for training."

Beary looked at him and smiled, "Ben you be careful of being around that old scoundrel. He has a habit of getting bears into trouble."

Ben looked at him but Beary and Caesar just laughed.

Caesar spoke next. "It's alright Ben the Chief and Beary have traveled some together. What he said was said partially in jest but the Master Chief is a legend in the fleet."

After the room was squared away the three left for their assignments. Ben was the first to report to the Chief.

The Legend Begins

Chief Grizlarge looked at the young Polarian. "Walk with me young Maritinus. Your brother, Major Maritinus is a great Marine officer. I hope you will live up to your brother's standards. We will start your arms training today."

Caesar was the next to report, "Chief Medical Officer Fang, I am Ensign 3rd Vantanus reporting as ordered Sir."

Dr. Fang looked up from his desk; "So you are Dr. Vantanus a good friend of mine tells me you are a great Doctor. We will see. Come let us see if you are as good as she believes you to be."

Caesar looked at him. "Sir, are you speaking of Lady Angelina."

Dr. Fang smiled, "So not only a student but perhaps a close relation?"

Caesar shook his head, "I am not related, per se but my family has long served the Maxumus clan. Lady Angelina took me under her wing. I owe her much. Also my brother is married to her youngest daughter."

"Well, my young Dr. Vantanus, we will see." Dr. Fang said "Come with me and I will test your knowledge and your procedures."

Three hours later, Dr. Fang looked at his testing results. "Dr. Vantanus, please go eat and come back in 90 standard time units."

After Caesar left the room, Dr. Fang picked up the phone. "Captain Atilus, this is Dr. Fang I just finished testing Dr. Vantanus."

"Well, Wu I am waiting. Did he meet your minimum standard?" Captain Atilus asked impatiently.

Dr. Fang shook his massive head, "Do I need to have the Captain come in for a physical. No? Then here is my report: the young Vantanus pasted with the highest score I have ever seen. He is more than qualified to serve as one of my surgeons."

Captain Atilus looked at the phone. "Alright, Doctor, thank you. Will you give my congratulations to the young Dr. Vantanus?"

Beary found Commander Centaures, "Sir, Cadet—I mean, Ensign 3rd Maxumus reporting as ordered."

"Come with me," Commander Centaures said, "we're going to take a little trip."

Beary followed him to the hanger bay. There were five Red Daggers and one Blue Dagger Attack Shuttles sitting there. The Commander walked over to Red Dagger 5. The name on the shuttle was Crimson Blade. Beary noticed it was fully loaded.

"Ensign Maxumus do you know how to fly one of these?" Commander Centaures asked.

"Sir I didn't know they were in production. I did help design the prototype. I have 40 Cycles in the prototype. MSU6 was part of the design team." Beary explained.

"Let me guess, the engines, and a few other features." Commander Centaures asked.

Beary nodded his head, "Yes Sir, and the separate shield and cloak generator. These Attack shuttles were designed to do Warp 4. The shield generator is designed to produce a shield strong enough to stop missiles and phaser fire."

"Good we are going for a little ride, and see if there are more surprises waiting for our ship." Centaures said with a gleam in his eyes.

Chapter 4

Carnise Asteroid Drift

Commander Centaures smiled at Beary and motioned to the pilot's seat, "Why don't you take the Crimson Blade out. I will play weapons officer."

Beary looked at him with surprise and said, "Yes sir, what courses do you want to take after leaving the hanger bay?"

Commander Centaures said, "Let's take a casual flyby of the ship and then we are going to set course for the Carnise Asteroid Drift. What is the maximum speed of this craft, Ensign?"

"Sir, the Red Dagger is designed to maintain warp four over a sustained distance. In an emergence warp 4.5 for about thirty standard time units." Beary recited from memory.

"Ensign, when you were a Marine, were you given a call sign?" the Commander asked.

"Yes Sir, my call sign is Spirit 6." Beary responded

"Good, I am Red Paw 2. The Saber Claw is Blue Dragon. Would you please notify command that we are ready to launch." Centaures requested.

"Yes Commander. Blue Dragon, this is Spirit 6. Red Paw 2 request permission to depart." Beary transmitted

"Spirit 6 you may begin roll out shuttle bay is open. Red Paw 1 gives permission for hot launch. Blue Dragon, command out."

"You heard the boss, Ensign, hot launch." the Commander Said.

Beary, didn't respond he just started the procedure. He fired up the lift engines rotated the Crimson Blade 90 degrees and pushed the sub light engines to 30%. The Crimson Blade shot out of the Saber Claw. He immediately set a course at a 260 degree axes and then turned and flew leisurely along the side of the Saber Claw. He marveled at the beauty of the ship. Had it just been three days since he first arrived?

"Good Job, Ensign!" the Commander said, "She is a beautiful ship isn't she."

"Very beautiful," Beary said absentmindedly, then getting back to business, "Sir, I am setting course 365, to Carnise Asteroid Belt Warp 3. Expected arrival time at Carnise Drift is 2 Bearilian days."

"Very good, Ensign Maxumus, set the auto-pilot and let's talk for a while. What do you know about the Arcrilians?" Commander Centaures asked.

"Sir, the Arcrilians are insectarians they are from the Arcrilis system. Their home planet is Arcritinian. There are six other planets in the system. Only the desert planet Bordux also has life on it. Bordux is the home of the Arachnid Scorpis. Which, they use as a tracking animal and beast of burden. They put control collars on the females which allow them to control up to six males. Normally they never have more than two males per female." Beary recited from memory.

"All that was text book answers. While correct it wasn't what I wanted to know. I wanted to know what you know. You have faced them in battle, and you have killed many of them. But do you know why four of the six planets are dead? Do you know why they never hold territory they take, but retreat back into their own system." Centaures asked.

Beary thought about his answer, then looked out the front view screen before answering. "I know they are ferocious fighters. The troopers follow the orders of their leaders without question. They never ask for mercy and they never give it. I know they destroy every planet they invade. I don't know why they don't hold territory. I do know they destroy everything they touch. They strip planets of everything until it becomes a dead planet."

The Commander took a small stone from a pouch. "This is from Pratis V. It was given to me by a little Girl we helped rescue.

It seems that we both share in that experience." He looked at Beary closely then continued, "If half of what I have read about what you did there is true . . . Did you know they call you the 'Ghost that stalks at night'? They swear they have killed you a dozen times. But you keep coming back. They have a huge bounty on your hide. Is that why you were seeking the safety of a ship, instead of that of a Marine?"

Beary looked at the Commander. "Sir, what are you talking about? I have never shirked my duty. Do you think it is easy to kill and to do it without any thought about the life that you are destroying? I have been fighting this enemy since I was 15 years of age. I am good at what I do. But what good has it done Pratis V? It's a wasteland. MSU6 destroyed the outpost but we still lost the planet. Captain Atilus and you fought off an armada. Yet we lost the planet. When you were with the famed Red Paw Squadron you defeated several fighter Squadrons of the enemy. Did it make a difference? I plan to make a difference somehow."

He had wanted to push Beary's buttons but the Commander found his own buttons being push. He realized that is why he made the decisions he made. He had turned down his own command to stay with Captain Atilus and to be the First Officer of the newest Bearilian warship in 30 years. He understood the drive of this young Cadet/ Ensign but he didn't understand the Cub.

After an extended period of quiet, the Commander spoke again. "I wasn't questioning your devotion, Ensign Maxumus, or your courage. But I made a decision to take you possibly into harm's way. So I just want to know who you are."

"I don't know what you want to know, Commander. You have read my file." Beary said

"Tell me what is not in your file." Centaures said with a smile.

"My Great Grandfather was Sir Augusts Maxumus the Hammer of Corsan. He was killed leading the Red Axe Knights in an attack against Arcrilians in an attempt to hold them off until the last transport left the planet. They say he was the last knight to fall. My Great Grandmother on my mother's side was Princess Maria Caesar. She was the only survivor after their transport was destroyed. Of a hundred and twenty clans, only forty remained. You know the rest." Beary said.

"So you come from an old and influential family. Yet you never chose to use that influence. Why?" the Commander asked.

Beary thought then said, "I am the youngest of seven cubs. I have three older sisters and three older brothers. All chose the careers my parents wanted. I was gifted it seems. My parents wanted me to do the things I had gone to school for. I wanted to be a soldier. As you know my father was against it. I haven't talked to him since I entered the Academy. My Mother is supportive but I know she would have preferred if I had chosen differently. I don't really understand why my father is and was so set against any of his cubs entering the fleet. As a Senator he has championed the building of new warships. He has even called for more resistance to the Arcrilian incursions."

Commander Centaures thought for a moment. "I remember when I first meet your father. I was a young ensign just out of the Academy heading for training as a fighter pilot. He walked up to the podium and explained that over half of us would flunk out of training and another quarter of us would be dead 6

The Legend Begins

months after we joined the fleet. He was right. Your Dad was the Wing Commander of the Golden Dragons. He would have been an Admiral by now. He just could not stand the weakness of our politicians so he resigned his Commission and ran for the Senate. He was a highly decorated pilot and one of my heroes."

Beary looked at him, "My Father was the leader of the Golden Dragons? He never told about his days in the fleet. I thought he had just been an academic, a professor in foreign affairs."

"You apparently are not the only one in your family that has their secrets. Your Dad was more than just a Fighter Pilot. He belongs to the society of the Sword Masters. Haven't you ever wondered about the ring he wears?" Centaures asked as he turned his own ring. "I have something I want to give you. Why don't you take it and get some rest. I will take the first watch and wake you in 8 cycles." He then handed Beary a small data card.

Beary relinquished the pilot's seat and moved to the back of the Crimson Blade. He pulled down one of the bunks next to it was a small computer and a data screen. He looked at the data chip and inserted it into the data port. Much to Beary's surprise it was a copy of his father's service record. As he read the details of his Dad's service he began to realize just how much he didn't know about his father's life. After about a cycle he turned off the computer and rolled over to sleep. As he slept his mind played over the events in his Dad's life. He woke up and saw Commander Centaures looking at the long range scanners and making a minute course correction. Beary looked at the chronograph 7.5 cycles had passed since he had given up control of the Crimson Blade. He got up and slowly prepared two ration plates and took one up to Commander Centaures. "Sir I thought you may be hungry."

Commander Centaures looked up, "Thank you, Ensign Maxumus. I think I could eat. Did you fix yourself something?"

Beary nodded, "Yes, Sir. May I ask a question?"

Commander Centaures nodded affirmative.

Beary cleared his throat, "Why did you give my Dad's file to me?"

The Commander shrugged, "There should not be secrets between fathers and sons. You were wrong to keep secrets from your father. On the other paw he was wrong to keep his past from you. You now know his secrets. It is time for him to know yours. If we survive this little trip I want you to contact your father and tell him as much as you can about the career you have already had and the one you wish to have. It may not change his mind but he should know that his son is not just a disobedient Cub but a Bear that has made his decisions like a mature Bear."

Beary thought about what the Commander had said. "Sir, I give you my word. I don't know if my father will talk to me but I will try. Thank you, Sir."

"Good, now to business. I picked up some anomalies on long range scan near three of the asteroids in the passage through the Carnise Drift. We will be in range of Arcrilian scanners in three cycles. I want you to cloak the Crimson Blade in 2.5 cycles. You may also want to turn on the shield generator any questions? Wake me in 8 cycles."

Beary said "Yes Sir. Sir, if we make contact do you want me to engage the enemy?"

The Commander smiled, "Only if you must we want to see what is going on hopefully without being seen."

Beary started studying the data on Carnise Drift it was a debris field that divided the Bearilian star system from the Tarsus system. The passage was the only clear path through the field it was also the perfect choke point. Years ago the Bearilian's had kept an outpost near the opening. Budget cuts had forced the fleet to abandon the outpost.

Beary thought about the outpost some of its automated systems might still be functional. All he needed was an access code. Of course Marine Special Units had such codes. Beary contemplated what he wanted to do. He could launch a receiving buoy, and then send a code to start up the outpost sensors. Beary realized he didn't want to turn on the electronic sensors. Instead he decided to use the optical sensors which would use very little power. By sending the data to a buoy he could make it look like they were being used by a research station on a planet in another system.

Beary launched the buoy and sent the code through it. At the outpost the optical cameras and telescopes turned on. What Beary saw caused a chill to go down his spine. Two Arcrilian destroyers with fighters riding piggy back were setting off from the old outpost's asteroid and were moving toward the next one in the line.

As Beary started recording the data and making notes, he reached down and turned on the cloaking device and the shield generator. He thought about waking Commander Centaures but thought better of it. He wanted to be able to give him a full report.

Little did he know, Commander Centaures, had been quietly watching him. The Commander smiled this Cub was smart normally such initiative would be discouraged but not in this case. He rolled over and went to sleep.

On Bearilia Prime a tall Kodacian Marine Major entered the officer of Senator Octavious Maxumus. The receptionist was an older Maxmimus female. She looked up and asked, "May I help you, Major?"

Major Valorous looked at her and smiled, "I would like to see the Senator, if you please?"

Looking at her calendar she stated, "I may be able to get you in next week, Major."

The Major, just shook his head. "My Dear madam that just is not acceptable. Please tell the Senator that Spirit 1 is here. He will see me."

She touched the communication device on her desk and spoke into it. "Senator Maxumus, there is a Marine Major here to see you. I told him I couldn't get him in till next week but he is insistent. He told me to tell you Spirit 1 was here to see you."

Senator Maxumus sat back in his chair and replied, "Tell that pirate to come on in, Deloris."

"Yes, Senator," She paused. "You may go in, Major." No one got to see the Senator without an appointment but somehow this was different. She then dismissed the thought. She had been with the Senator since her husband died. She knew there was a good reason for this breach in procedures and was smart enough not to ask why.

The Senator stood up and walked over to the major and shook his paw. "It is good to see you my friend. I see you have been promoted."

Major Valorous smiled, "Yes Sir all good things have to come to an end. They promoted me and broke up MSU6. Gunny is on the new Saber Claw as Chief of the Boat. The majority of the others were sent to training command."

"I see." The Senator paused. "But why are you here my friend. You didn't come all this way to tell me that."

"No Sir, I came here to show you this." Pulling a small data recorder from his brief case, he said, "I was ordered to bring you this. It is Top Secret Eyes only I must stay here while you read it and must return it to Fleet Headquarters."

The Senator turned on the device. It immediately scanned his eyes verified it was him then displayed the data. The Senator read the first few lines and looked up. Fire was in his eyes but he said nothing and continued reading. After 10 standard time units he looked up and said, "Major, are these documents and citations accurate." The major just nodded. "My son, was the one that rescued the marines on Pratis V?"

The Major sat a little straighter and then spoke, "Sir the Gunny led that mission. I had helped evacuate the last civilian Governor off the planet. When the request came in, the Gunny and Corporal Maxumus responded to the distress call."

The Senator looked at him dumb founded, "A two Marine squad destroyed the outpost and rescued the captured Marines?"

"Yes Sir. Your son is very good at what he does and the Gunny is the best tactician I have ever known." the Major then went on, "Sir, your son, as you know, joined the Academy. What you don't know is that he is on the Saber Claw. He has been promoted to an Ensign 3rd Class along with a Dr. Vantanus. They are now considered Five year Cadets finishing masters in fleet operations."

The Senator looked up, "Major, the Ensign 3rd program was done away with 10 Years ago."

"No, Sir just mothballed," the Major smiled, "General Zantoran and a few Admirals felt it needed to be reinstated."

The Senator's paws were shaking, then they calmed down, "My son did all this under my nose, and I didn't know it. I was angry at him when he joined the Academy. It wasn't the life I wanted for him. I can see that he is not a Cub anymore. How much can I share with his mother?"

The Major thought then responded, "Senator everything you read is classified. Tell her that Beary is a great Bear, and is living up to the standards set by his father and his father's fathers. Dr. Maxumus will understand. I have taken way too much of your time. Your gate keeper will have me removed if I stay any longer." With that the Major retrieved the data device and said his goodbye.

Back aboard the Crimson Blade Beary was preparing to wake the Commander. He fixed a quick meal and laid out his report. As he turned around the Commander was standing behind him. "Sir I was just preparing . . ."

Commander Centaures cut him off, "Smells good. It looks like you have been busy while I rested. So you took some initiative and accessed the optical sensors of the old outpost. Good job. Now what did you find." The Commander looked at the images Beary had collected and sighed. "It doesn't look good does it?"

Beary thought for a moment, "Sir there are at least 4 fighter Squadrons and 2 destroyers there."

The Commander asked "Have they discovered that we are monitoring them?"

Beary shook his head, "No, Sir. Even if they discover that the optics are being used they will trace the signal back to the Balthazar system."

"Excellent, Ensign Maxumus, this proves that I was right to bring you along. Now what would you do about this?" The Commander asked.

Beary pondered the question and weighed the options. Then said, "Sir we have two options. We can retreat and warn the Saber Claw and wait for orders, or we can launch a buoy with this information and use the capabilities of the Crimson Blade to break up the ambush."

"You want to crash this party knowing that we are outnumbered out gunned and have little or no hope of surviving am I correct Ensign." The commander asked.

"Yes Sir." Was all Beary could say.

The Commander laughed, "I was hoping you would say that.

Of course I am going to have to reevaluate how smart I thought you were. Okay Ensign we have three cycles to decide how we are going to do this and try and live through it. Launch the buoy with the information we have on encryption channel zeta 5."

The two got busy coming up with a plan as the buoy raced toward the Saber Claw. After one cycle the buoy started transmitting.

On the Saber Claw the on duty Communications officer started retrieving data. "Captain Atilus to communications immediately please for priority coded message."

Captain Atilus looked up from his desk. "Master Chief you had better join me. How is our young Polarian doing with his training?"

Grizlarge answered, "He is good and a quick learner. He will make a good security officer."

"Good." The Captain paused in thought. "What kind of trouble do you think they got into?"

The Master Chief saw concern in the Captain's eyes. "Sir, you know the Commander better than I. As for Ensign 3rd Maxumus . . . well trouble tends to be his middle name. Of course it usually is trouble for the enemy."

"Great, we sent a matched pair on a simple mission and my gut tells me it has become something else." They reached the communication section just as the decoding was finished.

"Sir you need to see this!" the communication officer said excitedly.

"Calm down, Lieutenant, let me see what we have." Atilus said. As he looked at the data on the screen he couldn't believe what he saw it was the perfect ambush being set up. If the Saber Claw had entered the Carnise Drift unaware they would have been destroyed. "How, was this data transmitted lieutenant." the Captain asked.

"It was transmitted by remote buoy, Sir." The Lieutenant responded.

"Oh crap they wouldn't!" The Captain turned to Grizlarge.

"Yes Sir, Ensign Maxumus would. The Crimson blade was fully equipped it has a cloaking devise and a separate shield generator. My guess is that they will attack the fighters and then run away as fast as they can." Grizlarge answered.

The Captain thought *that is how Centaures would play it also.*

"Okay, Bridge, this is the Captain. Set course to Carnise Drift warp 6.

How long will it take to get there?"

"Navigator to the Captain: it will take 1day 12 cycles to reach the Drift." The Navigator reported.

Atilus looked at the Chief. "Master Chief, inform all division heads to report to the conference room in one cycle. See to it that the ship is ready for action. Have Major Basil set a security watch in all sections. Go to yellow alert. Communications send the data to the Fleet Headquarters."

Everyone snapped into action. It was times like this a Captain was most alone. He had done his job; he had given the orders now it was up to the officers and crew to do theirs. He quietly returned to his wardroom off the Bridge. He had learned years before that there were times for the Captain to be seen and times to stay out of the way. This was the latter times. Soon he was lost in his own thoughts.

Chapter 5

Hit and Run Like Hell
Gunfight at Carnise Drift

The Commander looked over the plan. It was simple and direct hit fast, hard, and run away as fast as they could without getting killed. He also knew that like all plans it would fall apart when the first shot was fired. He looked over at Beary. The young ensign showed no fear only determination.

Beary looked at Commander Centaures and wondered at how calm the older Bear was. Beary wasn't afraid he had been in similar situations. Only his nightmares showed his doubts and there would be no time for sleep for a while. He did think about his friends on the Saber Claw. It was his duty to protect the Ship and his friends. To do that the Arcrilian forces would have to be destroyed.

Commander Centaures thought well it is time to get started. "Ensign Maxumus if you would take the helm please."

"Sir" Beary questioned?

"Look ensign I was a good fighter pilot but this is a drop ship. You have more hours and experience in this type of craft. You're our best chance, flying it. Besides I am a great weapons officer." Centaures smiled.

Beary took the pilot's seat and made a few course corrections.

The Crimson Blade was as agile as a fighter. The plan was simple use the asteroids as cover and pray the cloak worked as advertised.

Once they opened fire, even with the ability to launch the missiles in cloak mode, the Arcrilians would open up in every direction.

There was a good chance one or more of the enemy crafts might get in a lucky shot, and then there were the destroyers. Their only hope was to stay out of the way, launch their missiles, and run away as fast as they could. It should work, but only if they timed it right. Even though he looked outwardly calm, he knew the nightmares would come unless they didn't make it. Beary, let out a slow breath and angled toward the first asteroid. His mind raced as he moved the Crimson Dagger.

"Commander Centaures," Beary said slowly as he let the idea form, "We could detach one of the missile pods and set it up on one of the asteroids. Then set it off remotely, while we hit them from the other side. We might even get them to believe they triggered an automated defense system."

The Commander thought about it. "It just might work, Ensign. Can you land us on the second asteroid on the right?"

Beary smiled, "With my eyes closed, Sir, but I better do it with them open." Beary synchronized with the pitch of the asteroid and slowly lowered the Crimson Blade to the surface

"Okay hot shot," the commander said, "let's get this done."

They put on space suits and stepped out on to the surface of the asteroid. They quickly removed the missile pod and positioned the pod where an old launcher had existed. They set up a tracking system so they could remotely launch the missiles. They quickly gathered and stored the tools and reentered the Crimson Blade.

Beary pulled off his helmet and asked, "How did you know there had been an old launcher there?"

The Commander said, "I was flying support when they installed them. Now let's get out of here."

Beary jumped into the pilot seat. Centaures moved over to weapons control. He lifted, and then rolled the jump ship off the asteroid. "Where to Sir?"

"We covered right, so we go left just as you suggested." the Commander pointed down toward another asteroid. "Go below that one then work your way to the far side keeping the belt between them and us."

Beary skimmed the surface of each asteroid, as he worked the Crimson Blade to the attack position, the Commander had indicated. It took approximately 20 standard time units (STU) for the Crimson Blade to reach that point. As they prepared to start their run they noticed that one of the destroyers had parked directly over the missile pod. Beary looked over at the Commander, who just smiled.

With a stroke of a key Centaures sent the command to the remote launcher. In less than 30 Sub Standard Time Units (SubSTU) the missiles started tearing into the bottom of the Arcrilian Destroyer which immediately began to come apart. The other Destroyer pulverized the asteroid. The Commander smiled. "Well, that was a bonus. Ensign Maxumus, take us in. Then after we attack try and get us out of here alive if you please."

Beary moved the Crimson Dagger directly toward the fighter Squadrons. "Sir, we have 32 missiles and our phaser. We can fire the missiles cloaked, but the phaser requires us to uncloak."

"Alright, when we are in range we will fire one missile at each fighter that we can and strafe with the Gatling phaser. I want you to roll us over to get a good shot." The Commander ordered.

"Yes, Sir." was all that Beary said, as he moved toward the targets. He accelerated to attack speed. The Commander locked the remaining missiles on 32 of the fighters. He touched the keys and the missiles launched toward their targets. Once the missiles launched, Beary brought the Phaser to bear on the opposite row of fighters.

The Arcrilian fighter pilots started scrambling towards their fighters as the missiles arrived in a blink of an eye. Before it was over the missiles had destroyed 28 of the fighters and damaged 2 others. The carnage also included the Arcrilian pilots and ground crews.

As Beary rolled in on the other Squadrons he dropped the cloak. The Commander aimed the Gatling phaser at the other Squadrons and let out a long burst. Four of the other fighters exploded. That was when all hell broke loose.

The remaining Arcrilian Destroyer opened up. The aft shield of the Crimson Blade flared. If it hadn't been for the dedicated generator the shield would have failed. The remaining fighters started taking off. It didn't take long for more shots to be fired at the Crimson Blade.

Beary ducked under another asteroid and turned on the cloak. Beary knew this would only give them a little protection, but every sub time unit they kept from being spotted gave them a chance to escape. He kept spinning and dashing from one asteroid to the next keeping them between the Crimson Blade and the Arcrilian Destroyer. Beary knew the real problem would be the Arcrilian Fighters that were launching at this very moment to find them. He could feel the blasts as asteroids were pulverized around them. Since the Arcrilians couldn't see them on sensors they were lighting up every inch of space around the asteroids.

Centaures looked at Beary, "Ensign, get us out of here. Warp 4.5 toward the rally point." Just then they were hit by a phaser from a fighter that was firing blindly. Despite the cloak the shield flared.

Beary rolled 130 degree down angle and went to warp. After fifteen STU, Beary slowed to Warp 3.5. Arcrilian Fighters were short range and could only do Warp 2.5. That's why they had to be carried on the back of Destroyers.

Beary began picking up a homing signal from a remote buoy. He altered course and started heading to the new rally point. "Sir request permission to send an answering burst to the Blue Dragon." Centaures nodded and Beary hit the necessary keys.

Aboard the Saber Claw the communication officer received the coded burst. The Duty officer called Captain Atilus. "Sir Com, we have a response from Spirit 6."

Atilus looked up, "Com, what was the message?"

The Duty Officer reported, "It read kicked a stinger nest, coming home hot."

Atilus hit the ship wide button "This is the Captain. Set security situation Delta. Go to Red Alert."

Major Basil looked at the chief. "Gunny, I want 4 of your best Marines in engineering, and another four on the bridge. Security teams 2 and 3 will be ready to respond where needed. Team 1 will protect medical. Where do you want to be Gunny?"

The Master Chief thought, "I'll take Cadet Maritinus with me and I'll follow my gut."

"Okay, Chief" Major Basil said as he turned to deploy the rest of his security forces.

The Gunny turned to Corporal Black Star, a large Ursa Americanus. "Corporal Black Star, take your squad to the Bridge. No one gets to the Captain understood?"

"Yes, Master Chief Grizlarge." Corporal Black Star responded.

"Sergeant Goldson, take your squad to engineering." Grizlarge looked at the Gold colored Ursa Americanus. He was short but powerfully built.

"Yes Gunny. Don't worry; I'll stay out of Lt. Commander Tantous way. But no one will get into engineering." Sergeant Goldson smiled.

Grizlarge then turned to Ben, "You're with me, son." He then turned and handed him a hand phaser belt and a dagger.

Ben looked at the Master Chief and fitted the belt over his uniform. He could almost feel the light ting of red rise through his white fur as he anticipated the hunt to come. That is how he saw battle. In the Cold Seas of home, you either killed the prey or the prey killed you. "Sir, I will not fail you, my life on it."

Grizlarge smiled. *Polarians were different, but made excellent officers.* "I have no doubt Cadet that you will excel in carrying out your duties. Let's patrol near the Captains wardroom."

Captain Atilus sat down in his Command Chair on the Bridge

"Flight Crews report to Launch Bay. Midnight Dagger, take position 2 clicks out front. Ruby Dagger, fly cover for Midnight Dagger, Blood Dagger, and Scarlet Dagger fly Combat Air Patrol [CAP]. Flame Dagger, you will stay in reserve."

Ensign Pompey turned to Captain Atilus. "All weapon stations report ready. All divisions report manned and secure."

Atilus looked at the young and attractive Ursa Maxmimus.

"Thank you, Ensign Pompey." Everything was set. All he had to do was recover his lost lamb and retake the Drift passage.

"Dusk 1 to Blue Dragon, Lost lamb in sight Wolves tracking."

"Dusk 1 to Red Paw Two. Come to 340 we will cover."

Beary responded, "Acknowledge 340. Spirit 6 out." After another cycle Beary spotted the hanger Bay of the Saber Claw.

"Blue Dragon, Spirit 6, we are requesting permission to land."

"Spirit 6, Blue Dragon hot landing authorized." Beary thought *they want us to come in fast.* Okay, he hit the thrusters aimed at the landing lights. Once inside the hanger bay he flared the Crimson Blade fired the landing thrusters and sat her down on the same spot he had launched from.

The jump ship had hardly landed when the Commander said, "Come on we need to get debriefed."

Beary followed him out and caught a tube transporter to the Bridge.

Chapter 6

Destroyer vs. Destroyer

Once they arrived at the bridge the Captain motioned them over to his wardroom. "What are we up against Commander?"

Commander Centaures Started to explained, "Sir when we arrived at the Carnise Drift we discovered . . ." After a few moments Centaures concluded "Our sensors showed that the Destroyer had broken apart and was crashed on two asteroids. We also destroyed 28 fighters of the first two Squadrons and we destroyed 4 fighters of one of the other Squadrons. Then Sir it got real warm so we ran for home."

Atilus looked at the Commander, "Whose idea was it to use the optical tracking system of the old outpost?"

The Commander smiled. "That was Ensign Maxumus's idea also. He is an excellent pilot and should be given the Crimson Blade, since Ensign Darius is ill. He will need a gunner. I was thinking Ensign Artemus would be a good choice."

"Ensign Maxumus, go get some rest and eat. We may need you soon." the Captain ordered.

Beary left the wardroom, waved to Grizlarge and Ben, then moved to the nearest mess hall where he grabbed a couple of cold meat sandwiches and a cold drink.

In the wardroom Atilus was fuming, "Commander you are the First officer of the Saber Claw not a reconnaissance officer.

I don't plan on losing my First Officer on a job that should be done by Ensigns and Lieutenants. Do I make myself clear?"

Centaures looked at his friend, "Yes Sir, but what really bothers you is that it wasn't you out there. But you're right, it was a dumb stunt. I did learn what I needed to know. Maxumus is the real deal. He might even be a better pilot than me."

Atilus just sighed; he knew Centaures had just shrugged off his reprimand like he knew his friend would. "Okay, but if you ever pull a stunt like that again, I'll have you keel hauled." He smiled. "Now, about Ensign 3rd Maxumus, do you really think he should be given the Crimson Blade?"

Commander Centaures smiled, "Definitely, He has more experience in jump ships than any of our other pilots." Centaures pointed to his file. "You can check with Grizlarge, but it's there in his file."

Atilus hit the com button, "Ensign Maxumus, Ensign Artemus report to the flight hanger in 30 standard time units."

Artemus looked at his friend, Ensign Darius, "Looks like they have another stick jock to take over the Crimson Blade."

Darius weakly smiled up at his friend. "Doctor Fang says I am done flying jump ships. But I don't mind. Once I am cured I am going to be transferred to the astrophysics lab to work with Lt Commander Johansen. You know how good she looks in her uniform."

Artemus squeezed his friend's paw and left. As he walked toward the Flight Hanger he saw a tall Ursa Maxmimus moving the same way. He noticed that he was in a flight suit that looked a little ruffled. As he walked in he saw him talking to a flight chief. As he watched new missile pods being loaded, the same Maxmimus stepped out with a clean flight suit and walked toward the Crimson Blade.

Beary saw the Kodacian Ensign inspecting the installation of the missile pods. "Ensign Artemus, I am Ensign 3rd Beary Maxumus, your pilot, Sir."

"Ensign 3rd, are you sure you are qualified?" Artemus asked.

Beary shrugged. "I have a lot of hours piloting jump ships and I helped design the prototype for this one. But you may verify the orders, Sir."

Artemus went over to a com unit and called flight command.

"Sir, this is Ensign Artemus, I have an Ensign 3rd Maxumus telling me he is my pilot. I wish verification."

Lieutenant Talus looked at the orders in his hand. "Ensign Artemus, that is incorrect. Ensign Maxumus is your pilot, but as of 10 STU ago he received a field promotion to full Ensign. Please inform him."

Artemus just stared at the com unit then slowly responded, "Yes, Sir." He thought *who, is this young pilot and what is going on*. "Ensign Maxumus, you have been promoted to full ensign. I guess you are my pilot, and as such you are commander of the Crimson Blade. It was my best friends command I hope you're worthy of him."

Beary thought *what is going on*, but orders are orders. "I can fight and fly this ship Ensign Artemus, are you willing to fly with me?"

Artemus looked at him. "Who are you?"

Beary stared with penetrating eyes, "I am Dr. Beary Maxumus, co—designer of the engines that power this ship and the Dagger jump ships, plus several sub systems. I was also a Corporal in the Bearilian Marines prior to going to the Academy. Do you have any other questions?"

Artemus looked at his eyes. *He had heard the gossip, but here he was standing in front of him. Was this really the one the Arcrilians called the "Ghost"? He was little more than a cub. A good 5 years younger than himself.* "Well, I guess I should introduce myself. I am Savato Artemus and I am the best gunner in the fleet."

Beary smiled and stuck out his paw. "Well I guess both our skills will be tested soon. The Commander and I kicked up a stinger nest and I think they're going to find us or the Captain is going to find them. Are all our weapons reloaded?"

Artemus grinned, "She is ready. What is your call sign?"

Beary answered, "Spirit 6. As you know, regulations won't let us change them. What is yours?"

Artemus shrugged. "Darius was going to pick them. I guess it will be up to you."

Beary thought, *I won't keep this assignment but Artemus may be with the Saber Claw for years.* "Com request check for call sign assignment Crimson Blade weapons officer."

"None assigned." was all the communication room reported.

"Request call sign Spirit Blade 2, if available for Ensign Savato Artemus, of the Crimson Blade." Beary requested

Com responded, "Call sign is available. Standby, Ensign Artemus is now Spirit Blade 2"

Beary looked at Artemus, "Is that acceptable?"

Artemus nodded. Beary looked over the Crimson Blade she had taken two hits from Arcrilian phasers and suffered no damage. "I guess we report to the ready room."

In the Ready room the Flame Dagger's crew waited. Artemus introduced Beary to them. They had just begun chatting, when the klaxon sounded. Both Dagger crews raced to their ships.

Beary fired up the systems as Artemus turned on the weapon systems, Beary Reported "Com, Spirit 6 ready to launch." Beary immediately heard Flame 1 report in also.

Com responded, "Spirit 6, Flame 1 hot launch in order."

Beary rotated and shot out the hanger bay followed immediately by Flame 1.

"Dusk 1 to Spirit 6; take your section to 325, 1 click [a click is = to 250 SMU]."

"Spirit Blade 2 acknowledges Dusk 1, Section 3 to 325, 1 click." Artemus looked at Beary, "Well, section leader, I guess we go hunting.

Beary looked at him. "Verify cloak and shields are operating on both ships."

Artemus looked at him then verified Flame Dagger was also running shields and was cloaked. "Sorry, Ensign Maxumus, I over stepped . . ."

Beary cut him off, "Look Savato, I have done this before. This is not my first fight on land, sea, or space. I know I am not the partner you wanted. However, if we are going to survive this you are going to have to trust me and I you. Pick up the tracking data Dusk 1 is sending us and have Flame 1 take position to our right ¼ click."

"Blue Dragon to all units, accelerate to attack speed. Target the fighters and Destroyer."

"Dusk 1, to all units target and engage fighters."

The Arcrilian fighters began deploying from the destroyer. They could tell that there were 30 of the short range fighters and 5 of the destroyer's fighters. Each of the Red Daggers targeted the oncoming fighters with the Blue Dagger coordinating targets. From their cloaked positions the Daggers each fired one pod of missiles. 160 missiles flew toward the 35 Arcrilian fighters. In a matter of seconds, the Arcrilian fighters begin to explode. With over 4 missiles targeted per fighter it was not surprising that some of them started to die. When the first wave was over, 16 of the Arcrilian fighters were gone, yet nineteen survived. The Arcrilian fighters started to fire in all directions and dashed for the Saber Claw.

"Dusk 1 to all units, fire on remaining Fighters." Again 160 missiles streaked toward the 19 remaining fighters. With 8 missiles now targeted at the nineteen Arcrilian fighters. Once again the fighters started to explode. Yet 6 Arcrilian fighters still survived. Dusk 1 ordered section 2 and 3 to engage the remaining fighters.

"Flame 1 from Spirit 6, guns hot, uncloak, and attack."

"AB 1 to Scare 1, challenge the one on the left."

Four of the Arcrilian fighters peeled off to engage the Red Daggers, as two increased speed toward the Saber Claw.

"Blue Dragon, this is Dusk 1; we have two bogies in bound."

Captain Atilus turned to his weapons officer. "Launch missiles on the Destroyer. Gun down those fighters, bring the rail guns on line, charge phasers." 240 missiles launched against the Arcrilian destroyer which began launching missiles. Dusk 1 immediately began trying to jam the Arcrilian missiles. One of the Arcrilian Fighters launched its missiles just as it was destroyed by the Saber Claw's gunners. The Missiles struck the shield of the Saber Claw which absorbed the energy of the blasts. The other fighter was destroyed as it tried to penetrate the shield of the Saber Claw.

Master Chief Grizlarge and Cadet Maritinus were outside the Captain's wardroom. All of a sudden an Arcrilian Pilot materialized right in front of Grizlarge. Before the Chief could react, the Arcrilian pilot swung a knife at the chief cutting the arm that the Chief had put up to deflect the attack. As the Chief, fell back Maritinus grabbed the Arcrilian pilot and threw him up against the bulk head. With one paw Ben twisted the claw with the knife around and plunged it into the Arcrilian's chest. With his other paw Ben crushed the Arcrilian's neck. Ben noticed the smell of poison on the Arcrilian's blade.

"Chief, you have been poisoned! You must chew this." Ben pulled a small white object from a pouch and forced into the Chief's mouth. He also started putting an ointment on the wound and wrapping it with a field dressing. "Maritinus to Medical we have a medical emergency near Captain's wardroom."

Atilus heard the call "Cadet Maritinus report situation."

Maritinus looked up and hit his com device, and reported what had happened he then asked. "Do you wish me to stay here or go with the Chief? Medical has arrived."

Atilus thought quickly, "Major Basil, take a security detail outside my wardroom. The Chief has been attacked and we have a dead Arcrilian on board. Look for an explosive nearby."

Atilus watched the incoming missiles some had been diverted by the Blue Dagger and some were being destroyed by automated defense systems, but some were going to hit. "Shield to full strength prepare for impact." In 30 sub time units the remaining missiles arrived. The explosion against the shield could be felt throughout the ship. Still, the shields held.

In medical, Chief Grizlarge was fuming. Caesar just smiled at him. "Chief, calm down, you're going to live thanks to Cadet Maritinus."

"What did he give me and what was that abominable stinking stuff he put on me?" Grizlarge growled as the Doctor put an IV in his arm.

"Ben, tell the Chief what you told me." Caesar smiled.

Ben looked at the Chief. "I knew you had been poisoned with concentrated Scorpius venom. So I gave you a Borarachnid gall bladder and put Bovinus urine concentrate on the wound."

The Chief asked, "What is a Borarachnid?"

Ben smiled "It is a very large and poisonous water spider from my home land. If they bite you, you die. But they are very territorial so they developed an enzyme in their gall bladders that will neutralize most poisons. The Bovinus salve also draws poison from the wound and aids in healing."

Caesar then spoke up. "Chief the anti-venom I am giving you is really just the same thing. If he would not have done what he did you would have lost your arm if not your life."

Grizlarge sat back, "Okay, Doc, write it up just as you told me." Turning to Ben, "Thanks, Cadet, you saved my life. I will not forget. I take it the Arcrilian is dead."

Ben smiled. "I killed him with his own knife and my paw crushing his neck."

Grizlarge sat back "Is Major Basil taking care of the Arcrilian?" He saw Ben nod affirmative. "Good I think I will rest for a few moments." He said as he drifted off.

Caesar smiled at Ben. "Don't worry; I gave him a mild sedative. I needed him to sleep while he heals. You did good Ben."

The Red Daggers were in a fur fight with the Arcrilian fighters. Scarlet Dagger had suffered some minor damage when its shield failed over an empty launcher. The Arcrilian fighter moved in for the kill too quickly and was ripped apart by the Scarlet's Gatling Phaser. The other Daggers had destroyed their opponents also. The Scarlet Dagger tried to re-cloak but realized it couldn't. Scar 1, notified Dusk 1 and went to warp.

"Dusk 1 to all units, withdraw"

Artemus looked at Beary. "What now?"

"We need to get clear. We don't want to get between the two destroyers." Is all that Beary, could say.

As the missiles struck the Arcrilian Destroyer its shield started to buckle but only minor exterior damage occurred. Unfortunately for the Arcrilian's, their destroyers carried less than a third of the missiles that the Saber Claw carried. The Arcrilian's began racing to get into range of its energy weapons, as the second wave of missiles began to strike. This time the forward shields failed and 25 of the missiles exploded on the forward weapons array. Automated systems sealed the numerous hull breaches. The Arcrilian Captain just lost half of his weapons, yet, he still felt he could destroy the Saber Claw. Just a little more time and he would be in range.

Atilus ordered a third wave of missiles and ordered the rail guns brought to bear. He watched as the Arcrilian turned his port shield into the missiles.

Again the Arcrilian's shields failed and more damage was sustained to the Arcrilian Captain's ship. He was losing power and more of his weapon systems. It was time to withdraw He began to give the order as the first Rail gun shell ripped into the Bridge. He saw the bulk head disintegrate, and felt his body being pulled into the darkness of space. His last thought was *how could this happen*? After the Bridge was destroyed shells ripped into engineering and the Arcrilian Destroyer came apart.

Captain Atilus watched as the Arcrilian destroyer came apart.

He and his ship had won the day. Yet he didn't feel elated only very tired. "Commander Centaures you have the Bridge." Without another word he walked slowly to his wardroom. Major Basal was there. "Report, Major."

Major Basil opened his note book. "The Arcrilian had a small explosive device strapped to his body. When young Maritinus crushed his neck he snapped the spinal cord. We found the explosives on the body and instead of trying to defuse the bomb we just put him out an airlock."

Atilus nodded. "Good job, Major. How is the Chief?"

Major Basil smiled, "The old pirate is going to live, thanks to Cadet Maritinus. By tomorrow he will be able to return to duty, according to Dr. Fang."

Atilus nodded. "Were there any other casualties?"

Major Basil answered, "Nothing major. A few cuts and bruises and a couple of minor burns."

"Alright Major, Commander Centaures has the bridge. Thank you." With that he went in and lay down.

Commander Centaures turned to the Communication officer.

"Order all units to return to base."

"Blue Dragon, to all units return home."

Chapter 7

The next move

Soon the Daggers started to land. The first one in was Midnight Dagger. Then the Red Daggers landed, with Scarlet Dagger being the last to land.

Beary walked over to the Scarlet Dagger. There he met Ensign Horton, an Ursa Europus, "Scar 1, I presume," he said holding out his paw, "mind if I join you looking at the damage."

Horton took his paw. "Johan Horton and you are?"

"Spirit 6, Beary Maxumus." Beary answered. "Shall we take a look?"

The two Ensigns looked over the damage to the Scarlet Dagger. The missile pod had been destroyed. Luckily it was empty, or the resulting sympathetic explosions would have ripped the dagger apart. Their inspection also showed that the cloaking device had been severely damaged in the blast. Horton was amazed at Beary's knowledge of the dagger as they continued their inspection. Then Beary saw why the shield had failed.

Beary looked closer at the shield emitters, "Here's the problem. The aft emitters were not aligned properly giving you a weak spot over the missile pod." Beary turned to the Crew Chief, "The missile pod is a total loss; so is the cloak emitter. Also the shield emitters need to be realigned."

"Yes, Ensign Maxumus, the missile pod is not a problem we can scrap it. The cloak emitter will take 4 cycles to replace. I will personally realign the shield emitters." The Crew chief said.

Beary looked at Horton, "Can I buy you a cup of coffee?"

Horton looked at him. "Sure, I'll meet you in the mess hall. I need to take care of a few things. I'll just be a moment." After Beary left, Horton turned to the Crew Chief. "How did he know what was wrong with the emitters?"

The Crew Chief looked at Ensign Horton. "Sir Don't you know who he is? That is Dr. Beary Maxumus; he designed the engines and was on the design team for the red daggers."

Horton looked at his Crew Chief. "That cub, are you sure?"

The Crew Chief smiled. "Sir I worked with MSU 6 a few times. He was a Marine Corporal and one of the best pilots I have ever seen. You are right; I think he is 18 years old"

Horton just shook his head and headed off to collect that coffee.

On the Bridge, Commander Centaures was receiving a message from Fleet headquarters.

"Red Paw 2 reporting after action report as requested. Two Arcrilian Destroyers and four fighter Squadrons destroyed. One of the Destroyers was eliminated at Carnise Drift along with two Fighter Squadrons. Remainder was destroyed in Bearilian space this side of the Drift. We are awaiting orders."

"Red Paw 2, where is Red Paw 1? Gold leader 1, out."

"Gold Leader 1, Red Paw 1 is in his rest cycle. Do you wish him awakened?"

"Red Paw 2, No Need. Proceed to Carnise Drift secure and proceed as per orders, Gold leader out."

Centaures decided he better awake his friend to fill him in. "Captain, Bridge."

Atilus sat up, "Go, Bridge."

Centaures responded, "Orders from Headquarters: We are to secure Carnise Drift and proceed as ordered."

Atilus looked at his watch "Okay, you know what to do Commander. Wake me in 5 Cycles unless something comes up." He lay back down. He knew his friend could handle the ship as well as he could. He felt he needed to get some rest.

Centaures touched his com button. "Bridge to flight crews: stand down, get some rest. Ship wide, Yellow 4 Alert." With that, a third of the crew went to rest for 8 cycles. Others took a short break to eat.

Beary went to Medical to check on his mentor. Seeing Caesar he walked over to him. "How is Grizlarge doing?"

Caesar smiled "Thanks to young Ben he is doing fine. In fact, in another 12 cycles I am going to release him back on duty. How are you doing?"

Beary smiled a weary smile "I am fine; just fatigued. It has been a busy day. Can I see him?"

"Go ahead. I have a few more patients to see." With that, Caesar pointed to where the Master Chief was.

Beary stood by the bed, "Gunny, how are you doing?"

Grizlarge opened his eyes "I am okay Corporal . . ." Then he stopped and looked again. "Sorry Sir. I should say Ensign."

Beary smiled. "They threw them at me. I believe they are temporary. Doc said you're causing so much trouble he is going to kick you out of here in 12 cycles."

Grizlarge laughed, and then got serious. "Young Maritinus saved my life. I got careless, Cub. He killed the Arcrilian the hard way stuck its own knife in it as he crushed its neck. The Cadet may have saved the ship also."

"Gunny, I doubt you got careless. The Arcrilian just got in a lucky blow." Beary said reassuringly to his old friend.

Grizlarge smiled, "Okay, I won't retire today. Are you happy Sir?"

Beary laughed. "You're too young to retire. Besides, you know too much. Well, I better get some rest. Oh, by the way, they gave me the Crimson Blade. It's a great jump ship."

Grizlarge waved at his friend and closed his eyes. Things were moving too fast. Everything was out of control. He was afraid this little assault was just the beginning; and how did they know the Saber Claw was coming this way? He opened his eyes and hit his Com button. "Commander Centaures, Master Chief Grizlarge. Could I see you in medical, Sir, please?"

Centaures replied. "I'll be down in a few moments Chief.

Navigator, you have the Bridge." With that, he started for the ships hospital.

Grizlarge saw the Commander and tried to sit up.

Centaures said, "At ease Gunny. What can I do for you?"

Grizlarge asked, "Sir, the Arcrilian's knew we were coming? They were waiting for us."

"Yes Chief, I know. The problem is we don't know 'who'. That is partially what we are out here to find out." Centaures said.

Caesar went to the mess hall. He was hoping to meet with Beary and Ben. That's when he saw Ensign Pompey. He realized that she was the only other Ursa Maxmimus on the Saber Claw and she was a female. So he approached to give his greetings. "Ensign, I am Caesar Vantanus . . ."

Ensign Pompey cut him off. "I know of no such lineage among the clans. So you are either a liar or rogue."

Caesar was taken aback. "I am neither. My family name was Vantorious but my family gave me the honor . . . ."

Again she cut him off. "A servant family trying to start a new line that is even worse."

Beary had been standing by listening when he finally had enough. "And who are you to be so haughty? What was your family but sheepherders who gained prominence due to their wool? So who are you to question anyone's family?"

"Who are you to question my family or to call down dispersions on my family?" Ensign Pompey growled.

Beary smiled a wicked smile. "Your Ladyship, I am, Beary Maxumus Son of Octavious by Angelina, Great grandson of Sir Augustus Maxumus the Hammer of Corsan, and the Princess Maria Caesar. Next to my lineage your bears are nothing. So who are you to question my friend's lineage? Besides, since the destruction of our home world there are no longer serf families. You should know that!"

Ensign Pompey looked at him with her mouth open. No one had ever spoken to her like that and he did it with authority. She felt her face redden. She stood up, turned, and left without another word.

Caesar looked at his friend "I am sorry, Sire . . ."

Beary cut him off. "Don't you, ever call me that! You are my friend and are part of my family. Caesar, you are a gifted Doctor and your parents are the finest of our race. Don't you ever lower your eyes to anyone," he smiled, "or I'll tell my mother."

Caesar smiled. "You are your parent's son. They taught you well. Thank you, my friend."

Beary smiled, "Let's eat shall we?" The two friends sat down and started to eat. Just then Ben joined them. The three friends sat and chatted as they ate. Then they returned to their quarters.

When Ensign Pompey returned to her room she started crying. How could she have not seen his crest? He called her family a bunch of sheepherders. He was technically right but how dare, he! Beary Maxumus: the one bear who could say what he did! Yet she would not let the slight go without being answered! She would have to save face. She would challenge him to a duel in accordance with the old ways!

Ensign Pompey called the Captain. "Sir, Ensign Pompey. I am requesting permission to dual Ensign Maxumus."

Atilus looked at the com, "I do not understand, Priscilla, why would you want to duel Ensign Maxumus?"

"Sir, he dishonored my family." Pompey responded.

Atilus sighed, "Okay in the gymnasium, one cycle." Then he called Beary's quarters. "Ensign Maxumus, report to the Gym in one cycle."

Beary responded, "Yes, Sir. But may I ask why?"

Atilus answered, "You have been challenged to a duel by one of your race."

"The Lady Pompey I understand. I will be there, Sir." Beary turned off the com.

Ben looked at him. "I do not understand you are to fight a female of your race?"

Caesar spoke first, "Ben, this is my fault. But Beary will have to face her. Ben, the females of our race are fighters as much as the males. You should come and watch."

Captain Atilus was standing in the middle of the gym. He looked at his two officers. He knew Ensign Pompey was the ships champion with the pugilist sticks [fighting sticks about 5 feet long with padding on both ends used by the military to train close order combat]. Yet, she will be facing a combat trained Marine. She might just learn some humility.

"You will both start fighting when I say fight, and stop if I say stop. Do you both understand?"

Beary and Pompey both just nodded, and picked up the sticks. Beary twirled his and felt its balance. Pompey thought she saw an opening she charged and aimed at Beary's head. He easily dodged the blow and caught her across the back of her tail. She skidded across the floor. She caught herself and flew back at Beary spinning her stick and trying to catch him off balance. Beary blocked her blows with ease and then spun and caught her on the back of her shoulders hard enough to drive her to the floor. Pompey rolled and shot back up. Now she was angry she started circling Beary. Looking for an opening she saw him lower his guard and moved in. Before she knew what had happened, she found herself on her back with his stick at her throat.

Captain Atilus ordered "Stop!"

Beary, backed up and offered his paw to Ensign Pompey.

"You fought well Lady Pompey."

She glared at him, but took his paw and he lifted her up.

She started to leave when she heard him say. "Ensign, I am a fifth degree master in Bachee. Please believe me when I say you fought well." Beary said.

She turned toward him and bowed then left.

"Ensign Maxumus, did you say a fifth degree master?" Captain Atilus asked.

Beary smiled "Yes, Sir."

Atilus shook his head, "She never had a chance. Well played Ensign. Well played."

Beary walked to her berth and spoke into the com "Ensign Pompey, a word please?"

Priscilla opened the door "Ensign Maxumus, how may I help you? Or are you here to gloat over your victory?"

Beary could not believe how beautiful her eyes were or how beautiful she was. He cleared his throat. "I only wanted to make sure you were not injured."

She smiled. "In the olden days you could have demanded tribute for such a victory. Is that why you are here?"

"No, my Lady, for a tribute so won has no value. I only wanted to insure that you were well and ask if you would forgive me for my ill treatment of your family name. Caesar is my friend and his Parents are very close to mine." Beary said.

Priscilla closed her eyes and touched his face with her paw. "You pay me to high an honor, Sire Maxumus, and have faced my scorn with humility. I ask your forgiveness."

Beary smiled. "None is needed to be given. Goodnight my, Lady Pompey"

"Goodnight, Beary son of Octavious by Angelina." Priscilla sighed as she closed her door. *He really was the real deal.*

Atilus arrived on the bridge. "Fun and games are over. Navigator, head for the Carnise Drift passage. Launch multi—specter probes.

Atilus returned to his wardroom to catch up on the never ending paper work. This was the worst part of command. He looked up and saw someone sitting in a chair.

Ensign Pompey spoke first. "Sir, will you forgive me for the spectacle I made of myself?"

Atilus smiled back at his god daughter. "You have a lot of your father in you, girl. He always shot his mouth off before thinking. Yet next to Centaures he is my dearest friend, so you are forgiven. What do you think of our young Maxumus?"

Pompey sighed, "He has true nobility, yet a strength I have not seen in any of our kind in a long time. It is not just physical strength, but he has humility of heart."

Atilus looked at her and smiled *another victory for young Maxumus.* "Ensign you are not due to go on duty for 4 more cycles. Get some rest. That is an order."

Pompey smiled. "Yes, Captain." With that she returned to her quarters.

Chapter 8

Carnise Drift and Beyond

Atilus looked at the data coming in from the probes and from the optical sensors. There appeared to be no signs of an Arcrilian presence. He could see the dead Arcrilian destroyer. It was time to move in and reestablish the outpost. "Commander Centaures, notify Lt. Commander Vesuvius to join me in my ready room. Bring any files we have on the old outpost."

Centaures looked up from his breakfast. Never time to eat.

"Understood, Captain, see you in 10 STU. Lt. Commander Vesuvius meet me in the Captains ready room in 9 STU."

Lt. Commander Vesuvius, an Ursus Spelaeus, looked up. Well, it looked like the Captain was going to need his Civil engineers. "Yes Sir." He then turned to his 30 bear staff. "It looks like we are going to be put to work. Check over all the equipment and inventory all our materials."

Atilus was waiting for them when they arrived. Atilus looked up from the orders he had received. "Please have a seat. Lt. Commander Vesuvius, I have a large job for you. We have been ordered to reestablish the outpost on the Carnise Drift. What kind of support will you need?"

Vesuvius thought. "It depends on what is left of the old outpost. We need to know what still works and what doesn't. Will the outpost have a defense force or just automated defenses?"

Atilus said, "Both. They are sending two Companies of Marines to man the outpost, The Red Aces and Black Aces of the 307th Marine Regiment. We are looking at quarters for 66 Marines. Plus we need to set up several automated missile launchers, as well as gun, and other defenses positions."

Vesuvius thought for a moment. "Sir, first we will have to survey the Drift. Then we are going to have to see what we are going to need to replace any destroyed or worn out systems. I will need the Midnight Dagger for two Days and the use of at least one Red Dagger plus three space shelters for housing and workshops. We have all the necessary supplies and equipment. Do we have the time?"

Atilus looked at him. "I'll see that you have the time. Get your bears ready. We will be entering the Drift in one cycle. Dismissed, Lt. Commander Vesuvius, and tell your bears, thank you, for all the hard work they will be performing." Vesuvius stood up, saluted, and left.

Centaures smiled. "So, what do you want me to know that the Lt. Commander isn't privy to?"

Atilus shook his head. "Why do I even try? Okay, the Senate has decided to draw a line. We will no longer give up territory to the Arcrilians. The Fleet is being rebuilt. Soon, Fleet, will have new ships, like the Saber Claw, and larger ones built on the same design. Unfortunately, we are going to have to hold the line here by ourselves. The older fleet is being kept near the home worlds for now. How best do we do this with the resources we have?"

Centaures thought. "The Scarlet Dagger is almost fixed. I would pair it with the Midnight Dagger. Also, I think Lt. Commander Vesuvius was overly optimistic. His bears are up to the task but to really remap the Drift it will take at least four days. Also, the Drift was shot up pretty bad while we made our escape."

"Okay, it will take time. We have seven days before the Marines transport arrives." Atilus continued, "What about our

Ensign Maxumus, do we keep him with the Daggers or move him to other duties?"

Centaures smiled. "Both. We need him to fly, but right now they are not flying. So I keep him with me and teach him everything I know."

Atilus laughed. "That is what worries me. What should we do about Cadet Maritinus?"

Centaures shrugged. "I think we need to reward the young Polarian. Perhaps put him in for a Bronze Fang."

Atilus smiled. "I like it. It is unprecedented, but this whole trip is unprecedented. Write it up, Commander, and I'll sign it."

Centaures handed him the paper work. "The Chief already did. Major Basil and I have added comments and endorsed it. Well, I better get back to work. Where do you want me?"

Atilus thought, "In auxiliary control; I will be on the bridge. Take Ensign Maxumus with you."

With that they both left the ready room. Centaures saw Beary and waved for him to follow. They entered a turbo lift. "You're accompanying me to auxiliary control. I want you to observe everything. Ask questions. Learn as much as you can. Ensign Maxumus, you are not being reassigned, but for you this has become a higher level cruise. I need to teach you everything I can. We need to put three years of cruises into one cruise. I have been told you are a fast learner. I know you are a professional Marine, but this is different. You are being trained for Command, not to learn the rudiments of a system. Do you understand?"

Beary thought about what the Commander had said. "Sir, I will not let you down. Whatever, you ask of me, I'll do."

"Good. From now on you will pull a double shift unless you are flying. First Shift you will spend following me and learning every inch of this ship and its components. The second shift will be spent standing as a junior watch officer in various parts of the ship except engineering. You are already qualified there." With that they entered auxiliary control.

Auxiliary control was an exact duplicate of the bridge except it was located deep in the center of the ship. Commander Centaures sat in the center seat and Beary started going from station to station talking to the different operators. When he reached communications he stopped. Ensign Pompey was at the station. He walked over. "Ensign Pompey, I hope you don't mind but the Commander wants me to familiarize myself with all the subsystems."

Priscilla smiled. "I would love nothing more than to help you, Sire Maxumus."

Beary looked at her and smiled. In a quiet voice he said, "Please, Lady Pompey, don't call me Sire. Your Family is among the upper families of our race and your Father was a great pilot."

She quietly touched his face and quickly removed her paw. "In Auxiliary control we only monitor communications. The bridge handles all incoming and outgoing traffic but we have to be able to take control if the bridge loses communications. Also, it is my duty to keep commander Centaures or the watch officer informed." Ensign Pompey paused. "Commander, Bridge reports that we our entering the Drift."

"Thank you, Ensign Pompey, Ensign Maxumus, would you go over to plotting and show Lieutenant Lee our entry and exit path from the Drift?" Commander Centaures said.

Beary looked over at the small Ailurus Fulgens, his Red fur was bright against his blue uniform. While few in number, his kind, was known to be very good tacticians, they were able to solve multiple problems at the same time. Beary walked over. "Lieutenant Lee, I am Ensign Maxumus."

Lee smiled. "It is a pleasure to meet you, Ensign. Please tell me everything you and the Commander did from the time you entered the Drift till you returned to the Ship?" Beary related the story without leaving out anything. When he was done he showed the asteroids that were pounded by the barrage of the Arcrilian Destroyer and where the other Destroyer was demolished.

Lee closed his eyes, "You did well young Ensign. The Commander wants you to work with me and plot our movements into the passage. If there was still an Arcrilian presence where would you expect them to be?"

Beary thought about it and marked where he would expect trouble.

"Very good," Lee said, "You have done this before, I see."

Beary smiled, "Yes, Sir, I have, more than once."

"My position is as Watch Officer. You will act as the Junior Watch Officer." Lee motioned for Beary to take the console next to him.

On the Bridge, Captain Atilus was watching as they passed through each Choke point. Soon they reached the Asteroid that had served as the headquarters of the old outpost. It had suffered some damage but didn't look as badly hit as some of the others had been.

Atilus hit the com button "Lt Commander Vesuvius please report to the Midnight Dagger. Midnight Dagger and Scarlet Dagger prepare for launch; sealed orders on board." Dusk 1 and Scar 1 both reported that they were ready for launch. Atilus gave the order and the two daggers rotated and launched.

After 12 cycles the two Daggers returned. Lt. Commander Vesuvius headed for the Bridge. Upon arriving, he asked to see the Captain alone.

Vesuvius looked at the Captain, "The old headquarters was hit very hard. I will be able to refurbish it in about three days but it will take my entire crew."

Captain Atilus shook his head "Lt. Commander you have a day and a half. We need to get some weapon stations established. While you and your Crew do your job, the Midnight Dagger will finish the survey for you."

Vesuvius started to protest. "Sir, it will take time to do this job . . . ."

Atilus cut him off. "Lt. Commander, I know I am asking the impossible but we are all that stands between the enemy and our home worlds, and we are not going to give up the Tarsus system either."

"Sir, what if I split my team in half that would give us an extra team to work on the sensors and weapons. I will require help from other sections of the ship. Another thirty pairs of paws will make a big difference. There are at least 15 Bears in damage control that could do part of the work. The electronic shop also has at least 10 that are qualified, and some of the flight maintenance crew members could help." Vesuvius explained.

"Take who you need, just get it done. Lt. Commander, if I seem cross it is just that we are the tip of the sword, and the enemy has known our every move to this point." Atilus said. "Dismissed and get some rest."

Atilus thought about what needed to be done. One more thing needed to be examined: the remains of the Arcrilian destroyer. He knew the Chief was the best person to send and called him in.

"Master Chief, I have a job for you."

Grizlarge smiled. "You want me to have a look at the Arcrilian destroyer?" Atilus nodded, "May I pick my own team?" the Chief continued.

Atilus thought "Okay, Chief, who do you want?"

Grizlarge thought, "Security team 1, Cadet Maritinus, Ensign Maxumus, and Ensign Artemus. Of course, we will take the Crimson Blade. I would like to put Ensign Maxumus in charge of the boarding party."

Atilus examined him, "Why?"

Grizlarge shrugged. "Because he has boarded ships before but he has never commanded a team. Sir, I will be there to give suggestions, but what better way to teach him than a dead Ship."

"You have a good point, and I am sure Centaures would agree with you. I just hope we are not expecting too much from him." The Captain continued, "I will notify the Ensign. Get ready. Ensign Maxumus report to the Captains ready room. Commander Centaures please also report."

Beary looked up. *He had been asleep for what four cycles.* He quickly dressed and headed for the Captain's ready room. Along the way he met Commander Centaures.

"Have you had any rest, Ensign?" Centaures asked.

"About 4 cycles, Sir" Beary replied.

With that, Beary and Centaures reported to the Captain.

Centaures took his usual place and Beary stood at attention.

"Ensign, you are to lead a boarding party onto the dead Arcrilian destroyer. The Chief and his security team will accompany you and Ensign Artemus aboard the Crimson Blade. You will be in charge, but I suggest you take advice from the Gunny."

Beary looked at the Captain. "Yes Sir. You want us to collect any and all intelligence we can and possibly try and download the ship's files and the Captain's correspondence. Sir, I have been on boarding parties before, but I was always the point man."

Atilus smiled inwardly. *This one was smart; he knew what was expected but also had the ability to express his doubts.* "Ensign, most bears I have put in this situation have never boarded an enemy vessel before. Just remember, it is not your job to take point that is a Private's or Corporal's job. Your job is to lead and delegate. The Master Chief is there to help you, but you are in charge."

"Yes Sir. By your leave, Sir, I will prepare my team." With that, Beary saluted and left. As he went out the door he called Artemus. "Savato, it is Beary. Saddle up; we are going for a ride."

"Understood, Boss, Master Chief already informed me to get the Crimson Blade ready." Artemus responded. Well, one thing was sure: being around this guy was not going to be boring.

Chapter 9

Dead Ships, Ghosts, and Projects

Beary met the Master Chief as he headed toward the Crimson Blade. "Gunny, who is on the team going on the mission with us?"

Grizlarge answered back, "My Security team 1. Most have some experience, especially my two squad leaders. Both of them were with MSU 9. They're as good as they get. They do have a few young privates on the team, but it's a dead ship so it shouldn't be a problem."

Beary thought for a second. "A wise old Gunnery Sergeant told me once that nothing was ever as simple as it seemed. I think we had better treat this like we are boarding a fully manned and operational ship."

Grizlarge smiled to himself. *The Cub was thinking and acting like a leader not a corporal.* "You're right. Besides, it will make for a better training session if it is a dead ship. If it isn't, then we will be ready."

When they arrived at the Crimson Blade it was all ready to go. Beary waved to Artemus and approached Security team 1. Grizlarge introduced the team to the young Ensign. Ben just nodded to his friend.

Sergeant Blackpaw looked at Beary. "Sir, what is your call sign? I am Banshee 8. Squad leader of Team 1:1"

Beary smiled. "I am Spirit 6."

Sergeant Blackpaw looked at his friend Sergeant Nighthunter. Both flashed a sign of recognition. *So this was the Ghost.*

Sergeant Nighthunter saluted. "Sir, I am Sergeant Nighthunter, Banshee 9, and Squad leader Team 1:2. It is an honor to serve with you."

Beary nodded. "We have three objectives, download the information on the Arcrilian destroyer's main computer core, download the captain's log and correspondence, and gather any other intelligence information we can find."

Everyone acknowledge the objectives. Beary continued, "You all have been told this is a dead ship. The easiest way to get killed on any boarding party is to believe your enemies can no longer fight. We will treat this as if we were boarding a fully operational ship. I want everyone fully equipped for the mission. Is that understood?" Beary waited for everyone to acknowledge his orders, and then continued. "I want Cadet Maritinus and one marine from each squad to stay aboard the Crimson Blade to maintain security aboard the jump ship."

Ben looked disheartened. Beary smiled. "Ensign Artemus will take command of the Crimson blade when we transfer over. Cadet Maritinus will then act as weapons officer. Can you handle the assignment, Cadet?"

Ben straightened and said "I have been given instruction in the weapon systems. I will not fail you."

"Alright, we will split into three teams. Sergeant Blackpaw, you and three of your marines will secure the ships computer core. Sergeant Nighthunter, you and three of your marines will secure the captains log and correspondence. The chief and I, along with one Marine from each squad, will look for other intelligence. Does everyone understand their duties?" Beary waited till he got an affirmative. "Okay, let's board."

Artemus looked at Beary. "Ben will make an excellent weapons officer. He learned the system in just about two hours. Besides, as you pointed out, I can fly the ship and fight her if I have to. Thanks for leaving a small detail aboard also."

Beary smiled. "I have been there. It was on an old C Class; three Arcrilians beamed in on me. I was by myself, and I didn't much care for the situation. It will be harder for them to do it on a Red Dagger, but why not set a precedent."

Artemus shook his head "Remind me, how old are you? Oh never mind. As the Lady at the orphanage use to say, "It's not the years; it's the distance traveled."

Beary just smiled and climbed aboard and took the pilots seat, while Artemus ensured everyone was ready and returned to his seat. Artemus reported "Boss, we're ready."

"Command, Spirit 6 is ready to launch."

"Spirit 6, Command authorizes, hot launch. Good hunting"

"Acknowledge hot launch, Spirit 6 out."

Beary rotated the Crimson Blade and shot out of the hanger bay, rotated and headed away from the target. Once behind another asteroid he turned on the Shield and the Cloak, and headed for the Arcrilian Destroyer. The Engineering section had been ripped apart. The Engines were laying on one asteroid while the rest of the destroyer was crashed on another. Surprisingly, the main part of the ship looked intact. They flew past the engines.

Artemus looked at his instruments, "We have a minute power signal coming from the engine debris field. It could be a leaking auxiliary power unit."

Beary thought. "Mark its location and assign it a target number. Dedicate two missiles to it. This whole set up smells. I know we hammered this ship, but the back of my neck is tingling. We'll dock by that service port. Keep everyone on transporter lock, stay cloaked, be ready to pull us out and hammer the ship here, here and here." Beary pointed to strategic points on the Arcrilian destroyer.

Artemus noted the positions and dedicated missiles to each spot. Beary took them in and docked the Crimson Blade.

Beary looked at Artemus. "Take command."

Artemus saluted. "Command transferred. Good hunting. Cadet Maritinus, report to weapons control."

Ben got up and took the weapon officer's seat.

Beary reached to open the access hatch, when the Chief stopped him. Grizlarge whispered to him, "Not your job, Sir."

Sergeant Nighthunter swept past, stationed his three Marines, opened the hatch, and jumped through followed by his team. Sergeant Blackpaw followed with his team. The Chief led Beary through and the other two marines followed.

Blackpaw held up his paw. "I have movement." Sergeant Nighthunter also reported movement.

Beary thought quickly. "Set some claymores around the bend of both corridors." Beary ordered.

Two Marines dashed in opposite directions. They both flew back when their task was done. They both reported, "Sir, there are two male Scorpius coming down the halls one on each side."

The two monstrous beasts walked into the kill zone at the same time, with over 1000 small metallic balls tearing in to their hard exoskeleton. One of the beasts died instantly, but the one coming down the hall toward the left staggered around the corner one pincher and its poisonous tail whipping side to side. Sergeant Nighthunter fired a charged bolt from his crossbow into the head of the Scorpius. The animal reared up and then dropped dead.

Deep inside the ship came an angry scream that vibrated all through the ship as the Female Scorpius felt the death of her two mates. Then they heard the power surge throughout the ship as systems were being turned on. The Arcrilian Destroyer was only partially out of the fight. Beary and his boarding team had fallen into a trap.

Beary hit his com button, "Spirit 6 to Spirit Blade 2: launch target packages one through four."

Artemus acknowledged the order and turned to Ben, "You heard the boss, one through four."

Ben put the Commands into the fire control computer.

The first two missiles left the Crimson blade and raced for the engine debris field. Four more shot out and headed for the forward weapons array. Three more went for the area over which the female Scorpius was held. The last package of four missiles was aimed at the location of the ship's auxiliary control station.

The first missiles struck the engine debris field. Immediately the power went out on the destroyer. The forward weapons array was struck next, ripping major portions of the front of the destroyer apart. Bulkheads slammed shut, isolating the boarding party from the rest of the ship. The next group of missiles that struck near where the female Scorpius was isolated failed to kill her, but it did release her from her holding cage. Enraged, she attacked a group of Arcrilians nearby. Before they could react she had killed two of them with her front pincers tearing them in two. A third was skewered by her poisoned stinger.

The remaining Arcrilians opened fire on her. After killing two more Arcrilians she died of her many wounds.

The last set of missiles tore open the Destroyer's hull and smashed the area around its auxiliary control station. The Arcrilian Captain and his first officer were trying to get things back under control when the bulkhead behind them turned to molten ooze and burst toward them, killing them instantly as they became part of the burning mass of metal.

Beary and his team closed their viziers and sealed and re pressurized their boarding suits. Then Beary molded some thermite cord on the wall behind them. According to their diagrams there was an access tub behind the wall that would lead them to the computer core. The thermite burned through the wall and gave them access to the tube.

Sergeant Blackpaw and his team entered first, followed by Beary and Grizlarge. Once they were outside the computer core, Sergeant Blackpaw blew the door and three of his team entered killing the three Arcrilian technicians in the room. Sergeant Blackpaw set up a small APU [Auxiliary Power Unit] and a portable data storage unit and began downloading the Arcrilian computer files.

Beary and Grizlarge proceeded with their two Marines, through the next door into the communications room. They found the storage units for incoming and outgoing messages and started down loading the information.

Sergeant Nighthunter and his team had climbed up and found an access to the ship's bridge. Once inside, they were caught in a fire fight with twelve Arcrilians. When the fight was over two of his marines were down. Both were wounded. So he called the Crimson Blade and had them beamed off. He then started collecting the data they were sent to get.

Artemus beamed one of his security marines over to replace one of Sergeant Nighthunter's wounded men and then quickly evaluated the two wounded Marines. Artemus then contacted Beary. "Spirit Blade 2 to Spirit 6, I need to evacuate wounded to ship immediately please, advise?"

Beary thought. "Spirit Blade 2, Understood make best possible speed and return. Spirit 6 out."

Artemus turned to Ben and the remaining security Marine,

"Do what you can to stabilize them." He then turned to report to the ship, "Blue Dragon Control, Spirit blade 2; we have two WIA [wounded in action] request immediate transport to medical."

"Blue Dragon Control to Spirit Blade 2: acknowledge two WIA. Beam directly to Medical. Dr. Fang, we have two WIA. Prepare for beam in."

Centaures looked up and started toward medical. He arrived just as Dr. Fang and Caesar were cutting off the boarding suits. Both had been hit by energy weapons. One private's arm was badly burned. The other had taken a hit to the chest. The armor in his suit had absorbed much of the energy, but not all of it.

Dr. Fang gave Commander Centaures a quick "get out of here I am busy" look and started working to save the second marine private. Caesar was too busy working on the arm to even notice the Commander.

Centaures returned auxiliary control to try and get a handle on what was going on.

Meanwhile, Sergeant Nighthunter and his Marines planted explosives on all the vital command and control areas on the bridge and returned down the access corridor and to the entry point. Beary and Sergeant Blackpaw's teams set their explosives and returned to the entry point.

Just as Beary was starting to call Artemis, he heard, "Spirit 6, Spirit blade 2 ready for pick up." Just then, the hatch opened and the team rushed in to the Crimson Blade. As they pulled away, Beary hit the detonator and ordered a full spread of missiles launched at the collapsing destroyer. When it was over, only a debris field was left.

Once they had landed back aboard the Saber Claw, Beary sent the intelligence with Sergeant Blackpaw and Sergeant Nighthunter to the intelligence officer. Beary and Grizlarge made their way to medical to check on the two wounded Marines.

Chapter 10

Reports, Doubts, and Long Hours

Beary and Grizlarge reached medical just as Dr. Fang came out of the operating room. He smiled a tired smile and wiped his massive forehead. Looking at Grizlarge he reported, "Both of your Marines are going to make it. One took a blast to the chest his armor deflected about 60% of it; but still he took a hard hit. The other ones arm was hit but Dr. Vantanus did an excellent job repairing the damage. We are looking at least three weeks, at least, for them to return to duty."

Beary thanked Dr. Fang and then turned to Grizlarge. "Master Chief, I need to report to Commander Centaures. Why don't you get some food and rest?"

Grizlarge looked at Beary. "Cub, this wasn't your fault! You know better than anyone that boarding an enemy ship is dangerous. It is just part of the job, and we did retrieve the information we were after."

Beary looked at him. "Gunny, I know the risks, but it is different when it's your command. I hope the Intel was worth it." With that, he headed to see Commander Centaures.

Beary found him looking over some of the raw data they had retrieved. "Ensign Maxumus, reporting as requested for after action debriefing, Sir."

Centaures looked up. "Have a seat, Ensign. You and your team did a great job. The amount of information that was recovered will keep Fleet Intelligence working for half a year to digest it."

Beary dropped his head. "Most of the credit goes the Sergeant Blackpaw and Sergeant Nighthunter. They are excellent squad leaders."

Centaures looked at him. "Ensign Maxumus, snap out of it!"

Beary sat up. "Sir?"

Centaures smiled. "Ensign, you're worried about the two injured Marines. I talked to Sergeant Nighthunter and Sergeant Blackpaw. They said that they would follow you anywhere anytime. So did the other Marines. Ensign, you were the only one that realized that it might be a trap."

"Yes Sir," Beary stated, "and I still lead my team into that trap."

Centaures sighed. "Beary, if you hadn't, we wouldn't have the information we now have, and they would have ambushed the Saber Claw. I know that this was your first command. It is always hard to lead others in combat. You are responsible for their lives, and sometimes you have to risk those lives. Even worse, sometimes you might have to sacrifice the lives of some of your troops to save others. That is why it's called command. You have always been the one sent in. Did you ever question a command that could risk your life?"

Beary shook his head, "No Sir. All that mattered was the mission."

Centaures smiled. "That is always what matters Ensign, no matter the cost. Even if you're a ship's Captain, you might have to destroy your own ship with the entire crew on board."

Beary thought for a moment. "I understand, Commander; I just had doubts about whether I couldn't have done something different or better."

Centaures looked at him. "You will always have doubts. If you allow those doubts to control you, you will fail and get your team killed. Do you understand?"

Beary sighed. "Thank you, Sir."

Centaures nodded, "Get some sleep, Ensign. Report to Weapons Control in 9 Cycles. I want you to study the fire control systems."

Beary stood saluted and left.

Atilus came in. "Well?"

Centaures looked at his friend and Captain. "Do you remember your first command? He did well, but he felt he had failed the two Marines that were wounded. Still, I would send him out again and the Bears with him said they would follow him."

Atilus thought. "Are we being fair to him? He is only 18 years old. He is just a cub. We sent him out there expecting little more than a training exercise on a dead ship."

"Yes Sir, and he was the only one that expected a trap and he set up plans to deal with it. Isn't it better to find out how good he really is now, rather than in five years?" Centaures replied.

"Okay. Well, what did the expedition get us? Was it worth it?" Atilus asked.

Centaures just smiled, "Oh yeah, we hit the mother lode."

While the Captain and the First officer talked, Beary had returned to his quarters. No one was there, so Beary lay down and went to sleep. That's when the nightmares started up. After about three cycles he woke up covered in sweat. He still had six cycles before he had to report, so he decided to go to the ship's gymnasium. He dressed in his work-out uniform and headed out.

Ben waved to him and continued toward their berth. Beary stopped and called to him, "Have you seen Caesar?"

Ben turned. "He is in Medical. One of the engineers was injured and required surgery. Caesar decided to stay there and monitor him."

Beary smiled. "Ben, you did a good job out there today. Thank you." with that Beary continued on his way.

Ben watched his friend walk away. His chest swelled a little. *The Ghost had said he had done a good job!*

Beary arrived at the gym; he had decided to work on what his father called the Fast Knife technique. He pulled 20 knives from his bag and slipped them into his belt. He also placed two Hammer axes on his belt and started in on his targets. As he moved through them he released a barrage of knives. After 15 Sub Standard Time Units [SubSTU] he had hit all his targets in the bull's-eye and had sent or plunged a hammer into their targets. He stopped to review his exercise. His accuracy was perfect but he was still 5 SubSTU behind his Father's normal time. He just shook his head.

From behind him came a familiar voice. "That was amazing! What is that technique called?" Ensign Pompey asked.

Beary turned around and saw her standing there in her workout uniform. He was taken by how her eyes sparkled. "Lady Pompey. It is called the Fast Knife technique. My Father taught it to me."

She came over closer to him. "What are those strange looking weapons called?"

Beary smiled. "They are Hammers of Corsan which I modified by adding an ax blade to them. They are perfectly balanced so they can be thrown or used as a direct contact weapon."

Pompey looked at him "Sire Maxumus, you have told me I should not refer to you as such. Do you not think you can drop the lady? We are both Ensigns. Can you not just call me by my name: Priscilla?"

Beary looked at her. "But you are a Lady. I am just a cub."

She almost glared at him, and then softened. "Dr. Beary Maxumus, you are not that much younger than me. You have accomplished much in your 18 years and you are one of the humblest and sweetest males of our race. Or are you the most devious?"

Beary was taken aback. "I do not understand?"

She moved closer. "I see how you look at me. Can you not tell that I look at you the same way? I started falling in love with you that night you came to my quarters." She reached out and touched his face with her paw.

Beary placed his paw on her face. "You would honor me with your love, my sweet Lady Priscilla? You must know that I fell in love with you the first time I saw you. But these are dangerous times."

She placed her paw on his lips. "You know that does not matter. However, I do expect to be courted properly my dear Beary. That takes time." With that, she kissed him and said, "Can you teach me the Fast Knife technique?"

Beary went through his paces once more. Again his aim was perfect and his time was better by two SubSTU. He then handed her the weapons and instructed her on the technique. On her first try she scored almost a perfect score. Her time however was almost a full STU. Beary smiled. "That was very good especially for your first time."

Priscilla just beamed. "I had an excellent teacher." She smiled. "I need to shower and report to duty. Thank you, Beary." With that, she sprinted to the showers.

Beary checked his gear and moved toward the showers. He looked at his watch. He had just enough time to get dressed and eat before he had to report.

In the mess hall, he saw Caesar and sat down with him.

Caesar looked up. "You look like a cantarus [a horse like creature] heading the wrong way."

Beary laughed. "You must be looking in a mirror."

Caesar smiled. "Good, you sound like your old self. Did Lady Pompey find you?"

Beary looked surprised. "Yes, I was in the gym working on the Fast Knife Technique. Why?"

"I was never able to beat your Mothers time, 8 SUBTU, she was fast! My best time was 15 SUBTU." Caesar replied.

Beary shook his head. "My Mother taught you the Technique? Wait, that's not what I mean! 8 SubSTU, no, Ensign Pompey was looking for me?"

Caesar looked concerned. "Yes, yes, and yes. Do I need to take you to medical? You seem confused."

Beary just thought for a moment. "She says she loves me."

Caesar said, "Well that explains the symptoms. You do know she is Captain Atilus's God Daughter?"

Beary shook his head, "No, I didn't." Changing the subject, he continued, "How are you?"

Caesar shrugged. "I almost lost one of the civil engineers twice on the operating table. We could still lose him. It was a stupid accident. He was tired got careless and knocked over some construction plates. Crushed both legs and punctured a lung. He is stabilized. If we can fight the infection, and if we didn't miss more damage than we could see, he might survive."

Beary quietly asked, "Do you ever have nightmares?"

Caesar looked at his friend. "Beary, when I was an intern we had a transport accident come in. 350 Bearilians were on it. Your, Mother and I worked for 48 Cycles straight. We lost 30 of the patients. I had to tell 15 of the families that their loved ones had died. I see their faces almost every night. Yeah, I have nightmares. It's part of the job. We saved 320 that night I can't remember a single one of their faces. But the ones we lost still haunt me. Your mother told me it was part of the job."

Beary sat back. "Thank you, Caesar. Well I have to go to Weapons Control for a shift."

Caesar caught his arm. "The Captain is allowing us to contact our families tonight. You will call home, Beary. That's not a question; I will have your posterior locked in medical if you don't. I can do it, and Dr. Fang will back me."

Beary started to protest then stopped. "Well, I guess I need to tell them about the Lady Priscilla. After all I was informed by her that I had to court her properly."

Caesar's mouth dropped, and then he smiled. "Get out of here, you will be late."

Meanwhile, Lt. Commander Vesuvius was standing in front of Captain Atilus. "Captain, my Bears need rest. They have been working for three days without rest. We have already lost one engineer due to fatigue. All I am asking for is eight cycles so everyone can rest. We have almost half the defenses up and operational and the marine's quarters done."

Atilus looked at his Civil Engineer. "I understand, Lt. Commander. Give your troops eight cycles to eat hot food and rest.

But we must get this project done soon; it is vital to the defense of the home worlds."

Vesuvius's anger flared, "The stuffed shirts at fleet should have thought of that before they deactivated this site . . . ."

Atilus cut him off, "That will be enough, Lt. Commander! Go take care of your engineers and get some rest."

Vesuvius saluted, and then left.

Centaures waited for Lt. Commander Vesuvius to leave, "You know he is right."

Atilus turned toward him, "That's the problem. How would *you* like to take over?"

Centaures just smiled. "No, you're in command, I just want to bask in your glory and hold your coat."

"Keep talking like that and I'll insist Fleet give you a command of your own." Atilus fired back.

"You're not that cruel. Besides, you like my happy intellect." Centaures answered.

"In four cycles I want to open up the communication stations so our crew can call home. Make sure Maxumus calls his family. They need to talk, just in case I get their son killed." Atilus said.

"Yes Sir. Besides he needs to tell them about Ensign Pompey." Centaures said, watching his old friend.

Atilus shoulders sagged, and then recovered. "I was afraid it would happen. She approached him, didn't she?" He looked at Centaures. Accepting his silence for an affirmative he continued, "She could do worse. He is an exceptional young Bearilian. I just hope she doesn't become a distraction. We are pushing him very hard and fast."

Centaures shook his head. "I don't believe so. Lt Commander Dontanus just called from weapons control, while you were talking with Vesuvius. Our young Ensign found a problem in the fire control matrix and fixed it. Improving the efficiency of the fire control computers by 10%, Dontanus wants to keep him. I said no of course."

Atilus smiled. "I wonder if we could sneak him into engineering without starting a riot."

Centaures smiled. "You are the Captain, but I think Lt. Commander Tantous would try and throw us both out an air lock.

Besides, between flying, learning parts of the ship he didn't design, and courting our dear Priscilla, I don't think he has any time left."

Atilus looked at his First, "Don't you have work to do, you Pirate? If not, I could give you some of this blasted paperwork."

Centaures mockingly held up his paws in surrender and said, "Anything but that Captain, besides I need to check with our intelligence crew to see what else they have found." With that he got up saluted his friend and left.

Chapter 11

Calls Home, Calls for Help

Beary had finished his tour in Weapons Control and was headed for his berth, when he ran into Commander Centaures. Centaures motioned to him. "You're with me Ensign Maxumus."

Beary fell in beside the Commander. "Sir, if I may ask where, are we going?"

Centaures kept a straight face. "We are following the Captain's orders, Ensign. Also, what are your intentions toward our dear Ensign Pompey?"

Beary stuttered, "Sir? I, is there a problem with, I mean is it against regulations or . . . ."

Centaures just shook his head. "For a young officer with your record, education, and abilities you have failed to master the art of speaking, or is it the young Lady?"

Quieting his thoughts, Beary continued, "Sir, my intentions are honorable when it comes to the Lady Pompey. If you have any concerns about me, please tell me."

Centaures wanted to see if he would get angry, instead Beary had deflected the question with a question. He wanted to know if he was good enough. "You will make a fine pair. I was more concerned about her intention than yours, anyway. The females of your race are not afraid to express themselves."

"That is true, Sir. That's also why our marriages last. Sir, where are we going?" Beary asked.

"We are here, my quarters. You will use my com station to call your parents. That is not a request, Ensign. It is the Captains orders and I have been charged with seeing they are carried out." Centaures explained as he opened his door.

Beary looked around the room. It was almost bare except for a bed and a work station.

Centaures smiled. "I spend most of my time in my office or the bridge, not much need to fancy up this space. There is the com panel. It is time to call home."

Beary dreaded making the call. If he was lucky his mother would answer. He had always been able to talk to her. The Com link established and the Senators face materialized. "So my disobedient son finally decides to call home. Look at you, not even out of the Academy and you have received a field promotion to Ensign." Then his voice softened, "I read your file son I am proud of you. Your Great-Grandfather would also be proud. This isn't the life I wanted for you."

"I am sorry, Father, for having deceived you. It's just . . . ." Beary tried to say.

The Senator cut his son off. "No, Beary, it is I who should be sorry. You were always the one most like me. I put you in the position of disobeying because I was unwilling to listen. Did they put you in engineering?"

Beary smiled. "No Father, but that's a long story. Let's just say I am not welcome in engineering I am flying jump ships and learning all the other ship's systems."

"Who is your Captain?" Octavious inquired.

"Captain Atilus." Beary answered

"That reckless hot-head was given a Command! I almost flunked him out of flight school. Who was dumb enough to agree to be his First?" Octavious inquired.

"I was, Senator Maxumus." Centaures answered.

Octavious laughed. "My youngest son entrusted to a hot-head and a pirate. What is the fleet coming to? Let me get your mother. Angelina, our son wishes to talk to you. I love you, Beary. May the Creator's blessing, be with you."

Angelina's face appeared on the screen. "My son, you look well. How is Caesar doing?"

Beary smiled. "Mother, he is doing great. He has also been promoted. He is a great Doctor. I also need to ask you and Father to contact Sire Pompey for me. I wish to court his daughter, Lady Priscilla."

Angelina beamed. *So a young Maxmimus female had chosen her son*. "What does she look like, my son?"

Beary thought. "Her eyes are like sunrise over Lake Bora near home on a cool autumn morning. Mother, can you really complete the Fast Knife Technique in 8 SUBTU."

"Yes Dear. Now about the girl, is she also on your ship?" Angelina asked.

"Mother, she is a com officer and she is beautiful. I need to go, Mother, my time is up. Stay safe. I love you all." Beary turned off the Com link. "Thank you, Sir."

Centaures smiled. "It is Okay, Ensign, now go, and get some rest."

All over the Saber Claw the crew was calling their families. Priscilla called hers. "Hello Mother, Father, I am doing well. Captain Atilus sends his respects."

Her parents greeted her. "Daughter, we are so glad to hear from you. What is new?"

Seeing her opening, she said, "I have met one of our Races that I like very much."

Her Father exploded. "I suppose he is a low born country Maxmimus."

"Father, your opinion, cost me a humiliating loss with pugilist sticks. He defeated me completely." Priscilla allowed the statement to sink in.

Her mother looked pained. "He didn't demand tribute, did he?"

"Mother, you and Father taught me that I had to live by our customs." Sensing her mother's, pain Priscilla added, "But he was too much of a gentile Bearilian to demand tribute. The truth is that we are far beneath his family. He is the Son of Octavious and Angelina Maxumus and Great Grandson of Sir Augustus Maxumus and Maria Caesar. He has asked his parents to contact you."

Her father paled. "Senator Maxumus, is going to ask me for permission for his son to court my daughter?"

"Yes, Father, I expect you to be humble, for I wish to do this according to our customs. I will be his if he wants me, whether you agree or not. He has won the right according to our customs and your own rules. After all compared to his family we are mere sheepherders" This last tweak hit its mark and Priscilla knew it.

"I am sorry, Daughter. It will be as you say." was all he could say.

"Father, I love you. But you taught me wrong and it took one whose feet I should not even kiss to teach me humility." Priscilla added.

Her Mother smiled. *It was about time someone did.* "Do you love him?"

Priscilla looked at her mother. "Yes. I have never met anyone like him. His strength is unmatched and yet he has humility of heart I have not seen. His eyes . . . ."

"Daughter," Her mother gently interrupted, "You told us his family's name, but not his."

"Oh, he is Ensign Dr. Beary Maxumus; He designed the engines that propel our ship. He is brilliant and handsome." Priscilla added.

"Do not worry. I will control your father. He has already taken off to make plans for the meeting. You were not kind to your Father, Priscilla, but I understand. You will write him and apologize." Her Mother concluded, "We love you Daughter."

Priscilla dropped her head. "I love you and Dad also, I am sorry, but he made me mad. Tell him I am still his little girl and always will be. Goodbye mother."

She turned from the screen and started to cry, when she heard a knock at her door. Wiping her eyes she said, "Come in."

Beary opened the door. He saw the tears still in her eyes. "Are you alright, my Lady?"

She flew into his arms and wept. After a few standard time units she calmed down. "I am sorry; you should know I am known to be a shrew, with a sharp tongue. Your parents will not want me."

Beary pushed her a little away, and looked into her eyes,

"My parents will love you. In fact, my Father will contact yours tomorrow. Then I will court you properly. For now, will you have dinner with me?"

She fell into his arms again but this time without tears. "You know, I would have given you tribute according to our customs if you had demanded it. I am glad you didn't. Yet, I am yours."

Beary blushed. "My sweet Lady I . . . ."

Priscilla smiled. "The great Maxumus is embarrassed. Your Mother is a great Doctor. Did she not explain that females of our Race express their inner thoughts to the ones they love? I am yours, Beary, but you will wait will you not to take your prize?"

Beary stammered, "Of course, I mean . . . ."

She kissed him and said; "Let's go eat, shall we?" she took his paw and led him out of her room.

Ben called his parents. "Hail, Father, it is I, your son."

"Hail, my son. Have you brought honor to your, Clan?" His Father asked.

"I have killed an Arcrilian with his own blade and my bare paws. I also helped to destroy a crippled Arcrilian Destroyer. He who saved my Brother is on my ship he has honored me with his friendship and told me that I did well in destroying our enemy." Ben stated.

His Father let out a war call. "Tonight we will celebrate your victories and write them in the book. Hunt well, my son."

"Hunt well, my father." With that, Ben turned off the com link.

Caesar looked up. "You didn't talk long."

Ben smiled. "Tonight there will be singing and dancing in my village. They will feast and drink to our victories. Will not your family do the same?"

Caesar grinned. "Tonight my family will gather at the Maxumus chapel. They will pray to the Creator for our safety, and for my patients. They will also eat after the service."

Ben smirked, "Our Clans are different; we know the Creator will be at our celebration to enjoy the music and the songs. Yours will go to a Chapel to pray for the fallen. Will not the Creator help you to heal them or take them home? Why make your celebration solemn?"

Caesar thought for a moment. "It is just our way, Ben. It has been so forever." With that, they talked about many things.

Beary came in. "Who are you two? You vaguely look like my roommates."

Caesar smiled and spoke first, "Is that shade of lip gloss regulation?"

Ben laughed, and Beary blushed.

Beary thought quickly. "I talked to my father and Mother she sends you both her love and prayers."

Ben shook his head. "Your Race must keep the Creator busy with all your prayers."

Beary looked confused and Caesar laughed.

Caesar smiled. "I'll explain later." After talking a while, the three friends went to sleep.

For the first time in months, Beary's dreams were sweet.

After about 5 Cycles, the Klaxon went off throughout the Ship. The three friends sprang to their feet. Beary threw on his uniform and headed for Auxiliary Control. Caesar headed for Medical and Ben headed to be with Chief Grizlarge. He had decided that it was his duty to protect the Chief.

Beary arrived at Auxiliary Control and went to plotting. Centaures noted that Beary was at his station and nodded. He looked around turning to Ensign Pompey. "Please report Auxiliary Control manned and ready."

Pompey nodded. "Bridge, Auxiliary Control is manned and ready."

Atilus thought. "Stand down to yellow alert. Ensign Maxumus, Chief Grizlarge, and Commander Centaures please report to my wardroom."

Centaures motioned to Beary. "Come on, Ensign, I feel the excrement is about to hit the fan again."

When they arrived, Beary saw the Chief and Ben standing off to one side. "Commander, the transport carrying the Red and Black Aces was shot down over the Forest Moon of Tarsus 9. There may be survivors. Also, we need to be sure that the transport is destroyed so that there is no intelligence value to the Arcrilian's. Unfortunately we do not have a MSU unit aboard."

Beary looked at Atilus. "Sir, you do have an insertion team. The Chief and I have done this before. We would need the

Crimson Blade and a security person and a Medical officer. There are bound to be injured if there are survivors."

Centaures looked at his Captain. "It is our only option. I'll call Dr. Fang and see who is on landing rotation."

Atilus looked at Beary. "Who do you want for your security officer?"

Ben spoke up, "Sir, if I may?"

Atilus looked at Ben. "What is it Cadet?"

"Sir, I have been trained to operate the weapon systems of the Crimson Blade. I also took part in the raid on the Arcrilian Destroyer." Ben pleaded.

Beary looked at his friend. "Cadet Maritinus is capable. He would do well."

Centaures looked at the Captain, "Ensign Vantanus is the Doctor on call."

The Captain looked at Beary. "Then it is settled notify your team."

Beary hit his com button. "Artemus we have a mission. Load the Crimson Blade with half and half, air attack and ground attack missiles. We will also need small arms packages six and nine."

Artemus shook his head, "Got it Boss. Medical package ten has also been delivered." Artemus thought to himself, *well here we go again, once more into the breach*. He turned around and saw Ben running toward the Crimson Blade. "What is going on, Cadet Maritinus?"

"We are going to the Forest moon of Tarsus 9. We need to rescue the Marines that were coming to join us." Ben told him. "I am to be your weapons officer."

Artemus nodded. "Well, help me get the ship ready."

Beary, Grizlarge and Caesar arrived just as Ben was loading the last of the supplies. Beary, motioned his team into the small briefing room off to one side of the hanger bay, once they were all seated, he brought up a 3D image of the Forest Moon of Tarsus 9.

Beary started the briefing. "What you are looking at is Dryden the Forest Moon of Tarsus 9. It is an M class moon with an Oxygen and Nitrogen atmosphere. Breathing units should not be necessary however, I want them available.

Tarsus 9 is a gas giant; it has twelve other moons, three of which are capable of sustaining life.

The transport ship, Raven Star, was carrying two Marine Companies the Black and Red Aces. It was shot down and crashed landed on Dryden in the Central Mountain Range just south of the moon's equator. We believe there may be survivors but we are not sure.

Our mission is three fold: first destroy what is left of the Raven Star to ensure no intelligence information exists. Second is to rescue any survivors. Third is to engage any and all targets of opportunity necessary to complete the first two objectives." Beary looked around. "Are there any questions?"

Artemus looked at Beary. "Only one, Boss, how do we play it?"

Beary nodded. "Once we arrive at the crash site, the Chief and I become the insertion team. You will take over Command of the Crimson Blade. Search for survivors and take out any targets necessary. If you need to leave to save injured Marines or if you are full from recovering a unit do so at your discretion. But please come back for the Chief and me. The three of you are not to leave the ship unless it is to aid in evacuation. Are there any other questions? No? Okay, let's get going."

Chapter 12

Dryden the Forest Moon

They rotated out of the launch bay and headed behind a large asteroid. They engaged the cloak and the shield and went to warp.

Beary turned to Artemus. "Savato, when we get in range, let's start looking for a beacon and see if we can figure out what happened. Also start scanning for any Arcrilian communication in the region. We need to know what we're facing."

"No problem, Boss. But I was wondering if I could get some help?" Artemus responded. Beary nodded yes. Artemus looked at Grizlarge. "Master Chief, could you assist me?"

"Be happy to. What would you like me to do?" Grizlarge responded.

"Chief, could you do the monitoring of Arcrilian communication? I will monitor the beacon channels and scan for any activity in the area." Artemus said.

"Good. Don't forget the old lower frequencies. They might have used one of them." Grizlarge stated.

"Thanks, Chief." Artemus said.

With that, the team aboard the Crimson Blade started back to work. After about 4 Cycles they neared the Tarsus 9 system.

Suddenly they picked up a low powered beeping signal.

"Boss, I think I have something. It's on an old Q frequency distress beacon. It has to be close." Artemus reported.

Beary slowed the Crimson blade and brought it to a stop. "Which way do I need to go, Savato?"

"We need to go about 100 standard measurement units at 265 degrees." Artemus responded.

Beary eased the Crimson Blade over to the spot where the sensors indicated the beacon was located. Just in front of the Crimson Blade was a small canister. Beary extended the retrieval unit and brought it in to the Crimson Blade. They opened the canister and found three data crystals inside. One was the Raven Star's manifest; the next was a message for the families of the crew members and the Marines. The last crystal contained the captain's log.

The captain's log explained that they had come under attack by Arcrilian fighters and were being driven towards Dryden. The Captain planned to dive steeply into the atmosphere release the escape pods and then crash the ship into the southern mountain range. The engines had sprung a plasma leak and the engineer had locked himself in engineering. The four other crew members had been killed when the Arcrilians had boarded the ship. The Marines destroyed the boarding parties. The log ended there.

Beary looked at his team. "The Captain doesn't expect to survive and he knows his engineer was dying. If we can find the Marines we are going to bring them home." With that he headed for Dryden.

As they neared Tarsus 9, Beary ordered probes launched. A Red Dagger carried 1 orbital and 2 surface probes. He had the Orbital probe set to survey the Equator, and the surface probes to survey 30 degrees North and South of the Dryden's Equator.

It wasn't long before images of the Dryden surface started coming through. The Raven Star's resting place was clearly visible on the orbital scan. The surface probes started picking up Arcrilian transmissions. Beary maneuvered the Crimson Blade toward the location of the crash site.

As they approached the Raven Star's final resting place Beary spotted a platoon of Arcrilian troop transports. There were ten troop carriers, an artillery carrier, and a Command vehicle. Beary landed the Crimson Blade on a hill opposite of where the Arcrilians had stopped.

Beary turned to Artemus. "She is all yours. Set four missiles for laser guidance. The Chief and I will climb to the top of the hill and call in the strike. We will also use a couple of hand held rockets to attack the column. After you fire the four missiles get out of here and look for survivors. We will travel by foot toward the Raven Star."

With that, Beary and Grizlarge left the Crimson Blade and climbed the hill. Just as they reached the top of the hill Beary noted that five of the Arcrilian Transports were pulling out and heading back down the road. The Arcrilian Commander climbed to the top of his command vehicle. He was standing, barking orders to his subordinates when Beary released a bolt from his cross bow. The Bolt struck the Arcrilian in the side of his head, throwing him from his command vehicle.

As the Chief lined up the laser designators, Beary called Artemus and asked him to launch the missiles on the four targets. The missiles launched on cue. Once he had launched the missiles Artemus rotated the Crimson Blade and moved out on his mission. The missiles struck the command vehicle, the Artillery carrier, and one of the troop carriers. The last missile struck a tree and rained shrapnel down on the Arcrilians that were seeking cover outside of their vehicles. Beary and Grizlarge fired a few more shots and then headed for the Raven Star.

Down below, an Arcrilian Lieutenant looked over the carnage. His commanding officer was dead. So were many of the senior Non-commissioned officers [NCO]. The command vehicle and the artillery carrier were destroyed, as was one of the troop transports. When they had left this morning they had started out with one hundred and forty front line soldiers. Now seventy troopers were heading towards the central wasteland and thirty four lay dead all around him.

He mustered up the remaining 36 troopers and advanced on the hill where the attack had come from, but nothing was there. He then climbed into his troop transport and reported the loss of his commander and the others. He was told to standby for orders.

The Lieutenant in charge of the second echelon that had headed west heard the report. He immediately raised his antenna to verify he was to continue on the mission he had been given.

Artemus picked up the transmission and gained a fix on the second echelon and launched ground attack missiles. He had Ben launch four missiles at the Arcrilian formation.

The Arcrilian Lieutenant had just got his column moving again when the missiles arrived. The troop transport in front of his exploded. The next missile clipped the rear of his vehicle tearing the back off and rolling it over violently one missile missed and slammed into the ground just north of the last vehicle. The Driver panicked and turned into the fourth missile taking it in the front of the vehicle. The missile burned through the front armor and exploded in the crew compartment splitting, it open like a ripe melon.

When he came to, the Arcrilian Lieutenant found that he was entangled in wiring and the burnt metal of what had been his vehicle. Three of his troopers were trying to get him out.

The echelon Senior NCO ordered the troopers to scatter and dig in. He also ordered the two remaining troop transports to the outer edge of the line he established, leaving only the divers and gunners inside.

The lieutenant was finally freed and hobbled over to his NCO. "What hit us?"

The NCO looked at his Lieutenant. "Some type of missile system. We picked up nothing on the threat sensors. We lost 29 troopers in the attack and three vehicles. It is amazing that you and six others survived the strike on your vehicle, Sir."

"You have done well deploying the Troopers. Set a night watch, we will decide how to proceed in the morning." the Arcrilian Lieutenant responded.

Across the valley of the wasteland, on the side of a small mountain a group of Bearilian Marines watched the carnage. The Black Aces were the first to launch their escape pods. Most had fallen close to one another in these hills. The Marine Sergeant looked at the ten Marines with him and sent out a quick three letter burst over his emergency beacon.

Ben looked up from his weapons station, "Ensign Artemus I just picked up a three letter beacon burst, BA1. The signal originated on a small mountain 27 KSMU bearing 35 degrees true."

"Good work, Ben. Doc looks like we may have customers for you after all." Artemus said with a grin.

Ben got up and went to the weapons cabinet and put on a vest and weapons package 6. "I will assist the survivors and provide them cover if needed." Artemus started to say something, but Ben cut him off. "I cannot fly the Crimson Blade. You can. I cannot operate that is Caesar's job. I can fight in the woods for I was raised in the wilderness and know its ways."

Caesar looked at Artemus. "He has a point."

"Alright, Ben, bring them in. But be careful. Beary will skin me alive if you get hurt." Artemus said

Ben just smiled and dashed out of the hatch. Once clear he slowly moved toward the location of the survivors. He spotted one lying in the underbrush of a tree. Realizing that these Marines might be jumpy, he whistled a few notes of the Bearilian National Anthem.

The sentry almost jumped, but calmed down and whistled the next few notes.

Ben approached in the open until he was challenged.

The Sentry slowly rose up and offered the challenge.

Ben simply replied, "I am Maritinus of the Saber Claw. I am here to take you home."

A Marine Sergeant appeared "I am Sergeant Fontanels of the Black Ace Squad 1, 1st Platoon. It is good to see you. Some of my men are injured."

"We have a surgeon on board the Crimson Blade. But we must hurry. If we picked up your signal, the Arcrilians may have also." Ben responded.

Ben noticed that one of the Marines could hardly stand. Kneeling down, he told the Marine, "Grab on to the straps of my pack and I will carry you." With that done, he stood up and took off with the remaining Marines following.

Thirty STU later they were back to the Crimson Blade, Ben lowered the injured Marine onto one of the beds that Caesar had lowered. The Marines filed slowly in.

Sergeant Fontanels looked, at Ensign Artemus and reported in, "Sir, we are part of squad 1 Black Aces. We are still missing our Lieutenant and four others along with all of the Second squad."

"I understand, Sergeant, but right now I need to move this ship."

With that, Artemus lifted off and headed for higher ground.

Beary and Grizlarge had traveled fast without resting. They came to the top of a rise and saw the Raven Star broken and smashed beneath them. They quickly descended into the depression. First they moved through what was left of the Bridge. The Captain had died at the helm controls pinned beneath the wreckage. Beary picked up his broken body, carried it outside, and placed it in a small ravine that ran behind the debris field.

While he was doing that Grizlarge, downloaded any information he could find and set demolition charges to complete what the Captain had started. Then he moved across the debris field to where the engineering section was. This part of the ship had been damaged the least. As he opened the hatch, a plasma bolt hit the frame just above his head. He dropped and wheeled around just as a bolt from Beary's crossbow hit the Arcrilian. Beary, finished pushing open, the hatch and dived through. Grizlarge scrambled in and slammed the hatch closed.

Grizlarge looked at Beary. "Cub, that was too close. We had better get going."

"Go ahead, Gunny. I want to leave them a few surprises." With that, Beary started laying booby traps along the passage. He had stepped into the next section when Grizlarge called him.

"Cub, get down here quick! We are in deep!" Grizlarge had located the body of the Engineer and started to move it when he set off a dead man's switch.

Beary arrived and realized what had happened the engineer had set the engines to create a plasma build up. When it went critical, the Engines would blow apart. Just as he started to say something the first of his booby traps went off.

"Chief, we have to leave now. When this blows, it will take out the entire debris field." Beary said, picking up the body of the brave Engineer of the Raven Star.

The two raced to the back of the Engineering section and opened the hatch. Much to their relief they saw open country leading to the ravine. The Chief slammed the hatch close and followed Beary to the ravine. A few shots were fired at them but none came close. They threw themselves over the edge of the ravine and started digging into its side. Beary placed the two bodies next to each other and covered them with a radiation blanket. Beary and Grizlarge crawled into the hole they dug and wrapped radiation blankets around them. They also pulled out portable breathing units and waited for what they knew was coming.

The Arcrilian Major forced his way into the engine room. His troops quickly spread out around the room. Much to his surprise, no one was there. Then he felt a tingle on his arm. He looked up and saw a blue haze appear. He had just started to scream an order when the world around him disintegrated. A blue bubble extended around the engineering section then expanded beyond the ship. Then it collapsed on itself. The following explosion ripped across the forested hills, tearing trees and rocks apart. The Arcrilian troopers that were stationed around the Raven Star just ceased to exist.

The shock wave rolled over the edge of the ravine and slammed into the hill behind. Beary and Grizlarge could feel the ground around them shake as if a planet-quake had hit the area. After about 30 STU the area around them got deadly quite. Beary and Grizlarge slowly dug their way out of the rubble.

They placed the bodies of the dead Captain and Engineer in the hole they had dug and marked the site with a responder so that their bodies could be reclaimed at a later date.

After they were done, they said a silent prayer for them and their families. Having done all they could do, Beary and Grizlarge moved down the ravine until they reached the end of the blast area. From there they climbed a nearby hill to survey the area around them.

Beary looked out over what had been the crash site. The ground was blackened for up to three KSMU in every direction. If they hadn't made it to the ravine or if it would have been any shallower, he and Grizlarge would have been killed just the way the Arcrilian troopers were, "Gunny that was too close." Beary finally said.

Grizlarge, who had flopped down on the ground to rest, looked up at the young Ensign. "Cub, it was way too close, and I am getting too old for this!"

Beary was getting ready to join him on the ground when a noise just below the crown of the hill caught his attention. Grizlarge had heard it also and had moved to a covered position and drew his weapon. Beary moved over to a rock and took up a firing position.

A voice called out from under the edge of the hill, "You're surrounded. Surrender or die."

Grizlarge recognized the voice, "Sergeant Jedediah, you, and a small army couldn't take me and the Ensign."

Sergeant Jedediah, platoon Sergeant RA2, looked at the four Marines with him. He whispered, "Stay sharp!" Then called out, "is that you Horatio?"

Grizlarge smiled when he saw the strange look on Beary's face then replied, "Who else would they send to find your sorry tail?"

Sergeant Jedediah brought his four Marines to the top of the hill; one of the privates looked hurt.

Beary broke out water and rations for the Marines. "Sergeant, can you tell us anything about the rest of your unit?"

Sergeant Jedediah looked at the young Ensign. "Sir, we were the last five to jettison from the Raven Star. Private Brighthope broke his leg when his capsule hit. We have fixed him up the best we could. Corporal Horatius is our medic. He set the break but we are low on supplies."

"Okay, Sergeant, position your Marines around the crown of the hill. I'll call for your ride." Beary said, as he moved to the center of the hill.

Without being told, the marines spread themselves out. "Horatio, what gives with the Ensign? I mean, he is kind of young isn't he?"

Grizlarge started to laugh but caught himself, "That, my friend, is Ensign Dr. Beary Maxumus, and the best corporal I ever had. He started out with MSU6 when he was 15. Don't underestimate him. We'll get you out."

Using a burst transmitter Beary contacted the Crimson Blade, "Spirit Blade 2, this is Spirit 6 we have five for pick up."

"Spirit 6, Cutter 10; glad you're alive. We are busy right now will call back."

"Master Chief, hand out blankets and whatever else they need. Our friends are tied up." With that, Beary found a position on the hill and started watching for movement below.

Aboard the Crimson Blade they had witnessed the final death of the Raven Star. They also noticed artillery fire coming from north of their position. Artemus had taken off and noticed four Arcrilian skimmers racing toward a hill six KSMU away.

"Ben, target the Skimmers with two air to air missiles each.

I'll find and destroy the Artillery carrier." Artemus said as he lifted the Crimson Blade into the air.

Ben locked in on the skimmers and launched his missiles. The lead two skimmers exploded simultaneously as both sets of missiles found their targets. The rear two took evasive action just as the missiles arrived. The third skimmer avoided the first missile but turned into the second and spun into the ground. The fourth turned in the opposite direction. The first missile missed clean and also slammed into the ground. The last missile detonated behind the skimmer tearing large holes in the engine section the pilot flew his crippled ship toward his ground forces and ejected.

Artemus located the Artillery carrier and launched two missiles at it. The missiles slammed into the armored vehicle ripping it apart. He also saw Arcrilian troop carriers dashing for the hill that was being fired on.

He landed on a hill near it and again Ben was out the hatch. As he climbed up the hill, he heard movement below him. Five Arcrilian Troopers were making their way up the hill.

Ben took cover in a Band tree thicket. The Band trees are thin hard wood bushes with straight trunks. Ben's tribe had used them to make spears for centuries. He cut ten off at the desired length and fitted spear points on them. With that done, he started his hunt.

The Arcrilian Sergeant had maneuvered his troopers behind the hill and was now advancing. He had his troopers spread out two on either side. The one farthest on the left seemed to have fallen behind. He stopped his team and waited for the trooper to catch-up. After a few moments he and the other trooper on the left went searching for the missing trooper. They found him pinned to a tree with a spear through his neck. They immediately started back, only to find the other two troopers both dead with spears in their necks.

The Sergeant started to say something when his last trooper was picked up and thrown to the ground with a spear sticking through his chest. As he turned around the young Polarian was standing in front of him. The Sergeant went for his weapon as Ben's knife hit him between his eyes. Ben walked over, removed his knife, and pinned the Sergeant to a tree with one of his remaining spears. He then ran to the top of the hill. He threw himself down at the edge and called out, "Black or Red Aces come to me."

"Who are you?" a voice replied.

"Ben Maritinus from the Saber Claw, I am here to take you home." Ben said.

A Bearilian Sergeant stepped out from behind cover and approached Ben. "I have wounded."

"I will help carry them but we must leave now." Ben said.

When he reached the top of the hill he saw three Marines lying on stretchers. One was a Captain. The others it was hard to tell. A Marine Lieutenant approached; his arm was heavily bandaged.

"Sir, I am Cadet Ben Maritinus. I am here to lead you to the Crimson Blade. We have a surgeon on board. The Arcrilians will be here soon. We must leave." Ben reported.

The Lieutenant nodded, and then signaled his men to follow Ben. There were ten survivors in all. The healthy ones picked up the wounded and the Sergeant led the Lieutenant down the path. Ben led the way. The Marines stared at the dead Arcrilian Sergeant that was pinned to the tree as they passed. When they reached the Crimson Blade, the marines on board went out to help them in. They almost gasped at the site of their wounded Captain. The Lieutenant just sat down on one of the seats and collapsed.

Caesar ran over to him. The Lieutenant had lost a lot of blood. He laid him down and started an IV as he removed the bandage on the arm he quickly cleaned it and sealed the wound. He also gave the Lieutenant a dose of ant-venom just in case.

He then went to work on the other wounded. The Captain was suffering from a concussion, but his vitals were good.

The other two were more serious. He started immediately to stabilize them. One would require surgery to remove shrapnel from his chest. "Artemus, I need at least two Cycles before we can move."

"Doc, we have Arcrilian swarming the hill they were on, it won't take long before they get here." Artemus said

"I will buy you the time, Ensign Vantanus. May I take some claymore mines?" Ben said.

Artemus looked at him. "Ben . . . ."

Ben cut him off. "Sir, I am at home in the woods and the water. This is a job for a hunter, is it not? I can move quieter than most and I can survive if you must leave me behind. The others are at their end."

Artemus considered him for a moment, "Alright, but get back in one piece."

With that, Ben was gone again.

"I am going to be in deep excrement when the Boss finds out." Artemus thought out loud.

"Sir," the Sergeant said, "I don't understand?"

Artemus looked at him, "Sergeant who are you with?"

"BA2, Sir." The Sergeant responded. "Sir, he said he was a cadet? Should he be out there by himself?"

Artemus thought about that. "Probably not, Sergeant, but our job is to rescue you at our peril. He understands that. Also he sees this as a chance to get payback. His brother is Major Maritinus."

Ben slipped down the hill and started planting the mines. He also prepared several fighting positions as he fell back on the jump ship.

The Arcrilian major in charge of this group was on his com link. "No, Sir, I do not know where they went or who attacked our skimmers. I have to assume they had a portable missile launcher of some kind . . . . Yes, I Know that 1st Group was wiped out. I saw the explosion from where we are . . . No, Sir, we will not give up the search . . . Yes, Sir, we are pushing forward." The major cut the transmission, "Captain Acrnic, gather your troops and start searching those three hills."

The Arcrilian Captain called his three Lieutenants over and assigned each a hill to take their troops up.

Ben was watching them point at the two other hills. He scrambled down and planted mines on the approaches of the other two. He also set up three remote weapons along the ridge of the one to the south.

Then Ben crossed back as the Arcrilians began working their way down the hill. It wasn't long before they found the bodies of the scout team. Each Arcrilian Lieutenant had 60 troopers with him, leaving Ben out numbered 183 to 1.

Ben grinned. He didn't have to kill them all; just keep them busy for one and a half cycles. Ben watched as they advanced. To his relief the center section was moving slower than the other two. The Troops heading for the north hill hit the first line of claymores. The shallow ravine exploded as thousands of small projectiles filled the air. The first line of ten troopers was cut in half. The second line that followed ten SMU behind also suffered many casualties. When the Lieutenant looked up, 15 of his troopers were dead and another five wounded.

The Troop on the south hill hit the kill zone next but this time the mines were set on a delay so that one group would pass into the second group of mines before the first went off. The first ten troopers cleared the ravine then the second when the third group hit the center of the ravine, three lines of claymores went off. Again tens of thousands of metal projectiles sprang from the ground. The first, second, and third groups were annihilated. The fourth group suffered eight killed and the fifth and sixth group lost two each. This Lieutenant had been in the third group. The surviving Sergeant moved his troops back. Out of 61 troopers 42 had been killed. The Sergeant dug in his remaining 18 troopers and reported in.

Ben triggered the remote weapons and attacked the central group before they hit the line of claymores. The Remote weapon carried 12 high explosive rounds. Ben placed the laser designator near the center of the second group and launched six rounds. A Sergeant in the first group saw the flash and opened fire. Then the rounds fell in a line among the second group: all ten Arcrilian troopers were killed.

The major received the reports from his three groups. Believing the Bearilian Marines were on the south hill he ordered his other two groups to join the remainder of the Southern group and take the hill. As members of the Northern Group passed through the ravine they set off a line of claymores. Six more Arcrilian troopers were cut in half from the Northern group. The projectiles continued their path across the ravine and killed three of the central group's troopers.

Ben looked at his watch: one cycle to go. He fired two more rounds from the southern hill. These landed near a few troops that were working their way up the hill. To his satisfaction three of the five were blown from the hillside. The other two lost their nerve and retreated.

In the Crimson Blade, the Marines could hear the explosions.

The Doc was still operating on their friend. They begged to join the fight, but Artemus was firm.

With thirty STU left, the Arcrilians decided to attack in mass the Southern hill. One hundred and one Arcrilian troopers swarmed up the hill, firing as they went.

Ben triggered a second line of claymores. Again, twenty troopers fell dead, but still they pressed on.

Ben launched the last four projectiles from one of the remote weapons and guided them towards a group of troopers trying to work their way around a rock out-cropping. The shells hit the out cropping and started a land slide. Six of the Arcrilians were crushed by the rolling boulders. Another three were killed by the high explosives.

Ben looked at his watch: 18 STU left. He watched as the Arcrilians regrouped and charged again. This time he launched all twelve of the high explosive rounds from the second canister. The rounds fell among the charging Arcrilian. More went down, but this time they kept coming.

Ben looked at his watch: ten STU to go. He started working his way back up the hill.

The two Arcrilian lieutenants reached the top of the hill. But again the enemy was gone. Only 53 of their troopers had survived the attack. Their troopers were milling around. Some took cover and decided to rest. The two lieutenants found a rock out-cropping and sat beneath it to make their report.

Ben reached the top of his hill and set off the third canister. Twelve high explosive rounds went straight up and came back down on the top of the hill.

Luckily for the Arcrilians, most were away from the center and in slit trenches when the rounds fell. Still, twelve more were killed in this attack.

Ben reached the Crimson Blade, just as Beary's call came in. Artemus was helping secure the wounded as Caesar intercepted Beary's call. Ben slid into his seat and said, "If you please, Ensign Artemus, it is time to go!"

Artemus did a quick check, fired up the engines, and lifted off.

The Arcrilian Major saw a small cloud of dust rise from the central hill and cursed, "Your troops went up the wrong hill!"

Captain Acrnic looked at the Major. "Sir, I have lost one of my Lieutenants and one hundred forty three of my troopers trying to take that hill and they did it."

The Major looked at him. "Yes they did, but it was the wrong hill. And it was your incompetence that sent them up it." With that, the Major pulled his weapon and shot the Captain between the eyes.

Artemus looked at the carnage on the Southern hill as he flew north. "Ben, remind me never to get on your bad side."

Ben beamed. *His village would celebrate for a month over this victory.*

Artemus wondered what the Polarian was thinking, but thought *he had better contact the Boss.* "Spirit 6, Spirit blade 2 we are clear. We are awaiting orders."

Grizlarge had the watch. "Spirit blade 2, this is Spirit 2. Rendezvous at the following coordinates."

Artemus looked at the readout and responded "Spirit 2, Spirit Blade 2; twenty STU out prepare for pickup."

Grizlarge woke Beary up. "Sir, they're on their way."

The "Sir" sounded strange. Beary cleared his mind. "Alright Master Chief, get, the Marines up, feed them, and prepare them for pick up."

Grizlarge woke Sergeant Jedediah "Come on, your chariot is coming to take you home." The two NCO moved among the others getting them ready.

Corporal Horatius approached Beary, "Sir."

Beary regarded the medic. "Yes, Corporal, what can I do for you?"

"Sir, are you planning to evacuate also?" the Corporal asked.

"No, the Master Chief and I will be staying to try and locate other survivors." Beary answered.

The Corporal stood at attention. "Sir, your surgeon will have to return with the jump ship. I am requesting to stay behind with you and the Master Chief. Others are bound to be wounded. If your surgeon could give me some supplies I could be of use to you."

Beary studied the Corporal. "Corporal Horatius, my job is to get you out."

"Begging your pardon, Sir, but my responsibility is to the other Marines in my unit. If they are still alive you may need my help." Corporal Horatius pleaded.

Beary studied him, "Tell Master Chief Grizlarge you're staying. We will get you the equipment you need."

Horatius smiled. "Thank you Sir!" He then went over and talked to Grizlarge.

About that time, the Crimson Blade landed in the center of the hill. Artemus came out followed by Caesar.

Caesar inspected the broken leg of Private Brighthope and looked up at the young Medic. "You did a good job, Corporal. He is going to be fine."

Horatius considered Ensign Vantanus. "Thank you, Sir. I lost most of my Med Kit. Could you provide me with one?"

Caesar looked at Beary who just nodded. "No problem, but haven't you had enough of this paradise?"

"Sir some of my unit is still out there. They may need help before you get back from evacuating the survivors you have already picked up." Horatius said.

Sergeant Jedediah heard the conversation and asked Grizlarge to let him stay also, but the Master Chief just pointed to the Crimson Blade.

Artemus walked over to Beary, "Boss, we are almost full up with wounded. I need to get them back to the Saber Claw reload and get back. It will take twelve Cycles at least to return."

"More like twenty. You're going to need to rest before you come back." Beary said.

"Like H . . . ." Artemus caught himself. "Only if they make me, I can sleep while they reload the ship. Maritinus and the Doc can rest on the way back."

"Look, it doesn't matter. Captain Atilus will decide what is going to happen. Right now you have 28 wounded Marines to get back. Also, I want to check something. Master Chief, will you join us?" Beary asked.

Beary lead them to the Tactical 3D map. Entering the data that they had received, from the sensors, he began to explain, "All of the Arcrilian troops seem to be fanning out from one central location. When we take data from the orbital sensor we find a slight distortion in the moon's magnetic field."

The Chief looked at the data. "Just how big is the distortion?"

Beary looked at him. "Two KSMU squared."

Artemus said "What does that mean, Boss?"

Beary looked at them, and the Chief nodded, "It means it's a Hive ship. 200 skimmers, 50 long range fighters, and 20,000 troopers. That's a Hive ship."

Artemus smiled. "Well, they now only have 196 skimmers and a few less troopers."

"How many ground attack missiles do you have left?" Beary asked.

Artemus checked. "I have six ground and 24 air attack missiles."

"Okay," Beary said, "Here is what I want you to do. Pick six ground targets and empty your launcher. Then launch all but four of your air attack missiles at the energy field around the Hive ship."

"Alright Boss, then what do you want us to do?" Artemus asked.

"Simple: run and get back to the Saber Claw." Beary said.

Beary then took out a small down link computer and left the Crimson Blade. Artemus climbed into the pilot's seat and rotated the Crimson Blade off the ground.

Beary looked at Grizlarge and Horatius. "Let's go."

Artemus peered out across the surface of the moon and saw a cluster of troop vehicles under some trees. He locked four missiles on the cluster and fired. The missiles streaked in and exploded among the vehicles. The Command vehicle was blown apart, as were two other vehicles. The fourth missile slammed into a tent in the center of the grouping.

The Arcrilian Colonel stepped out of the woods with one of his troopers. He found most of his staff dead, his command vehicle destroyed and two of his troop carriers destroyed. Luckily for him the troopers were with him when their carriers were hit. As it was twelve of his staff officers were dead, along with three drivers and three gunners.

Artemus spotted a lone command vehicle crossing the wasteland, dialed in the last two ground attack missiles and fired.

The Major was racing back to the Hive ship. He was looking back at the hills he had just left. Then he looked the other way and saw the missiles coming in. Before he could react, the missiles exploded. The Major was ripped apart by the explosion.

Artemus then fired his twenty air attack missiles at the energy field. Much to his surprise, the field lit up like a sparkler. He then headed for the Saber Claw at warp speed.

After about three cycles, Artemus picked up two Arcrilian fighters heading in the direction of the Carnise Drift. He increased speed to get in range and launched his last four missiles. The two fighters exploded. Artemus called the Saber Claw. "Blue Dragon, Spirit Blade 2, destroyed two fighters in bound. We have wounded. Prepare weapon pods 15 and 16. We also need weapon packages six and eight, and medical package ten. We will be there in forty STU.

Captain Atilus looked at his team. "Flight, launch Midnight Dagger, and two Red Daggers. Sweep the asteroid Drift."

Midnight Dagger, Flame Dagger, and Scarlet Dagger rolled out of the launch bay.

They did a complete sweep, but found nothing. They stayed in position and patrolled the Drift.

The Crimson Blade received priority landing. When it came to a stop, medical and maintenance teams rushed in. Commander Centaures was waiting, as was Dr. Wu Fang.

Centaures called Artemus over. "Where are the Chief and Ensign Maxumus?"

"Sir, they are still on Dryden. We recovered 22 of the Black Aces and four of the Red Aces. We need to get turned around and get back." Artemus reported.

"What are you not telling me, Ensign?" Centaures asked.

"Sir, due to the number of Arcrilians we have encountered, Ensign Maxumus believes there is a Hive Ship on the Moon." Artemus handed him a data log with his report and sensor readings. Centaures asked a few more questions, and then headed for the bridge.

Artemus looked at Ben. "Go get some hot food and bring me back some. I want to leave as soon as possible."

Dr. Wu Fang examined Caesar. "You look beat. I can send another surgeon back out."

Caesar gazed at him. "Sir I am good trauma surgeon and I work well with this team. I want to go back."

Wu Fang thought about it. "Alright, Ensign, but get some rest." Much to his surprise, Caesar saluted him and reentered the Crimson Blade. When Dr. Fang went to say something, he found the young surgeon asleep on one of the jump seats. He smiled and thought *those were the days*. He wrote a note and went to Medical.

Chapter 13

Long nights, Hard Flights

After the Crimson Blade left, Beary, Grizlarge, and Horatius traveled fifteen KSMU until they found a spot on the map Beary had been looking for. Telemetry had shown that there was a lake and a cave system behind the water fall. As they approached, Beary felt they were being watched.

"I am going to check the water for purity. You two stay here." Beary said while giving Grizlarge a hand signal.

Grizlarge pulled the Medic into some bushes and signaled him to stay put. Then he disappeared into the underbrush.

Beary pulled a sample vile from his kit and tested the water. Just then, he felt a weapon pushed against the side of his head.

"Who are you?" The voice growled with a rasping sound.

Before Beary could respond, Grizlarge did it for him. "He is Ensign Maxumus, and if you don't lower your weapon now, marine, you won't get another chance."

The young Marine lowered his weapon and slumped to the ground. Beary caught him and called out. "Corporal, we have a bear down."

Horatius was by their side in an instant. "He appears to be dehydrated, Sir. I need to get him to someplace where I can start an IV."

Beary pointed to the waterfall. "There is a cave behind it. We'll take him up there."

When they got to the cave entrance, they were shocked by what they found. Fifteen Marines were lying on the floor; all appeared sick. Beary, Grizlarge, and Horatius immediately put on breathing masks. Grizlarge checked the air in the cave and gave the all clear, but the Medic asked them to keep on the masks until he could determine the problem.

All were dehydrated. So he started them on IVs of fluids and anti-microbial medicine.

The young marine, they first encountered, was also the first to respond to treatment. Horatius called Beary over. "Sir this is Private Thadeus Bonaventure of RA2. He can tell you what happened."

"I am sorry, Sir, I thought you were stealing our water. My friends need it or they will die." the young private said as he started to cry.

Beary growled at him. "Stop that, Marine!" Then in a softer voice, "Just tell us what happened son."

Grizlarge wanted to laugh. The private was at least a year older than the Cub.

Private Bonaventure composed himself. "Sir, we had traveled for days until we found this cave. We were out of food. At the other end of the Cave is an opening the slope is covered by berry bushes. The berries were so sweet we couldn't stop eating them. Then bears started getting sick."

Beary looked at Grizlarge, who took off for the other opening. He was back in ten STU.

"Coronas Diablo, the Devil's Fire. The whole ridge is full of them." Grizlarge reported.

Beary shook his head. "Doc, the berries they ate are not poisonous under normal conditions. But, if they were starving, and ate the berries by the paw-full . . . . , Then, the acids in the berries would cause; dehydration and a loss of electrolytes, Potassium, and Magnesium in the blood."

Horatius looked at the young Ensign. "Thank you, Sir, I had never heard of them before." He immediately began giving them shots of the minerals they needed.

Beary walked over to Private Bonaventure. "Private, how are you feeling?"

"Better Sir, thank you." Bonaventure answered.

Beary lowered his voice. "Tell me about your friends."

Bonaventure sat up. "Sir, most of us are with RA2. Our Lieutenant is over there. We are missing five no that's not right, Doc is here. I am sorry, Sir, we're missing four from our unit. We have four from RA1. They are all privates like me."

"Thank you, Private, now get some rest." Beary said. Beary walked over to Grizlarge. "Gunny, how close do you think we were?"

Grizlarge thought for a moment, "Some would have been dead in three or four cycles. The rest would have died in the next 24 cycles. The Private may have survived, though I doubt it. They were hungry and scared."

Beary thought about that. The Master Chief had just taught him another lesson even well trained troops can panic. Beary thought of the stress this group must have been under. "Thanks, Gunny." Grizlarge just smiled.

Back on the Saber Claw, the maintenance crew had finished refurbishing and reloading the Crimson Blade. Artemus did a walk around as Ben followed, watching the Ensign inspect the Jump Ship.

Centaures walked up to Artemus. "We are going to scrub the mission. Fleet orders."

Artemus looked at him in disbelief. "No, Sir, I won't leave those Marines on that moon, nor the Chief and Ensign Maxumus."

Ben's white fur turned red, "Are the Fleet Commanders dishonorable or just cowards?"

Centaures looked at them and smiled. "That is enough, Cadet Maritinus! You realize you can be Court-marshaled for disobeying their orders."

They both said, "Yes Sir."

Caesar stretched and said from the hatch, "What are we waiting for? I know a really good lawyer with a Senator for a father who isn't very pleased with the timidity of the Fleet higher ups."

Centaures smiled. "You left thirty STU ago and are under radio silent. So get out of here."

Ben looked at the Commander. "I am sorry, Sir."

Centaures nodded. "Cadet, we have all thought it. But you must never say it again, do you understand? Good, now get out of here." Centaures walked back to the main door as the Crimson Blade lifted off and shot out of the Saber Claw.

Atilus looked at his First Officer. "Well?"

Centaures smirked. "They left thirty STU ago under radio silent. We can't contact them."

Atilus nodded. "Make sure all the logs and telemetry shows they left thirty STU ago."

"Already did." Centaures said as they walked back to the bridge.

Ben looked puzzled, "Why did they say we couldn't go, and then let us go?"

Artemus started to answer when Caesar interrupted, "Ben, you have to understand they had to give us a chance to stay without fault. They also wanted us to know that we, and they, could face punishment if we fail."

Ben shook his head. "If we fail we will be dead. What difference will it make? Caesar, would you say I have killed many of our enemy with honor and courage? Would you, Ensign Artemus?"

Both said, "Of course."

"Caesar, there is a custom in my village: when one proves his worth as a warrior his shoulder blade is tattooed with the mark of our tribe. It is a red paw with claw marks radiating from it. Would you give me the mark?" Ben asked.

Artemus spoke up, "Ben, tattoos are banned by regulations."

Ben glanced at him. "Is it not within regulations to honor the Creator? Among my Clan, a warrior is a servant of the Most High. It was He who put the first mark on my Tribe, so that we would remember to protect the weak from the Dark One."

Caesar went to a computer and scanned the regulations.

"Artemus Fleet regulation 65-3 sub paragraph a gives a loophole and makes it permissible."

Artemus looked at him. "What, a doctor and a lawyer. What else, a Chieftain?"

"No, I just dated a very good lawyer for a while. She taught me to read the fine print." Caesar said.

"Fine by me, I sure hope you're in good terms with her we may need her before this is over." Artemus replied.

"Yeah we are. I was too young for her, so she married my Brother." Caesar replied. "Ben, let's get it done before we get to Dryden."

Back on Dryden, the Lieutenant of the Red Aces 2 had come around. Beary went over to talk to him. "Lieutenant, I am Ensign Maxumus of the Saber Claw. We are here to get you and your men home. Sergeant Jedediah and three others are already on the Saber Claw."

The Lieutenant looked up, "I am Lieutenant Jax. I am still missing a Marine."

"Corporal Horatius is with us; he wouldn't leave. All your marines are accounted for." Beary said.

Jax looked around. "My Marines got sick. Did any of them . . . ."

Beary shook his head. "No, we got to you all in time. Private Bonaventure bought you all just enough time. You ate Devil's Fire Berries. A few won't hurt you, but in large quantities they will dehydrate you and kill you. Lieutenant, as soon as you and your men are able we're going to have to leave you here so we can look for other survivors. I want you to set up fortifications inside this cave system. I know you're short on ammunition. We will leave you what we can. My jump ship should be on its way back, but we may need to have a base of operations."

Jax looked at him. "Thank you, Ensign Maxumus. How many have you found?"

Beary thought. "We're missing all but four of RA1 and your Captain. We are missing a Lieutenant and four marines from BA1 and six marines from BA2." Beary thought, *we have 15 here and another 24 to find.* "Get some rest and eat your soup it will make you feel stronger." Beary had given Horatius some emergency soup mix his mother had given him.

Beary looked at the Chief and signaled him and Horatius over to him. "I need to take a look around. They were running from Arcrilians when they found this cave. Maybe the Arcrilians got distracted but I need to see what we're up against. Gunny, I need you to stay here until a few of them are strong enough to help defend this place. Artemus should be getting back in four to five Cycles. Doc, how are they responding?"

Horatius looked at them and shook his head. "Ensign, they are in bad shape. That stuff your mom fixed up for you is helping. Still, only four or five are going to recover enough to be of use. Also, I am down to only two bags of saline solution."

"Okay, push the soup and do your best. Gunny, you know what to do." With that, Beary picked up his gear.

Grizlarge looked at him. "Cub, be careful out there. I'll take care of things here."

Beary saluted and left. The Chief held his salute for a moment and sighed.

Horatius watched them. "Chief, may I ask a question or two?"

"Shoot." Grizlarge said as he started messing with his equipment.

"You and the Ensign have been together for a while?" Horatius asked.

Grizlarge smiled. "He was the best corporal I ever had. I think he is going to make a fine officer. What is your next question?"

"This soup mix his mother fixed up and gave to him?" Horatius questioned.

"Oh, Beary's mom is Dr. Angelina Maxumus: a Nero-surgeon. She sent him a care package through Ensign Vantanus, the Surgeon you met on the Crimson Blade." Grizlarge said, "Now, I have things to do. Try and get me a few of these Marines going." With that, Grizlarge headed for the back of the cave.

Horatius walked over to his Lieutenant to check on him.

Lieutenant Jax sat up. "Hort, just who are those two?"

Horatius shrugged. "I am not sure; Lieutenant but I am glad they're here. Our best bet is to follow their lead. Now, Sir, please eat."

Beary climbed to the top of a mountain and looked around; things were quiet. Night had fallen on this side of the moon. Beary reached for his transmitter. "Spirit Blade 2, Spirit 6:" Beary, waited then he heard a low crackle, "Say again."

"Spirit 6, Spade 1." A voice said over the transmitter.

"Spade 1, Spirit 6; code in coordinates." Beary received the information.

Just then, Artemus came in. "Spirit 6, Spirit Blade 2."

"Spirit Blade 2, contact Spade 1 on bravo." Beary said.

"Spade 1, Spirit Blade 2; I have your coordinates. Can you move 300 SMU to the North-east of your position and await pick up?"

Spade 1, Lieutenant Bandar, looked at the eight Marines with him. "Okay Marines we need to move. Our ride is coming." The eight Marines got to their feet and followed Lieutenant Bandar to the North-east through heavy brush.

Artemus picked up the Marines as he flew over. He also spotted an Arcrilian Force of sixty troopers heading to intercept them. "Ben, set three missiles for air burst and launch at these coordinates."

Ben set the missiles and fired them. The three missiles flew toward the tree line and exploded above the Arcrilians. The explosion ripped through the trees, sending wood and metal splinters through the Arcrilian Troopers.

The Arcrilian Captain pulled a long, wooden splinter from his arm. Some of his troopers had not been as lucky. He saw one of his Lieutenants stretched out over a rock with a large limb of a tree on top of his chest. In all ten of his troopers were killed and twenty were wounded. He needed to get his troops moving again so he started barking orders. His troops slowly began to regroup.

Lieutenant Bandar saw the explosions not more than one KSMU away, and stepped up the pace. He reached the rendezvous point just as the Crimson Blade landed.

Ben jumped out and signaled the Marines inside. It didn't take long before all nine were in the Crimson Blade. Just before he jumped back in, he heard a voice cry out.

"Artemus, we have three more survivors, 200 SMU to our south." Ben yelled into the jump ship.

"Ben, can you get to them and get them to that hill one KSMU to the West, away from the Arcrilian?" Artemus answered back.

"It will be done!" Ben took off on a dead run through the brush. He grabbed a few straight branches and fitted spear points on them.

Ben spotted three Arcrilian lying in wait. He launched a spear into the first one and sliced the neck of the second before they knew he was on them. The third Arcrilian tried to spin around when Ben pinned him to a tree with his other spear. Without stopping he grabbed the injured Bearilian Marine and threw him over his shoulder and demanded the other two to follow before they knew what happened.

The two uninjured Marines hurried to catch up. Ben pointed to a hill one KSMU from where they were. "We need to get to the top of that hill fast; the Arcrilians are near."

In fifteen STU, they reached the Crimson Blade. Six Marines were waiting at the top to provide cover. Ben didn't stop; he hit the hatch and tossed the wounded Marine on a table and collapsed. He reached into his pouch and took two of the Arachnoid gall bladders. "Caesar, I think I am injured."

The Black Aces' Medic started working on the injured Marine as Caesar went to Ben. He found an Arcrilian blade stuck in his hip clear to the bone. It had just missed the main artery in his leg, but all that running had done its damage. He had two Marines place Ben on an operating table and began removing the blade.

"Doc, we have got to go. Can you work on them in flight?" Artemus asked as the last of the security detail jumped in.

"Ben is hurt bad, but I'll make it work. Go!" Caesar yelled back.

Ben said, "It is okay, Caesar, do what you must."

Caesar broke the blade taking it out. The tip was in bedded in Ben's hip bone. He had a Marine hold a bandage on his wound while he tested the blade. Luckily, there wasn't any poison on the blade. "Ben, this is going to hurt. I can't afford to give you a sedative. It is important you hold still."

All Ben could say was, "Yes."

Caesar went in and surgically removed the tip and began sewing the torn muscles back together and sealing the small bleeders he found. After twenty STU, he was finished.

"How is the other Marine?" Caesar asked.

"He will be alright. He has a dislocated back and some minor bruises. That flying shoulder ride probably didn't help, but he would be dead if it wasn't for that cadet. How is he?" The Medic asked.

"Lucky, if the knife had been a fraction of a SUBMU left or right it would have got his main artery and he would have bled out when he got here. As it is, he will probably walk with a slight limp. I checked him over; there were no other injuries. He will sleep for a few cycles." Caesar said with a tired voice.

Caesar moved forward and stood behind Artemus. "How long before we reach Beary's location?"

"Not long, but I am heading well south of their location before I come back. By my reckoning we have all the Black Aces and all of RA2 and four of RA1 located." Artemus responded.

Arcrilian skimmers were heading north in force toward where they had just been. Artemus said a silent prayer that his cloak would keep working.

Two cycles passed before he was able to head for the position Beary had given him.

Beary was starting to worry when he received two clicks on his com unit. He moved over to the landing spot. The hatch opened and Artemus stepped out.

"Sorry it took me so long Boss. We ran into some problems." Artemus explained.

Beary studied Artemus, "Where is Ben?"

Artemus appeared sick. "He was wounded while saving an injured Marine. Doc said he will be okay. I still don't know how he did what he did, Beary." Artemus explained what had happened. When he was done, Beary just nodded.

"Okay, I have more passengers for you. You need to get them back to the Saber Claw and come back." Beary said.

"Sorry, Boss. This is the last trip we have to get everyone out. We're facing possible Court-marshal when we get back.

Fleet ordered us to suspend operations. Commander Centaures left it up to us this time. Next time there won't be a choice." Artemus said.

Beary was angry but didn't want to show it. "Okay, get everyone into the cave. Power down the Crimson Blade and set its camouflage gear. You've probably been pushing the shield generators pretty hard. Besides, I need help."

Caesar came out while Ben and the injured Marine were carried into the Cave. Master Chief Grizlarge shot out of the cave.

"What by the moons of Bantine is going on here!" the Master Chief demanded.

Beary explained the situation and explained his plan. "What do you think, Gunny?"

"I think I would like . . . ." Then Grizlarge sighed, "Sir, this is your play. I'll back it any way you want to play it. We have saved a little over $3/4^{th}$ of the Marines from the two units. No one would blame you if we left right now."

Beary looked at his mentor, "I would. And Gunny, you couldn't live with it either. Not as long as there is a chance we can find the others."

A marine came over. "Sir, the Cadet wants to talk to you."

"Thank you, Corporal." Beary said, and headed for the cave with the other three following close behind.

"How are you, Ben?" Beary asked.

"I got careless. I should have made sure the third one was dead. I am sorry. If you will let me have a few minutes I will be ready to help you, Sir." Ben said weakly.

"Sorry, Ben, Caesar said you lost a lot of blood. Besides I have several sick Marines in here. Artemus will need your help protecting them." Beary said, patting his friend on the shoulder.

Ben thought. "It will be as you say if Artemus doesn't mind."

Artemus looked at him. "I would fly or fight with you anywhere at any time Ben Maritinus. Now get some more rest I am going to need you."

Glancing over at Ben he said to Beary, "That Kid might become as big a legend as you have become. He has killed over 150 Arcrilians that I know of in single combat."

Beary said, "If you get a chance write it up and get witness. Even if Fleet doesn't care, his tribe and village will go nuts. Now let's go talk."

Lieutenant Bandar came over. "Ensign you have a real mess here."

Beary looked at the Lieutenant, "Yes, Lieutenant, and it's even worse than you know." Beary went on to explain.

Lieutenant Bandar snarled. "What can my eight Marines do to help you? We're in good shape and we want a piece of the Arcrilians."

Beary looked at him, "Lieutenant Bandar you out rank me. Are you and your Marines willing to follow my orders?"

Chief Grizlarge was watching.

Bandar looked at the young Ensign. "It's your party Ensign . . . . ?" His voice trailed off as he waited for Beary to tell him his name.

Beary looked at him. "Maxumus, Beary Maxumus."

Bandar flashed some recognition, "Spirit 6? You were the young Corporal that got us out of Pratis V in one piece. I was a Gunny Sergeant at the time. I'll follow your orders, and so will my eight Marines."

"Feed your Marines and replenish your weapons and other gear. Get some rest. We're leaving as soon as it gets dark." Beary said.

Horatius approached Beary, "Ensign Maxumus, Sir?"

"Yes Corporal." Beary responded.

"Sir, I wish to stay with you and the Chief." Horatius said.

"Alright, Corporal, talk to the Black Aces Medic and tell him you were here first." Beary Said.

Night fell quickly; Beary gathered Lieutenant Bandar, Horatius, Grizlarge, and seven Marines. "From what I can tell, the escape pods of RA1 fell in this area close to the Hive ship. We need to try and locate them. Do you have any questions? Okay, let's move out."

As the dawn broke, they were fifteen KSMU from the cave. Beary stopped his small unit. The Marines spread out and dug in. Beary watched this group of marines closely. They never complained and took care of their equipment. Beary nodded.

The Master Chief came over. "How do you want to play it from here?"

Beary thought about it. "Let's rest here, until we can get an idea of the terrain. We should only be ten to fifteen KSMU from the edge of the Hive ship's energy field. They have been looking up North. It won't be long before they look in this direction."

Bandar came over and Beary explained his intentions. "Does my plan meet with your approval, Lieutenant?"

Bandar smiled, "Yeah, my Marines can use the rest. I told them to eat cold rations and rest up."

Beary nodded, "Good. We should do the same."

Not far away, ten Marines of RA1 were chained together being led by a troop of twenty Arcrilian troopers, three Scorpius with handlers, three carriers with a driver, and a gunner. They were making their way toward a group of trees that were to be harvested. The Arcrilians believed in slave labor. Besides, when they couldn't work any longer, they could always eat the Bearilians.

The Arcrilian lieutenant, in charge of the detail, thought he saw something on a ridge two KMSU away. But, He dismissed it, when he noticed a mica [a flexible mineral with a shiny surface that reflex light] outcropping just below its crown.

Bandar signaled for Beary. Beary crawled over. Bandar pointed out the group.

Beary rolled over. "Do you think you and four of your Marines can get to that ravine running parallel to the trail in front of them?"

Bandar surveyed the spot Beary was pointing at. "You got it. It will take 40 STU to get there but at the pace they are moving we can beat them."

"Good. Pick your men and get started." Beary said as the Chief slid next to him. Beary pointed. "We're going to hit them from this side. Bandar is going to grab the Marines and get them into the Ravine on the other side."

Grizlarge looked at him. "Let's do it Sir." Grizlarge signaled the four remaining Marines to follow him.

It took Beary and his group 35 STU to reach the spot where they planned to launch their attack. Bandar arrived in 38 STU. They could see the Arcrilians approaching less than twenty SMU away.

The Arcrilian lieutenant was getting upset. One of the Scorpius was acting up and his handler was having problems with it. He would have to deal with it if it continued, maybe by feeding a Bearilian or its incompetent handler or both to it. That thought brought a smile to his face. He noticed the blind curve in the trail, so he sent his three Carriers ahead to secure the other side.

The Carriers pulled in facing away from the ravine. The gunners were looking up the hillside for danger, not at the ravine.

The Scorpius that was acting up let out a high squeal and tried to attack the other male. Its handler hit its stun collar. The Scorpius whipped its tail but settled down.

The gunners looked back down the trail toward the sound.

Beary, saw the movement as Bandar and his Marines crept up on the carriers. The Gunners never knew what hit them. A moment later the Drivers were dead. The Marines propped two of the Gunners back up. But one Marine took the place of the third gunner. The others slid back into the ravine. The line of Marines cleared the curve with three Troopers in front of them. The others were watching the handler struggle to control the rogue Scorpius.

Bandar and his Marines killed the troopers quietly and signaled the other ten Marines to come to them.

On the hill, Beary fired an energy bolt into the third Scorpius, which he realized was the Female. The bolt entered her eye and exploded. She let out a death scream and the two males went crazy. The first to die were the handlers. The seventeen troopers were so busy firing at the Scorpius they didn't notice they were receiving accurate fire from the hill in front of them. The Lieutenant ran toward the carriers, calling for their support. As he approached the last one the main gun swiveled and fired.

The Lieutenant, felt the first rounds hit. He couldn't understand what happened as his world went dark.

Only six troopers were left when the last Scorpius fell. It was then they realized they were under fire. They tried to run, but it was too late. Beary, signaled Bandar to bring the released prisoners, back up the hill, when they reached the top one of the released marines broke into tears.

Horatius was giving first aid to a marine, when he called Beary over. "Sir, this is Corporal Longscar."

With tears still flowing, he looked at Beary. "Sir, they have our First Sergeant, Lieutenant, and Captain. They have been torturing them. You have to help them!"

"Alright, Corporal, we will do what we can." Beary said.

Bandar stared in disbelief. "Not even you would try and get into a Hive ship."

Beary shrugged. "The Master Chief and I have done it before. Take your troops and these Marines, three KSMU south and call Artemus for a pick up."

Horatius and two other Marines stepped forward. "Ensign, we want to stay with you. They're going to need medical attention if you do rescue them." Horatius said.

One of the other Marines spoke up. "Sir, I am Sergeant Fisher, a weapons expert. The Arcrilian carriers are full of very useful weapons. My loader, Corporal Moon-Scar, and I could do great things with all that equipment."

Bandar came up. "I contacted Artemus. He will pick us up. Ensign Maxumus, take them with you. They can help cover your escape. You did great, Marine."

Beary grinned. That was the best compliment he could have received. Grizlarge walked up. "You could always switch back to the Marines."

Beary shook his head. "No, but for a minute I thought about it."

Grizlarge stood up. "Well, one of us needs to say it: once more into the belly of the Beast."

Chapter 14

Into The Belly of the Beast

The three Marines loaded up all the equipment into one of the Carriers. Beary and Grizlarge climbed into one of the other Carriers. They started moving toward the Hive ship. When they got within three KSMU, they pulled off the trail.

Beary walked over to the other Carrier. "Find a place to hide the carrier. Stay vigilant. If we're not out in 45 STU, pull out and get to a point you can call for a pick up and leave."

"Sir" One of the Marines started to say.

Beary glanced at the Marine. "Marine, if we are not out of there by then we're not going to be coming out, and neither are the others. I won't leave them to the Arcrilians."

The three marines pulled into cover and set a string of snares to signal them if anyone was coming.

Twilight was falling and the setting Sun was in the Arcrilian Sentry's eyes. He saw the carrier coming toward him. He just waved it through; the Gunner even waved.

Beary and Grizlarge watched the flow of the traffic. Grizlarge pointed toward one of the shield generators. They parked near it. Grizlarge slipped out of the Carrier and planted enough explosives to destroy the generator. Then they moved into the flow again. They found a cave system leading below the Hive ship.

Beary pointed toward the entrance. "I bet they're down there." They pulled the Carrier over near the entrance. The two Guards walked over. Before they knew what happened, Beary had killed both of the Arcrilians.

Grizlarge flew down the passage. At the end was a guard station. Using his silenced weapon he fired three times; all three guards dropped. Grizlarge moved over and ensured they were dead, then took up a coverage position.

Beary flew up the right passageway. There were cells in this area. He heard the sound of a whip striking skin and a low moan of pain coming from one of them.

Beary's blood boiled. Drawing one of his Hammers of Corsan, he entered the torture room. The guard leaning near the door was the first to die. Beary smashed his head in with one blow. The other guard heard a sound and received a knife through his skull.

The Torturer turned around. Beary plunged his knife into the large Arcrilian and twisted, splitting the Arcrilian up the middle. Beary looked around the room; there were no more threats. He cut the Bearilian Officer down.

His eyes were swollen. "Please just kill me. Just don't hit me anymore."

Beary leaned in close. "It's okay. They will never touch you again." He lifted him up and carried him into the hall. Beary heard sounds coming from another room. Setting him down, Beary said, "It is okay, I'll be right back. Just rest and try to gain some strength." Beary gave him a shot to ease the pain.

Beary then flew back up the stairs to the room he heard the sounds coming from. An Arcrilian Colonel was standing over a map of the quadrant. Beary slipped in and went into the fast knife technique.

Five Arcrilian troopers laid dead. The Arcrilian Colonel tried to move. Beary pinned him against the wall, caught the Arcrilian's claw twisted it, and plunged the Colonels own knife into him, shoving it through him and pinning him into the wall.

Beary spoke softly. "You will not succeed at raping our planets anymore." Beary gathered what intelligence he could and set explosives then went back to the Bearilian officer.

"Who are you? I am Lieutenant Harden of RA1. I am sorry . . . ." Harden tried to ask.

Beary cut him off, "It's Okay, Lieutenant Harden. I am Ensign Maxumus from the Saber Claw. I am here to take you home. Where are they keeping your First Sergeant and your Captain?"

Harden whispered, "They were kept in the other passage. My men were kept in this one. I wish I knew where they are; they took them out earlier."

Beary smiled. "We have them. They are safe." Harden just sighed. The pain medicine had taken its effect: he was out. Beary placed him next to Grizlarge.

"I had to sedate him they were torturing him." Beary explained. "Here, keep these files Commander Centaures might find it useful."

Beary moved up the other passage he heard laughter from one of the rooms. The First Sergeant was hanging by his paws and kicking at his tormentors, much to their amusement. They stopped laughing when the first guard's head quietly exploded. Beary fired four more times and the room was clear.

The First Sergeant stared in disbelief as Beary cut him down.

"Who are you, Sir?"

Beary held up his paw. "Can you walk?"

First Sergeant Sealhunter said, "Sir, I can run if it will get me out of here. Did you find the Lieutenant and the Captain?"

Beary looked at him, "I found Lieutenant Harden; he is in bad shape. If you can head down this passage and report to Master Chief Grizlarge?"

The First grinned. "Horatio is here? Great, he owes me money." Then he took off down the passage.

Beary started looking in the cells. He almost missed him: the Captain was just a lump on the floor. Beary opened the door; they hadn't even bothered locking it. He carefully picked him up only to find a knife pointed at his gut. "Sir, if you don't mind."

The Captain squinted to see a Bearilian face, "Who are you?"

Beary smiled. "Spirit 6, I am here to get you out but we need to leave now, Sir." Beary finished picking him up and carried him down the hall.

"Chief, time is running out. We have to go." Beary threw a few claymores down both passages.

Grizlarge grabbed the Lieutenant and Beary carried the Captain. The First followed. They got back to the carrier just as alarms started going off. Grizlarge started the carrier as Beary climbed into the Gunners position.

As they started back out other carriers were heading in the other direction. When they hit the junction with the skimmer hanger, Beary fired a few shells down the tunnel. One shell hit a skimmer, and another, hit weaponry that was being loaded. The bomb went off just as the skimmer exploded. Several secondary explosions could be heard. As they passed the shield generator, Grizlarge set off the explosives by remote control. The other Marines were getting ready to bug out when they heard the explosions.

The weapons expert saw the shield fail on one side of the Hive ship. He launched twelve short range rounds against it. Four hit the Warp nacelle, three hit areas around the edge of the ship, and five hit the main part of the ship, causing minor damage. He saw the other carrier flying out of the entrance with six carriers chasing them. He locked on each one and fired the automatic gun. Shells started hitting the Arcrilian carriers.

This allowed Grizlarge to gain ground and turn the bend. Just as they got around it, the other carrier swung across the trail. The three Marines jumped out and raced for the other Carrier. They climbed through the hatch and they were off again.

The Arcrilian Major was screaming, "Where are the skimmers! What do you mean there is a fire in the hanger bay!" Just then they turned the corner on the trail. The driver couldn't stop in time. He struck the booby trap broadside. The whole area was lit up by the fire ball caused by the explosion.

An Arcrilian Corporal found the Intelligence Colonel pinned to the wall. When he went to pull him down he set off the explosives Beary had left behind.

Horatius started working on the Lieutenant and the Captain.

"Sir, I know it might be risky but we need immediate pick up."

Beary called Artemus. "Spirit Blade 2, this is Spirit 6. Load everyone up and meet us at this location."

"We are ready for lift off and are on our way, Boss." Artemus responded.

Caesar looked at him. "Are we going to be able to lift off?"

Artemus nodded. "We'll make it? How is Ben?"

"I am fine." Ben said, as he slid into the gunner's seat. "It is an embarrassing wound."

"Why? You killed the Arcrilian and he got in a lucky shot with his dying breath. You're alive, he is dead, and you saved an injured Marine and his buddies. I think it was worth the scar." Artemus said as he vectored into Beary's position.

They landed near the carrier and opened the hatch. Beary grabbed Harden while two of the Marines carried the wounded captain. The First ran to the hatch. Grizlarge threw a grenade into the carrier and jumped through the hatch and slammed it shut. Caesar and Horatius and the other Medic started working on Harden and Captain Quintus.

First Sergeant Sealhunter sat next to Grizlarge. "Horatio you owe me 25 Chits."

Grizlarge laughed and reach into his wallet and paid his friend. "Are you alright?"

The First Sergeant nodded, "They were not interested in me. So I wasn't tortured, just annoyed."

Beary took over the Pilot seat and Artemus slid into his seat. "Artemus, take out targets of opportunity as we go, but keep the air to air unless you need to use them."

Artemus started picking off targets as Beary took them into orbit, then into Warp.

Artemus scanned around them. No enemy fighters or ships were in range as they left Tarsus 9 and its moons behind.

They were beyond the stated capacity, but all systems were working nominally. "Boss, "Artemus asked, "We're over loaded. How long before we start having problems?"

Beary shrugged, "The engines could lift the Saber Claw and take it to warp 1.5. We over designed the rest of the systems to pull an extra 100% over capacity. Remember it was designed for this type of work."

Artemus thought, *of course it had been designed by Marines*. "Okay Boss, we're clear of the Tarsus system. No bandits in sight."

Master Chief Grizlarge moved over to Ben. "How are you doing, Sir?"

Ben looked strange. "Master Chief? I am just a Cadet. But I am well."

Grizlarge smiled, "No, Cadet Maritinus, you're a Marine and you are going to make a fine officer. I talked to these young Marines you saved. They would follow you even to the Moons of Bantine. You deserve the mark on your back. Your Clan has been greatly honored by you on this mission." With that the Chief moved to another spot.

"Artemus, did you reload the probes?" Beary asked

"Yes, Maintenance did. Why?" Artemus asked as he called up the probes command matrix.

Pulling up a map of the Region on his heads up display, Beary asked. "Can we place the probes along this axis to act as a weak sensor picket?"

Artemus looked at the map. "If I place them at these three coordinates we will get the best coverage. However, it still will be weak. It wouldn't pick up fighters or a small transport. But anything larger we would pick up."

"Do it then. I am not worried about the small ships at this point." Beary said.

Artemus typed in the commands and launched the three probes.

On Dryden, the Arcrilian Supreme Commander was having a fit. Reports of damage to his Hive ship were coming in. The No. 2 Warp nacelle had suffered damage. The fire and secondary explosions in his skimmer bay had destroyed half of his skimmers and most of their dedicated armory. Then the reports came in that his prisoners had escaped. One shield generator was destroyed and the other two had been slow to close the gap.

Then more explosions rocked the Hive ship. Reports that the cave structure that they had landed the ship on was starting to collapse was also coming in. It was time to leave before his ship was disabled. He gave the order for all units to get underway. Troops that were still in the field went to rally points to be picked up and returned to the hive.

Out of 20,000 troopers, 3000 were dead or missing. He smashed his front claw into the console in front of him. Turning to his helmsman he exclaimed, "Let's leave this cursed moon and let its name mean place of death".

The orbital probe picked up the lift off. Then it watched, as the Hive ship, limp out of orbit and into space. With its data collected it sent a signal to the Saber claw.

Atilus watched as the huge Hive ship limped into space.

"When should our lambs be home?"

Centaures checked. "ETA is one cycle."

"Good. Let me know when they make contact. I have paperwork to do." With a pained expression he went into his ward room.

They were approaching Carnise Drift, time to call home.

"Blue Dragon, Spirit 6." Beary called.

"Spirit 6, Dusk 2, welcome home. Drop your cloak and head to 215."

"Spirit 6, acknowledge 215. Cloak down for ID."

"Spirit 6, Blue Dragon control, requests your situation report."

"Blue Dragon Control, Spirit 6. Multiple wounded, and we are over loaded."

"Spirit 6, we are opening Bay doors. Hold position thirty SMU from doors. We will tractor you in. Please acknowledge."

"Control, we are in position. Bring us in, Spirit 6 out."

The tractor beam pulled them in and sat the crimson blade down near a hatch leading to Medical. They were barely down before medical teams were removing the wounded and sick. The five friends sat down near the Crimson Blade. Commander Centaures walked over. None of them moved or acknowledged his presence. They were all asleep. He motioned for some crewmen with stretchers, "Take them to the sick bay."

Chapter 15

A Few Day of Rest and Relaxation

Beary woke up when soft lips kissed his forehead. He looked up into Priscilla's soft eyes. "Doctor Fang, he is awake." Pompey called.

Beary sat as Dr. Wu Fang approached. "How are the Marines?"

Dr. Fang smiled, when Beary's stomach rumbled. "We almost lost Lieutenant Harden twice. They worked him over pretty hard, but he is stable now. The rest of your team is awake and taking nourishment. Are you hungry?"

Beary nodded, just the thought of food made his stomach rumble. "Yes Dr. Fang, I can eat."

"Good. I will place you in Ensign Pompey's capable paws. You may leave Medical and return to your own quarters." Dr. Fang waved as he went back to work.

Beary realized he needed clothes, and Pompey handed him a uniform. "Do you need help with these?"

Beary blushed. "No, I can do it."

"Oh well." She pulled the privacy curtain shut behind her and waited outside as he dressed.

She smiled as he came out, a slight blush still on his cheeks. Then she took him to the mess hall for food and a little talk.

One of the Marines Beary had worked with smiled. "Our young Ensign is a mad Boar as a fighter, but that little lady has him running scared."

The other shook his head, "No. He just is in unfamiliar territory. She had better watch out when he gets the lay of the land." They both smiled and went back to sleep.

Caesar, Ben, and the Chief were eating when Beary and Pompey walked in. Ben started to call them over when the Chief stopped him. "Ben, why don't we leave them alone for a while?"

Caesar smiled. "I need to get back and finish my report. And you my young friend need to have your stitches checked."

"Why? It is healing well." Ben questioned.

"Because, Ben, I say so, unless you want to spend the next five days in medical." Caesar responded.

"No, I will come with you now." Ben answered.

"Good choice, my young Cadet." Grizlarge added as they got up to leave.

Centaures came over, making sure he stayed clear of the young couple. The Master Chief started to stand, but Centaures waved him down.

"How was it, Master Chief?" Centaures asked as he set down his coffee.

Grizlarge looked up from his food. "Sir, I am getting too old for this. We accomplished our mission. Unfortunately, we were unable to recover the body of the pilot and the engineer of the Raven Star. We placed a beacon. The rest was in my report."

"How about the job our young Ensign Maxumus did?" Centaures asked.

"Sir, I can't really be objective when it comes to him; you know that. His leadership was excellent and he did what he was trained to do. But you need a more objective observer than I. I know his father would be upset, but sometimes I think of him like a son." Grizlarge said.

Centaures smirked. "So Master Chief Gunnery Sergeant Grizlarge has a heart."

Grizlarge smiled. "You caught me at a weakened moment over pie. By the way Sir, the intelligence he pulled out of the Hive ship was it useful?"

Centaures smiled. "More than you know, Chief. It answered a lot of burning questions."

On Bearilia Prime, in a seedy hotel room, in the coastal town of Delia, Admiral Benedict and two others were in a conference. "I want the Crew of the jump ship brought up on charges."

Admiral Brutus slammed his paw on to the table "Are you crazy? They are heroes. If we make such a move we risk exposure."

Admiral Santanus raised his paws. "What is done is done. Our friends will contact us again. We need to slow up the rearmament of the fleet. Brutus, can't you find a way to slow construction of the new ships?"

"Not for long, but small problems could accrue." Admiral Brutus said.

In a room next to the room occupied by the three Admirals, a team of fleet security personnel were listening.

Fleet Admiral Starpaw looked at the security team. "I have heard enough. Take them down now."

The security team kicked in the door: Admiral Benedict went for a weapon and was cut down.

The other two Admirals sat still.

The Security Captain kicked Benedict over and saw he was dead. He turned to the other two. "Do you want to resist? Please do, Scum."

Admiral Starpaw came in. "Take them away. I have bears that want to talk to them. Don't forget to take out the trash as you go."

Admiral Starpaw picked up a com unit. "General Zantoran, please. Zanny, you were right. We got all three. Benedict got stupid and is dead. The other two surrendered without so much as a whimper. I want Maxumus promotion made permanent and the Doctor's also. Do something for Grizlarge and Ensign Artemus. Also, did you read the reports on Cadet Maritinus? Yeah, I know it has never been done before. I want it done. The Silver Claw for saving Grizlarge, and a Golden Claw with combat cluster for actions on Dryden. Give the others whatever you think they deserve."

Zantoran turned to his Aide. "Captain Christiansen, I hope you have time to write some orders and dispatches."

Atilus was on the bridge talking with Centaures when the Communications officer turned to him. "Sir, there is a coded message coming in. It is marked Captains Eyes only."

Atilus signaled Centaures to follow and went into his wardroom. Centaures closed the door.

Atilus read the message. "I'll be a Bantoos' uncle, they got all three and on tape. Benedict dead went for a weapon. The other two are in custody. Holy . . . . you won't believe the rest of this." He let Centaures read the rest of the message.

Centaures looked at him, "That has never been done before." With an evil grin he asked, "How do you want to play it?"

Three cycles later, Atilus called Beary, Caesar, Artemus, Ben, and Grizlarge into his office. Knowing the Chief would explode if he wasn't in on the plan he had informed him beforehand.

The Five stood before Atilus's desk. "Gentlebears, I am sorry but Ensign Artemus, Ensign Vantanus, and Cadet Maritinus, are to be court marshaled for direct violation of orders. Ensign Maxumus you and the Chief are also to be charged for failing to abandon the mission when informed it had been terminated. I am sorry."

"Sir, I was in command; I will take full responsibility. Artemus and the others were only following my orders." Beary pleaded.

"I am sorry, Ensign, it is out of my paws. A summery hearing on the facts will be held in one cycle on the hanger deck so all testimony can be taken. That is all. Everyone, but Ensign Maxumus is dismissed." Atilus said.

After the door was closed Atilus said, "Ensign Maxumus, your father could use his influence to get you out of this."

Beary shook his head. "No, Sir. I am willing to strike a deal to get the others off."

"Sorry Ensign Fleet insists they get what they deserve. If it's any consolation, the Intel you gathered was right on. I will speak in your team's defense, dismissed Ensign." Atilus said.

Centaures shook his head. "That was just cruel."

Beary caught up to his friends. Grizlarge was talking to them and waved Beary over. "As I was telling the others show up in full Dress uniform. For you, Ensign Maxumus, that includes all your decorations. Remember: this is just a hearing to explore the facts. Come in confident. I have been court marshaled six times and beat the rap each time. Ben that Cadet Uniform will not do. You proved yourself a Marine. You're coming with me. Sirs see you in 45 STU."

Priscilla was waiting for Beary at his quarters. Caesar nodded and went in. Beary saw her and dropped his head. "I . . . . Priscilla, I, and my team are facing charges. I may not be worthy of you."

Priscilla leaned into him. "I do not care, Beary Maxumus. I love you. There will be no discussion." With that she gave him a very passionate kiss and ran down the hall.

Beary went into the room and sat down.

Caesar said "Snap out of it Beary. We have a more important date."

Beary started changing into his dress uniform and reached into his drawer and removed a small box he attacked three small Medals, a Bronze Fang, a Silver Fang and a Gold Fang with clusters. He then pulled a small blood red ribbon from a box on it was a blue medal with twelve Star points. He placed it around his neck. I guess I am ready Caesar."

Caesar stared at the Medal on his friend neck, snapped to attention and saluted.

Beary returned the salute, "Let's go."

Artemus was leaning by the door when they came out. He started to say something funny, and then he saw it and went to attention.

Beary smiled, "Let's go Savato."

As they walked down the hall other crew members moved and came to attention. Chief Grizlarge was waiting at the end of the hall with Ben. Ben looked as if he was in shock.

The two Ensigns saw the two Red ribbons on the Chiefs neck. They snapped to attention and saluted as did Beary. "Let's go Chief bring Ben along."

The three friends looked at Beary and Grizlarge, and followed them in. The hanger was filled. The entire hanger came to attention when Beary and Grizlarge came in.

Priscilla had been crying until she saw him with the red ribbon standing out from his neck. Then her chest swelled.

Beary positioned his Crew and faced the table and saluted.

"Sir, The Crew of the Crimson Blade reporting as ordered."

Atilus looked at the three Bearilian Stars that were in the room. The chief never talked about his two. Nor had Ensign Maxumus ever worn his till today just as he had planned.

"At ease, Ensign Maxumus do you have anything to say, before we begin." Atilus asked.

"No sir, but I am ready to defend my crew and our actions." was all Beary could say.

"Alright, then we will get started. Attention to orders." at that the entire hanger deck came to attention. Atilus continued, "For bravery before the enemy the crew of the Crimson Blade is awarded the Bronze claw. Five officers came forward and pinned the award on the confused crew.

"Cadet Maritinus step forward. For bravery above and beyond the call of duty you are awarded the following awards, The Silver Claw, the Gold Claw with Combat cluster, The Marine infantry Badge, and you have been promoted to Lieutenant 3rd class till you graduate the academy with all the honor and privileges thereof.

Ensign Dr. Vantanus you are here by appointed as a permanent Ensign, you have been awarded the Medical service cross, the Medical Service combat shield, and the Silver Claw.

Ensign Artemus, you have been awarded the Silver Claw with flying cluster, the Silver Fang with Combat cluster, and the Silver Blade for combat operations in a hostile environment.

Master Chief Gunnery Sergeant Grizlarge, you are here by promoted to Fleet Master Chief Gunnery Sergeant, with all pay and privileges. You are awarded the Silver Fang with Combat cluster and the Gold claw with palms.

Ensign Maxumus for leadership and bravery in the face of the enemy you are here by awarded the Gold claw with Combat Cluster and Palms, and the Gold Fang with palms. You are here by promoted to permanent Ensign.

The crew of the Crimson Blade is also authorized three days leave at Candaris Prime starting in six cycles." Atilus looked up, "Congratulations and thank you all." With that he saluted the crew and they returned the salute.

The Saber Claws crew filed out. Priscilla stood in the corner shaking when Atilus walked by. "What's wrong Pompey?"

She just looked at him with tears running down her face.

Atilus call Beary over "Ensign Maxumus do you have room for one more on the Crimson Blade."

Beary looked at him, "Yes Sir"

"Good you're taking Ensign Pompey with you. I think she needs medical leave. Oh be on one cycle alert, if I need you. Have fun see you in three Days." Atilus waved.

Pompey looked at him. Beary smiled, "You better get packed, don't forget your swim suit the beaches are beautiful at sun set."

Ben walked over as Pompey left. "Sir, what does it mean?"

Beary smiled. "It means your tribe will celebrate the day you were born. You have just brought the greatest honor to your tribe any Polarian could have. No Cadet has ever been so rewarded."

Ben pointed at the Bearilian Star, "But . . ."

Beary shook his head, "I was a Marine Corporal remember. You are a true cadet, excuse me Lieutenant 3rd Maritinus. Now go and get packed no one wastes three days of shore leave."

Artemus was checking over the Crimson blade then his wallet. 22000 credits should buy him some fun at the casinos.

"That's a large wad." Beary said.

Artemus smiled, "The Chief invited Caesar and me to go to the Casino with him."

Beary shook his head, "Just do me a favor stay away from the card tables, and don't play the Chief."

Artemus look puzzled, "Why, by the way what are you going to do?"

Beary smiled, "Savato, if you have ever trusted me do it now. As for me," He saw Ensign Pompey coming with a small bag, "swimming, and fishing."

Artemus smiled, "I see."

The Chief and Caesar showed up as did Ben. Ben had a stack of books and manuals.

Beary looked at him, "Ben, we're going on shore leave."

"Yes that is why I brought the books, I do not gamble and for me fishing and swimming are about work. I will sleep, read, and eat." Ben said

It took a few cycles to reach the resort planet, when they landed Grizlarge lead the two Ensigns to the casino. Beary checked them into the hotel. He and Artemus would share a room as would Ben and Caesar. Grizlarge and Pompey had their own rooms. Beary gave Ben his key card and went to join Pompey. Their bags had already been taken up to the rooms.

Beary had just reached Pompey and placed his arm around her, when a familiar sweet voice spoke from behind them.

"This must be the lovely Lady Pompey." Standing there was Beary's mother.

Pompey almost fainted she tried to curtsy, "Lady Maxumus I . . . ."

"Call me Angelina, dear. Son you are right she is breath taking." Angelina Maxumus said as she kissed her son.

"Mom I, Dad?" Beary stammered.

"He could build a warp engine out of two fang sticks and a piece of wire but he can't talk. Yes Son, your Father, and I are here. There was a Neurology Symposium here earlier in the week. I talked your father into a short vacation. We are over here Octavious." Angelina called.

Octavious saw his son and swept him into his arms, "We have to talk, its important." Pulling away "Let me look at you. Who is this ravishing young lady?"

Pompey felt almost dizzy. "Senator Maxumus I, I am Priscilla Pompey, Ensign Pompey."

"Lady Pompey you may call me Octavious or junior it is your choice." Octavious said with a smile.

Beary thought *Mom is always sweet but Dad is never this informal not even with his own cubs.*

"By the way Dear I ran into Caesar and that card sharking Gunnery Sergeant. He hit me up for the thirty credits I owed him from the last time we played cards." The Senator said.

Beary smiled, "That is Fleet Master Chief Gunnery Sergeant, Father."

The Senator mockingly shook his head. "What is the Fleet coming to?"

"Priscilla dear, the Gentlebears have to talk. Would you like to go shopping with me and perhaps we could get to know one another." Angelina said nodding to Beary.

Beary followed his father to his room the Senator pulled a small device from his case and swept the room then placed in the middle of the table and indicated for Beary to set as he did.

"Alright, Father what is going on especially with that junior bit?" Beary said.

"Was it that obvious?" the Senator asked.

"Dad, you were never that informal with us cubs. That bit about Gunny was pure bull. Last time you played you cleaned him out." Beary said.

"Alright I am a bad actor." The Senator began, "I am proud of you son. Do you know what was in that information you acquired on Dryden?"

Beary looked at him, "Sir, I don't think I can discuss that even with you."

The Senator smiled, he pulled a letter and a badge from his pocket. Beary looked at the Badge from the office of Senatorial investigation and a letter from General Zantoran.

Beary looked at his father, and then sat up. "Sir, is this an official investigation?"

"For now Son, let's just call it an exchange of information." the Senator said.

Beary sat back, "Dad, from the time we arrived at space dock someone had tried to destroy the Saber Claw. The Arcrilians knew we were heading for Carnise Drift and were setting a trap. The Raven Star's log said it had been diverted towards the moon Dryden before it was attacked. One instance is a coincidence. Three is a conspiracy. You taught me that. Then I saw the names on the Arcrilian messages. That is all I know."

The Senator nodded, "I had hoped for more. Son, three Fleet Admirals were conspiring with the Arcrilians to overthrow our government. Admiral Benedict tried to resist. He was killed the others surrendered without a fuss. The problem is that we don't know if it began or ended with them.

Oh that Arcrilian Hive ship you damaged was destroyed by the Antilleans when it strayed near their territory. Their wasp ships tore it apart. You and your men had caused a lot of damage. The Arcrilian's couldn't launch their fighters."

Beary smiled, "Good."

"Son, You cannot discuss what we talked about." The Senator replied.

"I know Dad. Dad I am sorry. I had to follow my own heart." Beary said.

"Son, you are a recipient of the Bearilian Star, and other awards for courage and selfless leadership. Yet I know you are humble about it. At 18 you are already being marked for greatness. I am proud to be your Father." The Senator said, "Let's go find your Mother before she operates on someone."

Angelina looked at Priscilla, "Dear do you prefer, Priscilla or Pompey."

"Lady Maxumus, I mean Angelina. Priscilla is my special name. Most of my friends call me Pompey. Of course if you wish you may." Pompey answered.

Angelina smiled. "You are a lot like my husband but a lot prettier. Pompey, my son is a great scholar, a great engineer and a strong warrior. He however hasn't had any experiences with the females of our race. Well other than three older sisters. You will have to teach him."

Pompey blushed. "I don't have any experience either. Your son taught me a lesson I needed to learn. I was a snob before he humbled me. My Parents taught me about the old ways and said we had to uphold them. When he defeated me I expected him to demand Tribute according to the old customs. Instead he asked if I was Okay. He was humble and sweet yet strong. I fell in love with him."

Angelina smiled, "Beary is my youngest. He is stubborn and pushes himself to always excel. Do you know he is madly in love with you also?"

Pompey smiled, "We were waiting for you and my parents to talk before we started courting."

"Octavious tried to talk to your father before we came. He acted strange and babbled. Your mother is a lovely lady. She gave her consent. I think your father did. He gave us a fine sheep." Angelina smiled.

Pompey dropped her head, "Lady Angelina I am sorry."

"Don't be. To tell you the truth my Husband is never that nice or personable to anyone, except me that is. Beary knew his father was not being himself. I think you disarmed him with your beauty and charm. We will be pleased to have you be part of our family." Angelina smiled.

Pompey didn't know what to say all she, could do was hug Angelina and kiss her paw.

Angelina smiled, "Our Boars are coming."

Pompey stood up, "Senator and Beary will you join us."

She moved over and allowed the Senator to set next to his wife.

After a nice dinner Beary's Dad stood up. "To Lady Pompey may our son always be worthy of you and your love."

Pompey bowed, "Lord Maxumus, may I always be worthy of your son and his love, and I pray that I can bring honor to your house."

Octavious smiled, "Thank you, Lady Pompey welcome to our family. If my Son proves worthy, if not you will still be welcome in our home."

Angelina touched her husband's arm, "Say goodnight dear." She stood up kissed Pompey and her Son. The Senator bowed and touched his Son's shoulder and followed his wife.

Ben was lying on a chair on the Beach as Beary and Pompey walked by, "Hail Sir Maxumus and Lady Pompey."

Beary smiled. "Hail Maritinus the slayer."

Ben grinned. "Where have you two been? I saved you some nice seats facing the sun set."

"We ran into my parents." Beary said.

Ben asked, "Beary could I meet your Parents?"

"Sure let me call them, I'll be right back." Beary walked over to the refreshment stationed and called.

Ben looked at Pompey, "Ensign what were they like?"

She smiled, "Lady Maxumus is just wonderful. His Father is a dear. You will like them."

Beary walked back over. "Can we have breakfast with them at eight in the morning?"

Ben beamed, "Beary what should I wear to have breakfast with your parents."

Beary smiled, "Just wear a nice shirt and pants, nothing fancy. Now if you don't mind I promised a lady a walk on a beach." with that they waved and headed down the Beach paw in paw.

Beary kissed Pompey goodnight and headed for his room. The other three also arrived at theirs. Beary waved to the Gunny. "Chief we have been invited to breakfast with my parents at Eight." the Chief acknowledge him.

Caesar smiled, "Angelina is here I mean Lady Angelina."

Beary smiled, "She is very anxious to see you also Caesar."

Artemus had already gone in. "Hay Beary."

Beary smiled, "My parents asked us to have breakfast with them."

Artemus looked at him, "Are they buying?"

Beary smiled, "That bad?"

"I lost 15,000 credits tonight." Artemus sighed.

The next morning they all got up and got dressed. The Five friends stopped and collected Lady Pompey.

Beary, knocked on the door, "Lady Pompey your escorts await."

She opened the door slowly and almost floated out of the room. Beary's mouth dropped as did the other young Bears.

The Master Chief offered his arm, "My lady."

It took the others a moment before they raced to catch-up.

Beary cleared his throat "Master Chief if I may."

"She is all yours Ensign Maxumus." Grizlarge said releasing her arm.

Pompey, took Beary's arm, and whispered, "The Master Chief is right I am all yours."

Beary squeezed her arm gently and blushed.

In a few moments they arrived on a veranda overlooking the beach. Beary's mother and father were seated at a single table set for eight.

When the group came closer the Senator and Lady Maxumus stood up. The five officers and the Master Chief came to attention and saluted the Senator.

Angelina said, "That is enough of that." as she walked over and kissed first Pompey, Beary and then Caesar. Then she walked over to Grizlarge and gave him a hug.

Then she walked over to Artemus and Ben. "Son will you introduce us?"

Beary walked over as the Chief pulled his Dad aside for a moment. "Mother this is Ensign Savato Artemus, my weapons officer and the best in the fleet. She shook his paw.

"It is a pleasure to finally meet you Ensign Artemus." Angelina said. Then she turned to Ben.

He dropped to one knee. "Lady Maxumus I am Lieutenant 3rd Maritinus of the Red Paw. My Clan wishes to give you this gift, if you would honor our Tribe by accepting them." With that he handed her a box. Inside was a necklace made of flawless blue pearls with earrings to match.

She looked at him, "Please rise Lieutenant Maritinus of the Red Paw tribe." She then kissed his cheek, which turned a light pink. "Your Clan has paid me a great honor and I will cherish them forever." Ben's chest swelled he would call home tonight.

"Friends and family please sit". Angelina said. They ate breakfast, and talk, telling stories and reminiscing.

After a while the Senator saw Caesars Crest. "Caesar your family sends their love. Your father has coffee with me most mornings before he goes to his Shop but he won't let me in do you know what he is doing?"

Caesar looked puzzled, "No Sir, I didn't even know he was back working. Since the accident I never thought he could form metal again."

The senator laughed, "He is even better now that he can't see. He clams the metal talks to him telling him how it wants to be formed. I see you have almost finished your family crest it is beautiful but why is the top right section empty?"

"I was unable to see you before I left for the Saber Claw. I was hoping to add the Line of Vantanus to the Maxumus family as my father's is." Caesar said.

The Senator rose up, "I would be honored, please present your Crest."

Caesar stood up and handed the Senator his Crest, "I Caesar Vantanus first of my line do here and for always tie my line to the House of Maxumus."

The Senator took the Crest, "By these witnesses, I Octavious Maxumus Head of the Maxumus clan, do here and forever more Claim the Vantanus line as part of our clan with all the privileges, rights and responsibility of the Clan Maxumus." With that He turned his ring over, "By the Hammers of Corsan", the ring glowed bright red and he placed his paw on the crest in the upper right corner the family Crest of the Maxumus Clan was etched in. The Senator smiled as he handed the crest back to Caesar.

Pompey had never experienced anything like it. She had read about it but this was amassing. She dropped her head next to these fine Bears we are sheepherders.

Angelina leaned over and whispered, "Remember my dear the Maxumus clan were a bunch of raiders and thieves before they become respectable. Even the First of the Caesar line was little more than a successful pirate. It is not who our ancestors were or the name of the clan that makes us who we are, but it is us, who make the name of the clan what it is."

Pompey leaned into Angelina and kissed her cheek. She now understood the difference between Beary's family and hers. His family embraced who they were but didn't dwell on it. Her Father was always trying to improve their name through money and influence. She got up and walked around to Caesar, and whispered in his ear, "Please forgive me Caesar, I was a snob will you allow me to name one of our Cubs after you if Beary approves."

Caesar, nodded his head yes and she returned to her seat.

The morning was waning, Angelina smoothed her dress. "Ben may I call you that," Ben nodded and she continued, "is your mother alive?"

"Yes, Lady Angelina, she is strong and well." Ben replied

Angelina removed a bright Red Star stone necklace from her neck. "Would you do me the honor of giving this to her for me? It was my Grandmothers and it would please me if she would accept it."

Ben was speechless as she placed it in his paw then put on the Blue pearls his tribe had given her. All he could do was kiss her paw.

"Well I don't know when I have had a more lovely morning but the Senator promised me some alone time and I plan to collect it. Beary we are leaving in the morning if you care to see us off, come Octavious." Angelina said.

Beary got up and kissed his Mother as did Caesar and watched as she led the Senator down the beach.

Ben was the first to speak, "I must see to Lady Maxumus wishes. My village will sing of her kindness and write about how she honored my Tribe and village." With that he took off.

Artemus looked at Beary and Caesar, "We have got to go to one of their parties."

Grizlarge laughed, "You three wouldn't last a day. They are one wild celebration."

Pompey quietly took Beary's paw in hers and leaned in to his Chest.

Grizlarge took the cue, "Come on you two cubs the Casino awaits."

Artemus stopped and handed Beary 5000 Credits "I don't want to go home broke." then took off.

Beary and Pompey walked down the Beach for a few KSMU and found a spot with a great view of the Sea. After a while she leaned deeper into his chest. "Your, Parents are wonderful, especially your mom giving Ben such a present for his mother."

Beary kissed her forehead. "Those pearls Ben's tribe sent her were worth a full year's wages for the entire village. Her necklace pales in comparison. But Ben's Clan believes the Creator used the Red Star stone to give their founder the Red Paw mark on his shoulder. His mother will be held in high esteem and they will all celebrate the gift."

"I am almost afraid of you meeting my parents," she said "they are different from yours. They believe you can buy nobility."

Beary laughed, "Priscilla you have great nobility and a great spirit. Your parents must have did something right."

She kissed him, "No, my dear Sire, it was you who taught me to be humble and your mother who showed me how to be a true lady. I will learn my lessons well." Then she snuggled down into the sand next to him to watch the sun set.

Beary's com went off on his wrist, "Boss, where are you?" Artemus asked.

Beary looked down as Priscilla woke up, "We are on the Beach. What's going on?"

Artemus smiled, "We have been recalled I have your location and your bags. We will pick you up."

Pompey, sat up, "What is wrong?"

Beary looked at her with sun in her fur, "We have to go back to work."

In Five STU the Crimson Blade landed next to them and they climbed in. Beary lifted the Crimson Blade off the sand and took her over the water before heading out of the atmosphere.

Ben came over, "My tribe says they will hold a weeklong celebration in honor of your mother and her kindness to my Clan and the great honor she has given us."

Beary smiled as he dialed in the Saber Claw Coordinates. "Tell them that my mother was very moved by their kindness."

Artemus looked at Beary, "Boss is that a new standard uniform."

Beary looked down and saw he was still in his swim suit. "Artemus take over for a moment." With that he walked back and pulled one of his extra flight suits from a storage compartment and pulled the curtain and put it on.

Pompey smiled as she said, "Do you have an extra one," Beary turned to see her standing there. He reached in and pulled out another spare. She kissed him, "This will do. Thank you now you better go fly the ship." as she closed the curtain.

Artemus smile, "Relinquishing control. Boss shield is on do you want to cloak."

Beary thought, "No we're just a ship returning, lets fly easy."

Pompey came out, the flight suit was a little big, but she took it in at the waist with a utility belt. "Ensign Maxumus we have a data stream message coming in. It's a priority message to all fleet units to stand to condition 2."

Beary looked at Artemus, "Bring weapons on line and cloak the ship." Beary pushed the engines to emergency power.

Midnight Blade picked up an incoming fighter, "Blue Dragon Control we have an Antillean Wasp II fighter in bound."

"Dusk 2 make contact, Blue Dragon Control out"

"Dusk 2 to in bound Antillean Fighter please acknowledge."

"Dusk 2, this is Death Wasp 1 requesting permission to see your Captain."

"Flame 1, Dusk 2 please escort our friends in."

Flame Dagger appeared off the Wasps II right wing,

"Death Wasp 1, this is Flame 1, please form up, and follow me."

Swarm Colonel Bantic smiled and told his pilot to comply.

Beary saw the Saber Claw and uncloaked, "Blue Dragon Control, Spirit 6 requesting instructions."

"Blue Dragon Control to Spirit 6 land hot we have incoming visitors."

Flame 1 heard the transmission. "Death Wasp 1, Flame 1 we have a jump ship landing hot it might be interesting."

Bantic turned toward the Saber Claw's massive cam shell doors as they opened a Jump ship was coming in at a high rate of speed it flared and rotated as it hit the Landing Bay pointing back out the door.

"Death Wasp 1 to Flame 1, he must be a very good pilot or have a death wish."

"Flame 1 smiled, "Death Wasp 1 I am handing you over to Blue Dragon Control, Safe wings and good crops."

"Thank you Flame 1, "May your cubs be close to the Creator"

"Blue Dragon control Death Wasp 1 requesting landing instructions."

"Death wasp 1, Blue Dragon control permission granted please land at your discretion Welcome to Carnise Drift"

The Colonel pointed to his pilot, "Take us in Lieutenant Juristic."

The Wasp II Fighter lightly landed almost without a sound. The Maintenance crew quickly pulled a boarding ramp over. The Flight Sergeant stood at attention and saluted as the Large Antillean Colonel returned his salute. The Flight Sergeant said, "Sir if you will follow me. Is there anything we can do for your fighter?"

The Colonel looked surprised, "Flight Sergeant does your maintenance crew know how to service a Wasp II fighter."

"Yes Sir my crew is fully qualified." the Flight Sergeant replied.

"Lieutenant Juristic, they have offered to service your fighter, please aid them." Bantic ordered.

Centaures walked over, "Colonel what an unexpected pleasure. May I, get you some nectar or perhaps some food."

"Commander Centaures I need to talk to you and Atilus.

But first may I meet the pilot that landed the Jump Ship. He is a fine pilot." Bantic said.

Beary and Artemus was checking out the Crimson Blade and securing her systems. When Centaures called him over "Ensign Maxumus, would you come here?" Centaures said.

Beary saw Bantic, and leaped out and called, "Uncle Ban," then he stopped himself, and came to attention and saluted, "Swarm Colonel Bantic it is good to see you sir", then in Antillean he said "Safe wings, and may your crops always prosper."

Centaures observed as the large Antillean took Beary in his arms and touched his head with his mandibles.

Then Bantic smiled, "It is good to see you Beary. I knew only a Maxumus would try a landing like that especially that last maneuver. You have grown well, how is your family?"

"They are well but wish they could again walk your fields in the mid-summer." Beary said in Antillean.

"Commander Centaures, I am sorry Beary lived with my family for a year on our farm when he was five. His Mother was working on a vaccine for Nero palsy that affected my Race. His father was also working on the treaty of Sonact." Bantic explained "May he join us, my Bearilian is useful but not perfect. Beary is fluent in both languages."

"As you wish Colonel, Ensign, can you change quickly and report to the wardroom." Centaures responded.

"Yes Sir." Beary saluted and headed for his quarters.

Artemus looked at Caesar, "Our young Ensign is full of surprises."

Caesar smiled, "You don't know the half of it. Do you have any complaints?"

Artemus smiled, "At first, but I was wrong now I don't even want to think about him leaving or you or Ben. We have made a great team."

Caesar smiled, "Thanks, by the way how did you make out last night."

Artemus sighed, "I gave Beary 5000 credits to hold for me, or I would have come home broke. The Chief broke even. How did you do?"

Caesar pulled out a wad of bills, "I did all right. Let me buy you lunch." He laughed.

Chapter 16

The Calm before the Storm

Bantic was talking with Atilus and Centaures, "We intercepted a damaged Hive ship that strayed near our territory. One of its warp nacelles was badly damaged and they couldn't maintain warp. We hit it when it dropped to sub light speed. They tried to launch fighters but the bay doors jammed only partly opened One of my Wasps put a missile through the opening. It looked like the entire bay exploded. Do you know how it was damaged?"

Centaures looked at Atilus who nodded his eyes, "The Raven Star was transporting 2 Marine units to man this Drift when it was attacked by Arcrilian fighters and forced down on Tarsus 9's moon Dryden. Ensign Maxumus lead a rescue team to the moon. They ambushed a group of Arcrilians who were holding Bearilian prisoners.

They discovered that 2 officers and a senior NCO were being held in the Hive ship. Ensign Maxumus and Fleet Master Chief Grizlarge made entry and secured the captives. They destroyed some systems on their way out. Then two Marines from the Black Aces laid down cover fire they purposely targeted the Hanger doors but they believed they had failed to cause any damage."

Bantic shook his head, "Will you give these to the two Marines. They are called in your language Honey stingers with Laurel leaves. Their actions saved many of my warriors."

Centaures looked at the beautiful Medals, "It will be done."

At that point Beary arrived and knocked on the door. The door opened, "Ensign Maxumus, reporting as ordered."

Atilus waved him to a seat. "Colonel Bantic wants to go over details of your encounter with the Arcrilian Hive ship. You may answer all his questions."

While Beary was giving his report Artemus finished talking to the crew chief and walked over to the Wasp II Fighter.

"Lieutenant that is a beautiful fighter, I am Ensign Savato Artemus."

"I am Flight Lieutenant Juristic. Your maintenance crews are excellent they are even repairing some minor battle damage." Juristic replied.

"Lieutenant may I buy you a Drink in our ready room." Artemus asked.

Juristic nodded, "Do you think they have Surmain nectar, Ensign Artemus."

Artemus smiled, "If not I know a Master Chief that probable can find some."

He led the Antillean Lieutenant into the ready room. "Sergeant Dark Paw, do we have any Surmain nectar."

"Yes Sir, I have one bottle, in the back." Sergeant Dark Paw said, and went to get it. He came back and poured a tall glass for both, the Lieutenant and Artemus.

Artemus sipped it was good, "This is a good choice. "May you fly fast and your crops, be abundant."

The Lieutenant clicked, "Thank you Ensign. I think I like your version."

Artemus Dropped his head, "I said it wrong, Lieutenant where do you live."

Juristic smiled, "I have a little farm, just 10 hectares of meadow above ground and 20 hectares of tunnels below ground. It is on our planet Hillane. Last year my brood grew 10 tons of fungi. It is a small farm but just big enough for my wife to run. I am not home enough. Artemus where is your home?"

Artemus thought, "I guess the Saber Claw is. I don't have any land to set my feet. If this situation with the Arcrilians ever gets settled Dryden might be worth settling. There are a few nice valleys."

Juristic looked at him, "You were part of the team that attacked the Hive ship?"

Artemus didn't know how to answer. "I wasn't one of them that attacked the Hive directly. I killed 4 Skimmers and several troop carriers. My job was to rescue the other Marines, we got them all out."

"Your team damaged a Hive Ship that had attacked our lands. Because of the damage it received we were able to destroy it." He thought for a moment, "Everyone needs a place to set his feet. You are always welcome in my meadow and tunnels. This card has a small speck of dirt from my farm. If you show this to my wife or one of my brood they will know to give you sweet rest on our land and sanctuary in our tunnels." Juristic handed him the card

Artemus took it, "I don't know how to thank you."

Juristic smiled, "Kill more Arcrilians." he then took another sip. "If you have another bottle of this I could take with me I wouldn't be offended."

Artemus signaled Sergeant Dark Paw who had been listening. He came back with a wrapped box a few minutes later. Just then Ben walked in and saw the Antillean Lieutenant.

Ben bowed slightly so his tattoo showed briefly. "Safe wings, genital breezes, and abundant crops always bless your lands, Sir."

The Antillean replied, "Warm sun, cold water and abundant game. May your children's children, bask in your honor warrior of the Red Paw."

Artemus said, "Well I guess I should introduce you. Flight Lieutenant Juristic of the Death Wasp Swarm this is Lieutenant 3rd Ben Maritinus. Ben killed 150 Arcrilians in single combat on Dryden."

Juristic stepped over and touched Ben's head with his Mandibles. "With your permission I will add your name to the scroll of Hillane Ben Maritinus of the Red Paw."

Ben smiled "You do me to high an honor."

Juristic said "Not so. You killed troopers of the Hive Ship Styx reaper."

Ben's fur turned red, "Sir if I would have known I would have killed many more."

Juristic smiled. "Your team damaged the Styx Reaper bad enough that my swarm was able to destroy it."

Ben's, joy over flowed. "Your Swarm will be remembered in song and written in the book."

Artemus finally had to ask. "Your Races have interacted before?"

Juristic smiled. "150 years ago the Styx Reaper attacked Hillane. They destroyed or took our crops and took many slaves. Ben's bears came to our aid. They brought us seed and fertilizer and food to help us till our planet healed. 10 of their warriors attempted to free the slaves. About half were freed. But all but one of the warriors was killed."

The three continued to talk and Drink Surmain nectar the Sergeant handed Artemus a small piece of paper. He looked at it. It was a bill for the gift bottle. 1200 credits. Artemus reach in his pocket and quietly gave the Sergeant the money.

In Captain Atilus's wardroom Beary had just finished his report. Colonel Bantic had asked several questions during the briefing.

"That was a good report Ensign Maxumus. I am proud of you. I understand your bears rewarded your crew. Our Government wishes to also with the Captains permission." Bantic looked at Atilus who nodded.

"Ensign Maxumus you know our customs, please give these awards to your bears quietly and solemnly." With that Bantic pulled five small boxes from his case. "We had been monitoring the transmissions from Dryden. We notified the liaison Admiral Benedict of our findings. He told us that a Bearilian Destroyer had been sent to the area. So we came prepared if we found the heroes of Dryden. These are for your crew.

Beary opened one of the boxes he saw the honey colored ribbon and the red rose medal. "Colonel this is too great an honor for me and my crew."

Bantic said, "Nonsense, besides would my own God-Nephew cause an incident between are two races."

Beary bowed, "No Uncle, but I know the importance of these awards. My Crew will cherish and try to live up to this honor."

Bantic smiled, "It is well that you showed humility my nephew. Again you honor us. Captain Atilus we found information in the wreckage of the Hive ship that indicated they planned to ambush you near Dryden. It was a trap you failed to fall into. Why did you not rush in with the Saber Claw?"

Atilus thought, "To be honest Colonel that option didn't occur to me. Our jump ships are designed to conduct rescue operations. Plus, we didn't know the Hive Ship was there. If I had I might have fell for the trap. Plus we received orders not to attempt any more rescues after the Crimson Blade dropped off the first group. Of course they were already on their way back before we received the orders."

Bantic thought, "They didn't know you would send in a dedicated rescue team. So by a fluke you didn't fall for the trap. But we had informed Admiral Benedict. Did he not inform you?"

Atilus looked at Centaures, "Admiral Benedict is dead. He and two others were plotting with the Arcrilian to overthrow our government."

Bantic let out an oath in Antillean, Beary nodded in agreement. Then he continued, "Captain Atilus were they the beginning or the end of the conspiracy?"

Atilus sighed, "That is what we do not fully know. We are interrogating the other two Admirals. Hopefully we will gain some knowledge from them. Or we will find a way to gain more intelligence somehow."

"You have my pledge that we will try and help you. Benedict betrayed us as well. I hope we together can push them away from our territories." Bantic replied.

"Your assistance will be appreciated, my dear Colonel." Atilus responded.

"Now my good Captain may I take some time to talk to Ensign Maxumus to catch-up on family matters?" Bantic asked.

Atilus looked at Beary, "Why don't you show the good Colonel around."

"Yes Sir," Beary responded, "Colonel, would you come with me?"

Beary and Bantic were walking down the hall talking in Antillean, when they saw Pompey. Beary called her over. "Swarm Colonel Bantic, it is with great joy that I present Ensign Priscilla Pompey, my betrothed." Beary said.

Pompey looked at him, "Beary Maxumus we have not been officially betrothed I have no symbol of it."

Beary looked shocked, "Uncle she is right. You know our custom where a member of the boar's family must be present? Well would you act as that member?"

The Antillean Colonel looked at Beary, "It would be a great honor."

Beary turned to Pompey, "Colonel Bantic is my God-Uncle, and he taught me how to fly a Candela skimmer. To my family he is family." pulling a box from his pocket he knelt "will you be mine?" He opened the box.

Pompey stared at it. In the box was a ring in the center was a large blue diamond. Around the diamond was a ring of Red Star stones. "I, I have never seen anything that beautiful."

Beary smiled, "It was my Great Grandmothers. My Mom thought you might like it."

"Beary, I love it and you. Yes I will be your betrothed." Pompey said with tears of joy in her eyes.

The Colonel reached over and touched Pompey's head with his mandibles. "If you will, you are now my God-niece."

Pompey looked into his eyes, "Colonel Bantic it would be my great honor and she hugged him. I am sorry. I am due at my duty station. Fast wings and abundant crops, my Uncle." with that she took off down the passageway.

Bantic smiled, "She will give you a good brood."

Beary flushed, "Thank you Uncle." with that they continued down the passageway."

Back on Bearilia, Admiral Starpaw and General Zantoran were looking through the glass. Colonel Mac Starland looked down his snout at Admiral Santanus. "Do you have anything to say to me Santanus?"

Santanus eyes flared red, "That is Admiral Santanus Coronal."

Colonel Mac Starland slammed both fists on the table, "You are nothing but a traitor. You are filth Santanus and if you give me any excuse I will break you in half. I swear it."

"You can do nothing to me. I have not been tried. The Citizens will rally to our cause." Santanus growled.

Mac Starland smiled, "The evidence we have found has already convicted you. The intelligence we gained from the Arcrilian's Hive ship proves you were working with them. You have already been convicted by the Bearilian Supreme Court you have been stripped of your rank and your citizenship. I can do anything I want to you, no one would care, and when I am done you are going to the prison planet Dragon Breath."

Santanus looked at him, "Do what you like. You will not break me. When our friends come it will be you who screams for mercy. But you will not receive it."

In another room Captain Aurelius was interrogating Admiral Brutus. Aurelius shook his head "Tell me Brutus do you wish to spend the rest of your life on Dragon Breath. You have already lost everything, your property, family, rank, and citizenship. All you have left is your worthless life. Why do you not talk with me? We could make a deal I could send you to another prison one with a less harsh environment."

Brutus looked at him his resolve weakened, "I was just following orders. Santanus was in charge, all I did was slow up the delivery of supplies to the contractors building the New Ships. Don't you see we can't defeat them? Even with the new fleet but we could make a deal. After all we have allowed them to harvest planets for centuries and always pulled back. Our government needed changing. Why there are even some in the Senate who supported Santanus's plan."

The Captain smiled, "Who are they and what are their names."

Brutus shook his head, "Only Santanus knows he was the contact between the Arcrilian and what he called the council of eight. He kept our actions compartmentalized. I work at slowing logistics Benedict reported ship movements and assignments and leaked Antillean reports back to the Arcrilians.

I think he also did dirty jobs for Santanus. He was upset over the activities of an Ensign Maxumus but he could not locate anything on him."

"Very good Brutus I will see you are feed and taken back to your cell. We will talk some more. If you are good and help the investigation, I will see you spend the rest of your life on a farming penal colony." Aurelius promised as he left.

Senator Maxumus looked at the Captain, "Do you believe him?"

"Yes Senator, he didn't lie. He is weak and his mind is easy to read. That is why he was not trusted by the other two and he knew it but they needed him at least for a while longer. Now Senator I must rest even a weak mind drains your body." with that Captain Aurelius left.

Octavious picked up a secured com device and called his personal secretary. "Deloris, Octavious here, find out what Senators had contact with Admiral Santanus on a fairly regular basses formally and informally. Look into any staff contacts also. Deloris, do this through your special channels not regular. We need to be discrete.

Also have Tiberius check and see if any Senators or their staffs have family involved in fleet logistics. Have him also see who has contacts with the Orion guilds or the Chameleons."

"It will be done Senator. How is Beary?" Deloris asked.

"Grownup, he has found a young female of our race. They are betrothed. Be careful Deloris and tell Tiberius also the Bears we are after plan to destroy our Government from within." Octavious said as he hung up.

He walked into another room Zantoran and Starpaw were waiting "We have at least eight senators involved but Brutus doesn't know who they are. Captain Aurelius probed his mind while he questioned him. Brutus was not trusted nor did he trust the others. He believed they thought him disposable. The key is Santanus, but he would not be susceptible to a mine prob. He was a member of SNU2 they trained in mental manipulation until the Fleet banned the program." Octavious explained.

Zantoran looked out the window. "We sent in a sapper team to Dryden. They found the pilot and engineer of the Raven Star and brought their bodies' home. They also sifted through the carnage that was left behind. We will know soon if it has any intelligence value."

With that the three tried to figure out where to go from here.

Colonel Bantic came into the ready room. "Lieutenant it is time we returned to our base. What is in the box?"

Juristic grinned. "Sir it is a gift a very fine bottle of Surmain Nectar. Thank you my friends. Oh pardon, Colonel Bantic this is Ensign Artemus the gunner of the Crimson Blade and lieutenant 3rd Ben Maritinus of the Red Paw."

Colonel Bantic smiled, "It is good to meet two of the heroes of Dryden. May the Creator, bless you and your prosperity."

Ben and Artemus stood and saluted the Colonel, "Safe wings, and may your crops be abundant."

The Lieutenant picked up his box and waved to his new friends and followed the Coronal out to the Wasp II Fighter.

The Flight Sergeant walked up and handed the lieutenant a list of repairs his crew had performed. "Sir, she is a magnificent fighter and she should be good as new. We have replenished your weapons so you have a full load, safe wings, good crops, and good hunting."

The Lieutenant checked over his fighter then Juristic turned to the Flight Sergeant. "Thank your crew they did a superior job." with that he climbed in to his seat.

Atilus showed up carrying a case. "Colonel Bantic, one moment please. I would like to give your swarm a gift it is a case of Rose-atine Nectar from my father's vineyards."

The Colonel looked at the label on the Box Atilus Prime Vineyard Red label Nectars. "This is a very fine gift Captain Atilus my swarm will be grateful. Good hunting. Captain you have a fine ship and a great crew may the Creator bless you all."

Atilus smiled, "Safe wings, and may your crops grow in abundance."

With that the Colonel Bantic closed his canopy. "Blue Dragon Control, Death Wasp 1 requesting hot launch."

"Blue Dragon control to Death Wasp 1, hot launch authorized Safe wings and good crops, Sir."

The Wasp II fighter lifted off as silently as it landed and shot out of the hanger bay and rotated up 90 degrees and was gone.

Atilus looked at Artemus, "The Crimson Blade will be on 5STU alert. Ensure she is prepped, Lieutenant Maritinus report to Master Chief Grizlarge. Artemus inform Ensign Maxumus to stand by."

Artemus said "Yes Sir, she is ready already and I'll inform the Boss."

Atilus smiled as he walked away, "So Artemus has accepted Maxumus, and they have become a good team."

Beary was in Medical, "Caesar can I see you for a moment."

Caesar came over, "Is something wrong Beary?"

Beary smiled, "No but I was going to have you stand with me when I gave Pompey the ring, but Uncle Bantic was here. It seemed important to make him part of it. Oh and he gave this to me to give you." Beary handed him the box.

Caesar opened the box, saw the honey colored ribbon and the red rose medal. "Beary do you, of course you do. But such an honor did we deserve it? Oh about the other, it is Okay."

Beary smiled, "Thank you Caesar, I guess we'll have to live up to the award. I have to find the other three. I'll see you later."

"Boss, Artemus we are on 5 STU standby please report to the ready room." Artemus said into his com unit.

Beary acknowledged, "I am on my way, ask Grizlarge and Ben to meet me there."

"You got it Boss." Artemus said then relayed the message."

Beary arrived a few moments before Grizlarge and Ben.

He went and got a drink of cold water. He watched as Grizlarge and Ben came in. He called them over and they took a seat.

Then Beary cleared his throat and in a quiet voice he handed the three friends each a box. "On behalf of my Uncle Swarm Colonel Bantic, of the Death Swarm and the Antillean Supreme Council I present these awards for your part in the destruction of the Hive ship Styx Reaper and its crew."

The three Friends opened the boxes. Ben and the Grizlarge both gasped when they saw the honey colored ribbon and the rose medal. Artemus saw it and knew it was beautiful but didn't grasp the significance.

Grizlarge spoke first. "Ensign Maxumus do you realize the significance of this medal?"

Beary smiled, "Yes Master Chief, it holds the same significance to the Antilleans' as the Bearilian Star does to us. That is why it is presented quietly and solemnly as their custom requires."

Artemus looked at him in shock, "Boss we don't deserve this high of an honor."

Beary smiled "To refuse it would bring dishonor to my family would you do that to me Savato."

Artemus looked at the card that Lieutenant Juristic had given him, "No Boss I just hope I live up to the honor they gave me."

Beary smiled, "So do I."

Ben was quite, "I am the second of my Tribe to receive this honor. My tribe will explode with joy over this it is a great gift they have bestowed on us." He got up "I must go and pray and ask the Creator to make me worthy of this Gift." with that he closed the box and left.

"Artemus is the ship ready?" Beary asked.

"Yes Boss, we can be out the door in, under 60 SUBTU." Artemus said.

Just then the com came on "Control to Crimson Blade launch in relief of Flame Blade. Beary and Artemus ran to the Crimson Blade. She started right up,

"Spirit 6 to control request hot launch."

"Control to Spirit 6, hot launch contact Dusk 2 on Delta."

With that Crimson Blade shot out of the hanger bay. Once on station Beary called, "Dusk 2 Spirit 6 on station"

"Spirit 6, Dusk 2 copy you are on station cloak and patrol section 2."

"Flame 1, Dusk 2 you are relieved. Return to base."

One cycle later Dusk 2 called, "Spirit 6, Dusk 2 passing baton to Dusk 6."

"Dusk 2 and 6 Copy Dusk 6 is in control Spirit 6 out."

Artemus checked his passive scanners, "Boss turn to 165 Mark 7 true 5 KSMU toward that small asteroid."

Beary brought the Crimson Blade to the new heading all at once they saw a hundred more canisters one started to race toward them. Beary shouted "Arcrilian sapper mines!"

Artemus blasted the first one and started picking off others farther in the field. The concussion of the blasts could be felt through their shields. Artemus had almost cleared the field when Beary asked him to leave one intact. Artemus selected one next to the asteroid to save and destroyed the rest.

Beary asked, "Have you ever deactivated one of those?"

Artemus looked at him, "If I can't blast them I don't touch them."

"Well, I have I guess I'll do it." Beary said.

"No Boss, this we call in." Artemus said.

"Blue Dragon Control, Spirit 6, be advised we have destroyed an Arcrilian mined field in Section 2. We have saved one mine for deactivation request permission to retrieve mine."

"Spirit 6, Blue Dragon control, Negative do not approach said mine we will send a robotic mine deactivation and evaluation unit. Please stand by in the area."

"Blue Dragon Control, Spirit 6 understood standing by."

"Thanks Savato." Beary said.

"Beary you are the best pilot I have ever flown with and you are a good leader. But remember you are not a Marine corporal, you are an Ensign. We have expendable machines to do that job."

The nonmagnetic drone arrived in about one cycle its microprocessor brain scanned the mine and sent the information back to the Saber Claw then it proceeded to disarm the mine as it was completing its task an energy beam hit it destroying it and the mine.

Four Arcrilian needle fighters cut through the gap and started frantically scanning for the jump ship they knew had to be there.

Beary swung the Crimson Blade around and launched 8 missiles at the fighters. The fighters caught sight of the missiles just before they arrived. Savato lined up on another fighter and fired. The energy beam slammed into the fighter as it tried to avoid the missiles. In a matter of moments 3 of the fighters were dead. The forth fired wildly one of his shots bounced off the Crimson Blade's shield. Artemus responded with two more missiles and a shot from his Gatling phaser. The needle fighter jerked into the path of the missiles and just came apart.

"Blue Dragon Control and Dusk 6, Spirit 6. Mine deactivation drone destroyed by four Arcrilian needle fighters. Fighters were engaged and destroyed with missiles and gun fire, standing by for orders."

"Blue Dragon control to Spirit 6 Drop long range sensor buoy and stand by."

Beary looked at Artemus, "Prepare the buoy, I'll take us in."

Atilus knew he was being stretched thin the crew of the flame Dagger was on rest cycle. Ruby Dagger and Blood Dagger were still flying support of the Civil Engineers who were being pushed to their limits Scarlet Dagger was flying cover for the Midnight Dagger, which was on its third crew rotation.

"Centaures you have the Con." Atilus said.

"First officer has the Con." Centaures repeated.

In his ward room Atilus picked up his com unit "Com, please have the on duty Communications watch officer report to my ward room."

After two STU, Pompey walked in and went to a panel and activated the Captains personal encrypted communication system. "Sir it is ready, whom do you wish to speak with?"

Atilus thought "Commander Fleet Operation security, Admiral Starpaw."

After a few minutes The Admiral appeared on the screen. "Captain Atilus what can I do for you?"

Atilus said "Sir who do I report to now that Admiral Benedict is no longer with us?"

Starpaw thought, "I am currently filling that position what do you need?"

Atilus cleared his throat, "Sir I need more troops and engineers. My civil engineers are worn out and are almost out of material. The Crimson Blade was patrolling the far edge of section two when they encountered four Arcrilian needle fighters. All the enemy fighters were destroyed but I am stuck in a stationary position and have no room to fight. Also, even though, most members of the Black Aces have returned to duty, some haven't. The Red Aces were hurt. If the Arcrilians launch a major push all we can do is slow them down, not stop them."

Starpaw smiled, "I can't send you much the 248th SCB is available they will ship out immediate from Darius II. With the 308th Knights Division plus equipment Colonel Remas will take over the installations on the Carnise Drift. The Black and Red Aces will be assigned to the Saber Claw if you don't mind them aboard. Also the tug Raging wind will bring in a launch bay for the Green Dragon II Fighter Wing. Will that be enough help?"

Atilus was stunned "I don't know if it will be enough but it will be a great deal of help."

"Captain Atilus you will be in operational command. I'll send more help as soon as I can. Just hold out Son. Your crew has already performed beyond any expectations."

"Thank you sir, we'll do our best." Atilus said.

Starpaw smiled, "Fleet out." The com went dead.

Atilus looked at Pompey's hand, "Ensign what is that planet on your paw?

Pompey blushed "It is a ring, Sir. Ensign Maxumus gave it to me."

Atilus smiled and opened the ward room door. "Centaures, come here."

Centaures came in, "What do you need Captain."

Atilus smiled "I need to know if this ring is going to affect the gravitational coefficient of our ship."

Centaures had a weird smile on his face. "I don't think so, but it will be close. May I ask where you got it?"

Pompey smiled, "I am betrothed to Ensign Maxumus he said it was his Grandmother's ring."

Centaures nodded, "Congratulations Lady Pompey."

Atilus looked at her. "You had better return to your duty station I need to talk to Commander Centaures."

After she left Atilus looked at Centaures. "What was that look?"

Centaures sighed, "I recognized the ring. I bet she hasn't. It wasn't just Beary's grandmother's ring that is the Star of Vandar the imperial ring of the House of the Caesar Clan."

Atilus, whistled. "We can discuss that later. We have help coming, the 248th SCB and the 308th Knights division and the Green Dragon II Wing."

Centaures grinned. "That is a lot of help. When do they start arriving?"

"Within the next 20 Cycles, then over the next 2 days everyone should be here." Atilus said.

Chapter 17

Storm Warnings

The first groups to arrive were; the 248th SCB [Space Construction Battalion] and the 308th Knights Division. Atilus called Lt Commander Vesuvius and Commander Centaures into his wardroom. Colonel Remas and Commander Laki were a great contrast. Colonel Remas dark fur stood out against his blood red uniform and Commander Laki light blue fur paled against his dark blue uniform. "Lt Commander Vesuvius, this is Commander Laki. His engineers will be taking over from your Civil Engineers. Please show him around."

"Yes Sir. Commander Laki if you will follow me. The Scarlet Dagger is waiting for us to take us out to the command post." Vesuvius said.

After they left Atilus turned to Colonel Remas, "I am glad your division is here. You do have your own Jump ships don't you? Atilus asked.

"Yes Captain, we have twelve Red Daggers and Two Blue Daggers. Sir, I understand you are in operational control. Where do you want my men?" Remas said.

"The Green Dragon II wing will be here in 36 Cycles. Until then we need you to fly Air Cover. My crew needs some down time. Our Blue Dagger has been rotating three crews on station for two weeks. It needs maintenance. My Red Dagger crews are also tired but I have rested them and their maintenance crews have been able to do some maintenance. Lieutenant JG White-Fang is one of my combat communications officers. He will act as Liaison officer between the ship and your staff." Atilus said.

"No problem, Captain my crews are very capable, we will do a good job. My Blue Daggers are Shield and Helmet. The red daggers all have various knight names. I'll give your communications officer all their call signs. We also have a new Green Dagger command jump ship it is a bit larger than the Blue Dagger and has capabilities of both the Red and Blue Dagger. Its call sign is Gauntlet.

I would love to meet the designer of the engines, a Doctor Maxumus. He also designed most of the systems on the Daggers. He sure knew marines and their needs. I bet he was one at one time."

Atilus smiled, "He was."

Rames looked surprised, "You know him?"

"Yes, I'll arrange a meeting Colonel." Atilus said.

Rames smiled, "Well since you are in such a giving mood I would like to meet the Crew that rescued the Marines of the 307th Aces."

Centaures smiled "The crew just landed I'll have them come up."

Centaures walked over and sent for Beary and Artemus. "They will be here soon."

Beary and Artemus knocked and came in and saluted.

Centaures smiled, "Colonel Rames this is Ensign Artemus the gunner of the Crimson Blade. This is Ensign Dr. Beary Maxumus pilot of the Crimson Blade and the designer of the Vallen/ Maxumus Engine and the Dagger jump ships."

Rames had disbelief all over his face. "I am sorry Ensign but you are what 18 years."

"Yes Colonel, I am. I designed the warp engines when I worked with Dr. Vallen at the Vallen institute when I was 14. I joined MSU6, when I was 15 and was a corporal when I went to the Academy. I was part of the Dagger design team because of my degree in engineering and experience in jump ships." Beary said.

Rames said, "Well Ensign you did a great job. Thank you."

Atilus looked at Beary and Artemus, "Gentlebears you are dismissed."

Rames shook his head, "He is so young."

Atilus decided to Drop the other bomb, "He is also the recipient of the Bearilian Star, and speaks fluent Antillean"

Rames said, "Okay he is smart and brave, and was a Marine. Thank you Captain."

Atilus and the Colonel continued talking and planning.

On the resort planet Saratine, eight Senators were setting around a table on a private white sand beach.

The tallest of the eight looked around the table "What do we do now? Admiral Benedict is dead and Santanus and Brutus are in custody?"

The Senator to his right, a small Moonarian looked up. "The death of Admiral Benedict is tragic, but I am more concerned about Admiral Santanus he knows we are all involved if he talks we will not survive. What should be done about Admiral Brutus we all know he is weak."

The Senator, across the table from him, "Shook his head Santanus will not talk as for Brutus he was weak but also a fool he never knew anything he only did what he was told by the other two."

"They will send him to Dragon Breath Prison. There they will break him no matter how strong he is." A small Red Pandarian said. The small senator looked for support from some of the other senators.

Soon seven of the Senators were debating the merits of their own plans for settling the situation. After several minutes of debate, the Senator at the end of the table stood up his dark graying fur and one marred eye set him apart. When he stood up the others stopped talking.

"Senators, we have worked long and hard for this day, the Arcrilian are willing to back us. We need not worry about Brutus he can always be dealt with. It is Santanus, that we need freed or dead. I would prefer if he was alive. He is very useful, but if he cannot be rescued then he must die. The plan is simple we hire pirates to attack the prison transport and free him if they can't then they kill him" said Senator Iscarius. "You can decide among yourselves who has the best contacts." With that he left the gathering.

The others were left to decide how to carry out his plan.

Two days later the rest of the reinforcements appeared, the Tug Raging Wind Arrived with the Hanger Bay of the Green Dragon II Wing. Captain Northern and his four Squadron Commanders reported to Captain Atilus. Atilus sized up the Polarian Captain he saw the strength he was hoping for.

"Captain Northern and Gentlebears welcome to the Saber Claw." Atilus said.

Captain Northern looked at Atilus, "Please Captain Atilus I appreciate the niceties. However at this point I just want our assignments so my Squadron Commanders can notify their flight Commanders."

"Alright Captain, I need you to take over Combat Air patrol of the Drift, allowing the Marines to use their jump ships for other purposes. A blue dagger will still serve as a command and control asset. Your fighters' main responsibility is to interdict enemy fighters" Atilus reported.

"Bottom line Captain, what are we expecting?" Northern asked.

"You want the truth Captain?" Atilus asked.

"Yes." Northern responded.

"Okay, three Bearilian Fleet Admirals, and some Senators have conspired to throw out the Government and allow the Arcrilians to take over. An Arcrilian fleet is probably only days away. This Drift, your Fighters and my ship is all that stands in front of them. My ship was a speed bump with the Marines and your fighters we are now a small picket fence. Do you now understand Captain?" Atilus looked into his eyes.

"Alright Captain you are right, I understand we are in deep." responded Northern. "My flights will be on patrol in four cycles."

"Good Dusk 1 will be on station at that time. Have your fighters report to him." Atilus said.

With that the Captain saluted and the Officers of the Green Dragon II wing left.

Centaures walked in, "Well that was interesting. So what does my good Captain think of our chances now."

Atilus shook his head, "20% better but if they come in force we won't last. Oh we'll hurt them but not stop them."

Centaures and Atilus were working on trying to work on strategy. When, Beary knocked on the door. Atilus turned, "Come."

Beary, looked at his captain, "Sir, where did the needle fighters come from?"

Atilus looked at him, "I don't understand Ensign you know as well as everyone that the Needles are long range fighters."

"Yes Sir. But they can't loiter. In a jump ship you could send me out for a week or more. I could eat walk around and even sleep. You can't do that in a fighter. They were waiting for someone to wander into the mine field." Beary said.

Centaures looked at him, "Sir he is right but why not follow up the attack?"

Beary said, "It's simple Sir. They are coming but they have a hive mind. If they would have followed up the attack, we would know and at that time in that narrow space we could have stopped a fighter wing. Wherever they are they can only hit us if we are occupied to our front then they will hit us from that passage."

"Alright Ensign you have told me the problem what is the solution." Atilus said.

"Simple, Sir we find them and hit them first." Beary said.

"What would you need Ensign," Atilus asked?

"An insertion team, a sapper team, and the Crimson Blade with an extra gunner, I would like lieutenant 3rd Maritinus. Sergeant Blackpaw and Sergeant Nighthunter are both trained in HALO [High Altitude low opening] jumps. As am I. Artemus is a good pilot He can put the sapper team in. Lieutenant Bandar and his team from BA1 have volunteered. Ensign Vantanus volunteered to act as surgeon." Beary explained.

"What about the Fleet Master Chief?" Centaures asked.

"Sir, if I am wrong the Master Chief might be needed here. If I am right and we get in trouble we'll need the Master Chief here." Beary explained.

"Alright Ensign, I'll trust your gut, only because I have enough air units on hand. Gather your team good hunting." Atilus said. With that Beary left.

Centaures looked at him "Why!"

"Because he is right and a few years ago that would have been us." Atilus said.

Lieutenant Bandar was waiting with his team in the ready room along with Sergeant Blackpaw and Sergeant Nighthunter. Artemus, Caesar, and Ben were preparing the Crimson Blade. Grizlarge was also in the ready room.

When Beary walked in Grizlarge spoke to him, "I wish, I was going too Cub. But as you said I am needed here right now. Stay safe." Grizlarge saw Pompey in the door. "You better say something to her Cub." With that Grizlarge moved over to talk to his two NCOs.

Pompey looked at him, "Why? They could send someone else."

Beary took her around the corner. "Priscilla this is who I am, and what I do. Only four members of this crew are trained in HALO jumps. The Chief is needed here and he is getting too old for the ride. I have done this before." With that he kissed her, "I'll, be back do not worry." with that he headed back through the ready room.

"Lieutenant if you please let's go." Beary said as he ran for the Crimson Blade followed by the team.

"Blue Dragon Control, Spirit 6 ready to launch."

"Good Hunting Spirit 6, you are clear radio silence is ordered, Blue Dragon out."

Beary lifted off and shot out of the hanger bay and headed for sector two. "Shield and cloak are operating. She, is all yours Artemus"

Artemus moved over, "I have control Lieutenant 3rd Maritinus you are now the gunner." with that Ben moved over and took his position.

Beary explained the plan it was simple; find the Base, HALO in deactivate outer defenses, and shields. Then land the sappers and then shoot anything that tries to fly out. He and Sergeant Blackpaw and Nighthunter would do the Halo Drop. Artemus would land the sappers and take off. Lieutenant Bandar and his Marines would blow up everything in sight.

The plan was simple they only hoped it would work.

Chapter 18

First strike

The Crimson Blade cleared the edge of the Carnise Drift and started quietly looking for the Arcrilian base. They passed down the edge of the Drift, and headed on a course of 035, mark 10.

Artemus looked back at Beary. "Boss just what are we looking for?"

Beary came forward, "We're looking for signs of Arcrilian activities, anything that will give us an idea of where they might be."

Artemus shrugged. "Not much help Boss. Could we launch a probe or two, I loaded 3 orbital probes."

Beary thought, "Okay, but let's think about how we want to do this."

Bandar walked up. "Ensign I have an Idea, if you don't mind."

Beary looked at him. "No Sir, I'd love an Idea."

Bandar smiled, "What if we launch one along the axis of the Drift a second on a 30 degree axis away from the Drift the third at 60 degree angle from the Drift."

Beary nodded, "Artemus you heard the Lieutenant make it so."

Artemus grinned, "Probes away, Boss. Thanks Lieutenant."

Bandar smiled, *the young ensign didn't feel threatened by his suggestion. That was good.*

Tiberius was following the prison transport carrying Santanus. Unknown to anyone Tiberius had planted three trackers on Santanus. He knew the Senators would either have Santanus killed or they would help him escape. He had warned the prison transport of his fears but the Captain brushed him off.

The Darius Pride had been a front line cruiser 100 years earlier and was still heavily armed, but it didn't have the fire power of a newer destroyer. It also relied more on armor plating than it did on plasma shields.

Tiberius on the other hand was in an ultra-top secret one Bear transport that was very heavily armed. He had two rail guns, three Gatling phasers, and 64 short range missiles and a cloaking system. His orders were clear he was only to follow and observe nothing else.

Tiberius picked them up at the same time the Darius pride did. Three blood clan Pirate ships and 50 fighters.

The Captain of the Darius Pride increased speed and turned away from the attacking ships. As he turned he launched his entire load of missiles. 78 missiles streamed toward the attackers, but instead of focusing on one target they had tried to hit everything.

Twenty of the fighters died. The three larger Pirate ships easily absorbed the few missile hits they received. Then it was their turn. The fighters each launched 2 missiles each and the three ships twelve each. 96 missiles streaked at Darius Pride. Its automatic defense system destroyed 30 of the incoming missiles others were absorbed by her shields and armor but 10 damaged her right warp nacelle.

The Pirate fighters swung straight into Tiberius path he launched 2 missiles at each fighter. He was so close when the fighters started exploding that he had to turn sharply away or be damaged by their explosions.

The main Pirate ships either didn't notice or didn't care that their fighters were no more. The three main pirate ships got in close and started trading blows with the Darius pride. One of the pirate ships lost a warp nacelle from three well placed rail gun shots, but the shields on the Darius Pride had failed. Pirate boarding parties went aboard. The fighting on the prison deck was fearsome. When it was over 30 Pirates were dead as were twenty of the Darius prides Security detail. Santanus was beamed aboard the lead pirate ship and it warped out of the area. The other two started circling their wounded prey.

Tiberius focused on the damaged Pirate ship and roared in.

He fired his four remaining missiles at the weakened shield near the damaged warp nacelle. They finished tearing it loose he then fired his rail guns and Gatling phasers at point blank range.

The Gatling phasers sliced open the area around the bridge while the rail guns punched through the engineering section. The Pirate ship started drifting then exploded. The other pirate ship turned and ran.

Tiberius called the Captain of the Darius Pride and offered assistance but the captain declined. Without another word Tiberius sent his report of the incident and started following the remaining pirates.

The Pirate Chieftain of the Blood Clan was angry. "Your freedom cost me 50 fighters and a ship not to mention 250 of my clansmen. Your friends will have to give me more in the way of compensation."

Santanus smiled. "Just name your price. They will pay it they, have no choice, for now except this as payment." He took off his prison jump suit and threw it at the chieftain. When he caught it he almost dropped it. Sewn into the lining were about a hundred small bars of gold and pressed platinum worth about 2 million credits. Santanus smiled "That should prove I am operating in good faith"

The Chieftain smiled. "It is a generous start at least." he figured he would hit the Senators up for eight million credits more. Yet Santanus had acted in good faith so he would be freed now instead of later.

After being clothed and fed Santanus was given a long range shuttle that had been relieved from a transport they had raided.

Tiberius noted the location of the Pirate base and sent the information to Bearilian Security Forces. He was sure that the Pirates would receive a visit and soon. He also picked up the signal he had been following and saw the shuttle head out into space.

After a few moments he started following the Shuttle to its next destination.

After 6 cycles the probe that was launched at a 60 degree angle started picking up Arcrilian fighters and traffic they appeared to be heading on a course of 5 degrees from the probes' location not toward the Drift but toward a small group of asteroids that circled the Tarsus Sun.

Beary pointed out the group of asteroids to Artemus then went back and called up a map of that area of Tarsus space. "This is where they are likely heading but I'd like to be sure. We should get some triangulation from the second prob. But if I was a betting Bear I would say that is their destination."

The Lieutenant looked at the map, "If it was me I would put the main base on the largest asteroid and one or two Squadrons for defense on these two. That could complicate things."

Beary thought, "I didn't want to use them but the Commander gave us two Asteroid busters that we can plant on the largest and split it in half. If their main base is there they will have tunneled into the Asteroid two of these will spit it wide open.

Of course we will want to be as far away as practical when they go off."

Artemus called back, "We have telemetry on the inbound fighters from the second probe and in and outbound communications. It is definitely coming from the target asteroids."

Beary looked at Lieutenant Bandar, "Artemus take us within sensor range let's try and see what we are up against."

Tiberius had his ship on auto pilot while he took nourishment. It was clear the shuttle was heading for the resort planet Saratine. He checked his computer. Senator Iscarius had a large estate on the planet and was hosting according to his sources seven other Senators at his estate. Iscarius' son had failed to receive the contract for the new warp drive engines when the Vallen/Maxumus engine outperformed the Iscarius/Bradius engine. Tiberius understood that the loss of the contract almost bankrupted his son's company but was that reason to commit treason? Of course the lust for power was always a prime reason for treachery. He decided it was time to play his hunch.

The Staff Sergeant knocked on General Zantoran's door. "General you have a call it is someone called The Scarecrow."

General Zantoran picked up his com unit. "This is General Zantoran please identify yourself."

"General my call sign is Scarecrow. Don't bother trying to look it up not even your clearance is high enough to find out who I am. I am tracking Admiral Santanus he is on his way to Saratine. Senator Iscarius and seven others are also there at Iscarius' private compound. Would you please inform Admiral Starpaw, and Senator Maxumus?" Tiberius said.

General Zantoran looked at his com device. "Where will you be, when we arrive?"

"Don't worry General I will be there and will give you all the intelligence that I can gather, Scarecrow out." Tiberius cut his transmission.

Zantoran picked up his secure line and made the conference call. Within 2 Cycles He, Starpaw and Senator Maxumus along with a strike team were on a transport heading for Saratine.

The Sensors showed that the Arcrilians had moved two wings of fighters to this asteroid group. Over 128 fighters were now prepositioned at this forward base.

Artemus checked the sensor readout again "That is a lot of fighters and at least half are bombers."

Beary nodded "They plan to attack through the small gaps and attack the marine positions. If we can stop this group we might slow the coming attacks."

They soon discovered that the main asteroid had a very powerful sensor array. It was also the main base for the fighters.

It was decided that the Crimson blade would come in at o degrees to the sensory platform.

Beary, Sergeant Blackpaw, and Nighthunter dived out of the Crimson Blade. They aimed for the top platform of the sensor. Beary flared first followed by Sergeant Blackpaw and Sergeant Nighthunter they quietly landed on top of the platform next to the sensor array. They put on their night vision visors and scanned the area. Off to their left was a guard post with two troopers inside. To the right of the path was another guard post with three troopers.

Beary looked at Sergeant Blackpaw and signaled for him to take the left guard post. He then signaled Sergeant Nighthunter to take the right guard post. He indicated he would take out the Sensor Command post.

Sergeant Blackpaw and Sergeant Nighthunter slipped quietly into the night. Beary lowered himself stealthily to the ground next to the door.

Beary slipped through the outer door and allowed his eyes to adjust. There were twelve Arcrilians around the room. Ten were at counsels. Two were standing just inside the door acting as guards. He pulled out his two hammers and prepared to attack. He pinned the two guards to the wall with the blades of the hammers. Beary then flew into the fast knife technique in a little less than 15 SUBTU all the Arcrilians were dead.

Blackpaw and Nighthunter moved into the building they slowly checked the dead Arcrilians.

Blackpaw was the first to speak up "What now Sir?"

Beary smiled, "We set it up so the bears down the line think everything is still up and working. Then we turn things off including the shield generators." as he pointed to a control panel

Aboard the Crimson Blade Artemus noted the shield Drop he moved the Crimson Blade into a landing position near the Sensor array. The Marines and Lieutenant Bandar quickly exited and spread out. Beary and the two NCOs met up with them.

Beary looked at the Lieutenant, "Lieutenant you and your Marines can plant the asteroid busters. We didn't destroy the shield generators we just turned them off. I have an Idea I want to try just as we leave. I set it up so that it shows their command post that everything is up and running. We are going to try and infiltrate the Arcrilian launch bay and see what intelligence we can gather."

With that Beary and his two NCOs took off toward an entrance that was shown on a map in the sensor post, while Lieutenant Bandar and his Marines looked for the optimal place to place their bombs.

Lieutenant Bandar noticed an exhaust port leading from the center of the asteroid he lowered one of the bombs down into the port till it was just above the bottom of the tube. They then found a fissure that ran the width of the asteroid and burrowed the second bomb into the center of the fissure. He then took his men back to the scanner station and started down loading its computer.

Beary and Sergeant Nighthunter slipped past the guards, while Sergeant Blackpaw stood over watch ready to kill the guards if they had started to raise an alarm.

Beary and Sergeant Nighthunter managed to slip into the hanger bay. They planted explosives among some of the ordinance that were on a cart near one of the fighters. Then they, moved towards a tunnel that looked like it lead to the command post. As they neared the hatch of the command post they heard movement in front of them so they ducked into another hatch surprising an Arcrilian trooper manning the communications station. Sergeant Nighthunter quickly and quietly killed him before the trooper could raise the alarm.

Beary found a computer terminal that gave him access to the Arcrilian's communications log and main computer. He started an immediate down load of the Arcrilian's central core computer while Nighthunter guarded the door.

Beary turned to Nighthunter, "It's time to go."

The Sergeant looked up and down the tunnel and lead out. Beary followed close behind. When they reach the hanger bay they worked their way to the exit as they turned up the tunnel they remotely set off the explosives they had planted on the ordinance cart.

When the explosives went off they set off the ordinance on the cart which started flying all over the hanger bay several fighters exploded and fires started everywhere. The Arcrilian troopers who had been in a sleep cycle started moving trying to contain the destruction.

Blackpaw killed the two guards at the end of the entrance.

Beary and Nighthunter came running out at full speed. Blackpaw threw a satchel charge into the entrance and followed the other two. The Charge went off closing the exit tunnel.

Beary called for Artemus who landed the Crimson Blade near the scanner and sensor arrays. Beary ran in and adjusted the shield generator controls so that they put a reverse shield around the asteroid. Once every one was loaded he set a timer and ran to the Crimson Blade.

Once he cleared the hatch, Artemus shot away from the asteroid. In a matter of moments the reverse Shield formed to prevent the explosion from escaping the initial blast.

Beary resumed command and Artemus the gunner's position. Ben moved over and manned the communications system.

The first Asteroid Buster went off inside the exhaust port sending shock waves and flame into the hanger bay. The concussion of the blast was reflected back against the surface of the asteroid which crumbled. The second bomb split the fissure in the rock of the asteroid carving it in half. Again all the force of the explosion was turned inward by the shields pulverizing the asteroid more. Then it happened the shields came apart and so did the asteroid. Several large pieces slammed into the other asteroids causing them to split or be crushed.

Artemus scanned for any surviving Arcrilian fighters. He found none. He planted a buoy inside the debris field nodded to Beary.

"Okay let's head home Team." Beary smiled.

Meanwhile the Marines of the 308th were planting mined fields among the various narrow entry points. It was a simple plan block as much of the Drift as possible and send the Arcrilians into specific kill zones. Hopefully a few Arcrilians will try and penetrate these narrow passages and die.

The Crimson blade turned for the main opening of the Drift.

On Saratine Tiberius found a place where he could set up a sniper position. He spotted the long range shuttle the Pirates had given Santanus. He watched as Santanus walked up and hugged Senator Iscarius. The other seven Senators also greeted him. At least 4 of the Senators were from outlying Districts. The Moonarian was Senator Black Moon from Tarsus 3. It made sense that he was involved. A tall Ursus Arctos with a badly scared face, it had to be Senator Scarden from Darius 4, walked toward the table on the beach. A Melursus Ursinus was setting at the table. Tiberius was sure it was Senator Lanki from Bandarius 7. Senator Helarctos a Sunnarian from Solaris 3 was also by the table. The other three were hard to make out.

Senator Iscarius waved over all the Senators to the table.

They took their seats. Soon they were eating and drinking.

Tiberius watched as they toasted each other. He slowly unsheathed his sniper rifle it was a beautiful weapon a small caliber rail gun. He then hit his com.

Admiral Starpaw answered his com unit, "Admiral Starpaw here."

Tiberius spoke quietly. "This is Scarecrow all targets are in place. Be advised there is armed beach security. They are not; I repeat not part of the Senatorial protection unit."

"Understood Scarecrow hostile targets on beach, all targets near beach," Starpaw out.

"Zanny who is this Scarecrow" Starpaw asked?

"I don't know my sources couldn't find out." Zantoran said.

Admiral Starpaw looked at his friend. "Send in, MSU14 tell them there are armed hostiles on the beach. We'll come in from the West side."

Zantoran signaled his marines and notified MSU 14. The Water Dragons of MSU 14 came out of the surf 3 of the 10 guards were dead before anyone knew what was happening. The other guards tried to return fire but were killed in short order. One Member of MSU 14 was down with a wound to his leg.

Santanus ran for his shuttle expecting to escape to Arcrilian space as he reached the door of his shuttle He pitched sideways into the sand. Near his right ear was a tiny hole that grew larger as it passed through his brain and out the other side.

Tiberius readjusted his aim but the main fighting on the beach was over. Two of the seven Senators were dead including Senator Scarden.

Tiberius watched as Senator Iscarius reached his villa. Marines were advancing, but all at once were pinned down by weapons fire from the villa. He made the call, "This is Scarecrow to all Marine units fall back now."

The Marines fell back as ordered. Once they, were back a safe distance Tiberius called out over the com unit, "Fire in the Hole."

Tiberius hit a remote control devise and the explosives he had set around the villa went off. As the flames leaped higher Senator Iscarius came out his clothing and fur on fire. Tiberius picked up his rail gun and aimed. The well placed shot through the Senator's heart stopped him in his tracks. Then he packed up and was gone.

General Zantoran was the first to find Santanus's dead body. He wondered where the sniper had been. It was a perfect shot. He also wondered about Senator Iscarius. Someone had set explosives around the villa which suppressed the fire his Marines had been receiving. Then Iscarius came out of the building on fire. He almost wished the sniper; this Scarecrow had not taken the shot.

Starpaw came over. General Zantoran turned toward him. "Whoever our friend is he is a good shot. He dropped Santanus as he was trying to board this shuttle."

"He also set explosives to take out shooters but despite a little fire that was put out by internal fire suppression systems, it did very little damage to the structure." Starpaw said.

Senator Maxumus walked over and smiled, "Four traitors are dead the others are talking, blaming each other. They are all hoping to make a deal. We of coarse will listen and promise nothing but a rope or Dragon Breath Prison. In the end they will all talk."

Zantoran looked at the Senator, "Senator Maxumus do you know who the Scarecrow is?"

Octavious thought for a moment his face got very serious,

"Yes. But if I told you I'd have to kill you." Then he smiled and laughed. "Come Gentlebears we have work to do." The Senator walked off toward the villa.

Zantoran looked at Starpaw, "He was kidding wasn't he?"

Starpaw shrugged, "I don't think I want to find out."

With that the two high ranking officers took off after the Senator.

The Crimson Blade landed on board the Saber Claw. Lieutenant Bandar, his troops, and Sergeant Nighthunter and Blackpaw disembarked. Centaures was waiting, "Well, how did it go?"

Bandar saluted, "We destroyed approximately two full Wings and all three asteroids. Ensign Maxumus asked me to give you the data we retrieved from the Arcrilian base and their Communication logs. Sir I never want to make him mad or be on the opposite side he is smart and totally ruthless. I would follow him anywhere and I am senior to him in rank and age. I do have a personal connection. I was one of the Marines he pulled off of Pratis V. Of course he pulled me off of Dryden also. So you can see I owe him."

Centaures smiled, "Our young Ensign does grow on you."

Bandar looked at the Commander, "Sir he may be an Ensign to you, but to me and my Marines he will always be a Marine. Sir I need to see to my Marines, with your permission."

Centaures smiled, "Get some food and rest for your bears and thank them for me."

Beary, Ben, and Artemus finished shutting down the Crimson Blade and stepped out. Artemus went to talk to the Crew Chief. Ben went to find the Master Chief and Beary walked over to Centaures.

Beary saluted, "Sir you might want to have the Communication logs checked first."

"I'll have the intelligence section start working on all of it immediately." He motioned an Intelligence NCO over and handed the data storage devises over. "Have these checked now. Ensign Maxumus you did a great job according to Lieutenant Bandar."

"Sir, most of the credit needs to go to Sergeant Nighthunter and Sergeant Blackpaw and Lieutenant Bandar and his Marines." Beary said.

Centaures smiled, "Ensign your modesty will serve you well, but the truth is you have performed your duties above the Captains and my expectations. Go see that Lady of yours. Have your crew take some down time. A storm is coming and we might not survive. By the way do you know the history of the ring you gave Pompey?"

Beary's expression changed slightly. "Sir, the ring and its secrets and history belong to my family. But yes I now all of its history. If you do Sir, I respectfully ask you to keep it to yourself."

Centaures looked at his eyes. "Ensign I will speak of it to no one other than the Captain. He will say nothing either I promise."

Beary nodded, "Sir it is a personal thing, but it is just a thing. The significance of the ring died years ago. Now it is just a family heirloom." with that Beary saluted and left.

Centaures shook his head. *The Maxumus Clan could hold power over the other clans of their race and others just by controlling the ring, but they never tried.*

Back on Saratine the surviving traitors were being questioned. Senator Maxumus watched as Captain Aurelius questioned Senator Black moon.

Aurelius looked at the Moonarian, "Now Senator you will tell me what I want to know. When is the attack to take place and where will it come from?"

Black Moon opened his mouth, "I will not answer your questions you have no right to question me?"

Aurelius shook his head. "You do not understand you are a traitor the proof is irrefutable. You can answer my questions or you can leave. Of course you will be shot trying to escape and join the other three dead Senators and the traitor Santanus who is still rotting on the sand."

Black Moon looked around the room. "Don't you see we cannot defeat the Arcrilian the only way we can survive is to make a deal? We would have given them territory in exchange for peace."

Aurelius shook his head. "What would this peace give you Senator?"

Black Moon shrank, "I would have been given a position of elevated importance in the government. Iscarius would have been the head of the new government. We were only doing what needed to be done. Don't you see the Arcrilians, are coming in force, they have a Base on Dryden. What are we going to fight them with a nonexistent fleet?"

Aurelius smiled, "The Hive ship Styx Reaper is no more, and Dryden is secure. The Carnise Drift is rearmed. We will stop the Arcrilian Fleet."

Black Moon screamed, "You have only delayed the attack they will be coming any day now; with Battle Cruisers, heavy Cruisers, Fighter Carriers, and Destroyers. What do we have to stop them a few Marines and a single Destroyer? It is you who are the fool not I."

Aurelius leaned in and spoke quietly. "If they come you will die. I promise you, your traitorous actions will not be left unpunished."

In different rooms the surviving senators were being asked the same questions. The answers were all the same.

Starpaw sighed, "Inform all new fleet ships to head to point Alpha. Inform the Saber Claw to go to Red 4 alert."

Atilus looked at the message, "To all crew members we are going to Red 4 Alert. All flight crews stand down for rest. The Crew of the Crimson blade is on twenty four cycle mandatory down time. All weapon systems are to be serviced and prepared for Battle. Medical, transfer all casualties to the medical shuttle Mercy immediately."

Pompey came in to operate her com position. Atilus looked at her. "Ensign Pompey I want you to take a twenty four hour rest cycle starting now. Ensign Torres will take your shift." Atilus walked over to her. "Pompey, go find your young Boar and spend time with him. It is going to get bad."

Pompey nodded and headed for her cabin.

Chapter 19

A Moment of Peace

Captain Atilus call in Commander Centaures to the wardroom. "They captured or killed the Council of Eight. Senator Iscarius and Admiral Santanus along with two others were killed.

We can expect a major attack on the Drift in 2 to 3 days at max a week."

Centaures nodded, "The Drifts defenses are up, and running the 284th also put out a string of sensor buoys between the Drift and Tarsus 11's orbit. They are scheduled to leave in 5 Cycles.

2 Platoons of the 266th Blood Knife Division is due in 3 Cycles. They are bringing 3 new plasma cannons and two new, 386 Rail Gatling guns. They can fire 50 rounds per STU. It will help."

Atilus shook his head, "It helps, but we may be facing twelve Destroyers, 6 Heavy Cruisers and a battle Cruiser with fighters. Even with the help we have we're nothing but a small speed bump. At least each of the Drifts gun emplacements and Command posts has improved shield generators."

Centaures looked at his friend, "What do you want to do?"

Atilus shrugged, "We aren't a gun emplacement we're a fast attack destroyer. I plan to put us in front of the Drift and attack the enemy until we destroy them or more likely they destroy us."

Centaures smiled, "Works for me."

Atilus smiled. "Notify the crew, that everyone gets to call home when off duty. Open up more stations if necessary. Also evacuate the Cadets."

Centaures looked at him, "Does that include Vantanus, Maxumus, and Maritinus."

Atilus shook his head, "Maxumus and Vantanus no. They wouldn't go anyway without being stunned besides there fleet ranks are permanent. Give Maritinus the option. Lord knows he has done more than his share."

Centaures nodded, "He won't go. Even if I told him he had no hope of survival. He would see leaving as an act of a coward."

Beary arrived back at his berth. Ben looked up and smiled. "Ensign Pompey has called looking for you many times."

Beary smiled, "Ben would you call her and tell her I need to clean up and I will be by soon."

Ben smiled, "It will be my honor."

While Ben was calling Pompey, Caesar came in and plopped down.

"Ensign Darius was med-evacuated on the last trip. I called Artemus. They said their goodbyes. The other cadets are being evacuated in 30 STU." Caesar reported.

Ben looked at him in shock. "What of us?"

"Ensign Maxumus and I are no longer Cadets. We have permanent ranks so we're staying. I wouldn't have left anyway. I doubt Beary would leave." Caesar continued.

There was a knock on the door as Beary excited the bathroom. Ben answered it. "Sir, will you please come in." Beary and Caesar came to attention.

Centaures said, "At ease, I need to talk to you. Ensign Maxumus and Vantanus we will be facing extreme odds soon.

Our likely hood of survival is slim. But you are deemed too valuable to this ship to evacuate. Lieutenant 3rd Maritinus you have performed above and beyond the call of duty as a cadet. You have already been put in harm's way more than ever anticipated. It is your chose to stay or evacuate."

Ben lowered his head, "If I am to die Sir. It is preferable to me to die with my friends."

Centaures smiled, "Thank you Lieutenant." With that he left.

Beary looked at his friends, "Well I have a lady waiting." He waved and left the room.

Caesar was tired, "Ben you could have gone home with honor. No one would have questioned it."

Ben looked at Caesar as he laid down, "I would have Caesar. Rest well no one will disturb you."

Caesar fell asleep with those words in his ear.

Beary arrived at Pompey's berth and knocked. When she opened the door she was wearing a beautiful flowered sun dress. She smiled, "We're eating in tonight. I made lamb thorn apple with greens. I hope you will like it."

Beary kissed her gently on the forehead, "Sounds great. Priscilla what if I could get you, evacuated off the Saber Claw would you go and stay with my parents?"

Pompey's eyes flashed, "You are the second person who has asked me that! I will tell you the same thing I told him. NO!!!

I know the odds it's the same odds we always face. Would you Beary Maxumus turn tail and run if I asked you to? No, I didn't think so. The Females of are race are warriors also. Do not forget 6 Valkyries died with the Red Axe Knights. Three fell defending your grandfathers back at the end."

Beary did the only thing he could he took her in his arms and kissed her. Her anger was spent and replaced by something else as she returned his kiss.

She pulled away from him, "That wasn't fair. Nice but not fair."

Beary put his arms around her, "I love you Priscilla that is all I was trying to say. I know you are needed here just as I am. But I . . . ."

She placed her paw on his mouth. "It has been decided. Not you, Captain Atilus or your father will change my mind. If we are to die in this battle then we will die. It is in the Creators hands not ours. Now let us eat so you can decide if my cooking meets with my Sires approval."

Beary bit into the lamb in thorn apple sauce it was sweet and tangy. The lamb was so tender it almost melted in his mouth.

The fresh greens were served with apple vinegar dressing. The flavors exploded in his mouth.

Pompey poured him a glass of cherry apple nectar and smiled. She delicately ate her portion as she watched as Beary savored every bite. As he started to finish she brought out a tart with a dark berry center. She sat it down and lit the center which caramelized then she cut it in half and gave him part of it.

Beary again savored the rich flavor of the dark berries when he had finished eating he smiled. "My lady that was the best meal I have eaten in years."

Pompey blushed, "Sire, do not tease me."

Beary walked over and looked her in the eyes. "You will make a fine wife. But I will have to work out more or become fat and lazy."

"Now that we have dinned, what do you wish to do?" Beary asked.

The Legend Begins

Pompey said in a quiet voice. "I wish to call our parents together, if you don't mind."

Beary and Pompey put through the call to Beary's home; when the image materialized it was Alexa Maxumus who appeared. "Little Brother, how are you and is that ravishing young lady, our dear Lady Pompey?"

Beary smiled at his oldest sister, "Alexa this is Priscilla my betrothed. Priscilla this is my oldest Sister Dr. Alexa Maxumus a Cub doctor. What are you doing at the house?"

Alexa smiled "Beany is in labor. I am here to deliver the Cub. Mom is up stairs now I'll call her. Hopefully I can do the same for you Priscilla." Her face faded.

Pompey looked at Beary, "Beany?"

Beary smiled "My sister Beatrice she is older than me by 4 years. I had trouble saying Beatrice, so I called her Beany, it stuck. She is married to Caesar's brother."

Angelina appeared, "Hello my loves. How are you?"

"Lady Maxumus, thank you for allowing Beary to give me this beautiful ring."

Angelina smiled, "It is Angelina dear. Also it was Beary's to give he is the youngest of our children and it will pass to your youngest at the proper time. Now tell me how you are. Octavious will want to know when he gets home."

Beary thought, "I am stuffed and ready for market. Not only is Pompey beautiful she is a great cook."

Pompey broke in, "He is much to kind Lady, Angelina I am sure you are better."

Beary and his mother laughed, "Dear," Angelina said, "I am arguably the best Nero surgeon in the galaxy but I can't boil water and get it right. Despite that Octavious loves me as my son loves you. Oh I just heard a cry! Stand by." In a moment Angelina returned holding a small cub in a blue blanket, "Beary and Lady Pompey met the newest member of or clan Caesar Beary Vantorious."

Beary smiled, "I will inform Caesar, tell Beany I am honored and that I love her. Caesar Beary Vantorious may the Creator of the Universe bless you and your family."

Pompey said, "Praise to the Creator of all. Lady Angelina I must call my parents. Thank you. "

"Nonsense my dear you are always in our hearts. We love both of you, may the Creator, keep you safe in his hand." With that Angelina severed the com link.

Pompey smiled, "While I make the call to my parents you better tell Caesar."

"This is Lieutenant 3rd Maritinus Ensign Vantanus is asleep." Ben answered the com.

Beary smiled, "Ben, it's Beary, wake up Caesar I have news from home."

"As you wish" Ben said.

A sleepy voice came on the com. "You had better be bleeding or dying Beary or you will be."

Beary smiled, "Uncle you better set down Beany had a cub."

Caesar woke up, "What did you say?"

Beary explained, "Caesar Beary Vantorious was born STU's ago. According to both Dr. Maxumus Cub and mother are well."

Caesar looked into the com unit, "Beary I hope you don't . . . ."

Beary laughed, "Caesar you know better than that. In my drawer is 70 credits take Ben to the ready room find Artemus and have a toast to our new Nephew. I will be toasting with my lady."

Caesar smiled "I'll add 70 of my own and do it right."

Caesar grabbed the 140 credits and headed for the ready room he called Artemus to join them. "Come on Ben tonight we Celebrate the birth of a new cub."

Beary turned to Pompey as the connection was being established. He handed her a glass of nectar, "To Caesar Beary Vantorious." They both drank the glass and broke them against the wall. A small robot came out and cleaned up the broken glasses.

Soon Pompey's Mom appeared. Beary spoke first. "Greetings Lady Sirena Pompey, I am, Ensign Dr. Beary Augustus Maxumus, the betrothed of your daughter, the Lady Pompey. It is my pleasure to meet you over the com link."

"By what right do you have of calling my daughter your betrothed? By what symbol have you given?" Sirena Pompey demanded.

Pompey broke in. "By giving his love and by this ring." She held the ring up to the view screen. The Blue Diamond caught fire and the red star stones glowed."

Sirena Pompey almost fainted. She called her husband. He stopped when he saw the ring.

Sire Pompey asked, "Where did you get that?"

Beary broke in, "It was mine to give. It belonged to my Great grandmother and then belonged to me. Do you have any questions." it wasn't a question but a warning.

Sire Pompey looked at the young Maxmimus and shivered. "You are the Young Ensign Dr. Beary Maxumus?"

"I am, Sire Pompey. I look forward to our face to face meeting. Your daughter is an excellent cook, very brave and beautiful. I love her very much." Beary said He could tell he didn't like his future father in law. He hoped that would change. Sirena Pompey seamed Okay.

"Pompey, are you happy and well." Her mother asked

Pompey answered, "Happier than I ever have been mother."

Sirena Pompey, looked at Beary, he was young strong and brave. "Beary, by Octavious and Angelina, please accept my daughters Paw in yours." Beary took Priscilla's Paw, "As

Sirena of the House of Pompey as is my right according to our Bedouin Customs I give my daughter to you. I look forward to our meeting may the Creator increase your flock and give you many Boar Cubs."

Beary blushed, "I accept your daughters paw, Sirena Pompey. I will keep her warm and safe with my life."

"Goodbye my daughter." Sirena Pompey hung up the Com.

Pompey nuzzled into Beary, "According to our customs I am now yours."

Beary looked at, her, "Not yet." He opened a come link

A Bear appeared. "Samuel, may the Creator bless you."

Samuel looked in the com link, he was an old Maxmimus, no one knew how old. "What can these old bones do for the Great Bear?"

Beary smiled. "Can you sell me 250 of your best Hazel Ewes, and five Rams?

Samuel beamed, "For you anything. Where do you want them delivered?"

Beary said, "To Sirena Pompey, as a gift for the paw of her daughter. The gift is to her alone."

Samuel raised one eyebrow. "I understand. The gift will cost you two hundred thousand credits it would be more but the discount is my gift to you."

Beary smiled hit a few buttons, "The credits are in your account."

Samuel verified the transaction. "May the Creator's blessing, be with you and your lady, great one."

"And with you my old friend." with that Beary hung up.

Pompey looked at him in disbelief. "Beary that was too much!"

Beary smiled, "Why?"

"I am not worth two hundred thousand credits." Pompey said.

Beary smiled "Your right. The regular cost is four hundred thousand credits. Two hundred thousand was a gift."

Pompey had tears running down her cheeks. "What will your Parents say or think all that money?"

Beary laughed, "Pompey I make 2.5 Million credits a year on proceeds from my patents. I am a Boar of means without my family's money."

"Why would you love a sheepherder's daughter?" She said with tears in her eyes.

Beary cupped her face and kissed her. "Because, I see so much more, your Mother needs to show that she was not taken by a name. Besides is it not part of your custom for me to pay a brides price?"

Pompey looked at him. "I hope it is not a fool's price."

Beary smiled, "I think it was a bargain."

Back on Bearilia Prime Pompey's father was furious, "You didn't even ask for a price for our daughter's paw we will be a laughing stock. My business associates will laugh at me."

Sirena Pompey stood up, "By our custom it was my right.

I saw how you looked at the ring so did the young Maxumus."

"It was the Star of Vandar the Imperial ring! Do you know the advantage that will give us?" Sire Pompey said.

"No. if you try to play it that way the young Maxumus will have you disgraced. I saw his eyes and heard his tone." Sirena Pompey warned.

Two days later an old Maxmimus arrived at their village with a young boy and 250 ewes and five rams. He saw a young lad. "Cub, come here."

The young Bear approached. "Yes Sire,"

"I am Samuel. I look for the home of Sirena Pompey." Samuel stated.

"I will show you, ancient one, to her home." The young Cub said with respect.

As they approached, the Pompey house, Sirena Pompey came out with her husband.

Samuel bowed, "I am Samuel. These ewes and rams are a gift to Sirena Pompey, from the Great Bear, Beary Maxumus, and great grandson of my liege Augustus Maxumus."

Sirena Pompey bowed. "Ancient one, this must be a mistake. You mean they are for Sire Pompey."

Samuel spoke in a large voice. "Sirena Pompey these, Hazel Ewes and Rams, are a gift for you, as matriarch of the House of Pompey and to no other. This Cub is in service to me. He will serve you for a few weeks, until one of your own shall become their Shepherd. His name is Issac you will treat him well." Samuel looked at Sire Pompey with ageless penetrating eyes.

Pompey's father shrank before his eyes. Sirena Pompey said, "He will be treated as a guest in our home. I swear it before our village."

Samuel raised his hand. "Peace, be with you and may the Creator increase your flock Sirena Pompey."

Without another word Samuel turned and headed out of the village. The boy Issac bowed, "Sirena Pompey where may I take your flock."

Sirena Pompey motioned to a cub. "Take him to the south pasture please. You will become responsible for this flock."

"It will be my honor Sirena." the male cub said.

Two days earlier back in Pompey's berth, Pompey smiled. But she was troubled. "Beary will you tell me why my father and mother reacted the way they did when they saw my ring."

Beary thought shrugged, "They must have recognized it. It is the Star of Vandar."

Pompey looked at it and shivered. She took off the ring and handed it to Beary, "I cannot take this," She cried "it is the Imperial ring. I am still yours. You have paid the bride's price, even if I am but your consort."

Beary smiled, and put it back on her paw. "You are never to remove it again till you give it to our youngest son or daughter."

"You don't understand my father . . . ." Pompey began.

Beary stopped her, "Your father will not be a problem. You are to be my wife do you understand."

She fell into his arm crying. "It will be as you wish my liege. I hope I prove worthy of you."

Beary lifted her face. "No my love, I hope, I prove worthy of you."

They talked for a few cycles. Pompey looked at the time. "You have only eight hours before you return to duty. You need sleep you can stay here my love." Pompey said.

Beary kissed her. "I cannot, if I do, we will regret it. You know that."

Pompey kissed him even harder. "I belong to you and you may claim what you own."

Beary smiled, "As long as you wear my ring, no one owns you my lady, not even me."

She kissed him again. This time even more passionately. "Then sleep well my love and dream of what is yours."

Beary left and went back to his berth. Caesar was waiting with two glasses of nectar. "Beary here is a toast to our nephew."

Beary drank the glass as did Caesar then they broke the glasses.

Ben rose up, "I did not know you could celebrate but it was a good celebration. I thank you now goodnight."

Beary and Caesar talked quietly for an hour and drifted off.

Pompey was curled up in the dark in a chair of Captain Atilus's room. He walked in and turned on the light. He saw she had been crying.

"Pompey what is wrong?" Atilus asked

"My mother gave me to Beary. He ordered 250 Hazel Sheep and five Rams. It cost him two hundred thousand credits. He didn't even blink. He said he makes 2.5 Million credits a year just in royalties for patents." Pompey said.

"So your mother approves and asked a high price. That is good." Atilus said.

"She didn't ask any price. My father saw the ring she did also. Beary stopped my father from asking questions. So I asked. I tried to give it back. He wouldn't let me. It is The Star of Vandar. I told him I belonged to him. I tried to get him to stay with me." Pompey said.

Atilus said, "And did he?"

Pompey looked at him, "No, I am still untouched. But we are going into battle what if . . . ."

Atilus looked at her. "Then you go to his family you give them the ring back. Then it is up to you return to your father or stay with the Maxumus clan."

"I would rather die than live without him. Why did he not . . . ."

Again Atilus stopped her. "Beary loves you he wants it to be right, for you to be joined in front of his and your family at his family's chapel in front of the Creator. To him it is important for you to be honored. Then he will claim what you give him not what he takes from you. Willing or unwilling he will not force you. He wishes only to love you. That is why he gave you the ring. As long as you wear it, you are no one's property. Not even his." Atilus said.

"That is what he said. Sir, I still hurt for him. I still want him. Is that wrong?" Pompey asked.

Atilus smiled, "Not wrong but he is right especially now. None of us may survive. Pompey trust me he is right and you will be happier if you wait."

Pompey left and returned to her quarters a dozen roses were in a vase. The card read "May your dreams be sweet my lady." She kissed the card and held it next to her chest.

Beary smiled to himself, he would sleep well.

Eight cycles later he got up and got dressed and headed for the ready room. Artemus met him there.

"Congratulations Uncle." Artemus said

"Thank you Artemus. Is the ship ready?" Beary asked.

"Locked and loaded. Ben is putting in a shield between the passenger compartment and the flight deck. It was one of the Chiefs ideas." Artemus said.

Pompey walked in "Ensign Artemus," then she kissed Beary a genital kiss, "Thank you my love.", then she walk out and headed for her duty station. The other flight crews looked at Beary.

Beary smiled, "Her mother gave her blessing to our engagement. I sent her some flowers."

Artemus smiled, "Boss . . . You continue to amaze me."

Beary looked at him, "Who are we partnering up with?"

Artemus got back to business, "Blood dagger. Ensign Ismael and Flag, both are good."

"Who is lead ship?" Beary asked.

Artemus smiled, "We are section leader, Boss."

"Okay, well let's go over and discuss how we want to do our job." Beary said.

Ensign Ismael stood up and presented his paw Beary shook it. "You must be Spirit 6."

"You must be AB1," Beary said, "Do you have a problem with me being section leader."

Ismael laughed, "I requested it. Look Beary, I am good and so is Flag. However you are better and Artemus has never been out shot. I'll be happy to follow your lead."

"Alright, I have some ideas to bounce off of you." Beary said. The two crews talked for a Cycle and then went to check their ships one more time.

Ben smiled, "The shield is up the door is in place and working properly. We could have a hull failure in the passenger compartment and still fight the ship. Of course if we take a hit up here we die."

Beary smiled, "Good work Ben." Beary continued to inspect the installation it was perfect. "Ben, have you done this before?"

Ben shrugged, "It is similar to what we use back home to protect our villages from the ice wind."

"Okay we are as ready as we can be control placed us on 1 cycle alert. The marines are patrolling for us. Get some rest and food." Beary said to his crew.

Sergeant MacIntosh walked up; He was the crew chief of the Crimson Blade. "Sir anything else you think she needs?"

Beary laughed, "Not that would fit on her."

Sergeant MacIntosh smiled, "Sorry Sir the new Gatling rail guns they brought in are as big as a dagger. We could load some seeking mines to her arsenal. They are basically useless, but if you want them I have them."

Beary thought, "In a pinch they might help. Sergeant thank you and your crew she is a great jump ship and you have kept her in great shape."

Sergeant MacIntosh beamed, "Thank you Sir."

Beary waved and headed off to the ready room.

Captain Atilus waved him over, "Ensign, walk with me."

Beary fell in beside him, "Sir what can I do for you?"

"I want to thank you for treating Pompey with so much respect. Another Boar might not have. Ensign her Dad is my friend. He was once a good pilot. His parents died and he had to resign his commission to take over the Family business. He has grown that business. He is a wealthy Bear. But he is still seeking more power and influence. He has become greedy.

Pompey is afraid once you realize his plan you will reject her. She of coarse has nothing to do with it neither does her mother." Atilus said

"Sir, I am not marrying her father. That is why I gave her the Star of Vandar. While to me it is just a family trinket, to others it is important. I love her; I want to honor her, besides my family already loves her." Beary said.

Atilus smiled, "Alright Ensign I'll mind my own business."

"Not at all Sir, I appreciate your concern. May I be of any other service?" Beary asked.

Atilus thought, "Kill a lot of Arcrilians and don't get killed yourself."

Beary nodded "That is an order I will do my best to carry out Sir."

Atilus returned Beary's salute and walked away. His opinion of this young officer was confirmed. He hoped they all survived long enough for his goddaughter's dreams to come true. In war bad things happen and the storm clouds were gathering.

Chapter 20

Storm Clouds Gathering

Green Dragon 24 and 25 were on a reconnaissance mission. They were long range two bear fighters equipped with long range sensors. They flew past Tarsus 9 and the forest moon of Dryden. They noticed activity on the surface and went in for a closer look as they were about to enter the atmosphere a Green dagger appeared.

"This is Blood Knife 1 to unidentified fighters please state your business."

"Blood Knife 1, this is Green Dragon 24, we are on recon."

"Green Dragon 24 understood, have a good day and good hunting."

With that the Green Dagger recloaked and Green Dragon 24 and 25 headed away from Dryden.

They flew on and headed toward Antillean space when they neared the boarder they heard a voice.

"Bearilian, fighters this is Death Swarm Control do you require assistance?"

"Death Swarm Control, Green Dragon 24, we are out hunting."

"Understood, Green Dragon 24 no game present safe wings."

"Thank you Death Swarm Control, Safe wings and abundant crops. We will, proceed elsewhere, Green Dragon 24 out."

The two fighters turned toward Arcrilian space. As they reached what was supposed to be Bearilian space they picked up Arcrilian communications signals. Green Dragon 25 dropped two listening buoys and they turned towards The Vandar system.

The two fighters cloaked and headed in till their sensors went crazy with signals. Green Dragon 24 dropped three sensor buoys and headed out of Vandar space, with 25 following. When they felt it was safe they hit the relay activation button and data started streaming to the Saber Claw. Green Dragon 24 and 25 went to Warp 2.

On the Saber claw Ensign Pompey began receiving the data burst transmissions from the buoys. "Commander Centaures, please report to Auxiliary Control."

Centaures arrived a few moments later. Pompey had rerouted the data transmissions to his computer which automatically scanned the data and correlated it.

Centaures scanned the data, and called over Lieutenant Lee, "Lee what do you make of all this?"

The Red Pandarian scanned over the information and pulled up the Vandar star system. Lee turned to Centaures, "Sir if the Arcrilian are in the Vandar system as the data may indicate I think they are hiding their fleet in Red Solaris belt between the first and second planets. As you can see this is a strange radiation belt. You could hide a large fleet in there and the class V buoys the fighters carry would have a hard time giving us more than they are."

"Okay, Lee what do you suggest?" Centaures asked.

"We need more information the only way to get it is to send a reconnaissance team to the Vandar system. The Red Daggers are equipped for such a mission. Their class one probes could gain the information we need." Lee said.

Centaures thought, "We can't ask the Marines to send one in they need all of theirs, which means we send one of ours." He looked at Pompey who turned white.

Lee shook his head, "You realize, Sir that even with our cloaking ability, which might be compromised by the Red Solaris Belt, it is basically a suicide mission for one ship."

"Yes, but if we're right I can't spare more than one. I'll take it up to the Captain it will have to be his decision." Centaures said as he watched Pompey.

As he left Pompey grabbed his paw, "Please no." she whispered.

Centaures leaned in close, "It's not my call but you, and I both know he is the best one for the job. At least his crew might have a chance. Anyone else might get the job done, but get killed in the process. Beary and his crew would be my pick. They are just that much better."

Centaures left the control room with her still whispering, "No, please no Commander."

Atilus looked at the information Centaures gave him. "Is there any other way we can do this?"

Centaures shook his head. "The Red Solaris belt makes it impossible without getting up close and personal. The Fighters don't carry the right type of sensor buoy. We have to send a Red Dagger in. I could do it."

Atilus shook his head, "No, your job is to help me fight this ship this is a job for an Ensign, not a Commander. Who do you have in mind?"

Centaures shook his head. "It's at best a suicide mission. Though I think any of our crews would volunteer."

Atilus looked at him, "You want me to make the decision." that was a statement not a question.

"This time yes, Sir you didn't see her eyes, or . . . . No your right they are the best chose." Centaures said.

Atilus dropped his head. "I am the Captain it's my job. You know she will hate us both if anything happens to him."

Centaures looked at him, "Do we send all three or just pilot and gunner?"

"I won't do that to Maritinus. He would see it as a lack of faith. If one goes all three go but no more. You and the Chief are restricted to the Saber Claw itself is that understood?" Atilus said, with a penetrating gaze.

Centaures nodded "I will relay your message to the Master Chief. Do you want to tell them or do I?"

Atilus thought, "No, It is my responsibility, have them report to me."

Centaures ordered the crew of the Crimson Blade to the Captain's wardroom. After 5 STU the three friends arrived.

Beary saluted for the crew. "Crimson Blade reporting as ordered."

Atilus had them seated. He then explained the situation and the risk, then asked, "Any questions."

Beary looked down deep in thought then spoke quietly. "Sir this could be a one bear mission. I am capable of flying and fighting the jump ship . . . ."

Artemus cut him off. "No. Sir I am almost as good a pilot and I have a lot less to lose I could do it . . . ."

Ben cut him off, "I cannot fly the jump ship but I am almost as good as Ensign Artemus. I can fight the ship no matter who flies it I will go."

Beary said, "Sir I am the commander of the Crimson Blade . . . ."

Atilus ended the discussion. "I am the Captain. You have all spoke your mind. Ensign Maxumus and Artemus, I understand your concern. Even if I tried to send only one of you, which I would not do, Lieutenant 3rd Maritinus would sneak into the ship and go. This mission requires a full three bear crew and you both know it. Ensign Artemus, I appreciate your selflessness. But I am the one that will have to answer her questions not you. Of course since it is as close to a suicide mission as you can get, you could refuse. After all this crew has done most of the heavy lifting on this deployment."

Beary shook his head no. "Sir you asked us first for a reason. I know there isn't a flight crew on this ship that would not take this mission. But you figure we have the best chance of survival even if it is by the slimmest margin. We'll, take it when do we leave."

Atilus looked at him, "Four cycles. Tell your crew chief the situation. He might have some ideas, eat, and write a letter home you know the drill."

The three saluted and said, "Yes sir."

When they left the wardroom Artemus looked at Beary, "Boss don't you ever try and leave me behind again. Now do you want me to talk to the crew chief or do you?"

Beary looked at Artemus and Ben who was quiet, "I apologize to both of you. Artemus you talk to the crew chief. Tell him to throw in everything he thinks we might need and still be able to fly and fight the Blade."

Artemus smiled, "You got it Boss come on Ben let's see what we can steal from the arsenal just in case."

Ben smiled and turned to Beary. "I know you were only trying to protect us. But we are a team we must live or die as a team."

Pompey was standing in the hall as Beary neared his berth. She looked at him. "No, no you could have refused!"

Beary open his door and led her inside. "Stop it!" He said in a soft but firm voice. "You knew they would send us and you knew I would say yes. I am a soldier and I am good at it. So is

Artemus and Ben, would my female dishonor me with tears. If you are going to cry at least wait until I am dead." Then he kissed her gently on the forehead.

Pompey looked at him. He was in his element this was who he was. Not the brilliant scientist or the brilliant engineer. But a brave and confident soldier, "I am sorry my liege. I forgot myself and my place."

Beary kissed her. "My Lady no one is your liege. Not even the boar that loves you. You wear the ring."

She looked at him, "Then I chose to put myself in your arms and under your control. This ring gives me that right."

Beary was about to answer when he was interrupted.

Centaures said. "Ensign Maxumus you have an incoming message from Bearilia Prime. You have permission to take it on channel delta."

Beary said, "Understood Sir."

Sirena Pompey appeared, on the screen. "Sire Maxumus may I ask a question?"

Beary smiled, "Yes Sirena Pompey, if it is in my power to answer it."

She straightened, "Was this gift from your own resources or your families?"

"Sirena, the brides price was paid from my personal resources my family had no part in it though, they would have paid it. They hold your daughter in honor and love her. Also, the gift was for you and you alone. As Sirena it was my right to give it to you to honor you before your village and in your House." Beary said.

Sirena Pompey pondered his words, "I am pleased that my daughter pleases her liege."

Beary shook his head. "Your daughter has no liege. She wears the ring. She is subject to no one but the Creator of the universe that rules us all."

Sirena Pompey was taken back had she heard him right. "I do not understand?"

Beary smiled, "Your daughter is to be my wife. I am the guardian of the ring. She is its wearer as is the custom. She is the Star of Vandar. As such she is subject to no house or Clan. Only I the Guardian can change that arrangement or when our youngest cub becomes its guardian"

Beary's words hit Pompey and mother like thunder and lightning. *What had he said, Pompey was the Star of Vandar?!*

Pompey's mother looked at her daughter, "Your Highness."

Beary then turned to the Sirena, "Sirena Pompey you are to receive 50,000 credits a year for life as additional payment of the brides price for your daughters paw. The money is yours and no one else, also if something happens to me prior to our wedding Pompey will receive 500,000 credits a year for life. This money is from my resources and no one else. Now my lady I must go."

Pompey looked at Him. "You cannot mean what you say. I cannot. You cannot . . . ."

Beary smiled, "Your babbling, my love. First, yes you are the Star of Vandar and subject to no one. Second only I can remove the ring from your possession or the next guardian, which would be my youngest sister, if I die. It would be her choice. Yes, I have established a fund for you if I should die. It should allow you to live free. Also my family would accept you as one of the family, even if anything happened to me. I have also made out a will, which makes other provisions for you. Ben and Artemus witnessed it. It has been submitted to the fleet. This is your copy."

She took it shaking. "Why, why have you, did this for me and my mother?"

Beary looked at her and shrugged. "I have no one else to give it to. My family doesn't need it. I left some to my nephews and nieces. A little goes to a charitable foundation my family runs." He took her in his arms. "If something happens I want you to be happy and live well for the both of us. Now if you would kiss me. I need to go."

"Can't you stay for a little while? We are alone." She said shaking.

"No my love, besides the sooner I leave, the sooner I get back. We can start planning our life together then." Beary said kissing her.

"Will we have a life together? Or will I be a widow before I am married." She asked in a weak voice.

"Only the Creator knows Priscilla. If you, have a chance say a prayer for all of us. Now please I must go." Beary said gently and left her in the room.

She lay on his bunk smelled his scent and cried after a few moments she raised up. Wiped her eyes straitened her uniform.

No she would not act like a heart sick cub. Her boar was a warrior a Knight of the Maxumus clan. The Guardian of Vandar and the feared Ghost that stalks the Arcrilian's in their sleep. She would prove worthy and left for her duty station. Lieutenant Torres was coming on duty. Pompey stepped over. "Tor, take an hour and a half break I owe you."

Torres looked at Lee who nodded. Lee turned to Pompey. "Are you Okay?"

Pompey turned toward Lieutenant Lee. "Sir I am the Star of Vandar and my betrothed is its Guardian. The one he loves. I will honor my Boar. I am fit for duty."

"Crimson Blade to Control we request hot launch."

A familiar voice came on, "Control to Crimson Blade may the Creator protect you. Hot launch expedite authorized silent running communicate by remote burst transmissions. Come back my love. Control out."

Beary launched the Crimson Blade out at high speed barrel rolled and headed for the Vandar system.

Once they cleared Carnise Drift he turned on the shields, cloak, and went to warp 3.

Ben sealed the command section and started listening to the various signals.

Artemus checked over his systems and the probes. "Boss I have green on all boards and sub systems."

"Thanks, what did the crew chief put in here we are heavier than normal I had to adjust our center of gravity." Beary asked. While technically a jump ship was weightless in space the internal dampening fields that provided gravity to the crew were affected by the increase in mass.

"He said you could build a new ship if you needed to." Artemus laughed. Little did he know just how true that statement would almost prove to be?

They entered the Vandar system Artemus started scanning as they passed the outer four planets. Then they passed through an asteroid belt the debris of several old transports and warships were scattered in the field.

Beary lowered his head and said a prayer for the souls of the dead. "Here lies my race."

Artemus looked at him. "Beary?"

"This is where my race is from. Those are ships of the houses of our race. They were killed in the first incursion." Beary said.

Artemus checked his scanner, "We have plant and animal life on the 6th, 5th, and 3rd planets. The fourth planet seams to cross the path of the 3rd planet."

Beary looked at him, "That's impossible. We were told that those planets were dead."

"Maybe a few hundred years ago, but they're not now. Do you know their names?" Artemus asked.

"The 3rd planet is Andreas Prime my home world. The fourth is Andreas Beta. The Fifth is Cascadia and the sixth is Pacifica the water planet." Beary answered.

"We are heading for the Red Solaris Belt between The first and second planet. Does it have a name?" Artemus asked.

Ben spoke before Beary could, "It is the Guardian of Vandar, Corsan the hammer, the forge of the Red Star Stones."

Artemus looked at Beary, "Boss?"

Beary looked at him, "Shield and cloak to max start laying probes and buoys. Set up for burst relay transmission. We're going in."

Artemus fired two small class 1 probes into the field all of a sudden ships started appearing in the data. Beary entered the Solaris field.

"Boss cloak is down to 10 % efficiency shield is at 60%.

I am picking up multiple targets and they are all big!" Artemus said.

"Ah . . . launch all spectrum buoys and probes set on auto burst and let's get out of here." Beary ordered.

"Buoys and probes launched. We are being targeted by a Battle Cruiser. I am firing, twenty death hawk missiles. They have acquired us. They are firing their main gun." Artemus said.

Beary rolled to the right just as the energy beam hit. The energy beam pushed through the weakened shield. It hit the Left warp nacelle and punched a hole through the passenger compartment of the Crimson Blade.

The twenty death hawk missiles struck the Arcrilian Battle Cruiser knocking out its main gun and a few small ones.

Beary checked his panels, "How bad?" he asked as he exited the Red Solaris Belt.

Ben answered, "We have a 2 to 3 SMU hole in our left side in the passenger compartment. I can see stars. I can also see plasma leaking from what is left of the left warp nacelle. Passenger compartment is depressurized. I am trying to establish a containment field. The containment field is established structural integrity at 69 %."

Beary shut off power to the warp Drive and closed the plasma intakes. "Put on your helmets in case the internal shield fails and we lose containment. Artemus weapon status."

Artemus answered "I have a green board on remaining missiles and the gun. Sensors are at 70 %. Shield and cloak is back to 98 %."

Beary looked at his crew. They should be dead, but by providence they had survived, a direct hit from a main gun. "We are heading for Andreas Prime. Watch for fighters and pray. It will take 5 cycles at our present speed." the ship felt sluggish at any faster speed.

Artemus spoke next, "Boss, I don't think we can make it back to the Saber Claw like this. I am not sure she would hold together."

Ben added, "Communication Systems are out, except the intelligence package. I am still able to receive Arcrilian traffic"

This star field is beautiful." as he looked out the hole in the Crimson Blades side.

Artemus smiled, Ben always finds a blessing in something. "Boss what now?"

Beary thought, "Now I return home, we are going to try and land on Andreas Prime. When we get close enough scan the Northern Continent and the third high mountain range for a castle like structure."

"Sorry Boss, I launched all the Probes back there." Artemus said.

Beary shrugged "That's what they were for. We'll have to do it the old fashion way."

On board the Arcrilian Battle Cruiser Harvesters pride. The Admiral was livid. "What has happened Captain to my Flag ship?"

The Captain cleared his throat, "We picked up the shape of a Bearilian jump ship. We fired at it with the main gun. We believe we destroyed it nothing that size could have survived. Unfortunately it launched missiles in close our shields are compromised by this field. The main gun was severely damaged and its control room destroyed. Some minor damage was sustained by other forward weapon systems. We are attempting to repair the systems."

"Captain how did it happen, How could a Bearilian craft get this close? I want the debris from that ship found and studied now." The Admiral said with a sneer.

After a Cycle what debris that could be found was brought in, part of a warp nacelle and some shards of the outer skin of the Crimson Blade. The Admiral looked at the debris "Is this all they found."

The Captain was nervous, "So far sir but we are still looking."

"You incompetent slug send out a fighter Squadron have them look for this dead jump ship. If they don't find it I will personally throw you out an airlock." The Admiral fumed.

Artemus looked at his sensors, "Boss we have company coming. A Squadron of Arcrilian Sabot Fighters just cleared the Solaris field and is fanning out."

"Alright Artemus they are fishing. How, are the cloak and shields operating?" Beary asked

"Cloak is at 99 % and shields are still at 98.5% efficiency. The cloak might fail when we enter the atmosphere. Artemus reported.

Beary thought they want to find something. "Can we detach a missile launcher set it to launch its missiles by proximity at the fighters?"

Artemus smiled, "Good idea. We have 16 missiles left in the 2nd launcher we could use it."

"Do it Artemus then set it up so it clears the cloak easy so it doesn't give us away. We want them to find it." Beary said.

Artemus did his magic and released the missile launcher. It detached from the blade and floated away. Then a small booster pushed it out of the path that the Crimson blade was traveling.

Beary eased more power out of the sub light engines. The Blade was hurt but she was still holding together. They were now getting within 2 cycles of Andreas Prime.

"The fighters are searching away from us they have not yet found the launcher. They are heading toward the asteroid belt that separates the inner and outer planets." Ben reported

"Good they are thinking we are a bigger threat than we are. They will leave part of the Squadron there in ambush and the other half will sweep back this way. By then we might be on the far side of the planet." Beary thought.

The STUs passed by as they did Andreas Prime grew from a distant dot to a large class M planet.

Artemus focused a very narrow sensor beam at the planet. "We have a good oxygen, and nitrogen atmosphere. I cannot get a clear picture of the surface yet but there is atmospheric disturbance in the south central part of the planet."

Beary looked at the information that should be the Delinian Ocean. "I bet it is a Hurricane or other large storm that should be an ocean."

Artemus shrugged "I can't tell for sure the upper winds seem to be around 200 KSMU/Cycle. I hope you are not planning to fly us into that."

Beary thought, "No, if the Crimson Blade was in one piece and not holed I might. Besides we are heading towards the other side."

The Arcrilian Squadron Commander reached the asteroid belt he took one flight in and sent one to another point. The two other flights turned back. After 30 STU one of the fighters picked up something on his scanners and reported the debris.

The two returning flights turned toward the launcher. There were 16 Arcrilian fighters and 16 missiles the computer brain on the launcher picked 8 fighters and waited. The Arcrilian fighters got within 100 SMU when the missiles started firing. Two missiles lost lock and chased after another fighter but they missed. The others bored in 6 of the Arcrilian fighters were destroyed the seventh took damage but survived. The launcher went dormant its internal computer degaussed itself and shut down. The Arcrilian fighters reported the find and towed the launcher into the Harvesters Pride. They arrived at the same time the Crimson Blade reached Andreas Prime.

On board the Harvesters Pride the Admiral looked at the Captain. "You think this is debris from a dead ship?"

The Captain stood straighter. Yes, Sir I do."

The Admiral looked at him. "We lost 6 pilots and fighters retrieving a missile box. And you think this is good?

We are being played by this Bearilian." The Admiral walked over to the ship's Captain "You are worse than useless." With that he pulled a phaser and shot the Captain. The first Officer stood up.

The Admiral looked at him, "Are you smarter than this one was."

The First officer nodded.

"We will see. Find the Bearilian and remove this trash from my sight." The Admiral snarled.

Beary angled the Crimson blade to the far side of the planet and started scanning the Northern Continent. The Mountain ranges were lush with vegetation. He began his descent the reentry was tricky the shield took most of the buffeting but the crew could tell the Crimson blade was on the verge of ripping itself apart. Then they broke through the outer atmosphere.

All three took a sigh of relief. Beary turned to Artemus, "Do you see that third internal ridge of Mountains. Scan for a structure in the middle saddle."

Artemus focused his beams. "Got it, we have large stone structure. I am picking up no sign of Arcrilian presents."

"Good I am going to try and land in the court yard near the wall. That way we can camouflage the ship." Beary said.

Beary brought the Crimson blade slowly over the court yard and lowered the ship slowly down the vertical thrusters were sluggish and they landed harder than he wanted.

Artemus and Ben both laughed, Artemus said, "I'd give that a C on the landing."

Beary smiled, "I lost one thruster at the last moment. Sorry."

Ben smiled, "We are alive. Where are we?"

Beary pointed to the faded crest on the far wall. He felt strange as he looked at the wall with the Crests of the families of the clan. He sighed "Welcome to the House of Maxumus the hall of Corsan, Home of my clan. Let's see what we can do."

Ben opened the internal shield door and deactivated the containment field. Beary stepped into the compartment the hole was exactly 2.5 SMU in diameter luckily the damage was only to the shell of the ship. Other than the left nacelle and at least one thruster no other critical components seamed damaged.

Artemus looked over the damage, "Remind me to send a thank you note to the manufacturer."

Ben pulled weapons from the storage unit handed Beary and Artemus a standard armament belt. He also grabbed a large multi barreled magnetic rail gun. "I will find a place to put this, Boss." Ben saw a tower that appeared to have a 360 degree view of the approaches to the castle. He climbed the worn stairs and arrived at the top. He placed the Rail Gun toward the pass. And looked around the view was excellent.

Beary looked at the spare parts the crew chief had put in the ship. Two of the most important were parts, for a nacelle and the same panel material the internal shield was made from.

Artemus pulled out some emergency rations and water.

"Beary I have the camouflage on we need to do two things, first eat then prioritize what we fix."

Beary looked at him, "Good Idea. I can fix the nacelle with what the crew chief gave us. And I have an idea for the hole. We should be able to limp back at warp 2."

Artemus smiled, "What no fang sticks and gum."

Beary smiled, and held up a new plasma injector and controller "No, but this is a good start."

Artemus smiled, "I'll take food and water up to Ben."

Beary opened his pouch, "Thanks Artemus."

Artemus climbed the tower. At the top he found that Ben had set a table and a few chairs near the rampart "Great view."

Ben smiled, "Yes, is he alright."

Artemus looked back into the court yard. Beary already had the warp nacelle off. And had pulled a bench over from what must have been an old black smith shop. "He won't rest till the engines fixed. I can repair a few of the electrical systems including the communication systems."

Ben said, "If I had some of the shielding panels I could fix the hole."

Artemus smiled, "We do. I think we have three panels."

Ben smiled, "We each possess one of the expertise needed to fix the ship and get us home. Beary needs to know it is not all his responsibility."

Artemus finished his ration and smiled, "I'll tell him after I get the electronics fixed you can seal the hole. Enjoy the view."

Ben patted the rail gun, "I will."

Artemus returned to the Crimson Blade. "Boss, Ben says he can fix the hole. I am a pretty good electrician, so I am going to replace the damaged communication equipment."

Beary smiled, "Thanks we have about three hours of daylight left. We don't want any lights showing so when it gets dark we rest."

"I'll be done with my part by then Boss." Artemus said. Artemus went in he found that the Crew Chief had put in extra spare parts for the communication system. He pulled out the main panel which was in the passenger compartment to save room on the flight deck. Artemus removed the damaged systems and started checking the fiber optic cables that connected the panel to the flight deck. All six bundles suffered some shrapnel damage. Artemus disconnected the bundles from the command panels on the flight deck and marked each one and the receiver.

After two hours he had rewoven the new bundles threw their channels and started reconnecting them. He then moved the panel over a few SUBSMU and connected the bundles to the panel with three STU to spare he slide in the last replacement panel.

Artemus came out, "Communications should be fixed I need to check the top array but as per your orders I am done for the night," Pointing towards the horizon, "time to quit."

Beary looked up, "Your right, I have the nacelle taken apart I need to form a new casing luckily I have the tools I need in there. I have all the internal parts I need but if you find some chewing gum and fang sticks hold on to them."

"Where do we sleep Beary?" Artemus asked.

"Ben has the right idea we sleep in the tower, one of us on watch every three cycles. Ben should get some rest. We need him sharp tomorrow to seal that hole."

Pilot and gunner walked to the tower and climbed the ancient stairs, Beary felt strange being here. They reached the top.

Ben smiled. "Great sun set," as he peered through the slots in the rampart wall. "We are staying in here tonight?"

Beary nodded, "Safest place, each of us take one three hour shift yours will be near sun rise. Artemus called this shift so you and I go to sleep now I get the middle shift." Beary took one more look out over the green mountain slopes and valley below. Why had they been told the planet was uninhabitable?

On the Saber Claw Centaures was looking at the data from the probes. There had been a release of energy from an Arcrilian main gun and what appeared to be explosions on the Arcrilian ship. Later Bearilian missiles were fired and some Arcrilian fighters died. The Arcrilian's were looking for something.

He looked at Pompey, "Pompey, I am sure he is alright. He won't try contacting the ship till he is clear of the space they are controlling."

"Sir they are overdue but they planted the probes we are getting vital data." She dropped her head, "Something has happened I can feel it but I also know they are alive I feel that also." Pompey said.

"Okay, you were officially off duty, 10 STU ago go, get some rest, that's an order. Lieutenant Torres do you need an engraved invitation to take your station." Centaures growled.

Lieutenant Torres looked at him. "No Sir, I am ready for duty."

Centaures growled, "Good."

Lee came over, "Sir, may I show you something."

Centaures came over, Lee handed him a small book. "You need to go rest and find peace."

Centaures looked at the pocket size *Word of the Creator*. "Alright Lee your right, but I might have sent those bears to their death."

Lee shrugged "And tomorrow or later it may be our turn. It is a risk we all take to serve. There is no greater love than to lay down one's life for his friends or Race. They understand that and so do you. Go Sir, please I have auxiliary control covered."

Centaures nodded. He left the room and headed for his office. All of a sudden he thought about *The Book* in his Paw, and headed for the chapel.

When he entered the chapel he saw Caesar and Pompey and Grizlarge praying he slipped into a seat. He opened *The Book and read the passage marked Greater Love has no one than this that he lay down his life for his friends*. He closed *The Book*. He then lowered his head and prayed for the first time in years.

On Andreas Prime Artemus was watching what appeared to be faint lights dancing in the forest near the top of the pass, they didn't approach the Castle but were just there.

Beary was sleeping but in his dream a voice kept calling his name and saying come find me and what only you can wield. Release me and claim the Hammers and the ring that only you can wear. Come find me look in the darkness under the keep, in the secret chamber." Beary woke up and walked out on to the rampart.

Artemus looked at him, "What's wrong?"

Beary shook his head, "Something is calling me I can still hear it in my head."

Artemus stretched, "I am good if I get tired, I'll call Ben. Go find the voice I have been watching what my bears use to call spirit lights."

Beary looked toward the pass and saw nothing. The voice kept saying look in the dark places under the keep. Find me Guardian of Vandar.

Beary started down the steps Ben looked at him, "Beary do you require me?"

Beary smiled, "I am just chasing ghosts of the past sleep well Ben."

Ben, laid down in his head a voice filled his mind sleep in peace Maritinus the slayer, all is well, sleep as if you can hear the cold waters of home. Ben opened his eyes then fell asleep.

Artemus was the next to hear a voice in his head, Do not fear the lights they watch over you. Stand your watch at ease Artemus, of the lost. Peace, be in your mind. Artemus looked around but could not help but feel at peace and safe.

Beary entered the keep and followed the voice. He came to a wall at the end of a long corridor. The voice said enter through what is not seen. Beary felt the wall his paw touched a block and the wall slide open then closed behind him.

Beary could make out stairs carved in the far wall he edged around the landing and took the stairs they lead down into the mountain. He came to a large metal door with three huge screw locks.

Again the voice called out to his mind; speak the ancient words Son of the Maxumus clan. His mind wondered back to when he was a child Samuel had taught him a poem or was it a song. Beary began singing the ancient words. The translation to which was the waters still, the flame subsides all find peace in his protective hands. The three screws backed out as he sang the song.

The door creaked and he swung it open. As he entered deep red and purple flames engulfed and danced around him but did not touch him. The Creature came forward and again sent flame dancing around him. Beary stood still but felt no fear.

The Creature spoke "I am Gamey the Brave by what right do you enter my home."

Beary stood tall "I am He the Son of the Maxumus clan the Guardian of Vandar."

"What do you seek young one?" Gamey asked.

"To free you and to learn what you told me to seek." Beary responded.

"The ancient tunnel is blocked how do you plan to open it?" Gamey asked.

Beary looked at him, "Show me," The Dragon moved slowly down the tunnel. Beary looked at the walls near the cave about twenty SMU from the entrance, "Can you fuse the rock around the slide"

The Dragon breathed in then released a fine blue flame that melted and fused the rock.

Beary then inserted the first six shaped charges, and backed away. The Dragon slowly followed. Beary hit the remote. The slide moved as if it had been shot out of a shotgun.

Beary, again moved forward and had the Dragon fuse the exposed ceiling. He planted more charges this time lower and deeper into the bottom of the slide. Again he retreated and the Dragon followed.

The next explosions opened the cave entrance. The Dragon fussed the ceiling and then the floor of the entrance. He spread his wings and leaped the wind caught his wings and he soured. The moons reflecting on his wings giving off a slight glow of purple and red, after a few moments he landed and lowered his head.

"Young one, touch my head." Beary felt heat pulse through his body, Gamey licked his head. You have freed me. May the creator bless your off spring and make them great. Now that which is yours, go down to the Hall of the fallen. Beary turned down a winding corridor that seemed to end at a great Hall. There interned were the bodies of his ancestors. Next to a crystal stone formed by Dragon breath was an ancient trunk and a jeweled box.

He opened the box in it was two Red Hammers made of a strange metal Beary had never seen. Also in the Box was a ring with the symbols of his clan he put the ring on and raised his hand the ring glowed and a bright red sword appeared in his paw. On it was an ancient inscription that translated said I am Star Fire the defender of truth and the weak.

Beary marveled at the sword its balance was perfect yet it was light as a feather. He twisted the ring and it disappeared he found it in its scabbard next to Justinian the Great's tomb he collected it.

He went to the trunk other family treasures were there including the Book with the family names and history. He put the Scabbard over his back and the ring in the box with the hammers and the trunk.

The Dragon was feasting on 10 Talus deer he looked up as he swallowed half of one of the Deer. "Will you eat with me young one."

Beary nodded then said, "How about my crew?"

The Dragon smiled and held up a young doe which had been cleaned and he roasted it with his breath and sliced some off for Beary. Beary savored the fresh meat that was surprisingly cooked to perfection.

"Thank you Gamey the brave. Thank you for also entombing my Great grandfather. And thank you for the fresh meat for my crew." Beary said

"Young one morning approaches if you can come and see me before you leave. Tell your house I will protect their home till they return." Gamey said.

Beary nodded threw the rest of the doe over his shoulder and grabbed the two boxes and climbed the stairs. He exited the keep. Ben and Artemus could smell the roasted meat, and saw the boxes Beary carried and the sword.

Artemus looked at him, "What were those explosions."

Beary smiled, "I was freeing the cook."

Ben saw the shadow of the Dragon and looked up his Purple and red scales flashed in the sun light. "He is the voice I heard."

Beary nodded, "Come on let's eat and get to work."

Ben sliced the meat and put some in a storage unit to keep fresh. Then he examined the hole. I can fix this with what I have available. It will not be a problem.

Artemus looked at Beary "What do you want me to do."

"Go rest and watch the sky. You got your part done." Beary said. He could tell the array was realigned.

Beary stepped into the old forge. Inside he found some Fine metal he tested it. It would work fine for forming the new casing for the nacelle. Soon he had the metal formed and he took it out and welded it to the damaged section. He then aligned the plasma injectors and controls he waved Artemus over "Help me attach this to the ship. After six cycles the repaired nacelle was on. Beary then went in and checked the actual engine all was in working order.

He looked at his friends, "She'll fly."

Ben stretched "I need two more hours and the hole will be fixed but I still wish I could put a metal skin on the outside."

Beary thought, "There is a sheet of some type of metal in the blacksmith shop it should work."

Ben went in and carted the sheet out. "This will do well."

As night fell Ben finished his repairs Beary looked at his crew "Get everything ready we will leave as soon as I get back."

Ben retrieved the rail gun but still climbed back up the tower.

Artemus checked and rechecked his systems. All was ready. Yet he remembered the haunting words. What had the voice meant by Artemus of the lost?

Beary followed the path to the ancient doors which were open. He saw the Dragon and spoke. "Gamey we are ready to leave."

Gamey looked up from his meal 6 large Terra hogs, "Young one thank you for coming, there is one more box I had to give you." Inside was the Imperial Necklace and Crown of the House of Caesar.

"The Imperial family is no more. Only my Great Grandmother Maria Caesar survived and she has passed beyond." Beary said.

Gamey lowered his head then roared and bowed to Beary. "Your clan then is next in line does one still exist that is a direct descendant."

Beary thought, "My mother was given the royal jewels by her grandmother."

Gamey smiled, "Then the House of Caesar and the house of Maxumus were united. Give these to your mother."

"It will be done." Beary said.

Gamey once more breathed fire around him. "Take the South Pole then, exit the atmosphere, Head for the Dragons eye." Gamey placed a picture of a star map in his mind. "Go young prince. May the Creator of all, bless you."

Beary returned to the Crimson Blade. He carefully lifted off and headed for the South Pole. Once there he headed for the Dragons eye.

Artemus looked at him, "Sir, where are we going?"

Beary smiled, "Home."

Atilus looked at Centaures, "The Crimson blade is four days overdue. We have to believe that they were destroyed."

Centaures said, "Yes sir, but they accomplished their mission."

Atilus lowered his head, "Call it in three cycles we will have a memorial."

"Com to the Captain, come to the bridge!"

Atilus stepped onto the bridge and went over to the com section.

"Spirit 6 to Blue Dragon control requesting landing instructions."

"Spirit 6 authenticate DW6"

"Blue Dragon, NC5."

Pompey flew onto the Bridge.

Atilus looked at her, "Red Paw 1 to Spirit 6, you're late."

Beary looked at the Saber Claw, "Red Paw 1, Spirit 6 we had to stop for gas. Request slow landing."

Atilus nodded.

"Blue Dragon Control to Spirit 6, land at your leisure."

Beary brought her in slow and carefully maneuvered to a spot near the repair bay.

The Crew chief saw the damage and the repairs and ran over. "Sir, by all that is Holy what happened?!"

Beary shrugged, "Main Gun from an Arcrilian Battle Cruiser. 2.5 SMU hole and a shot up nacelle. That's about it. Thanks for the spare parts they got us home."

Centaures flew in and hugged Beary, then Ben, and Artemus. Then He saw the patch work repairs to the side of the Crimson Blade. "What . . . . ?

Beary smiled, "Big Gun made a big hole. If the internal shielding hadn't been in place we would have been dead. We had launched just before it fired. Our missiles apparently damaged the main Gun."

Atilus had slipped in while Beary talked to Centaures. He walked over to the Crew Chief, "Well, what do you think?"

Sergeant MacIntosh shook his head, "Sir, most of the important sub systems they repaired. I would like to at least paint and smooth out the patch that they installed. Ensign Maxumus did a great job repairing the nacelle but I want to put a new one on. Give me two days and she'll be good as new if not better."

Atilus looked at the patch and the damaged interior he saw how they had used spare internal shield panels to cover the hole and add to the ships structural integrity. The welds were not pretty but were strong. He noticed the other crew chief inspecting the damage. He stepped out of the Crimson Blade. "Sergeant MacIntosh can you fix her and still keep her flyable."

MacIntosh nodded, "Sir it will take my Crew 3 Cycled to replace the nacelle, and one cycle to fit a new shield and cloaking devise. These two are still working but they are due for periodic maintenance. We can do the rest and still keep the Crimson Blade available. She won't be able to carry troops though till we are able to fix the interior. That will take time."

"Alright Sergeant get it done." Atilus walked over to Beary. "You are late."

Beary looked at the Captain. "Sorry sir, I had to stop and do some sightseeing. Can I speak to you and Commander Centaures alone?"

Atilus looked at him. "Be in my office in 2 cycles."

"Also, Sir is there by any chance a priority shuttle going back to the Bearilia Prime." Beary asked.

Atilus asked, "Why?"

Beary showed him the box containing the necklace and Crown, "I need to get these to my mother. They belong to her."

Atilus' eyes popped, "If those are what I think they are I'll send a security officer with them. I have a Marine from the Black Aces that needs to go home. His father is ill."

"Thank you Sir, could this trunk also go with him?" Beary asked.

Atilus looked at the ancient trunk, "No problem what of the other box and the sword."

"Sir they stay with me. I'll explain I promise." Beary said.

"All right go get cleaned up." Atilus said.

Beary headed for his berth when he got there Ben was coming out of the shower. Ben spoke, "You are scheduled for a physical in 5 cycles. You need to get cleaned up also."

Beary said," Thanks, also thanks for all you did to help get us home. I'll make sure your skills as a hull repair expert is mentioned."

Ben smiled, "I have some meat to deliver to our Crew Chief and his Bears with your permission."

"Great idea, Ben, besides I can't think of a better use for the meat." Beary said.

Beary, stripped and headed for the shower.

While he was in there Pompey slipped into the room. She saw the box and opened it she saw the Hammers and the ring. She then pulled the sword from its scabbard. She found that she could hardly lift it She read the Ancient inscription I am Star Fire. She slipped the blade back in and set it down.

Beary walked out with a towel draped around him. Pompey smiled, and flew in to his arms Beary tried to hold her and his towel.

"I thought I had lost you." she said as she kissed him.

Beary kissed her and then pulled away, "I need to get dressed."

Pompey smiled an impish smile, "Don't let me stop you."

Beary shook his head and grabbed his uniform and went into the restroom.

Pompey pouted, "Your no fun."

Beary laughed and came out fully dressed, "I love you." and he kissed her. "Let's go eat I have to go and see the Captain in a Cycle and a half."

Beary arrived at the wardroom, "Ensign Maxumus reporting." He had the Hammers and the Sword with him.

Atilus looked at him, "Set down, Ensign. We have some questions."

Centaures spoke next, "Your path back to the ship was not from Vandar but from within Bearilian space."

"Yes, Sir, We left Vandar through the Dragons eye." Beary said.

Atilus shook his head. "That is impossible no one knows its location."

"Sir Gamey the Brave put its location in my mind and told me to take it. I have marked its exit point if the fleet put even an old cruiser there it could destroy anyone that came through. Shields, weapons, and cloaks are disabled for 1STU. That would be more than enough time to destroy an intruder."

"Alright I'll call it in do you think the Arcrilians know its location?" Atilus asked.

"I don't know." Beary responded, "Sir why were my bears told our home worlds were destroyed?"

"Beary I don't know you would have to ask someone who knows more than I do." Atilus said.

Centaures spoke next, "Why haven't the Arcrilian attacked yet. By the data we are receiving the fleet is enormous, at least 4 Battle Cruisers, 8 Heavy Cruisers and 12 Destroyers and 3 fighter carriers. That's 400 Fighters. They could roll right over us."

Beary thought, "They are waiting for someone or something. I just don't know."

Centaures spoke next. "They caught the Admirals and the council of 8, their done."

Beary thought, "What if they were not the only conspirators. What if we missed the most important one?"

Atilus thought about that, "I'll report your suspicion to Admiral Starpaw. Now about the trinkets you brought back."

Beary opened the box, "These are the Hammers of Corsan. This is Star Fire. Beary pulled the sword and showed it to them." Beary handed Atilus the sword and he could hardly lift it yet Beary handled it like it was a feather.

Beary remembered the words that were spoken only you can wield. "Sir I do think they will come, and soon. The buoys we planted should give us some warning."

Atilus said, "Okay Ensign, pop quiz you are facing overwhelming odds with little or no chance of survival. How would you face them?"

Beary thought, "Their coming from the Vandar system. They have to pass through or by the Palisades Drift. If a small force of Jump ships could do a hit and run attack. Sir that's what they are waiting for Troop transports. The heavy ships can't take planets or launch land attacks. Instead of taking the heavies head on we hit the troop transports, with the jump ships.

The Arcrilians attack formation will have the 4 Battle Cruisers in the center. With 4 heavy cruisers on each side, Then 6 destroyers on each side. Forming an arrow head, The Fighter Carriers will form the shaft.

If the fighters could hit them near the far orbit near Tarsus 12 as they enter Tarsus space that leaves the Saber Claw and her jump Ships. We start hitting them trying to draw off some of their destroyers. If our attack on the transports works they might even split their force."

Atilus thought about it, "Not a bad plan Ensign get some rest."

After Beary left, "It's a good start but needs some refinement. We need to find out about troop transports." Centaures said.

An Antillean shuttle requested permission to land. Control gave it permission.

Atilus and Centaures went to the hanger bay.

A tall Antillean exited wearing a dark suit. "Captain Atilus I am Granitic pro council of the Antillean Council. We have information for you. One of our scout ships followed twelve Arcrilian troop transports entering Vandar space near our Provence that boarders the Vandar system. I am here to offer you what little help we can. If the Arcrilian attack us instead we will need our fleet. But we can spare two fighter Swarms and a Destroyer."

Atilus smiled, "Would your destroyer commander mind commanding the strike force on the transports."

"I am sure it would be his pleasure, Captain." Granitic said, "I will have my commanders contact you immediately." With that he returned to his shuttle and left.

Centaures, have LTJG White-fang come to my wardroom.

Caesar finished looking over Ben and Artemus and pronounced them fit for duty but gave them a 48 cycle down time borrowing an attack. Then Beary walked in. Caesar called him over and hooked him up to the machines.

Caesar rechecked his readings. Beary's heart muscles appeared stronger as did his skeletal structure. "Beary I need to run some more tests would you go over to the step machine."

"Sure Caesar" Beary got up and climbed on. He started pumping the steps. Caesar increased the resistance but Beary didn't seem to notice. He cranked up to the maximum resistance still Beary's heart rate and blood pressure never changed.

"Beary I want to check your bone density." Caesar said.

"Is there a problem?" Beary asked.

Caesar smiled, "I am just following protocol." Caesar checked his findings again. Beary's bone density had increased 30%, "Dr. Fang can you come here please." Caesar and Dr. Fang looked over the results of the test.

"I have never seen anything like this. Ensign Maxumus was a unique specimen before but now." Dr. Fang looked at the young Maxmimus.

Beary looked at the two Doctors. "Sir what is going on?"

Dr. Fang shrugged, "Ensign Your bone density and muscles have changed but not your weight. You are probably 30% stronger and faster. But I don't know why?"

"A Dragon's blessing. He had me touch a spot on his head I felt heat pulse threw my body." Beary said.

"What Dragon?" Caesar asked.

"Gamey the brave protector of the Maxumus estate," Beary said.

Dr. Fang shook his head, "That is just nonsense there has to be another answer but for now you are given a 48 cycle rest but are fit for duty."

Caesar looked at Beary, "Our home world?"

Beary smiled, "It is beautiful."

Caesar smiled, "Go see your Lady you are on mandatory down time."

Beary checked the time; Pompey would be on duty for another 3 cycles so he went to check on his other lady the Crimson Blade.

LTJG white-Fang had contacted Colonel Remas who was now in Atilus's wardroom. "It is a crazy plan, but if we gun down the transports, even if they broke through what good would it do them. Alright I can give you half of my red Daggers and Major Tan Wu with the green dagger."

"Will the Major mind following orders from an Antillean Destroyer Captain." Atilus asked.

"No we have worked with them before. Besides the Black Swarm is a good bunch." Remas said.

"Okay here are the rendezvous point, wish your crews the Creators speed." Atilus said Remas got up and headed back to the Drift.

Centaures waited till he left, "That was easy."

Atilus smiled, "No, but twelve transports of Arcrilian troopers is bad news. Even are dear Coronel would rather kill them away from here."

Beary looked at the Crimson Blade the shield and Cloak generators were being replaced and were being aligned. A cart with a brand new nacelle was rolled up and ready to be installed. The patched nacelle was on a cart next to the repair shop.

"Your Crew did a fine job Sir. " Sergeant MacIntosh said.

"Thank you Crew Chief, did Ensign Artemus mention the hard landing on Andreas Prime." Beary asked.

"Yes, Sir the number three thruster was damaged. You had no way to fix it. We replaced it and are ready to install the new nacelle. Give us two more cycles and she will be in fighting shape. Another day and she will be beautiful again." The Sergeant said.

"Thanks Sergeant, tell your crew thanks also. I'll get out of your way." Beary said. He went to the gym.

Pompey finished her shift and went looking for Beary. She had called his berth and Ben had said that he wasn't there. Next she checked the Gym He had his top off and his fur caught the light even more than before. He had been lifting weights. "Hi Sailor," Pompey said.

Beary turned and sat down the weights. "Hello my lady, How may I serve you?"

"No Sire, it is I who wish to serve you." She said impishly.

"Then would you favor me with a kiss?" Beary said.

"Gladly Sir Knight," with that Pompey kissed him.

Grizlarge had just walked in. "Don't be taken in by that rogue my Lady."

Pompey turned and blushed, "Too late, kind sir."

Grizlarge came over and hugged Beary. "I thought you were dead Cub."

Beary looked at him, "We almost were. But Providence was on our side."

Pompey gave the Master Chief a sly look.

"Well I have, work to do unlike some gold bricking Ensign I know." With that Grizlarge laughed and waved goodbye.

"You have been through a lot with him?" Pompey said quietly.

Beary thought, "Yeah, He has been like a second father to me, especially when tension developed between me and my father. He always set me straight even when I didn't want to listen."

"Come I will fix dinner for you." Pompey said.

"I had better shower first and get a new uniform." Beary said.

"Won't be necessary I have a shower and one of your casual uniforms. The shirt might smell a little like me but it's clean." Pompey smiled.

Beary put on his shirt and followed her to her berth.

Pompey smiled, "Go get cleaned up extra towels are inside the door. You can even lock it, if you don't trust me."

Beary smiled. "It is I, not my Lady that I do not trust." With that he went in and locked the door.

She smiled, quietly unlocked the door, and placed the clean uniform on a bench for him. She sighed and quietly closed the door.

She was fixing dinner when he came out. She smiled at him.

"The food is almost ready."

Beary smiled, "May, I ask a question?"

Pompey smiled, "Yes, my love."

"Was this uniform on the bench when I went in?" Beary asked.

Pompey frowned, "You locked the door didn't you?"

Beary shrugged, "What can I do to help?"

Pompey pointed, "Set the table if you don't mind."

Beary complied and soon they were eating and talking. After they ate Beary helped clear the table and put the dishes in the auto cleaner.

"It is getting late my Lady" Beary said.

Pompey looked at him and took him by the Paw. "Sit with me; tell me about what you saw and what happened to you. I need you to hold me, and confide in me."

Beary sat down and told her all about Andreas Prime and Gamey. They talked and soon she nuzzled into his chest.

"Please just hold me my Prince." She whispered and closed her eyes. Soon both were asleep.

The next morning Beary awoke with a start Pompey's alarm was going off. He looked down at her resting against his chest. He kissed the top of her head. "Pompey it is almost time for you to report to duty."

She rose up and kissed him, "I better get dressed for work."

"I had better go." Beary said.

"You don't have to." Pompey said.

"Yes my love I do. As the Guardian I am to protect you, even from me." With that he kissed her, and left.

Atilus was walking by when he saw Beary exit her room.

"That's not your berth Ensign."

"No sir, we fell asleep talking. I am sorry Sir." Beary said.

Atilus smiled, "It happens. The fleet took your suggestion the Grey Sword and two old Escort Destroyers are on station at the coordinates you gave them."

"I am glad. I have a feeling the Arcrilian were looking for it and that they will somehow find it." Beary responded. "Sir did my package get off to my Mother?"

Back on Bearilia Prime the young Marine Sergeant entered The Bearilian Medical Institute. He saw a young receptionist at a desk.

"Please Miss, I am Sergeant Fisher, I am carrying important items for Dr. Maxumus." Sergeant Fisher said.

The Receptionist looked up" Do you wish to see Dr. Alexa or Dr. Angelina Maxumus"

Sergeant Fisher checked his orders, "Dr. Angelina Maxumus."

The Receptionist looked at the box and old trunk he had with him. "If you wish you can just leave that stuff here and I'll see it gets to her."

"No Miss, my orders are clear I am to place these items into her paws and her paws only." Fisher said.

The Receptionist just shrugged. "Her office is on the sixth floor room 6110. Take the third elevator on the right."

Fisher nodded, "Thank you."

Fisher walked down the hall, and took the proper elevator. He looked at the numbers on the doors and moved down the hall to the left. He came to a door marked Chief of Nero—Surgery Dr. Angelina Maxumus. He opened the door.

Inside the first door was a desk and an older Kodacian was setting at the desk. The name plate said Mrs. Rebeca Maro.

"May I help you Sergeant." Rebeca said.

"Yes Mame, I am Sergeant Fisher, I need to see Dr. Maxumus" Fisher said.

"Do you have an appointment?" She asked.

"No Mrs. Maro., But I am under orders to put these in Dr. Maxumus Paws only." Sergeant Fisher said.

"Who's, orders" Rebeca said impatiently?

"Captain Atilus of the Saber Claw they are from her son Ensign Beary Maxumus. I am to guard these with my life till I give them to her." Fisher said.

Rebeca was stunned at the mention of Beary's name, "Is he alright" Rebeca asked with a shaky voice?

"He was when I left the ship Mame" Fisher said.

Angelina opened her door, "Bec is everything Okay?"

"Yes Lady Angelina this young Marine has something from Beary for you." Rebeca said.

Sergeant Fisher stared at Angelina, the light from her office window made it look like she was radiating the light like an Angel.

"Sergeant would you come in please," Angelina said with her softest voice.

Sergeant Fisher came in and saluted, "Lady Maxumus I am Sergeant Fisher. I was rescued by your son on Dryden."

Angelina smiled, "Call me Angelina, Sergeant. Now what is so important that Captain Atilus would send an armed Marine to bring me?"

Sergeant Fisher handed her the jeweled box. She took it and slowly opened it. She almost dropped the box but regained her composure "Sergeant do you know what you were guarding?"

"No Lady Angelina. I was only told to guard these with my life till I put them in your Paws." Sergeant Fisher said.

"Sergeant Fisher, was that the only reason you came to Bearilia Prime?" Angelina asked.

Sergeant Fisher dropped his head. "No, my Lady, my Father is ill they say he may die. He lives in a poor village twenty KSMU from here. The doctor there has done all he can do but can't find the cause of his illness."

"Bec come here. I want you to give Mrs. Maro your father's doctors name and your father's address Sergeant." Angelina ordered. Rebeca came in and got the information from the Sergeant. Then Angelina said. "Send an Ambulance, have Dr. Torrance go with it and bring his father and mother here. Call the High Ridge and put the Sergeant and his mother in a nice suite."

Rebeca went out and made the calls. Dr. Torrance and the ambulance rolled out in 5 STU.

Sergeant Fisher was in shock, "Lady Angelina, my parents and I can't afford the High Ridge and I know that my parents can't afford medical care here at the Institute."

Angelina picked up the phone, "Billing all medical expenses for Mr. Jubal Fisher are to be charged to me. Yes all expenses.

There that is done. Your rooms have already been placed on my account with the High Ridge Sergeant."

"Lady Maxumus you can't do this, we could never repay you." Sergeant Fisher said with tears in his voice.

"Nonsense Sergeant, this is a small gift for what you have done for my family. For me this is a debt of honor would you dishonor me by not accepting it?" Angelina said in a voice so sweet that he thought he heard singing.

"On my life, my Lady, I would never do anything to dis-honor you, your son, or your family." Sergeant Fisher said.

Angelina reached into her purse. "Here are a few Credits to help your family till we can find out what is wrong with your father."

Sergeant Fisher looked at the 12,000 Credits she gave him. "I . . . ."

"Remember your promise Sergeant. Now I need to go to work I will see you soon." Angelina said and showed him to the door.

Sergeant Fisher looked at Mrs. Maro, "Why?" He showed her the money. "This is over a year's salary for my rank."

Mrs. Maro smiled, "Sergeant Fisher, she is a Maxumus. You met her Son does this surprise you."

Sergeant Fisher thought, "Her son went into the belly of a Hive ship like he was walking into a room saved two officers and a first Sergeant that were being tortured. He did it like it was nothing more than a training exercise. That though was his duty. This?"

"Her duty is to try and fix the ill; she learned a long time ago that healing the body was sometimes not enough." Maro said.

With that the Sergeant saluted, and went to meet the ambulance and his parents.

In her office Angelina opened the box in it written on a piece of metal was this message, *"These belong to you my Empress*

Angelina Maria Maxumus Empress of Andreas Prime and the House of Caesar, Augustus and Maxumus. Gamey the Brave waits to serve you and the young prince. She looked at the blue diamond necklace with red star stones and the Crown and the ring of Andreas Prime.

She picked up the phone still shaking. "Tiberius this is Angelina please come to my office immediately."

Tiberius put down the phone and headed for the Institute.

After 15 STU he walked past Mrs. Maro who just nodded.

"My Lady, what can I do for you?" She showed him the contents of the box. Tiberius Dropped to one Knee, "My Empress."

Angelina looked at him, "Tiberius knock it off I am just Angelina."

Tiberius stood up. "No my Lady, you are not. How may your servant serve the house of Maxumus and my Empress?"

"Tiberius, take this to our home and put it in the special vault. You are not to speak to anyone about this. I will inform Octavious myself. Also please take this trunk to Octavious, I ask you." Angelina said.

"It will be done, my life on it." He said bowing. With that he left.

She picked up a secure phone, "Octavious, I have Tiberius delivering something to you. Will you meet me at home for a late lunch? 2:30 that will work. I love you."

"Rebeca have we heard from Tory?" Angelina asked.

"He thinks there may be more than one problem, He has asked for a full blood screen and a cat scan of his brain and spine. Do you want to see the patient?" Rebeca asked.

"Not just yet. Dr. Torrance is very good he doesn't need me hovering over him. He will let me know when he wants my advice." Angelina said.

Chapter 21

The Storm Hits!

On Andreas Prime Gamey the Brave pondered what he should do. He had placed the plan in the young Prince's mind but would the Bearilian Fleet believe him. If the Arcrilian's fleet was not split up there was no way the young Prince and his ship mates could survive. They just had to believe him he reached out with his mind at the very edge of the Dragons eye he felt a presence. It had to be a Bearilian Warship. Okay then he would do it and pray to the Creator of the Universe that he was right.

The Arcrilian Admiral was furious; His Captains had failed to find the jump ship. Two had died because of his wrath. He had scout ships searching for the Dragons eye all had come back with negative reports. To top that off the troop transports had been delayed while their escorts chased a ghost signal.

He stared out into space. Then he saw it clear as could be the Dragons Eye the back door into the Carnise Drift. A brilliant plan formed He would split his force He would take half through the eye and send the transports and the other half to launch a frontal attack. He called in his Commanders.

On board the BAF Grey Sword, an old Bearilian Battle Cruiser, Commodore Dansong, looked at his small fleet all were ready to be retired, including him. If the intelligence was right he and his crews would have a fine time and retire with honor if not, it would not be the first wild goose he had chased.

"Mr. Sang please bring the fleet to red alert charge all weapons bring the main rail guns on line if you please." The Commodore said.

"Yes Sir all ship report ready." Lieutenant Sang replied.

"Please inform the Captains we have 1 and only 1STU to do maximum damage, before their ship can regain weapons and shields." The Commodore instructed.

On the Antillean Destroyer Death stinger, the Black swarm commander, Colonel Dantic and Major Tan Wu and Captain Redantic looked at a map of the Palisades Drift.

Captain Redantic spoke "It will be hard to let the main warships pass us but our job is the transports. If by some chance they are not heading to Bearilian Space It will be good to kill them here, there are twelve transports and four small escorts. Do not underestimate the escorts or the transports themselves they are armed."

Major Tan Wu spoke up, "Sir my Green Dagger is equipped with sensors that can determine the frequency of the enemy shields and feed it to shield emitters in our missiles which allow them a chance to pass through."

Dantic smiled, "Are you carrying the Mark 3 or the Mark 4 Death hawk missiles?"

Major Tan Wu smiled, "We Just upgraded to the Mark 4."

Dantic's mandibles grinned even wider. "So did we, can you feed my fighters the frequencies as well?"

"Not a problem." He replied

Captain Redantic smiled, Bearilians were good creatures.

"I will allow you two to work out your attacks on the transports. I will handle the escorts."

On board the Saber Claw another meeting was being held.

Colonel Bantic arrived. "Captain Atilus, I place my swarm under your command."

"Thank you Colonel. I believe you have met most of my staff. It is my intent to place one Blue dagger with each fighter group. Ours will go with the Death Swarm. Colonel Rames one of yours will accompany the Green Dragons. The Third will remain with you if that is okay?"

"Helmet would be a good choice. That crew has been exercising with the Green Dragons." Rames replied.

"Good now if we can proceed. Colonel Rames you are in command of the Drift and its defenses The Green Dragons and the Death swarm will launch hit and run attacks to try and Draw off the destroyers. The Saber Claw will Attack the Heavies. If it is possible we will then fall back to this area in front of the Drift and try to draw the Arcrilian's ships into Coronal Rames's kill zones. If for any reason one of your Commands cannot return to this area escape into Antillean or Bearilian space and join up with those fleet units." After more discussion Atilus ended with, "We are a thin line drawn in space the Arcrilian's must not pass. Thank you; please return to your Commands."

Centaures looked at him, "Well?"

Atilus looked at his friend "You should, have accepted your own ship."

Centaures smiled, "Never wanted one. Captains have to be respectable First officers don't."

"Alright put all Daggers on alert were moving away from the Drift. Atilus said.

Centaures went to the com. "Red Alert set condition one all Dagger crews report to the hanger deck and stand by."

The Saber Claw came alive.

Pompey saw Beary, and stopped him "Just a kiss for luck." with that she kissed him.

Beary smiled, "Stay safe my love." with that both raced to their duty stations.

Artemus was already at the Crimson blade the Crew Chief and his crew had kept their promise she looked good as new, If not better. Ben arrived about the same time as Beary.

Artemus laughed, "Take a detour like you did last night."

"What?" Beary asked.

"Ben told me you didn't come home last night and your wearing lip stick." Artemus said.

Ben looked sheepish, as Beary looked at him, "She fell asleep on my chest while we were talking I couldn't just wake her."

Artemus shook his head, "You are a great warrior Beary Maxumus and a great pilot, but you know nothing about females.

Ben it must be the truth. His kind can't lie."

Ben smiled, "It is true. Females are tricky."

Beary shook his head, "Alright let's get to work, Com and weapons check."

Ben checked his systems, "I have green on all communication systems."

Artemus checked his board, "I have a red light on missile number 4, launcher 1, and a red light on missile 16, launcher 2."

"Have them pulled and replaced." Beary said.

The Armors were listening to the conversation and immediately sprang into action.

Artemus watched as the missile board went all green.

"Weapons are now all green, Boss."

Sergeant MacIntosh stuck his head in, "Bad arming switches, missiles were replaced."

"Thank you Crew Chief. Tell the Armors thank you." Beary said.

"Command and Control systems are green. Preliminary checks complete." Beary said report to Control.

Ben stopped "I do not have a call sign."

"Spirit 6, to control I am requesting call sign Lieutenant 3rd Maritinus, as Slayer 3."

"Control to Spirit 6 Command suggests Slayer 1."

"Understood, Slayer 1 confirmed, Spirit 6 out."

Ben smiled, "Control, Slayer 1 Crimson Blade all systems checked."

Beary shut down the systems and looked at his crew. "Let's go get some food and Drink and talk with the other crews."

Dusk 1 came over "Ensign Maxumus, I want you to take your, section to the left side of the Saber Claw. Ruby will fly cover for me. Scarlet and Flame will take the right."

Beary looked at him, "No problem."

On Bearilia Prime at the home of The Maxumus Clan

Octavious followed Angelina down to the Special vault. "These came by armed messenger from Beary." Angelina showed him the Box and the note.

Octavious looked at the note and the crown and necklace, "So Gamey the Brave lives and the home worlds are livable. What is your wish my Empress." He winked.

Angelina smiled then her face changed, "I don't want this. Our home is here."

"Yes, but Beary's is not he may wish to return to Andreas Prime. Others might also. We would only have to open up the house as a vacation residents. The other is your duty and responsibility." Octavious said. "You want me to check it out."

"Not, now it's in the middle of a war zone." Angelina said. "What did Beary send you?"

"The trunk was filled with family history and papers, including the Book. It will take some time to look through it all." Octavious said.

The Arcrilian Admiral split his forces he would take his flagship 1 other Battle cruiser and 4 Heavy Cruisers and six destroyers and 1 Fighter carrier.

The other task force followed by the twelve troop transports and its four escorts. This task force would be commanded by Vice Admiral Locatus: two Battle Cruisers, 4 Heavies, and 6 Destroyers, and 2 Fighter Carriers.

They discussed their plans. "I will have heavy cruiser Bringer of Death lead the way. Then I will follow with the Harvesters Pride. The other ships will follow in staggered formation." The Admiral said.

"Then we will catch them in a vice and destroy them." Vice Admiral Locatus said. "The troop ship will follow 1 Cycle behind my section.

"Good let us go." The Arcrilian Admiral said with glee.

On the Grey Sword, Commodore Dansong smiled as he saw the first hint of the forming of a worm hole. "Mr. Sang tell the Captains to fire as soon as they have targets then pour it to them." Dansong said.

"Ay, Commodore all ships are ready." Mr. Sang reported.

The Arcrilian Heavy Cruiser Bringer of Death began emerging from the worm hole.

"Fire" Commodore Dansong whispered.

The first shells started exploding as the nose of the Cruiser started through. The Captain of the Bringer of Death was screaming to reverse Course but the worm hole only went one way its tidal forces pushed the cruiser out. Missiles and rail gun shells ripped the cruiser apart then it exploded.

The Harvesters pride came through next. The Admiral started to yell an order when a 1 SMU rail gun shell ripped through his Command post. He was sucked into the darkness of space. Soon the Battle cruiser was ripped apart.

Each ship fell one at a time. Till the fighter Carrier was the last to come through. The Carrier tried to launch the fighters. Several fighters got out but their weapons and shield did not work.

In less than 1 STU the Carrier and all its fighters were dead and had turned into space junk.

Commodore Dansong smiled, this is a good victory for a tired old ship. "Mr. Sang please tell our Captains Congratulations. Send the message to fleet Happy Days."

"Com. to Captain Atilus, Fleet sends happy days"

Atilus looked at Centaures, "Our young Ensign must be a mind reader."

"No he is just a good tactician." Centaures smiled.

On board the Green Dagger Gauntlet Major Tan Wu smiled, the message happy days was received. Com, inform Captain Redantic and Colonel Dantic we have received confirmation of happy days.

Redantic reminded both commanders that there job was still the transports. Yet as the Heavy cruisers, Battle cruisers, six destroyers, and Carriers passed, his hiding place in the Palisades Drift, he wanted to hit them. Again he reminded himself that twelve Transports and four escorts were going to be a hard nut in itself.

"Inform the Blue Dragon they have 2 Battle Cruisers, 4 Heavy Cruisers, 6 Destroyers, and 2 Carriers heading towards them. Tell them good hunting and may the Creator give us all victory." Redantic said

Admiral Starpaw was on the new Battle Cruiser Broad Sword. "Well, the old Grey Sword Drew first blood good it's fitting for the old warrior to end its service with a great victory."

Captain Berserker looked at the Admiral, "Sir shouldn't we move up to help the Saber Claw. After all our force is ready."

The Admiral shook his head. "The Saber Claw is on its own. I am sure there is another fleet out there. The council of 8 was expecting more than just one fleet. We have to wait for the second wave."

"Sir I don't like it. Atilus is my friend. I feel I am deserting him." The Captain said.

The Admiral looked at him, "Do you think I like it? No, I don't that ship has done the work of an entire fleet. Yet, I have to follow my gut. Can you understand Captain? This is my call my responsibility."

Berserker looked at the Admiral, "Yes Sir, I understand."

Atilus looked at the report from the Death stinger. "Commander Centaures call battle stations inform Col. Bantic, launch the Daggers."

Centaures hit the com. "Battle stations, battle stations this is not a drill. Dagger crews to your ships expedite launch Creators speed and blessings."

He turned to Pompey, "Please inform the Green Dragons and the Death Swarm."

Pompey pressed the com, and sent a predetermined code, "Good Hunting."

Captain Northern signaled his wing. Then gave thumbs up to Colonel Bantic. The Bearilian fighters were not as elegant as the wasp II but they were sturdy and could take a lot of damage. Now came the hard part waiting.

The Helmet was scanning for the Arcrilian's he was protected by both a Green Dragon and Death Swarm Fighter. Four cycles latter the pips started to appear he started recording the shield frequencies this information he gave a target designation and fed it to the fighters.

On the Saber Claw Atilus's small formation of destroyer and daggers swung around Tarsus Twelve. Helm, bring us up to attack speed take us in Mr. Darkclaw Weapons control line up on the trailing Destroyer. Tally ho!"

The Daggers were the first to launch from their cloaked position. Each dagger launched ten Mark 4 Missiles at the trailing Destroyer.

On the Destroyer Torturer the Weapons officer picked up the incoming missiles "We are under attack." He activated his defense Systems.

Fifty missiles were streaking in the anti-missile guns and missiles picked off 25 of the incoming missiles the Shield stopped ten more despite the shield emitters on the missiles. Still fifteen slammed home. Four damaged the warp engines and started a fire in Engineering the others hit the outer spaces. Three of his anti-missile launchers were knocked out. Still the damage was considered minor.

The Arcrilian Captain turned into the attack. That's when he saw the Saber claw rushing in. He launched forty missiles and fired his main gun.

The Saber Claws Defensive systems intercepted twenty of the incoming missiles the other twenty struck the shield and exploded. Still the shields held. The Arcrilians main Gun plasma shell exploded on the front shield its efficiency Dropped to 70 %.

Atilus ordered return fire; ninety missiles and four rail gun rounds went down range as the phasers fired.

The Arcrilian Destroyers front shield began to fail from the onslaught. Forty of the incoming missiles were stopped but fifty struck the front weapons array ripping apart the main gun the phasers tore into the other smaller weapon stations the four rail gun slugs ripped into the hull below the Bridge. One smashed all the way to auxiliary control killing all the Arcrilian's stationed there, the others exploded in storage and computer spaces.

The Arcrilian captain launched thirty more missiles as the Saber Claw past down its port side.

On the Saber Claw Atilus braised for the impacts and ordered the launch of sixty missiles. The automatic defense system picked up fifteen of the Arcrilian missiles and exploded them fourteen were stopped by the shield but one punched through and exploded against the armor plating. The explosion ripped a small hole in one of the storage compartments. Damage control robots went to work to seal and shore up the damaged section.

The Arcrilian wasn't as lucky all sixty of the Saber Claws missiles struck. Ripping apart the warp Drive and sub light engines. The structural integrity of the ship was starting to fail. The warp core went critical and the Arcrilian Destroyer disintegrated.

On the Arcrilian Battle Cruiser Harvesters Reward he heard the call of an attack on his trailing destroyer He ordered two more destroyers, to peel off, secure the rear, and to destroy the attacking ship. He then increased the speed of the other heavy warships.

The Carriers were already maxed out on their sub light engines as the gap increased the two carriers came abreast of each other.

Dantic and Northern saw their chance and launched their attack on the closes carrier. Thanks to Helmet they had their Mark 4 shield emitters dialed in. The two fighter groups launched simultaneously. Over 288 mark 4 missiles launch against the nearest carrier.

On the Arcrilian Carrier Deaths Wings the Captain heard the warning klaxon. Before he could react the missiles struck. The first wave of 144 missiles past through his shields and exploded in his hanger and launch bays. Fighters and weapons started exploding adding to the carnage. The second wave smashed into the engineering spaces ripping out his sub light engines and his warp Drive. Somewhere deep inside the carrier the weapons storage area started cooking off. The explosions began a cascading effect splitting the Death Wing apart. The Captain died before he could react.

The Captain of Death Song turned away and launched his 100 fighters.

Bantic called Northern "Captain we will take on the fighters you get the Carrier, Safe wings."

"Understood Colonel Safe wings, Green Dragons attack formation delta 4. Tally Ho." Northern called out.

Helmet feed as much information as it could to the fighters.

The Death Swarm dived into the Arcrilian Fighters. Missiles and phasers slashed through space as a fur fight rolled through space.

Twenty Arcrilian fighters broke off and headed for the Green Dragons. 3rd Squadron turned and met them head on.

The other three Squadrons attacked the Death Song. 96 missiles were launched.

The Death songs defenses picked off thirty of the missiles but much to the Captain's surprise his shields had no effect. 66 missiles slammed into his hangers and weapons stations and engine spaces. Luckily all his fighters were off the ship yet carelessly secured weapons were set off. He was losing power. He tried to turn his ship into his attackers but the ship was sluggish. 48 more missiles slammed into the Death Song this time it was the bridge that was slammed into. The Captain and his ship died at the same time.

The Green Dragons turned back to the fight. 3rd Squadron had lost four Fighters but had destroyed twenty of the enemy.

The Death Swarm was fairing about the same the fight had been fast and deadly 25 of the death swarms fighters had been destroyed. But they had destroyed eighty of the enemy.

Helmet was trying to find and pick up survivors. Three Bearilian and fifteen Antillean pilots were recovered.

The two fighter groups headed for the rendezvous point.

Both Colonel Bantic and Captain Northern counted their losses.

For the Bearilians one confirmed dead four fighters destroyed. The Death Swarm had lost ten dead and 25 fighters lost. The Arcrilians had lost two Carriers and 200 fighters.

The Saber Claw was in a slugging match with two Destroyers. The Ruby dagger had taken a near miss that tore one of her nacelles off.

The Crimson Blade was down to twelve missiles when he saw one of the Destroyers open up its hanger bay.

Beary turned to Artemus, "Time to see how good a shot you are."

Artemus looked at Beary, "You're not Planning? Oh H . . . . go for it"

Ben looked wide eyed as Beary accelerated for the opening Shuttle bay door of the Arcrilian Destroyer.

An Armed Shuttle was exiting as The Crimson Blade was entering. Artemus split it open with the Gatling phased.

Beary fired ten missiles straight down the hanger bay as Artemus cut loose with the phaser.

Beary turned the Crimson Blade around and started exiting the Shuttle Bay doors just as they started to close. Artemus launched two more missiles, blowing the doors out into space. The Crimson Blade shuttered as its rear shield was hit by a phaser from the rear of the Destroyer Artemus returned fire as they cloaked.

The ten missiles buried themselves deep into the interior of the Destroyer. One slammed into the engine core, which started it to go critical. The engine room crew was killed when the missile went off.

All of a sudden the plasma containment system failed. The Destroyer turned blue then denigrated.

On the Saber Claw Atilus ordered a turn into the second Destroyer. "Fire all weapons!" Four rail gun shells, six phasers, and sixty missiles leaped out at the enemy Destroyer.

The Arcrilian responded with his remaining weapons. Both ships shuttered with the impacts of the weapons.

The Saber Claws shields were on the verge of failing as it passed down the side of the Arcrilian Destroyer.

The forward attack had smashed the Arcrilian destroyer the Captain died when two rail gun shells ripped through his bridge. The Arcrilian destroyer started drifting its shields were down. Its engines smashed.

The Saber Claw limped to the rendezvous point. Soon they started the recovery operation of the Daggers. The Ruby Dagger was tractor beamed in. Then the others started landing, the Crimson Blade was the last to land.

Dusk 1 ran over, "What was that stunt you pulled!"

Beary shrugged, "I saw an opportunity and took it. Our job is to take pressure off the Saber Claw. We were all almost out of missiles these Arcrilian Captains were smart they cycled their shield frequencies. Only a fraction of our missiles were scoring hits plus we were busy fighting their attack shuttles. I saw a chance and took it."

Dusk 1 realized, Beary had thought it out. "Just don't go and get yourself killed."

Medics pulled a marine Sergeant out of Ruby Dagger. Ruby 1 stepped out shaking "We got boarded. He killed three troopers after they wounded him. He is hurt bad. I didn't even get his name when he reported."

Beary, put a paw on the pilots shoulder, "He knew the risk it was his job."

The Crew Chiefs immediately started servicing and rearming the Daggers.

Atilus sat down, just as all sections began reporting in. The ship had sustained damage, most of it was considered minor, but some systems were off line. The repairs, it was estimated, would be completed in about four cycles. Medical reported that there were sixteen injured two of which were critical.

At Palisades Drift, the troop transports were coming into range. The escorts were in a diamond formation around the transports. The transports were in a two-four—four—two formation.

Redantic's plan was simple; hit the end of the column, where the transports had no defenses, roll them up and try to scatter the formation. He gave the order to attack as the last escort passed by.

The first escort never knew what hit him thirty missiles and five rail gun shells ripped the small attack craft apart.

The Dark Swarm hit the right transport from the rear its engines failed as did its shields. The skin of the ship was ripped open and Arcrilian troopers were pulled into the darkness of space. In a Blink of an eye the first transport died.

The right rear transport tried to turn away and ran into 75 missiles. The bridge was obliterated as was its steering control. The transport shot past the daggers and plowed head long into an asteroid the daggers of the 308th Knights concentrated next on the center right transport of the next group while the swarm launched against the center left.

The two side escorts were slow to react so the Death Stinger fired on the left outer transport. Its plasma pules cannon over whelmed the shields and smashed into the hull of the transport then its missiles arrived soon the transport was torn in half.

The Knights launched 20 missiles at the center right transport. Its Captain panicked, when he saw the outer left transport explode and the one next to him taking hits. So he turned to port. Just then the missiles arrived and the collision alarm went off. The two right transports had turned into each other. Then the missiles arrived both ships died in a flash of blue, as the plasma containment fields failed.

The three escorts formed up and raced to the back of the column as they had the transports scatter. Of 12,000 elite troopers 6000 had died without knowing what had happened.

Redantic contacted his forces, "They are splitting up help take out the escorts, and we will chase them down."

The Gauntlet had his forces fire on the left escort as it cleared the debris field ninety missiles leapt from their launchers.

The escorts automated defense system stopped twenty but a small fast frigate wasn't designed to take this much punishment especially with its shields ineffective, it simple denigrated under the force of 70 missiles. The other two died a similar fate.

One Dark Swarm fighter was damaged and its pilot ejected his escape capsule was picked up by the Red Knight which transferred him to the Death stinger. Now the chase was on the transports had scattered. The Wasp II fighters and Daggers took turns landing on the Death stinger to rearm. As they, chased after the fleeing six transports.

Vice Admiral Locatus was approaching the Carnise Drift He was starting to worry He had lost contact with the two destroyers he had sent back and the carriers. Now His Communications officer reported garbled reports that the troop transports were under attack. That and he had not heard from the task force that went through the Dragons eye. Yet his sensors said that the Drift had already been attacked. He made a decision he would send the other Battle Cruiser back with two Heavy cruisers and a Destroyer to find the Transports. The Harvesters Option and two Heavy cruisers dropped back and turned around. The destroyer followed in their wake.

The Saber Claw was heading at best possible speed back to Carnise Drift while servicing the Green Dragon and Death Swarm Fighters. The wounded had been transferred to sick bay.

Artemus saw, Flight Lieutenant Juristic and went over to him. "Safe wings and good Crops my friend."

Juristic smiled, "I heard mummers that you were dead. I am pleased they are not true."

"We had a close shave but we made it. How are you?" Artemus asked.

Juristic shrugged, "Still alive. Ten of our Swarm and one of your pilots are not. We lost 25 Fighters but the Helmet picked fifteen of our pilots up. Four of your fighters were destroyed, but three pilots were rescued."

Artemus said, "I am sorry for your losses."

Juristic said, "It is a soldier's risk we all take. I am afraid more will die before this day is out."

The Crew Chief interrupted them "Sorry Sirs, but your fighter is ready, Flight Lieutenant."

Juristic nodded, "Safe wings my friend."

Artemus replied, "And a bountiful Harvest."

With that Juristic sprang to his fighter and took off.

For as hectic as it was the flight deck crew had serviced and reloaded one hundred and fifteen fighters in less than two cycles.

"Bridge, this is tracking, we have two transports in bound no escorts."

Atilus ordered, "Launch Daggers. Have them and the Swarm hold back in case support arrives. This will be an echo attack plan."

The Saber Claw accelerated to attack speed and launched seventy two missiles against each transport the missiles were equipped with miniature cloaking devises instead of shield emitters, making the missiles invisible till they struck the shields.

In both case the Arcrilian Shields were able to absorb half of the missiles as they struck a single point in the shield but was unable to absorb more than that and 36 slammed into both of the transports. The missiles were set to explode at different depths of the ship on the first transport one punched through and detonated on the other side. The others rippled through the transport exploding and ripping the ship in half.

The second transport took the hits in the front of the ship destroying the bridge and the weapons storage area which pealed open the transport from front to back.

The Arcrilian destroyer had been dispatched to round up these two transports when he saw them explode. The Arcrilian Captain flew into a rage and charged head on toward the Saber Claw. He never heard the warnings from his staff about the fighters.

259 missiles were launch from the red daggers and the fighters, at close range. The automatic defense system beat fifty before being overwhelmed. Sixty missiles destroyed the main gun and the areas around it. Others slammed into the warp nacelles and the weapon systems the Arcrilian Destroyer was burning.

Its Captain was thrown against a bulk head as equipment fell around him. His bridge crew was dead. He opened a passage way and made it to an escape pod and left the ship. From the escape pod he watched his ship die.

He waited till the Bearilian Forces left the area and he headed for Arcrilian space.

The Arcrilian Commodore in charge of the Harvesters Option was getting irritated he had picked up two of the transport on long range scan and had sent a Destroyer after them now he hadn't heard from any of them. He had the two Heavy Cruisers fan out to try and pick up the other transports.

The Death Stinger and its task force had caught up with two more of the transports and destroyed them. Without anyone knowing two of the Transport Captains had lost their nerve, and return to Arcrilian Space as fast as their ships could travel.

The Troop transports were now out of the picture.

The Death Stinger and the Saber Claw joined up at point Delta. The Dark Swarm, the Death Swarm, the Green Dragons, and Daggers now gave them a sizable task force. Everyone was rearmed.

Midnight dagger and Scarlet Dagger and Black Knight dagger were out front of the formation when they picked up an Arcrilian Battle cruiser. Heading in their direction Dusk 3 started recording the shield frequency; he also launched a jamming buoy toward the Arcrilian Battle Cruiser to jam its sensors and Communications.

Atilus conferred with Redantic and Major Tan Wu and Colonels Bantic and Dantic. "I want to hold the two swarms in reserve and hit them with the Daggers. Major Tan Wu you and Gauntlet will lead the attack fire from cloaked concealment Hit them with everything you got then leave. Then The Saber Claw and Death Stinger will charge in. I want the Swarms to watch our back he should not be alone."

Atilus continued, "I am down one Dagger Ruby will be out of action for a while. That leaves me with four plus your seven.

That should give you a descent attack group."

Major Tan Wu smiled, "Eleven is my lucky number. We will hurt her for you."

Back at Carnise Drift Vice Admiral Locatus was marveling at the damage he could see. It was apparent the Drift had been destroyed and he had to catch up with the other task force.

"Com, try and contact the fleet!" Locatus ordered.

"Yes Sir," the com officer responded, "Sir the weapons they used to destroy the Drift have created a radiation belt the interference is to great we cannot get a signal out.

Colonel Rames smiled from his command post the suggestion from the Captain from the of the 3rd of the 266th to camouflage the Drifts and to put out destroyed decoyed guns in placements and even sending out a fake signal mimicking the effects of radiation was working.

The Arcrilian warships were floundering waiting for their Commander to decide his next move. One of the destroyers launched his four fighters to find a good route through the Drift. The Flight Commander took them farther down the Drift and turned through one of the small passages.

The flight leader was following his three other fighters.

All of sudden searcher mines launched from the surface of two of the asteroids. Two attached to the cockpit of the first fighter and exploded. The Second Fighter spun into an Asteroid when its engine section was damaged by three mines. The third was disintegrated when five mines attached to its structure.

The Flight Commander had one attach to his weapons package, which he jettisoned, before it exploded. The explosion tore at his fighter. He brought his damaged fighter back to the destroyer.

The Flight Commander reported the mines and the loss of three of his four ships, to the Destroyer Captain.

The Destroyer Captain tried to report the incident to the Harvesters Reward, but couldn't get through the interference. Then he though the main fleet would not have tried to clear all the mines they just swept through.

On the Drift Rames kept his bears quiet his plan was working he just needed to draw them in closer.

The Red daggers formed up on the Green Dagger. Major Tan Wu put five red daggers on either side of his ship. He had maneuvered his ships to form a semicircle in front of the

Arcrilian's Battle Cruiser. He continuously feed the daggers the shield frequency of the Arcrilian's Battle Cruiser.

When the Battle Cruiser was within 120 SMU, Major Tan Wu gave the signal, 660 missiles were launched from the Daggers at point blank range and emerged from the cover of the cloaking devises less than 100 SMU from the Harvesters Option. The missiles covered the distance in less than 2.5 SUBTU. The Arcrilian automated defense system managed to intercept thirty of the missiles before they started exploding. Another 150 were defeated by the Arcrilian shields, but 480 slammed into the Battle Cruiser. The Armor plating stopped another 200 but still more barreled through. The remaining 280 missiles started doing damage. The main gun was destroyed. As were the forward missile launchers and the phaser control room. Fires were breaking out and several decks were depressurized and had to be sealed off.

The Commodore was bleeding from several wounds caused when part of the ceiling on the bridge collapsed. He was carried to auxiliary control. His Communication Officer was desperately calling for help but all her frequencies were being jammed.

He ordered the launch of his eight fighters. As soon as they cleared the launch bay they started exploding. One was hit and crashed back into the ship causing more damage. The shields were failing. It was at this point the Saber Claw and Death Stinger launched their attack. The Death Stinger fired its plasma cannon and rail guns, which buckled the shield and smashed the Armor plating above the bridge, ripping a hole in the ship. Killing the ship's Captain and the remainder of the Bridge crew. The rail gun shells ripped deeper into the ship hitting the weapon lockers, which exploded. It was obvious to the first officer that the ship was doomed. He ordered the Commodore loaded into escape pod and had it launched.

Captain Atilus didn't waste any missiles he just poured rail gun shells and phaser fire into the Harvesters Option. The rail gun shells ripped through the warp engines and the sub light engines the phaser fire hit the engine room destroying most of its systems. The Engineer saw the plasma core was failing and dumped it in to space it floated away and exploded causing more damage to the Harvesters Option but the explosion also affected three of the Daggers.

On board the, Green Knight, Blood, and White Knight Daggers, several systems were knocked off line. The Blood dagger developed a slow leak in its hull and had to return to the Saber Claw. It was followed by two damaged Knight Daggers.

The Saber Claw called off the attack and the task force resumed its coarse back to the Drift.

The few survivors of the Harvesters Option manned escape pods and departed the dying ship. Six cycles later, one of the Arcrilian Heavy Cruisers, came along. They found the derelict ship and recovered 68 of her crew alive. The Commodore was found in his escape pod and brought in. The Arcrilian medics raced to his side, as he asked his last question, "How?"

The Arcrilian Heavy Cruiser moved away from the area towards the last known location of the troop transports.

The other Arcrilian heavy cruiser came upon two of the shattered troop transports that the Death Stinger had tracked down. Its Captain continued away from the Drift trying to locate any survivors.

Vice Admiral Locatus decided he couldn't wait any longer and started moving. He had his two remaining destroyers lead off followed by the two remaining Heavy Cruisers. The Harvesters Reward held back.

The Destroyers ran into the first mine fields. The Destroyers' shield deflected the energy from each of the mines. But each explosion had an effect on their shields. It wasn't long before their shields were on the verge of failure. One turned down the right passage. The other followed the left. The Destroyers passed deeper and deeper into the Drift.

The two Heavy Cruisers also entered the Drift. The Drift left little room for the big ships to maneuver. The Battle Cruiser held back.

Remas was smiling now he wanted the Battle Cruiser but he was happy to settle for the other four ships. The 266th waited two plasma Cannons and one Gatling rail gun was lined up on one Heavy Cruiser. Two Gatling rail guns and plasma cannon were aimed at the other.

The Guns of the 308th Knights lined up on the Destroyers. The Jump ships were being held in reserve.

Colonel Remas decided not to wait any longer. "All stations fire." The Destroyers all of a sudden were smashed by missiles and Phasers and rail gun. The Destroyers shields failed the phasers and rail guns and missiles ripped open the destroyers they couldn't react due to the closeness of the asteroids.

The Heavy Cruisers came under fire from the plasma cannons as the Gatling rail guns ripped at the shields. Then came the missiles the heavy cruisers had been maneuvered into a closed in channel between asteroid and couldn't turn their main guns on any targets So they did the only thing they thought they could do they beamed Troopers on to a few of the Asteroids to destroy the attacking weapons. They were met by the ground forces of the 308th knights. The Knights were specifically trained to fight in this environment. The Arcrilian's troopers were not as well trainer in this environment.

The Fighting was fast and deadly thirty Arcrilian troopers were killed while eight Bearilian Marines were killed and five were injured.

It didn't take long before all the asteroids were cleared.

The Arcrilian ships were dead. On the Harvesters Reward Vice Admiral Locatus hesitated his task force was destroyed or missing. He started to prepare to launch an attack. When the Jump ships of the Knights launched their attack, 384 missiles were rippled launched at the Harvesters Reward.

The Arcrilian ship managed to knock down 200 of the incoming missiles still 184 burned through. These missiles impacted on the outer part of the warp and sub light engines. The Battle Cruiser still managed to fire its main gun which destroyed two of the remote missile launchers. The smaller weapons destroyed a manned phaser location.

The Saber Claw and Death Stinger arrived just as the fire fight started. The two destroyers launched 584 missiles and ten rail gun shells into the Harvesters Reward. The automatic defenses knocked down eighty missiles but 504 missiles exploded destroying the main gun and several other weapon systems. The rail gun shells burst through the enemy ship tearing apart the center part of the ship. The Guns on the Drift also fired ripping through the bridge and auxiliary control. Soon the Harvesters Reward came apart.

All of a sudden the fighting was over; casualties on the Drift had been relatively light. Fifteen Bearilian Marines dead and 37 injured.

The Death Swarm had lost ten and the Green Dragons one pilot.

The Arcrilian's had lost ten troop transports, twelve destroyers, six heavy Cruisers, three Carriers, and four Battle Cruisers. The enemy at least for now had been stopped.

Around the rouge planet Tarantian a small planet setting between Tarsus and Antillean space two hive ships and their escorts waited for the signal to invade.

A small craft inside Bearilian space transmitted a no go signal. The Bearilian Traitor informed the Arcrilian's of the complete loss of the first wave of attack ships. Then ceased transmission and headed back to Bearilia.

Tiberius had stationed himself in the Tarsus system and picked up the Transmission but was unable to pick up its source but he did locate the Arcrilian fleet and some of their new orders. This information he transmitted to Admiral Starpaw, "Scarecrow to Winged Dragon Priority alert."

"Scarecrow this is Wing Dragon Go."

"Arcrilian's not moving on Carnise Drift. They were warned off by BT. They, are formed up at point Delta/Foxtrot, and plan to move on friendlies at Romeo/ X-ray. Scarecrow out"

Starpaw pounded his seat. "Com, inform Antillean Command of attack on Romeo/ X-ray from Delta/ Foxtrot. Captain Berserker please have Commodore Son Wang Take his destroyer Squadron and relieve the Saber Claw tell the Commodore to issue order 98-3A. All other ships are to form up on us and head for Romeo/Foxtrot at maximum speed."

The Saber claw had redistributed her available weapons. Captain Atilus shook his head, "We have enough for one good pass. We do still have twelve Photon Torpedoes left. Thanks to the marines we have twenty rail gun rounds and the four missile launchers are full. Our phasers are still good, but that would not be a slugging match I want to get into."

Centaures said, "The Death Stinger is in the same situation. The Fighter Wing and Swarms are good for one sortie. After that they and our daggers are down to guns. Fighter on fighter would be one thing but against ships not so good."

"Captain, we are picking up a formation of ships coming up the back of the Drift!" a young ensign on the long range scanners reported.

Atilus looked, "Battle stations. Inform Colonel Rames and Captain Redantic and the Swarms."

"Sapphire Dragon to Blue Dragon we are approaching your location from vector 180 Mark 6."

"Blue Dragon to Sapphire Dragon Authenticate GGW"

"Blue Dragon we Authenticate ZZG."

"Sapphire Dragon Welcome to Carnise Drift"

The New Heavy cruiser pulled alongside the Saber Claw . Commodore Son Wang beamed over, Captain Atilus saluted.

"Sir it is good to see you and your little friends."

Son Wang smiled, "Sorry we were delayed could you have the Various Commanders meet with me in your wardroom."

Atilus nodded, "Yes Sir, and nodded at the Com officer, this way Sir."

In a short time Colonels Bantic, Dantic and Rames joined Captain Redantic in Captain Atilus's wardroom Centaures was in his usual place.

Commodore Son Wang smiled, "My friends you are relieved. As we speak the Arcrilian's are being met by the combined fleets of the Antillean's and Bearilian Federation near Tarantian. Your stand here forced them to give up their attack on the Bearilian home worlds. They then decided to attack Antilia Prime. The Antillean Fleets along with our main Battle fleet were placed into intercept points.

To our Antillean Friends I hope you will accept these battle flags for your units for the defense of the Carnise Drift. Also if there is anything we can do for the families of the warriors you lost please tell us, also Colonels Bantic, Dantic, and Captain Redantic if you would accept the Star of Tarsus, as a symbol of your courage and that of your Swarms and Crews.

"Commodore, we are honored by your recognition of our efforts, as for those we lost we will inform their families of your willingness to give them whatever aid they may require. The Saber Claw and its crew though were instrumental in our combined victory." Bantic replied

The Commodore smiled, "Thank you for reminding me Colonel Bantic. The Saber Claw is to return to space dock for retrofit as a Command Destroyer. It and its crew have also been awarded the Carnise Defense Flag as has the Green Dragon II Wing and the 308th and the 266th that were here. As well as any members of the 307th that was still on board. Captain Atilus is to be promoted to Commodore and given command of Destroyer Squadron 9. Commander Centaures is to be promoted to Captain and given the Saber Claw. Since we don't have another Cruiser to give you we thought you would prefer to have the Saber Claw as your Command ship Atilus."

Atilus was shocked, "Yes Sir."

The Commodore nodded, "Centaures we will give you a list of officers who are eligible to become First Officers. Also your Crew is to be given a three month shore leave during retro fit. That will give both of you a chance to fill out your command sections."

Off point Romeo/ x ray, just a map coordinates in space, the three fleets converged. When the battle was over the Arcrilian's had lost both hive ships and several capital ships and ten Destroyers. The rest retreated back into Arcrilian's Space.

The Bearilians lost two destroyers and a damaged heavy Cruiser and half a Wing of fighters. The Antilleans' lost 3 heavy Cruisers and a portion of a swarm. Still it was a great victory.

Of the five known Hive ships three had been destroyed. The Arcrilian's would not be able to launch another attack for several years. They also now knew that Bearilian and Antillean Space would be defended. The cost might be too great to attack this coalition of Territories.

Goodbyes were said the 266th and 308th. These units returned to their base on Darius II. The Green Dragon II wing and its carrier were also returned to their base.

The Death Stinger headed home with the Dark Swarm and most of the Death Swarm.

Colonel Bantic and Flight Lieutenant Juristic stayed behind. "So it is now Commodore Atilus. It has been an honor to serve with your ship. I hope we may work together again or at least meet again under pleasant circumstances."

"I would also like that. Thank you for all your Swarm did for us. Would you join me in a glass of nectar?" Atilus asked.

While they talked Juristic went to find Artemus. He found him working on the Crimson Blade.

"I guess she will be yours when Ensign Maxumus leaves the Saber Claw." Juristic said.

Artemus looked at him, "I don't know I am a gunner not a pilot. They will probably just find another flier. It will be hard to find one better than the Boss though. Hay I am done here would you let me buy you some food and a drink."

Juristic shook his head. "No this time I will buy you food and drink."

Artemus smiled, "Alright."

Ben came into their berth smiling. "We are being given three months off before we return to the Academy. You two will join me and Artemus and the Chief for a celebration with my Tribe will you not?"

Beary looked at him, "I will try. I have to meet Pompey's family and prepare for the wedding she does not want to wait. You will stand with me and Caesar as escorts will you not I plan to ask Savato also.

Ben smiled, "You honor me. Pompey is invited to the celebration also."

A small fast ship approached Andreas Prime. It landed in the court yard of the old Maxumus Castle a small security detail disembarked; Tiberius was the next to step out and scanned the area. "It is safe to disembark Senator."

Octavious stepped out. "I have to go alone from here Tiberius. Have your men put a lookout on the tower."

Octavious followed the ancient stairs down below the Castle till he reached the ancient doors, which were open.

"Who enters the Keep of the Maxumus Clan unannounced?" Gamey asked.

"Brave one; I am Octavious Maxumus head of the Maxumus clan and husband of Angelina." Octavious said.

"Present and prove yourself worthy." With that Gamey sent out a blue and purple flame that engulfed Octavious who turned his ring and a blue sword appeared. He held it up as the flames split around him.

"I am Octavious Justinian Maxumus Jr. I am the wielder of the Blue Sword of the Maxumus clan, Gamey, the Brave Protector of the House of Maxumus." Octavious repeated.

Gamey bowed, "Sire you are the husband of the Empress Angelina and the father of the young Prince who wields the Sword Star Fire. I recognize you as liege."

"Gamey the Brave you are family. I plan to rebuild our home but I hope to give it to Beary and his attended if you approve." Octavious said.

"You also own the Caesar Castle its Dragon wishes to know if she can serve the Empress Angelina Maria Maxumus." Gamey asked.

Octavious thought, "Her highness wishes to continue her life on Bearilia, However we will restore the Castle and use it as a retreat for the Maxumus family and her highness. Will she accept the Maxumus clan as owners of the House of Caesar?"

Gamey let out a roar and a Golden and Silver Dragon flew in. "This is Widja the Wise."

Widja spread her wings, "I am Widja protector of the House of Caesar that lives on in the Empress Angelina Maria Maxumus. What do you wish of me?"

Octavious looked up at her. "I wish for you to join our family and serve us."

Widja lowered her head, "It is better to serve a live house than a dead clan."

"Widja, Gamey the Brave is the head protector of our house you are an imperial Dragon. Will you serve us under his lead?"

Widja smiled as only a Dragon can, "I can do that only if Gamey will take me as mate. Would you allow such a union?"

Octavious tilted his head, "Only if Gamey wishes such a union."

Gamey let out a planet shaking roar, "Sire I would gladly take her as my mate!"

Octavious nodded, "Do you wish to be united by one of your own or by a Priest of the Clan."

Gamey and Widja looked at each other and discussed it in the Ancient tongue. Gamey turned to Octavious, "By the Priest of the Clan before the Creator."

Octavious thought, "Perhaps a dual wedding. In three months' time it will be done."

They both lowered their heads. "Sire, touch our heads." Octavious placed his hands on the center of their heads he felt the warmth travel threw his body.

"I am leaving a small detachment of security bears to guard the keep till workers come. I will have Tiberius also have a security group from our clan go to the Castle of Caesar/Maxumus, with your permission Widja the Wise." Octavious said.

Widja nodded. "To have members of our clan in our castle will bring happiness."

"Tiberius, come here please." Octavious said Tiberius reported in a few minutes.

"Sire," Tiberius said.

"Tiberius this is Gamey and Widja they are members of our family. You will work with them to rebuild both Castles." Octavious said.

"I will send a security team to the Caesar/ Maxumus Castle as you have ordered Sire." Tiberius said.

"Prepare both for wedding Ceremonies. Gamey and Widja are to be wed." Octavious said.

"It will be done." Tiberius said. With that he left to accomplish what he had been asked to do.

"Sire what of the other Dragons who lost their entire Houses." Widja asked.

Octavious thought, "The Augustus family still exists their Dragon should be told.

The Pompaius family still exists, their Dragon also."

Gamey and Widja both sneered, "The Traitor is dead. Did you not know that the Pompaius family gave the Arcrilian's the ability to attack our world? The Dragon Council has confiscated their lands. The Empress will have to determine what is to be done with their land. Will she meet with the Council?"

Octavious talked with them more. "I must leave. I know she will meet with the Council. I will return soon. Tell the other Dragons we will help any who have lost their families."

A mysterious figure approached two Chameleons. "My Master wishes for you to eliminate a problem for him. The Target is an Ensign Beary Maxumus. He will be arriving on Bearilia Prime in 6 days. Be sure you kill him. Here is a down payment."

The Chameleons took the money.

Beary approached Commodore Atilus, "Sir It has been a pleasure serving under you. May I ask a favor?"

"No ensign I can't keep you from going back to the Academy. They already have the classes you will be teaching next Semester. Believe me I tried." Atilus said.

"That wasn't the favor, Sir. Could you give Artemus Command of the Crimson blade? He is almost as good a pilot as he is a gunner." Beary asked.

"That is not my call, it will be Captain Centaures. But I'll, put in a good word." Atilus said.

"Also Sir, will you and Captain Centaures attend Lady Pompey and my wedding." Beary asked.

"I, and I am sure, Captain Centaures will be there." Atilus said.

"Thank you Sir." Beary said. With that he left and went to find Pompey.

The Senator signaled Tiberius, "The Pompaius family was stripped of their lands by the Dragon Counsel. They were traitors. They may still be traitors. Inform the Augustus family that their Dragon has protected their Ancestral home. Help inform other families discreetly also, but none with ties to the Pompaius family."

Tiberius nodded, He walked away to contact some of his operatives to check out the information.

Octavious took one more look and boarded the ship.

Two days later Artisans arrived with two Architects. They both marveled at the pristine conditions of some parts of the Castles. They of coarse had to update the Castles. The first thing they, did was meet with the Dragons.

"We will be home in 3 days, and then we can go and meet with your family. Maybe a week later we can meet with my Parents and we cannot forget the celebration at Ben's Village." Pompey said.

Beary smiled, "We could go and see your family first."

"No, I want to talk to your Mother and Father first." Pompey said.

"Ensign Maxumus, you have an incoming call." com reported, "Take it on Delta."

Beary turned on the communication system, "Hello, Father."

Octavious smiled, "Hello, Son is Pompey with you."

"Yes, Senator," Pompey said.

"Oh good you look ravishing my dear. I was wondering if we could have the wedding on Andreas Prime." Octavious smiled.

"You said in your letter you wanted to be married soon. Would three months be alright?"

Pompey said, "If that is alright with Beary?"

Beary said "That is fine Father?"

Octavious smiled, "It will take that long to renovate the Castles. As a wedding gift you are being given the House of Maxumus."

Beary was speechless.

Pompey shook her head. "It is too much. I am . . . ."

Octavious smiled, "The gift is from Gamey the Brave, and Widja the Wise who are also to be wed. We are also renovating The Caesar/ Maxumus Castle for the rest of the family."

Beary nodded. "Give Mom my love."

Pompey looked puzzled. "What does it all mean?"

"It means you are going to have a big house in the country my love." Beary smiled.

The rest of the trip was quiet and busy as preparations were made to hand over the ship to a dock crew for retro fit.

The Saber Claw arrived at the space dock at 0800 Cycles in the morning. Ben was one of the first off so he could run some errands at the space port. Artemus collected his gear.

"Ben invited me to come up to his village during our shore leave. It sounds like fun." Artemus said.

"Don't forget the wedding." Beary said.

"Not on my life." Artemus said.

Caesar smiled, "We'll see you at the celebration at the end of the month."

"According to Ben, we have at least six Celebrations before that one." Artemus smiled.

Pompey came in and kissed Artemus and Caesar then Beary. "I am checked out are you three?"

Caesar and Artemus nodded.

Beary smiled. "I am all yours my lady." With that the four headed for the shuttle. Beary took one more look at the Saber

Claw she was a magnificent ship. He then looked at Pompey's eyes. "Are you sure you want to leave the service?"

Pompey shook her head. "No, but they cannot promise to keep us together. I know you will not leave the service. One of us needs to. Besides I can find work. Your Father has already offered me a position."

Beary smiled. "He could use someone with your skills."

Caesar stretched, "We are arriving. Artemus I will help you with Ben's stuff."

Beary and Pompey got off at the end of the line and headed for the exit. "Our ride should be here soon."

Beary saw Ben and waved. That's when he saw the shooter. Beary wrapped his body around Pompey just as the shooter fired. The plasma bolt hit his back and exploded against his back. The blast singed his fur as his head slammed into a beam.

Ben saw the shooter and tore his arm off and sank his blade into his throat. The Chameleon died instantly.

Tiberius saw the other shooter and grabbed him. He placed his hand on the Chameleon's throat, "Turn into your true form, or you die."

The Chameleon changed into his true form. Tiberius looked at him. "If the young Prince dies it will take you a year to die I promise. Also you will tell me everything I want to know, do you understand? He handed him over to two other security officers.

Pompey screamed as Caesar and Artemus pulled Beary off Pompey. She was crying she knew Beary was dead. He had died saving her.

Beary opened his eyes. "Is Pompey alright?"

Ben looked at him, "You are alive! Your attacker is dead. Pompey is well."

Pompey looked at Beary and gently fell into his arms. "I thought you were dead."

"No but it does hurt." Beary said.

Tiberius came over, "You are alive!?"

"Yes Ti, I'll be okay, I have been hit worse." Beary said.

Caesar ordered, "Take him to the base hospital. I want to check him out. Ben, you and Artemus protect Pompey."

Ben looked at him. "With my Life! Lady Pompey, please come with me."

Tiberius handed Artemus two phaser pistols. "Take the second car. The two Bears are part of my team they can take over for you."

"You heard the Boss, Pompey is our responsibility till he says different. Your bears want to tag along that's fine but we don't leave her side." Artemus growled.

Tiberius held up his paw, "Understood. We will take the Prince to the Medical Institute."

Caesar looked at him, "Tiberius I said the base hospital, and I meant it. You can take it up with Angelina, but for now I am in charge of Beary. You just make sure there are not any more surprises."

Tiberius felt a sting of anger, but knew Caesar was right.

"If anyone else had talked to me in that tone my friend I would have punched them. Your right Caesar it was my fault."

Caesar smiled, "You know better come on help me get him on the gurney."

The Ambulance drove them to the Base Hospital. Once there Caesar ran tests. He had just finished when Angelina came in.

She looked around. There were armed Marines and family security all over the place. That is when she saw Pompey. She went to her. "Are you alright my Dear?"

Pompey fell at her feet, "My Empress I am so sorry."

Angelina reached down and pulled her up, "Stop that nonsense Priscilla. I am to be your Mother-in-law. Besides you keep up the Empress stuff I'll give you the Crown and all its headaches. Now are you alright?"

"Yes, Beary covered me with his body." Pompey started shaking.

"Ben, thank you. Would you get Pompey a glass of water, have her take these." Angelina said.

"Yes my Lady, it will be done." Ben said.

Angelina touched Artemus face as she went by. He nodded.

In the room Caesar was looking over the chart when she walked in. "Lady Angelina or should I say your Highness."

"Caesar if you start that I'll have you shipped to the outer planets." Angelina smiled.

Caesar smiled then got serious. "Anyone else would be dead. He has a second degree burn that is already healing itself on his back where he was hit, a minor concussion from his head hitting a beam, and internal bruising around his spine."

She smiled. "Dr. Vantanus someone trained you well. Can he be moved to the estate?"

Caesar nodded, "I do wish to ask about this point on his spine."

Angelina looked closely at the CAT scan. "He has some swelling of the spinal cord. We'll give him some anti-inflammatory medicine and watch it. You were planning to come home anyway?"

"Yes Angelina. I'll arrange transport. Nothing against Tiberius or his Bears, but there are a lot of very angry Marines around here they will insist on guarding him at least until he is home." Caesar explained.

Angelina smiled, "Tiberius will you have your team escort Lady Pompey and our friends to the estate. Have rooms prepared and put Lady Pompey in the room next to Beary."

"It will be done." Tiberius said. He signaled five of his bears over, "You will protect the Lady Pompey with your lives. Follow the orders of these two officers and take them to the estate."

A Marine Lieutenant came over. "Lady Maxumus I am Lieutenant Bandar. My unit will escort you and the Ensign home.

I promise you on my life and that of my Marines you will have no more trouble today."

"Thank you, Lieutenant, but only on the condition that you and your men allow me to show my gratitude." Angelina said.

"That will not be necessary my Lady. Your, Son and his team saved my Marines lives. It is us who owe him." Bandar said.

"None the less, you and your men will accept our hospitality. Now let us get started." Angelina said

Chapter 22

Home Comings

Beary woke up in his bed. He started to get up when a voice stopped him.

"Don't you dare get out of bed," Pompey said. "Your Mother said you are not to get up for three days."

Beary was embarrassed. "I need to use the facilities."

She picked up a bed pan, "I'll help you."

Beary shook his head, "No!"

About that time Caesar walked in. "He needs to use the facilities but the baby won't let me help him." Pompey said with a pout.

"That's okay Pompey; I need to check him out anyway. Lady Angelina wanted you by the way." Caesar said.

Pompey gave Beary a kiss and floated out of the room.

Beary tried to clear his head. *It must be the drugs.* "Caesar, please help me into the rest room."

Caesar smiled, "You are a baby. She was strong enough to help you. Come on."

Beary did what he needed to do. Then Caesar helped him back to the bed. "Caesar what happened?"

Caesar explained, "The swelling on your spine is going down and your hair has grown back in, even thicker and more metallic.

Give it another day. You hit your head on the way down, but the concussion seems to have cleared up."

"Who and why," Beary asked?

"That is Tiberius job, mine is just to get you healed up." Caesar replied.

Angelina was in the drawing room when Pompey walked in. The room was filled with Maxmimus. "Come in my dear." Angelina smiled that angelic smile, "Pompey my dear these are members of our family. You met my oldest over the com, Alexa. This is Augustus my oldest son, Benjamen my third child, Maria my fourth child, Isaiah my fifth child, and Beatrice my youngest daughter."

Pompey looked at them Beany was holding her young cub.

"It is a pleasure to meet you all. Beary talks about his family especially his older siblings."

Augustus spoke up, "Please don't hold anything he said against us. He tends to exaggerate."

Pompey smiled, "Not at all. He said he was lucky to have such wonderful brothers and sisters."

An older Gentlebear walked up to her. "Lady Pompey I am Servitous Vantorious, Caesar's father. May I touch your face?"

"As you wish Sire" Pompey said.

He gentle followed the lines of her face, "You are very beautiful my Lady. My forges will be at your service."

It was then that Pompey realized he was blind. "Thank you Sire Vantorious."

Angelina walked over. "If you are up to it my dear, I would like to introduce you to the other clan members that are here."

Pompey nodded, "As you wish Lady Angelina."

Ben and Artemus came in to see Beary, who was setting up. "It is good to see you are mending." Ben said.

"For a moment you scared us, Boss." Artemus said.

"Thanks, to both of you. Ben you may have saved my life."

Beary said. "Tiberius told me you watched over Pompey, Artemus."

Artemus smiled, "Ben and I were just following Caesar's orders. That was right after you passed out again."

"I still don't know how . . . ." Beary started to say.

"Join us at the Celebration of the New Moon." Ben smiled.

"We're leaving in the morning, if you don't object. Ben's tribe is waiting for us." Artemus said.

"Pompey and I will be there at the end of the month." Beary smiled.

"Well your gatekeeper gave us five STU we'll see you before we leave." Artemus said as they left the room.

The next morning Pompey came in wearing a light robe and night gown. She kissed his forehead and sat down on the edge of his bed.

Beary opened his eyes. "You look like an angel."

"Your Mom lent it to me. It fits real good." she said as she stood up to show him.

"You better behave you'll raise my blood pressure." Beary said.

Pompey kissed him. "Do you feel like getting dressed. I can take you into the garden."

"Sure just give me a moment to get dressed." Beary said.

"I'll just go into my room and slip something else on." Pompey said and slowly walked into her room allowing the light to play along her robe and night gown.

I have got to talk to Mom, Beary thought as he quickly dressed. He could tell his back was healed.

Angelina was talking to Ben and Artemus. "Ben, will you accept this gift from me." She handed him a small box with the Imperial seal. Inside was a small pin of the order of the Dragon.

Ben's eyes widened, "My Lady I cannot accept such an honor."

"Ben, it is mine to give by right. Will you dishonor my pleasure?" Angelina said.

"No my Lady, I only hope I can live up to this honor." Ben said in a soft voice.

Angelina kissed him. "You already have Sir Knight."

"Savato Artemus, will you also except this small gift and please know you will always be welcomed in the House of Caesar/ Maxumus." Angelina said.

Artemus saw the same pin Ben received, "My lady I . . . ."

"Nonsense, Beary has told me you are two of the noblest Bears he has ever met. I agree." With that she kissed Savato, and walked off.

"She doesn't allow any argument." Artemus said.

"An Empress doesn't need to." Ben said.

"Artemus after this and everything else we have been through, I hope you are in good shape. My village will go nuts the celebration won't stop till after the new moon." Ben smiled.

"Ben, I will try not to let you down more than twenty times. I am new at this." Artemus said, with a smile.

"Good. I will try to last at least that many times." Ben said.

Beary came over with Pompey, "Ben, I slowed you and Artemus up. Tiberius will take you home. Also Artemus you can't go empty handed. I had Tiberius load twelve casks of Fire Cherry nectar in the transport for you to give to Ben's village."

Artemus smiled, "See you in a month, if I can still see."

Ben smiled, "I will take care of him."

Ben and Artemus arrived at Ben's village. The crew of the transport unloaded the casts of Fire Cherry nectar.

Ben's father walked up. "Son who is this you bring to our village?"

"Father this is my friend, Savato Artemus, a good pilot and the best gunner in the fleet. He has taught me to also be a good gunner. He is also a brave and honorable Bear." Ben said.

"Sire Maritinus, I hope you will accept this small gift of twelve casks of Fire Cherry nectar."

"A fine gift, you must bring great honor to your village." Sire Maritinus said.

"I have no village or family Sire." Artemus responded.

"I am sorry. Please except my full hospitality, Savato Artemus the brave." Sire Maritinus said.

"You, my Son, have you brought more honor to your family?" Sire Maritinus asked.

Ben showed him the small box with the Caesar/Maxmimus Imperial seal and the pin of the Order of the Dragon. "Artemus has the same honor."

Sire Maritinus, let out a yell. "We must celebrate!!"

Ben smiled and turned to Artemus, "I told you."

Artemus saw them bring in a field dressed polar wild Pig, "Oh my."

Angelina checked her Son out. "Well you are all healed. Well?"

"Well, what Mom?" Beary asked.

"Did you like the nightgowns I have lent Pompey?" Angelina asked with an impish smile.

"Mom, we shouldn't be talking about such things." Beary said.

"Beary, I am a Doctor. I talk about such things with others." Angelina said.

"What others?" Beary asked.

"Patients and Pompey," Angelina said.

"Mom" Beary said!

"Well since you are so uptight. I will take Pompey shopping for your trip up north." Angelina smiled her special smile.

"Mom, that doesn't work with me" Beary said.

"Of course not dear," She said with even a more radiant smile and kissed him on the forehead.

Octavious walked in.

"Well I am off. I am taking Pompey shopping." She said with a wave.

"Dad" Beary said.

"Son, we have been married for 69 years. I have never won an argument. I don't expect to in the near future. I have someone I want you to talk to." Octavious said.

Beary followed his father down to a holding cell. The Chameleon was restrained. "You tried to kill me."

The Chameleon shuttered. "You are dead!"

"No. I am not. You failed. Now you will tell me who hired you." Beary smiled.

"I do not know his name. He was one of you." The Chameleon said.

"A Bearilian," Beary asked?

"No, one of you, like you. He had a scar on his left eye that runs down his face." The Chameleon said.

"If you lied to me, you will learn why the Arcrilians call me the Ghost. If you told me the truth you will live." Beary said.

Beary and his father left. Octavious looked at him. "Well?"

"He was telling the truth Dad. It was one, of our own kind." Beary said.

"Tiberius agrees with your assessment. He is trying to run down the rogue." Octavious said.

"Father there was another traitor, one pulling the strings. But apparently only Iscarius or Santanus knew who they were taking orders from. Our friend was an errand boy not the true traitor. He must be someone powerful." Beary said.

"Yes Son and one of us. I fear it is the head of the Pompaius Family. The Dragon council took their land on Andreas Prime and killed their Dragon, as a traitor. They claim they were the ones that allowed the attack to accrue."

In a shop in downtown Bora near the lake, Angelina looked at Pompey. "Dear, have you found nightgowns you like."

Pompey blushed, "I have found some that fit me very well."

Angelina smiled, "My Pompey, Beary is a great warrior but he is not well versed in the art of love."

Pompey blushed even more. "My lady . . . ."

"Good, you are as naive as he is. But not quit." Angelina smiled.

Pompey lowered her head. "I have never known a Boar. My mother did say that it was a female's job to please her husband."

Angelina shook her head. "You are going to be a wife of a Maxumus. You need to be passionate in love and passionate in deed. You must be strong in your positions. Also remember you are the Star of Vandar. Not a concubine."

"I don't understand." Pompey said.

Angelina smiled. "Though I don't plan to use my position as Empress, It is my destiny, such as it is. You are the Star of Vandar. That is your destiny. You bow to no one; you are part of the Imperial family."

Pompey's eyes widened, "I don't . . . . I am just a sheepherder's daughter. How can I be?"

Angelina smiled. "The Guardian chose you, which was his right. My Son loves you."

Pompey looked at her, "I love him also, more than life itself."

Angelina dropped her head. "That is the curse, of the wives', of Maxumus boars. They will fly into battle without fear, leaving us to fear for them. You have held up well my dear."

"I hope I never disappoint you my Lady." Pompey said.

"You won't. Now let's go spend some more of your young Boars money. You want to look fabulous when you visit your parents and when you go to Ben's village." Angelina smiled.

On a small planet in the Darius system, Dontanus Pompaius looked at his servant. "Your assassins failed. The young Maxumus still lives."

"Yes, Master he was injured but recovered. No other assassins will attempt attacking the Maxumus tribe." The servant said.

"Stop the wedding between Maxumus and Pompey. Tell them we command it." Dontanus said.

Beary and Pompey were a cycle away from her family's village, when a mysterious Maxmimus approached the village. He asked to speak to the Sirena.

"Sirena Pompey, you will call off the wedding between your daughter and the Maxumus youth." The mysterious Servant commanded.

"Who are you, to come into my village, and command me?" Sirena Pompey responded.

"Silence female! I am the servant of the Great Pompaius, you will obey his command." The Servant said.

The Sirena rose to her full height. "We are free bears, we owe no one allegiance." The Sirena responded.

"I told you to be Silent!" With that he struck the Sirena in the mouth.

Sire Pompey saw him strike his wife. He charged in. Sire Pompey caught the attacker's paw, as he started to strike the Sirena again, with his Shepherd's hook.

The Pompaius servant went for his blade. That was his last mistake.

Sire Pompey, hit him across the face with the blunt end of his rod, and then pressed a button. A spike extended from the rod and he twirled it and stuck it threw the heart of the servant, who died instantly.

Beary and Pompey arrived just as the battle ended. Beary jumped out and ran over.

"Sire, Sirena are you alright?" Beary asked.

Sire Pompey twirled his staff and started to attack Beary believing he was an attacker.

Beary touched his ring and Star Fire appeared and blocked the blow. The sword flared and drove Sire Pompey back. Sirena Pompey caught Sire Pompey's arm.

"It is our Son in-law." Sirena Pompey said in a soothing voice.

Beary touch his ring and the sword disappeared. "Forgive me Sire Pompey."

"It was the blood fever. I killed this one after he attacked my Junia." Sire Pompey said, "That was Star Fire, the Sword of Justice?"

"Yes Sire, it was." Beary responded, "May I look at this rogue?" Beary turned him over and saw the scared eye and the gnarled face. "Sir, I must contact my family. This one paid assassins to kill me and Pompey."

Sirena Pompey said, "He served the Great Pompaius, the pig. He ordered me to forbid your marriage. Not even if the Empress so ordered!"

"She wouldn't, she loves your daughter. Sire Pompey, your lands on Andreas Prime, is free again." Beary said.

Sire Pompey looked at him. Pompey walked up. "It was him?"

Beary nodded, two Maxumus security bears came forward. "With your permission, Sire Pompey, these Bears will remove this trash, and unload our gifts to you and the Sirena."

"You have my blessing to do so, my Prince." Sire Pompey said.

Beary turned to the two security bears. "Unload our things and take this trash to my father. Give him this."

Pompey turned to her mother, "Let me tend to your face."

"Thank you my daughter." Sirena Pompey said, once they were inside, Sirena smiled. "It has been a long time since your father has showed his true self. He was the Boar I married."

Pompey smiled, "You do love him, don't you Mom? Why did Dad change?"

"He became obsessed. Your father attacked business the way he flew fighters. Then I failed him and only gave him one child. Don't misunderstand. Your father loves you. But he also wanted sons. I became sick and was unable to have more children. His business became his lover. At least he did not take another wife." The Sirena said. Mother and daughter continued talking.

Sire Pompey looked at Beary, "My daughter says you are an honorable bear. I know you are not a fool. You saw how I looked at the ring. You knew I hoped to use it to my advantage. You saw that I could not do that. You elevated my Wife and saw that she was financially secure without me. Then today that cull attacked my wife. I realized that my priorities were so wrong."

"Sire, it was not that I wanted to dishonor you. However, I could not allow you to use my Lady." Beary said.

"Or my daughter, you were right. By giving her the Star of Vandar you elevated her above our status." Sire Pompey said.

"I elevated her above myself. I am the Hammer of Corsan, the Guardian of the Star of Vandar." Beary said.

Sire Pompey looked at him. "Then you did not just make her a concubine?"

"No Sire, I have honored her and I will be marrying her at our ancestral home, which has also been given to us by my family." Beary said.

"I am sorry, my Prince. I have become what I thought you would be." Sire Pompey said as he dropped his head.

"Sire, I brought you this with my respect." Beary handed him a golden ring with the Pompey crest emblazoned on it.

Sire Pompey, looked at the beauty of the workmen ship of the ring. The luster of the metal, "I am not worthy of such a gift."

Beary smiled, "You're wrong, you proved your worth today. You are the Boar, my father said, was a great pilot. Now can we join our Ladies?"

After they joined the ladies they had a light meal. Tonight the village would have a celebration to welcome the young couple. Beary and Pompey gave the rest of the gifts they brought with them including fifteen casks of Honey Peach nectar.

Sirena Pompey looked at the young couple, "You should rest before the celebration. Your room is made up I'll show you to it." She led them up the stair. "This will be your room."

Beary looked at her. "Sirena where is my room?"

The Sirena looked puzzled, "Beary, you paid the Brides price. According to our custom if you are not in the same room it would shame my daughter. You have not consummated your relationship?"

"Mother by his family's custom we must wait till we are wed before our families and the Creator. Yet I know Beary, will not dishonor our custom. We will stay in the same room." Pompey said and took his paw.

Pompey smiled, and led Beary into their room. It was a large room. "See Beary there is plenty of room, for both of us. You can sleep over there, and I can sleep over here. See we can keep both our families happy. Now why don't we take a nap?"

Beary laid down on one of the beds and Pompey nuzzled in next to him. "It is only a nap."

Beary wrapped his arms around her. "Just a nap." soon both were a sleep.

As evening fell Pompey got up and changed. Then went and kissed Beary. "It's time for the celebration. I hope you like my dress your Mom picked it out."

Beary rose up. "It is beautiful on you my Lady. You are absolutely stunning."

Pompey beamed, "I laid out your dress uniform. Please to honor my Parents will you wear it and all your decorations."

Beary thought *if my Lady wants me too*, "It will be as you ask."

Pompey left the room and crossed the hall to a small veranda; she looked out over the village. She also saw a small Marine detachment guarding the perimeter of the village.

Her Father joined her. "The marines are here to insure your safety and that of the village. A Lieutenant Bandar sends his regards. Did he agree to my request?"

"Yes father he did. Why did you wish it?" Pompey asked.

Her father looked at her she was so beautiful. "I have been a fool daughter. I worried about what I didn't have or what I could acquire. I failed to see what I had. I want our bears to see what you have. Not just a Cub with a powerful family and wealth, but a true hero of our Race."

Beary stepped out the blood Red ribbon with the Bearilian Star and the Honey colored ribbon with the Red Rose Medallion, plus numerous other awards.

Sire Pompey came to attention and saluted. "Thank you." he said in a quiet voice.

Beary looked out and saw Marines preparing positions.

Sire Pompey shrugged, "Lieutenant Bandar said it was just a precaution."

Beary smiled, "If he is here your village is safe. I am sorry, if I have endangered your Tribe."

Sire Pompey saw the sword on his hip it was Star Fire. "Ensign you are dressed in full dress uniform."

Beary smiled, "My lady requested it."

Sire and Sirena Pompey led the way as Beary and Pompey followed behind as they reached the end of the stairs and turned towards the banquet hall an old man stepped out.

"Charlatan and thief, would you dishonor our lady by giving her a fake ring, as fake as the sword you wear?!" The old Bear screamed.

Sire Pompey turned red with anger, "Omar be still!"

Beary put his paw on Sire Pompey. "Let him speak Sire. If he said it others are thinking it."

Beary turned to the old Bear. "Please speak your thoughts Ancient one."

"You wear a Sword that resembles Star Fire. A Sword that was lost. Besides no one can wield it, not even Augustus the Hammer could touch the sword. If it is counterfeit then the ring is counterfeit." The old Bear screamed!

Beary spoke in a soft but strong voice. "It is Star Fire, and my lady is the Star of Vandar."

"Prove it!" The old one screamed even louder.

Beary spoke even softer yet everyone could hear him. "What proof do you require?"

"Place the sword in my paw." Omar said with a sneer.

"As you wish," Beary pulled the sword from its scabbard twirled it around and handed it to Omar.

The old man touched the pommel of the sword. He almost dropped it do to its weight. Then a burning sensation went up his arm.

Beary could see his discomfort and touched his ring the sword returned to his paw and he sheathed it, "Are you satisfied, I speak the truth?"

Omar looked frightened, "Please my Sire, do not destroy your wicked servant."

Beary looked at him with compassion, "Be at peace Omar, the Ancient one. You were trying to protect your village. Do you believe I am who I say I am?"

Omar stood up. "You are Corsan the Hammer, Guardian of the Star of Vandar, and my young Prince. Our young Lady Pompey is the Star of Vandar. Forgive me My Lady."

Pompey kissed him, "Omar my teacher and friend none is needed."

Beary turned to his Father-in-Law, "You staged this to prove to your tribe that this was real."

Sire Pompey grinned. "If it were your daughter would you have played it different?"

Beary smiled, "Well played Sire. Well played."

Sire Pompey beamed. "Let the celebration begin!"

Beary leaned over to Pompey and kissed her cheek. "Remind me never to fly a fighter against your father. He is very good at what he does."

Pompey smiled, and leaned over and gave him a passionate kiss, "So are you."

The Village went wild and called out kiss her; kiss her, every few minutes.

The Celebration lasted till 0700 Cycles in the morning. The villagers slipped off to bed or chores.

Lieutenant Bandar strolled over, "Must have been an interesting party?"

Pompey grinned. "Oh it was fairly mild." She said with a sleepy voice. "Did your Marines get fed properly?"

Bandar smiled. "Yes my Lady. A few were reprimanded. It seems some of the young Ladies thought the kiss her, meant them. Some of my young Marines obliged them. It was probably good for moral but not discipline."

Pompey beamed, "Please, don't be too hard on your young Marines. It is part of our custom."

Bandar smiled. "As you wish my Lady. We are going with you to Ben's Village."

Beary grinned, "If you think that was wild last night you better hold on tight to your Marines when we get up there."

"If you will excuse us, we need some sleep, before we leave later tonight." Pompey said with a smile and took Beary by the paw.

Bandar smirked; *Ensign Maxumus was the luckiest bear he had ever met. Okay, he had to give some young marines a reprieve.*

Beary hung up his uniform and put on his pajamas. *It needs to be cleaned*, he thought. He packed everything else away.

Pompey came out in her night gown. "Do you like it your Mom picked it out?"

Beary blushed and smiled. "You are stunning."

Pompey kissed him. "Good you will have good dreams." She said as she climbed into bed. She couldn't have been more wrong.

Beary saw the shooter but this time he moved too slow and the bolt hit Pompey. Then her village was attacked. The Marines and the villagers were slaughtered. He stood helpless unable to do anything. He screamed her name over and over. He couldn't leave the dreams, each seemed worse than the next.

Pompey rushed from her bed and tried to wake him. Finally she crawled in next to him. She kissed his forehead and held him. Soon the terror passed. His breathing became more regular. She held him and went to sleep.

Beary woke up when Sirena Pompey knocked and came in.

She smiled when she saw her daughter in his arms. "I hope you slept well it is almost time for your transport. Wake her gently." She then closed the door.

Beary gently brushed her face and kissed her. "Pompey." She woke and stretched and nuzzled him. "What happened?"

Pompey smiled. "Nothing my love, you woke me. Your mind was troubled. So I came over and held you till the terror in your mind passed. Then I fell asleep."

Beary remembered the nightmares and shuddered. He composed himself. "I am afraid your Mom has a different picture. She came in and found you in my arms."

Pompey smiled. "Good, I will tell her I had my way with you."

"Pompey!" Beary said.

She smiled an impish smile, "Behave or I'll show you what your mother bought me to wear on our wedding night. She looked at the time. "Go shower and get dressed I will order us some food."

Beary smiled and went in and showered. Again he locked the door. Again towels were placed on a bench that he swore were not there before. Yet the door was still locked. He dressed.

Pompey went in after him. Fifteen STU later came out dressed in another stunning outfit. "Do you like it? It was made by my father's company."

Beary smiled. "It is wonderful."

Their meal arrived; they sat down, and started eating.

Pompey could still see the effects of the night terrors in his eyes.

"Your dreams were not good?"

Beary dropped his head. "No. I had hoped you wouldn't see them happen."

Pompey realized that the fear in his eyes wasn't from the dreams. It was something else. "What happened in them?"

Beary shook his head. "I can't talk about it."

Pompey looked at him. "I have never seen fear in your eyes before. Even when you knew you might be heading into certain death. What are you afraid of? Please tell me."

Beary dropped his head. A small tear fell from his eyes. "I am not strong enough. What if I fail to protect you? You were almost killed. A moment slower and that bolt would have missed me and hit you."

Pompey got up and went to him, "I am a warrior too remember. I am not afraid. Also you have never failed. Can you imagine how I felt when that bolt hit you and you went limp, I thought you were dead. I wanted to die too."

Beary looked at her and the tears in her eyes. He reached up and kissed her.

Then there was a knock on the door. Pompey looked at his eyes. They had returned to the calm cool eyes he always had. She straightened her dress, "Come in," She said.

"Daughter your transport has come. Your father has asked that they load twelve lambs onto the transport to honor your friend's family." Sirena Pompey beamed.

Beary stood up and kissed Sirena Pompey on the cheek. "Thank you for the gift of your daughter. There is no finer Lady in the Universe."

Sirena Pompey swelled with pride. "Thank you Beary." She said as she kissed his cheek back.

Mother and Daughter embraced then walked down stairs.

Sire Pompey shook Beary's Paw, "We will see you in six weeks on Andreas Prime."

"Sire, thank you and please be careful." Beary whispered.

Sire Pompey grinned, "The marines were nice to have here, but my son we are Shepherds. We know how to protect our flock." he then winked and went over and kissed his daughter.

Beary smiled, "Maybe not as good as his father was, but he bet it would be close. Real close he had the look."

Beary and Pompey boarded the transport, He went and talked to the pilot and Lieutenant Bandar and came back and sat with Pompey.

As they lifted off Sire Pompey took his wife's paw, "Junia, can you ever forgive an old fool?"

She replied by kissing him and leading him into their home.

At Ben's village Artemus looked up at his friend, "You and the Master Chief just take me out, and bury me."

Grizlarge laughed "I wish I had got here sooner."

Artemus just groaned.

Ben smirked, "I know what you need." He helped him into his swimsuit and carried him to a hot springs.

Three Polarian females climbed into the spring with him and messaged his legs and back.

Artemus looked at Ben, who had also got in and was being messaged. "I am dead and you didn't tell me and this is heaven."

Ben smiled, "No but it is close."

While Ben, Artemus, and Grizlarge were at the hot springs Beary, Pompey and their entourage arrived at Ben's village.

Beary, Pompey, and Bandar were the first off the Transport.

"Sire Maritinus, I am Beary Maxumus. This is my, Lady Pompey and Lieutenant Bandar of the 307th Aces. We are friends of your son Ben Maritinus the slayer." Beary said with respect.

The old Polarian hugged Beary then Pompey. "You are all welcome to my village. Lieutenant Bandar you are not here to celebrate?" Aleut Maritinus said.

"No Sire, we are here to protect the young couple. Someone tried to kill them, then attacked Lady Pompey's mother." Bandar reported.

"Your marines may remain armed, but no Marine, comes to my village and not receive my hospitality. I will place 20 of my Warriors under your command. They will help you in your duties while you allow your Marines to enjoy at least part of our celebration." Aleut Maritinus commanded. He then signaled a young bear. In less than 15 SUBTU 20 tall Polarians responded. "This is Lieutenant Bandar; you will follow his commands and protect our guests with your lives." Aleut Maritinus commanded.

Beary nodded, "Thank you Sire. Please except these humble gifts twenty casks of black berry nectar. Lady Pompey's family also sends you twelve lambs for your table."

The older Maritinus beamed, "Such fine Gifts! You honor us."

Pompey smiled "Sire, Ben, and Artemus where are they?"

"They are at the hot springs would you two like to join them?" Aleut asked.

Pompey smiled, "Yes Sire, if it is alright."

Aleut beamed, "For you Lady Pompey anything. Boy, take their luggage to their lodge. Sister, bring their swim suits to the hot springs. These two Boars will show you the way. You have your orders." The two Polarian boars bowed.

The larger of the two turned, "If you will follow me."

When they got to the hot springs they were shown too dressing rooms. Beary was out first and headed for the springs. He saw Ben, Artemus, and Grizlarge relaxing and being tended to by nine young Polarian females. Pompey followed shortly behind him. Already three more young ladies were moving towards him.

"Ladies, I will tend to his needs, thank you." She said.

The three young girls giggled and backed away. Beary grinned. "You're no fun."

Pompey smiled. "You might change your mind. my lord." They stepped into the hot springs.

Ben smirked, "It is good to see you. Our friend Savato needed to be revived."

Artemus smiled, "Boss, you tried to warn me." One of the young girls served him a drink of glacial water.

Pompey grinned. "Yes, I see how horrible it has been for the three of you."

Grizlarge smiled, "I have only been here three days." He watched as three marines slowly spread out not too far away. He looked at Beary, "Cub?"

Beary nodded. "It is just a little precaution. Someone attacked Sirena Pompey before we arrived. Pompey's father ended the problem permanently. Just enjoy your time off Master Chief."

Ben and Artemus looked at each other. Ben spoke up, "You and Pompey will be safe in my village."

Pompey answered, as she moved over and lightly kissed her two friends and the Master Chief, "Of that I have no doubt."

Beary reclined back into the water. "Now back to the sorry state of our dear friend Savato."

The five friends talked for cycles enjoying the water of the hot springs.

On Andreas prime the work continued and preparations for the two weddings were being finalized.

Angelina was meeting with the Dragon Counsel. "Are you sure of these charges."

Gray Talon the head of the counsel answered. "Empress Angelina there is no doubt."

Angelina nodded. "The Facts are clear. The Pompaius Castle is to be emptied and raised. Their property sold and the proceeds to be given to the Counsel. Also the Pompaius Lands are to be given to the Dragons as a place of rest and solitude."

Gray Talon looked at her in surprise. "My lady, you are giving us their lands?"

Angelina smiled a radiant smile. "Is it not my right to reward those that preserved our heritage? Will the Counsel deny me this right?"

Gray Talon and the others bowed their heads low and foiled their wings over their heads. "No, my Empress we will accept your gift and call it Angel land."

"My lady, there are other issues. The Pompaius family was the treasures of the old Imperial house. As we have determined, we seized over 93 billion credits belonging to you. Also my Lady we have had no clergy on the planet to teach the young about, *The Way and the Book, of the Creator of the Universe*. The churches are in disrepair." Gray Talon continued.

Angelina smiled, "A group of young Clergy and missionaries are preparing to come." Use whatever funds you need to rebuild the Churches."

"My lady, who will you put in charge of the royal treasure?" Gray talon asked.

Angelina looked at the Counsel. "You have earned that right. The counsel shall replace the Pompaius family. Now are their other concerns?"

A younger Dragon spoke up, "My Empress several of our families are no more. What is to become of us?"

Angelina thought, "You have protected these lands."

"Yes My Lady." Dawn Star replied.

"We have been developing new lines. Some have chosen to tie themselves to their original clans others have not. Members of these new lines will petition the Dragons that have protected the land. If the Dragon agrees, the land will become their land

and the Dragon's family. Till then any Dragon without a family will hold the land in trust and serve me." Angelina said.

Red Fire an ancient Dragon spoke, "Your Highness, your faith in us is over whelming. All this has never been done before. Your generosity and trust is unprecedented. You are treating us as equals not servants."

"Is it not the responsibility of the Dragon to protect its family? Why would a slave do that? But one who is a member of the family shares in its triumphs and failures. Does not this counsel have rights? No, my dear Red Fire, Dragons are not slaves but important members of each family." Angelina said.

The old Dragon lowered his head. "You are truly a wise and kind Empress. I pledge myself to you."

A Dogon from the Southern Continent spoke next. "Empress Angelina, I represent the Dogons of the southern continent. We have protected our flocks for all these years. Now we have two problems. The flocks have grown too large and we have a horrible feral hog problem."

She looked at the strange mixture of Canine and Dragon that the Sheepherder's used to protect their sheep. "Would you allow the Dragons a one day, hunt on your sheep herds especially those that have turned wild and a two day hunt on the wild pigs."

Armon the Dogon smiled, "If our brothers would except a three day hunt on the pigs and allow us to hunt the spring bucks.

We are all tired of wild pig."

Grey talon smiled, "It is agreed."

"Now friends, I am getting tired. Can we put any other business off until tomorrow?" Angelina said.

"As you wish Empress Angelina," Gray Talon said.

Angelina stepped out of the Cave that served as a meeting hall. A Maxmimus security guard stepped up to her.

"Are you alright my Lady" The guard said.

"Yes Alexander, but I would like to go and take a nap." Angelina said.

Alexander signaled for her transport and helped her in.

Once back at the castle Angelina climbed the stairs and went to her room and slept.

The Dragons on the counsel were talking. One raised his voice. Let us sing and write songs of Empress Angelina the Wise and generous." Dragon songs filled the air.

Beary dressed casually, in Ben's village. It wasn't necessary for him to bring out the decorations or other finery. Aleut Maritinus walked up to him.

"You have a fine Lady, Sir Maxumus." Aleut said.

"Thank you. Sire Maritinus. Please call me Beary." Beary said.

"Then you must call me Aleut. You and Grizlarge saved my oldest Son and his Marines?" Aleut asked.

"Yes, we were the team sent in. It was just our job." Beary said, "Your son did the same on Dryden."

"But you lead that mission also, did you not?' Aleut said.

"Yes, but it is always a team effort." Beary said.

"You are a holder of the Bearilian Star, at 18 years?" Aleut questioned.

"Yes, I am. Why are you asking these questions Aleut?" Beary asked.

Aleut smiled, "Your Mother gave my wife, the Red Fire Stone necklace, of Empress Alexa of your Race. It has brought great honor to our family and my village. I have no such thing to give you, but would you accept this." He handed him a carved box inside was a fine blade knife with a carved bone handled.

Beary looked at the intricate workmanship of the handle and the sharpness of the blade. He felt its balance. "Aleut not even the armors of my Clan could make a finer weapon. Thank you." Beary said.

Aleut beamed, "Good, let us join the others. It is time to eat and celebrate."

Bandar talked to his Marines. "Half of you at a time may join in the celebration. You must be able to still conduct your duties. The First group has three cycles the second group will go at the end of that three cycles."

One of the Polarians smiled, "Lieutenant, you should go and enjoy yourself. There will be no trouble. My warriors have set up a perimeter If anyone tries to enter we will know and stop them."

Bandar smiled, "Okay, I will."

Pompey was setting next to Ben's mother, "You are Pompey, dear."

"Yes, my lady Maritinus." Pompey smiled.

"Call me Lunara dear. You have a very handsome Boar."

"Yes Lunara. He is very dear and a great Bear." Pompey said.

"You are very much in love with him. But I also see fear in your eyes." Lunara said.

"Someone tried to kill him. He covered me with his body. I thought he was dead, but he survived the attack and healed quickly. I am marring a warrior. I should not show fear, it dishonors him." Pompey said.

"No dear, it proves your love. Do you have another name?" Lunara said.

"Yes, unlike Beary's clan, we of the Southern Continent were nomadic herders. Like you, bears of the land, wild and free. At least that is what I have been told. Our secret name is used between mother and child, Husband and wife, and of course between lovers." Pompey smiled.

Lunara smiled, "May I know this name or is it forbidden."

Pompey smiled, "No I may tell it to whom I please. It is Priscilla, Lunara."

Lunara smiled, "I will call you Pompey, in public, but when we are alone, Priscilla, it is a beautiful name."

Aleut came over, "Lady Pompey are you getting enough to eat. Or is my wife talking you to death?"

Pompey smiled a radiant smile, "The Lady Lunara has been charming and wonderful company, while you Boars have been trying to prove your strength to one another."

Aleut smiled, "Yes and your, Beary has bested all my best warriors. You should be proud of him."

"Truly Sire I am." Pompey said.

Just then Caesar arrived. "Sire Maritinus please forgive my tardiness, to your celebration, but I was detained. A female Polarian in a nearby village had a medical emergency and I was diverted. I am Ensign Caesar Vantanus. Please except these gifts." Six Medical cases were unloaded.

"I am Aleut Maritinus welcome Dr. Vantanus to our village. Come eat and celebrate." Aleut said as his PA looked over the equipment and medicines and beamed.

"It is about time you got here." Artemus said, "You can give it to me straight, I am really dead and this is just heaven."

"Ben, you better put him to bed, he is done." Caesar said.

Ben signaled four young females over, "Please see to my guests comfort and insure he rests easily."

Pompey came over, "Ben, if Beary needs such help, I will provide it."

Ben smiled, "Of course lady Pompey."

She just winked back.

Caesar smiled, "I did get here late."

Ben smiled, "Not at all. The evening is yet young."

Out in the marsh three figures approached. They thought they were undetected until they found themselves upside down hanging from three poles and their weapons striped from them.

Bandar walked over, "Who are you?"

"It is none of your business who we are?" One said as he tried to free himself.

A large Polarian hit him in the ribs cracking two. "You will answer his questions or die by our custom."

Bandar smiled he might be in charge but this was their territory and it was their rules that applied. "You heard him answer my question."

"No I would rather die." The Pompaius mercenary said.

Bandar shook his head, "That is your choice." Two Polarians stabbed him to death.

The second mercenary stared in horror as did the third. "We will talk!"

"Cut them down. If they try to escape, kill them. Take them over to our transport." Bandar ordered.

"By your command," the Polarians said and carried out their orders.

The two security personnel had just completed their interviews. "We have all we need. The Pompaius family is behind the attacks. We have enough to arrest them and seize their assets. We are going to leave. Tiberius will return with a new transport." The head security guard said.

Aleut came over, "Lieutenant is there a problem?"

Bandar smiled, "Nothing your warriors couldn't handle. One intruder chose death the other two are talking and are being taken back for more questioning."

After 12 Cycles of constant celebration Beary was exhausted, "Aleut would you mind if I called it a night?"

Aleut smiled, "Not at all, you can join back in when you have rested." He started to signal some young Ladies, when Pompey appeared and shooed them off.

"Sire I will attend to Beary's needs with your permission." Pompey said.

Aleut smiled, "Of course my Lady."

Lunara came over and punched him. "Aleut, what were you up to?"

"Just an experiment my love, to see if all wives was like you." Aleut said.

"Did you tell her, that by taking him into the lodge at this time, that by our laws they were wed?" Lunara asked.

Aleut smiled, "No, our young warrior seams confused by such things. Why confuse him more we will tell them in the morning."

Pompey led Beary into the lodge. She went into a small room and changed as Beary did. She came out in pajamas.

"I am afraid these are not as alluring, as the other nightwear I have, but they are warm." Pompey said.

"You look radiant my Lady. You take the pallet. I will sleep on the ground." Beary said.

Pompey put her paws on her hips." Would you dishonor me before Ben's family?"

Beary looked at her, "I don't understand?"

Pompey looked at her ring and said in a soft voice. "Am I the Star of Vandar?"

Beary said "Yes." still clueless.

"Are you not my Guardian, the Hammer of Corsan?" Pompey said.

"Of course" Beary said.

Then in an even softer voice, "Do you love me?"

Beary was befuddled, "You know I do."

Pompey said with a tear in her eye, "Then do not disgrace me in their eyes. Share the pallet with me. If you are worried we can place some skins between us."

"As you wish, my lady" Beary said.

Pompey wrapped a skin around her then covered her and Beary with another. Soon both were a sleep.

Beary had pleasant dreams for half the night then the terrors returned. His breathing became erratic and he sweated profusely. Pompey woke up, with him moaning. She stroked his head and sang songs in the ancient language. The next morning she got up early and looked for Caesar.

Caesar was setting outside drinking coffee his eyes were blood shot, "Pompey how nice to almost see you, Coffee?"

She smiled, "Some big tough warriors, I hang out with. Caesar I need you to come and check Beary out."

Caesar raised an eye brow. "Why?"

"Please, before the rest of the village stirs." Pompey said.

Beary was up washing his face. Pompey led Caesar in.

"Caesar what's wrong?" Beary asked.

He saw the fleeting fear as Beary's eyes returned to normal.

"Your Mom, just wanted me to give you a once over. Pompey said I could do it now before things get started again." Caesar said looking at Pompey.

Beary smiled. "Alright then the Hot springs."

Caesar checked where his wound had been and his vitals.

"You had a bad night last night didn't you?"

Beary looked at Pompey, "Yes, same bad dreams."

Caesar looked at him, "Don't be angry at Pompey. I saw the fear leave your eyes. You're going to have to face them."

Beary dropped his head. "Alright Caesar I'll try. Now can we hit the hot springs?"

Caesar smiled. "Put a big smile of satisfaction on your face, and hold your lady in your arms as you leave the lodge. I'll sneak out the back. You were just married by their custom do not dishonor their gift."

Beary nodded and kissed Pompey. "Maybe by the third time I'll get it right."

Beary stepped out smiling and holding Pompey to him. Aleut and Lunara came over and put a flowered wreath on Pompey's head and a wreath around Beary's neck and tied their paws together with strings of flowers. Everyone in the village cheered. Aleut turned to his tribe. "I give you Sire and Sirena Maxumus."

"Now you may continue to the hot springs. We will celebrate your wedding tonight!" Aleut said beaming.

Beary smiled. "Thank you Sire Aleut Maritinus for this great honor."

Pompey kissed Aleut and Lunara's cheeks. "Thank you both."

They walked silently, "Ben told me what to do." Pompey said, "You did well for having it dropped on you."

Beary smiled, took her in his arms, and kissed her. She sighed and melted into his arms. He stroked the back of her neck. "When you have been married to the same female as many times as I have you start getting used to it."

They reached the hot springs Ben smiled, as did Artemus, Caesar, and Grizlarge. Ben said, "We thought we would skip this wedding and wait for the next."

Beary slid in as did Pompey. Pompey smiled, "My name at least here is Lady Pompey Maxumus" she said with a twinkle in her eyes. "Tomorrow we all leave for Andreas Prime." She lowered her self-deeper in the water and nuzzled into Beary's chest.

Dontanus Pompaius was in his study trying to grab what he could. He had been tipped off that his assets on Bearilia were seized and that the Security forces were coming after him. A few of his loyalists family members were preparing to defend his estate. He heard the front gates blow open as a division of marines stormed his home. He ran for his personal transport only to be cut off by Octavious Maxumus.

Octavious spoke in a low quite voice, "You tried to have My Cub and his attended murdered Dontanus. That cannot go unpunished."

"Do you think a Maxumus dog can take a Pompaius Lion?" Dontanus challenged.

"Let us see." Octavious said calmly.

A Green sword appeared in Dontanus's paw as did a Blue one in Octavious's paw. Dontanus charged at Octavious who easily parried the blow and countered attacked. Both swords flared as they struck each other. Their battle raged as the Marines moved through the estate. Here and there fierce fire fights broke out. The battle went on for 15 STU, and then just as Dontanus thought he had won Octavious reversed his sword and Drove the blade deep into Dontanus's neck severing his spine.

Octavious removed the green ring and the sword and walked out on a balcony, "Dontanus the traitor is dead! Drop your weapons or die." The remaining Loyalist surrendered. The Marines disarmed them and led them off.

Colonel Rames walked over, "Senator thank you for allowing us to help."

Octavious looked tired, "Did you lose many bears?"

The Colonel smiled, "A few minor injuries, nothing serious."

Octavious sighed "The first and the last of the traitors, so collapses the House of Pompaius."

That night in Ben's village the celebration was off the charts there was entertainment, food, nectar of all kinds, and wild honey on the comb. Again, Artemus was the first to say goodnight followed by Caesar and Grizlarge.

Ben came over "It is time for Lady Maxumus to take you to your lodge, Sir."

Beary looked at him, but Pompey just stood up and offered her paw, which he took. She seemed to float with him holding her paw, as they entered the lodge.

Pompey smiled, "What would my husband ask of me?"

Beary smiled, "To wait just six more days. Until we are wed in our Ancestral Chapel"

Pompey smiled, "As you wish." She went in and put on the warm Pajamas.

She came out Beary was dressed for bed. She pulled back the Skins. "Husband tonight you rest in my arms."

Beary looked at her, "But."

Pompey looked at him, "If the bad dreams come I don't want to fight to get to you. According to my customs and Ben's village we are husband and wife. So come and rest."

Beary knew he had just lost their first disagreement. That night he got the best sleep he had in a long time.

The next morning Tiberius arrived with the shuttle that would take them to the Andreas Dream a fast transport. Pompey had got up early and dressed. She found Artemus talking to Aleut.

"You are a lonely bear. Why not take one of our females for a wife? There are several who would desire you." Aleut smiled.

Artemus smiled, "I would, but I have no land, and no place to walk, or lay my head, I am a Bear of the stars. Perhaps someday that will change."

Aleut smiled, "If not, you are welcome always in our lodges."

Pompey turned away and found Lunara. "Lunara thank you for all your kindness." Pompey said.

Lunara smiled and kissed her. "Where is your Boar?"

"He is still sleeping it is the first goodnight he has had in a week." Pompey said.

"He has dark dreams?" Lunara asked.

"Yes, missions that went well in real life go badly in his dreams and he is powerless to change it. He calls out in his sleep." Pompey said.

Lunara looked at her. "Pompey there is only one cure for the night terrors. You must love him hard and with all your heart."

Pompey smiled, "I will do as you say."

Bandar came up, "My lady it is time to go. Your luggage is loaded. Ensign Maxumus is saying his goodbyes"

Pompey kissed Lunara, "Thank you."

Ben came up and kissed his mother, "I shall return mother before I return to the Academy."

"Stay safe my son." Lunara said.

Beary came and kissed Lunara's paw, "Thank you Lunara."

Tiberius said, "All aboard Bears we are on a schedule."

The trip to the Andreas Dream was fast the Marines were given first class berths. According to Beary it was because that would be the last place a boarding party would look. Artemus, Ben, Caesar, and Grizlarge were given suite berths.

Pompey and Beary's suites were attached. It was a five day trip.

Beary was resting, his mind was wondering and the terrors started up. They were preparing for the wedding all of a sudden Arcrilian fighters attacked. All their guests and family lay bloody at his feet. Pompey slumped in his arms. He screamed.

Pompey flew to his side. This time she started kissing him.

Slowly he woke up. He held her tight and cried as he kissed her.

"It is alright my love I am here." She held him close and hummed.

Slowly Beary came out of it, "Pompey you are alright!"

He looked around. "I am sorry my love."

Pompey smiled, "Let's go eat my love."

Ben and Artemus had set up a small party for the couple.

Artemus smiled. "I guess I missed Beary's bachelor party. I think I was passed out."

Ben smiled, "It was a great time. I really enjoyed it everyone else gave up too early."

Grizlarge smiled. "I am not as young as I use to be."

"As a Doctor I need to stay alert." Caesar protested.

Pompey smiled, "Hello my friends."

Artemus said. "Will you two join us?"

Beary smiled, "We would love to."

Food was brought and the friends talked for cycles. They were still setting when dinner was served.

Beary walked Pompey to her room. He kissed her gently "Goodnight my love. We will see Andreas Prime soon."

Pompey smiled, "Goodnight."

Beary walked slowly to his room and went in. He went in and showered and got dressed for bed. He opened up his bathroom door. Pompey was in her Pajamas. The sheet was pulled back. Beary looked at her. "Pompey, you shouldn't be in here."

Pompey smiled, "Come lay down you need a goodnight's sleep. Besides I need a goodnight sleep. I will sleep better in your arms."

Beary nodded, "Alright my dear."

Beary slept well. He kissed her gently, "Good morning my Lady."

The Andreas Dream landed a few days later in the early morning of the Northern Continent. Beary and Pompey stepped out. Two Dragons floated to the ground. Gamey and Widja bowed their necks "Welcome young Prince, and our Lady."

"Pompey this is Gamey the Brave and..?" Beary said.

Gamey smiled. "This is my betrothed, Widja the wise. We are to be married on the day before."

Beary beamed. "This is great news."

"Sire, we will escort you home." Gamey said.

Artemus and Ben looked at the House of Maxumus. They noticed it looked a whole lot better. Ben turned to Artemus, "It cleaned up real good."

Artemus grinned, "I wonder if they did much to the tower."

Gamey smiled a Dragon's smile, "Artemus of the lost, you can find rest in our halls."

Artemus looked at the purple and red Dragon, "Thank you Gamey the brave."

Gamey nodded then looked at Ben, "Ben Maritinus the Slayer, Peace, be with you."

Ben smiled, "Congratulations to you and Widja may the Creator bless your union."

Gamey roared in Joy.

Caesar saw the black smiths shop and the armors work shop. *This was where his ancestors did their work.*

"Dr. Vantanus welcome home." Gamey said.

"Thank you. Gamey will you place my crest below my families." Caesar asked.

"Please present it to me." Gamey said.

Gamey looked at it and breathed on it then turned to the wall and with a fine flame etched it into the wall. Caesar saw that it had changed. In the Center was a Dragon holding a medical staff. Gamey handed the original back it too had been changed.

Caesar lowered his head. "Gamey, may I live up to the honor of a Dragons blessing."

Gamey smiled, "I know you already have."

"You, Fleet Master Chief Horatio Grizlarge, will you touch my head please." Gamey asked.

Grizlarge put forth his Paw. He felt a flame of heat pulse through his body. "May the Creator, bless you." Gamey said.

Grizlarge felt a change in his body. "Thank you, Gamey the Brave."

"Now, your attendants will show you, your rooms." Gamey said with pride.

Once inside Grizlarge took Caesars arm. "Doc something has happened. I feel 30 years younger."

Caesar smiled, "A Dragons blessing Master Chief. Come to my room in a cycle and I'll check you out."

In a Cave near the Castle a young Priest looked at the Dragon chapel He would be the first to perform such a wedding in 250 years.

Angelina came in "Is everything alright Nephew?"

Father Jacob Augustus turned and kissed his Aunt. "My Empress it is beautiful. It is a great honor."

Angelina smiled, "Jacob, drop the Empress routine, I am just Angelina, the same Aunt that used to change your diapers and wipe your nose."

Jacob smiled, "But even then my dear Aunt you were an Empress to me."

Angelina smiled," Were the renovations to the House of Augustus acceptable."

"Yes and you should see the library! Johnathan is so excited. Old Grey Beard has been helping him find all the hidden records. Father sends his love. He is in the Talus system on a dig. Grandfather joined him." Jacob said.

"We have managed to open six Dragon Chapels and three Dogon. We need more ministers and missionaries." Jacob said. "There are rights to be held for the fallen. The Dragons want proper funerals for the ones they have lost. Not to mention our own." Jacob continued, "But first a wedding!"

"Then another," Angelina smiled.

Jacob smiled, "I am excited about that one also. How is my Cousin?"

Angelina smiled, "He has his war face on, calm and cool. He is scared to death."

Jacob smiled, "I have to get back to work. Don't forget The Empress must attend in full uniform."

Angelina smiled, "Thanks."

That evening the Dragon Counsel arrived and followed Angelina in. Armon the Dogon approached Pompey.

"Lady Pompey, I am Armon head of the Dogon counsel.

Your family's flocks have grown. Some will be culled in a day or two by the Dragons, to prevent sickness. This was arranged by the Empress. Your family's Dogon was killed by a traitor. A young Dogon, Timothy, has been assigned. If he pleases you, he will continue as your family's protector."

"Sire Armon, I will meet with you and him in three days." Pompey smiled. "You and he will please attend my wedding tomorrow but business must wait, as is our custom."

"Armon howled in pleasure, "As you command my Princess." Armon said.

The cave chapel was filled to capacity. Dragon song, in the ancient tongue, filled the air, as they sang to the Creator of the Universe and his Word.

Jacob stood and approached the two Dragons. He placed his paws on their Heads. "We gather here to join Gamey the brave of the House of Maxumus to Widja the wise Protector of the Royal family together. Does anyone challenge this union? The Chapel was quite. Do you Gamey in the presence of family and friends and the Creator above give witness to your love and fidelity to Widja."

Gamey swelled, "I so give my word to protect her with fang and talon, and to raise our young to serve the Creator."

Jacob continued, "Do you Widja submit to Gamey as Sire joining not only yourself to him but also as a remnant of the House of Caesar to the House of Maxumus. Do you pledge your love and fidelity to Gamey in front of family and the Creator?"

Widja swelled, "I give to him all my love and submit to him as my Sire. I will give him a fine brood and will teach them to love the Creator of the Universe."

Jacob continued "By the power given me by the Creator, I pronounce you Sire and Sirena. May you, receive his blessing." A surge of power transferred from one Dragon to the other and back again through his body.

Jacob smiled. "I give you Sire and Sirena Caesar/Maxumus."

The Chapel erupted in songs of praise. After a few moments Jacob raised his hands. "The couple has requested a sermon to be given. I will keep it reasonable. In the beginning was the Word . . ."

When the sermon and wedding was over Grey Talon approached Jacob. "Father Augustus, thank you. We have tried to keep the faith but many of our Dragon priests have past. Would you consider opening a seminary to train Dragon and Dogon priests?"

Jacob smiled, "It can be done if we have a place to build the school."

Grey Talon smiled, "The Empress has given us land we call it Angel land in her honor. A school could be built there."

Jacob nodded "Then you and I will have to see that it is done."

Dragon Celebrations almost rival Ben's villages. Ben dove right in fully enjoying the games and festivities. Artemus took it slower but didn't want to offend his hostess. Widja came over. "Artemus are you enjoying the celebration?" Widja asked.

"Sirena Widja, I am enjoying it very much. However, I have learned to take it slow after spending a month with Ben at his village." Artemus said.

Widja blew a small gold and silver flame around him. "Except a Dragons blessing, Artemus of the lost. Be at peace."

Gamey found Beary who was talking to his father, "Sire Maxumus and young prince, peace and rest."

Octavious smiled "Gamey we are family, are we not, by right you can call me Octavious and Beary by his given name."

Gamey roared in pleasure, "Father, I will serve my family with all my strength. So will my brood, serve our house."

Octavious smiled, "May you be blessed, with many sons and daughters."

Gamey smiled, "Father, may I speak to my brother?"

Octavious nodded and walked away.

Gamey looked at Beary, "Beary this is your house now what do you wish me to do."

Beary thought. "Gamey you are protector of the House. I am a warrior I cannot be here all the time. You will select a staff from the family to run the house and my affairs. Lady Pompey will be here more than I. You will protect her at all cost."

Gamey placed his talon over his heart, "With my life brother."

"Also Gamey as Regent you will give yourself proper compensation as you will the staff." Beary said.

"The fields and slopes will produce a bounty for my brother." Gamey said.

Angelina picked up the com unit.

"Doctor Maxumus's office, Mrs. Maro speaking," Rebeca said.

"Bec it is Angelina I wanted to check with Torrance about Sergeant Fisher's father." Angelina said.

"Dr. Torrance wanted to talk with you." Rebeca said.

"Can you put me through, to him?" Angelina said.

Dr. Torrance picked up his com unit, "Hello, Angelina good to hear from you. Sergeant Fisher's Father has a small tumor in his spine. It is operable if we do it soon. He also had a high level of toxins in his blood. I found it in his well that he used to shower. He was the only one that used it. All other water to the farm was clean. I had to clear his blood and get his strength up. We also sealed the well."

"Can you do the operation?" Angelina asked.

Dr. Torrance had done several. But she was always there if he messed up. Of course he never did. "Yes Angelina. I can remove the tumor. He will require weeks of therapy after the operation."

"No problem, tell Bec to pay all bills he and his family have had to this point. Then keep them current. I don't want them to want for anything." Angelina said.

"You're the Boss. Enjoy the wedding if there are any problems I'll call." Dr. Torrance said.

The morning of the wedding approached. The Star Vandar shined almost as bright as did Pompey. Angelina and Junia were busy preparing her for the Ceremony.

Pompey smiled. "This will be my third wedding in two weeks."

Angelina looked puzzled.

Pompey smiled, "By our Custom we were actually married, when he paid the brides price, which he paid way too much. The contract was completed when a celebration was held. Then in Ben's Village we were married by their customs, now this wedding."

Angelina smiled, "Did anything happen?"

Pompey smiled, "No, I was willing Beary wasn't. He won't have an excuse tonight."

Junia smiled and laughed so did Angelina. "It will be fine my daughter. The Creator will fill your heart with love and knowledge. Just let it happen. Did not the Creator say go forth and multiply."

Beary was very nervous, "Father, I . . . . . . "

Octavious smiled, "I taught you how to be a warrior, and a scholar. I guess I never had any time to explain other things.

Beary it is better you and Pompey, learn these mysteries for yourselves."

"Thanks Dad." Beary said.

Grizlarge was watching "Your Dad is right. Some mysteries need to be discovered on their own."

Ben and Artemus came in wearing their dress uniforms the honey colored ribbons could be seen. Grizlarge came to attention and saluted his Two Bearilian Stars and his Red Rose medallion around his neck.

Octavious helped Beary on with his awards. He carefully placed the Bearilian star and the Rose Medallion around his neck. He stood back and saluted his son.

Colonel Bantic came in, every one saluted him. Then Beary smiled. "Uncle you made it."

"It is good to see you Nephew. And you my friends." Bantic said.

"Sir, is Juristic also here?" Artemus said.

"Yes he is here. He is partaking of drink and food." Bantic said.

"If you will excuse me please," Artemus said. "I'll meet you at the wedding."

The wedding party was coming into the Chapel. Juristic was setting at a table outside when Artemus saw him.

"Juristic, safe wings, and abundant crops" Artemus said.

Juristic smiled. "May the Creator's blessings, be with you."

Father Jacob Augustus looked at Beary and his friends. "May I have a word with Beary?"

"Hello, my Cousin." Beary said.

"Beary do you know your vows?" Jacob asked.

"Yes, I know them. Jacob, have you met Pompey?" Beary asked.

"Yes Angelina introduced us she is beautiful, and intelligent." Jacob said. "You are a very fortunate Boar."

"Yes, I am Jacob." Beary said.

"Beary, Pompey tells me you are having trouble sleeping." Jacob said.

"Just bad dreams, Jacob" Beary said.

"Beary do you trust in your strength or the Creators?" Jacob asked.

"In His strength Jacob" Beary answered.

"Then share your fears with him and with the help mate, he has sent you. Hide nothing not even your fears about tonight." Jacob said.

"Jacob?" Beary responded.

"When two are united by the Creator their spirit and flesh become one. Do you understand?" Jacob said.

"Alright Jacob I will try." Beary said.

The hall was filled. Even a few Dragons and Dogons were in attendance. Pompey was introduced to Timothy by Armon she immediately liked him. "Timothy, will you continue as the guardian of my families flock." Pompey asked.

The Dogon smiled, "It will be my pleasure my Lady. I pledge my life to you and the flock."

Pompey smiled and said. "I will have my Father send you shepherds, to assist you."

Timothy howled in joy. "I will have a true family."

Angelina took Pompey's arm, "Excuse me it is time to go."

Timothy bowed, "My Empress."

Beary took his place with his Best Bears Caesar, Ben, Artemus, and Grizlarge. He looked around the chapel, Commodore Atilus and Captain Centaures was setting on Pompey's family's side of the chapel Lieutenant Bandar and his men were forming an honor guard to escort Pompey and her mother and father in. His Mother was dressed in her ceremonial robs and was seated with his father in her place of honor. His Brothers and sisters and their families were in the front rows on his side. The Dragons and two Dogons were in their places. Members from various houses filled the Chapel.

Jacob took his place and smiled at Beary. The music started playing the Marines came to attention, as a young girl passed through them dropping flower peddles. Pompey and her father appeared Bandar stepped forward and saluted. His Marines formed up and escorted her wedding party down the aisle. When the Party reached the Front of the Church Bandar saluted and he and his men peeled off.

Jacob asked, "Who gives this Female to this Boar?"

"I Sire Pompey and her mother Sirena Pompey do give her paw in marriage." Her father said. He then kissed her and sat down.

Beary stepped forward and took her paw in his. He looked at her. *She wasn't just beautiful he tried to think of a word that covered how she looked. There just wasn't any she was like watching a new star being born.* "You are wonderful. "He whispered.

Pompey blushed and smiled. "Thank you my Liege."

Jacob started talking. "We are gathered here to bring together Beary Maxumus and Priscilla Pompey into the state of holy Matrimony. Does anyone have knowledge of a reason these two should not be joined." The chapel remained silent. "Marriage is a holy state created by the Creator of the Universe that joins two beings into one. To share the good times and the bad times, triumphs and heartaches, laughter and pain. Do you Beary Maxumus swear your love and fidelity to Priscilla Pompey for the rest of your lives?"

Beary looked at Pompey. "I so swear, to love her for the rest of my life, to protect her with all my strength and to raise our cubs in the way of the Creator."

Jacob continued. "Do you Priscilla Pompey swear your love and fidelity to Beary Augustus Maxumus for the rest of your lives?"

Pompey looked into Beary's eyes. "I swear to love him with all my being and strength. To stay always faithful, to rear our cubs to love the Creator, and to serve their family and race."

Jacob smiled, "Give me the rings. By these symbols of love our races are joined. Beary, place this ring on Pompey's paw. Pompey, place this ring on Beary's paw."

Jacob continued, "The rings having been given, and the vows exchanged. By the power given to me by the Creator, I pronounce you Sire and Sirena Beary Maxumus. You may kiss the Bride"

The chapel erupted with applause. Angelina looked at the crowd. "Guests please join us in the banquet hall and court yard to celebrate the union of the young couple."

Angelina and Octavious lead the possession out of the Chapel each of the guests found a place to sit and bears or Dragons to talk to. Food was passed around as was nectar. The young couple came out and mingled with the guests. Gifts were given the young couple.

Commodore Atilus walked up and kissed his goddaughter.

"I guess I have lost a fine Communications officer."

Octavious was standing nearby. "Yes, but I have gained a great language expert and a communications specialist, for my staff. Not to mention a great Daughter-in-law."

Beary walked over. "Thank you for coming Commodore."

"Beary, I brought your orders you are to report in four weeks to the Academy. Base housing is being furnished. You will be teaching Engineering and Astrophysics. You also will be taking your flight training at the same time." Atilus said.

Centaures walked over, "I signed off on command and control and certified you as an officer of the deck. By regulation you still have to make one more cruise next rotation to graduate. So the Academy has you for two years. That is your punishment."

Beary smiled, "Could be worse it will give Pompey and me more time together before I ship out again."

Angelina stepped forward on one of the balconies. "Dear guests you have all been assigned rooms for the evening. Please enjoy your food and drink. It is time for our young couple to say goodnight."

Pompey took his paw. "The Empress has commanded us to retire my husband."

Beary looked at his Mom, yeah she meant it. "We must obey." with that he said goodnight.

Pompey led him up the stairs to a master bedroom and closed the door.

Beary looked at her she was so radiant. "Priscilla, I don't know what to do."

Pompey smiled, "I don't either, but we will figure it out together my love."

That evening they shared each other's passion. Beary fell asleep as she sang to him an old nomadic hymn. The next morning he kissed her forehead. She nuzzled into him.

Pompey looked at him, "What time is it my love?"

Beary looked at the clock on the wall, "0630 cycles."

Pompey smiled "Good we have time to explore the mysteries of love a little more."

At 0800 cycles the young couple came down stairs breakfast was being served. Coronel Bantic and Flight Lieutenant Juristic said their goodbyes.

Ben and Artemus had gone with Pompey's father and Timothy to check out the sheep herd and to do some wild pig hunting.

Commodore Atilus, Captain Centaures, and Fleet Master Chief Grizlarge were leaving in the afternoon for the Saber Claw.

Artemus still had a week of leave coming. He was going to explore Andreas Prime with Ben and Johnathan Augustus.

Angelina held her husband close as they stood on a balcony. "We have to move some stuff into the new castle."

Octavious looked at her, do you want to move here permanently."

Angelina looked out at the sun rise, "No, not now. I will have to set up communications links with the Dragon council and I may have to take a short leave of absence from the hospital for a few months. I have the vacation time built up. Also I can be back and forth in a day or two if need be. I wasn't expecting this responsibility but it is mine."

Octavious smiled, and kissed her forehead, "You will make a great Empress my love."

Two days later Angelina joined Gamey, Widja, and old Gray Beard at a small tower fortress called the hub. It sat at the point where the Houses of Caesar, Maxumus, Augustus, and Angel land met.

Grey Beard spoke, "My Empress this would be a good location for the young Dragons to set up their family. From here they can protect all three lands. I am getting old and am hoping that their first born can be given to me as an apprentice so it will be able to take over my duties."

Angelina smiled, "I agree the hub is to be given to Gamey and Widja. The last request is theirs to make."

Widja spoke up. "It would be my honor to have the egg I am carrying to be instructed by the Great Grey Beard."

Angelina beamed, "You are with child?"

Widja smiled, "Yes, but we need to build a layer to lay our egg."

Angelina smiled. "Then from this time on let the hub, be known as the Layer of Caesar/ Maxumus, and to be handed down to your family. Gamey design a crest and bring it to me when it is done."

"My lady no Dragon has ever had a crest. Only land owners may have crests." Gamey said.

Angelina smiled, "As empress is it not my right? Have I not said that Dragons are no longer slaves but members of the

Family? This fortress now and forever belongs to you along with the responsibility to protect our lands. As family members, joining the house of Caesar and Maxumus you need to have a crest."

Old Grey Beard smiled, "The Empress is a wise leader. May the House of Augustus, be of assistance in designing the crest and a new Crest for your Highness?"

"If you would like to, it would please me." Angelina said.

Chapter 23

Epilogue

Dr. Torrance was successful in his operation on the elder Mr. Fisher. Sergeant Fisher was able to return to his unit.

Artemus returned to the Saber claw and was promoted to Lieutenant Jg and was given command of the Crimson Blade.

Ben arrived at the Academy. Only to find he had been moved to bachelor officers' quarters. He would continue to attend classes but he had also been assigned to teach a class on field craft, and fighting with natural resources.

The Saber Claw had finished retro fit and had left for the Darius system with 6 new destroyers to patrol for pirates.

Sire Pompey had supervised the Dragon curling of the sheep herds. The Dragons got to eat their fill of sheep and the herds were returned to a healthy state.

The Dogons got their wild spring bucks and other wild game.

Sire Pompey put Timothy in charge of his daughters flock and assigned 5 Sheepherders to work with him.

Other families sent young members of their families to manage their flocks and to work with the family Dogons.

Angelina worked out a schedule where she could handle both her responsibilities. She found it was easy to find young members of the Clan that wanted to act as her staff on Andreas Prime.

Work on a Seminary was proceeding along with other needs such as a medical facility for both Maxmimus and Dragon.

Beary and Pompey had explored their home on Andreas prime then headed to the Academy.

They moved into base housing. Beary, checked in, he found out that he wouldn't be taking any more classes at the Academy. Instead he would start Flight training at the nearby Fighter field. Also he would be teaching two undergraduate classes.

He walked into his first Class. He was in his winter uniform with his ribbons on. One cadet saw the ribbon for the Bearilian Star and came to attention soon the entire class came to attention.

Beary had them take their seats he looked around the class. Ben was setting near the back smiling at his friend.

Six months later Beary came home from ground school. Which, he had to complete, before he got to start flying. Pompey had dinner ready.

She smiled a radiant smile. "Beary, I have some news."

"What is it Pompey?" Beary asked.

"We are going to have a Cub." Pompey said.

Beary sat down. "How" Beary asked?"

Pompey smiled an impish smile. "Come upstairs, and I'll explain it to you."

Main Characters

Now I would like to introduce you to our main Characters:

Beary Maxumus, youngest cub of Octavious and Angelina Maxumus a Cub prodigy by 13 he finished his first PHD in Astrophysics by the age of 14 he had received a second PHD from the Vallen Institute for Warp Engineering, where he helped design the Vallen Maxumus CX Warp engine and all its subsystems. At 15 he traveled with his father and had a Marine special Unit assigned to protect him. MSU 6 soon discovered that the young Cub had talents.

Without his father's knowledge they helped him join the Marine reserves at age 16. He took part in several operations including the rescue of a marine unit captured on a planet designated as Pratis V.

For this action he received the Bearilian Star the highest award given for bravery. At the beginning of our story he is between his first and second year at the Bearilian Astrofleet Academy. For his first cruise he has been assigned to a new destroyer The BAF Saber Claw. Call sign Spirit 6.

Octavious Maxumus father of Beary and head of the Maxumus Clan. He is a ranking member of the Bearilian Senate. In his younger days he had been the Commander of the Famed Golden Dragon Fighter Wing but left the military to fight for a change in the way the Bearilian government treated its military. He became head of the Senatorial Investigative service.

Doctor Angelina Maxumus granddaughter of Princess Maria Caesar her maiden name was Augustus. She is also Beary's mother. Angelina is the Chief Neurosurgeon at the Bearilian Institute of medicine. She has 6 other Cubs:

>Alexa a cub Doctor;
>Augustus an Architect;
>Benjamen, a Collage Professor of History;
>Maria, an Elementary Teacher:
>Isaiah, a Foreign Service officer with the Bearilian Government and;
>Beatrice (Beany) a young Lawyer married to Caesar's brother.

Caesar Vantanus the Seventh son of Servitous and Candas Vantorious, A young Doctor trained by Angelina Maxumus and now going through fleet training.

Ben Maritinus, a young Polarian Marine Officer Candidate he is the youngest son of the Chief of the Red Paw Clan. His brother, Captain Dontanus Maritinus was in charge of the Marine Company that fought a rear guard action to give time for the civilian population of Pratis V to evacuate, was rescued by MSU 6.

Aleut Maritinus the Chief of the Red Paw clan and Ben's father.

Lunara Maritinus, Ben's Mother.

Ensign Savato Artemus gunner of the Red Dagger jump ship Crimson Blade. Best Gunner in the fleet. An orphan at a young age knows nothing about himself. Call sign Spirit Blade 2

Commander Jax Centaures, First Officer BAF Saber Claw, also its intelligence officer and longtime partner of its Captain many see him as the counter balance to Captain Atilus. Call sign Red Paw 2

Captain Darius Atilus, Commander of the BAF Saber Claw. He had been the Captain of the BAF destroyer Dagger Claw that held off three Arcrilian Battle cruisers for three days during the evacuation of Pratis V. He loves action but hates the paper work of command. His call sign is Red Paw 1.

Master Chief Gunnery Sergeant Horatio Grizlarge, Chief of the boat BAF Saber Claw. Was the Gunnery Sergeant of Marine Special Unit 6 (MSU 6). He is a heavily decorated Marine with two Bearilian Stars for bravery. He was Beary's mentor and friend, Call sign Spirit 2.

Ensign Priscilla Pompey a female Ursa Maxmimus. She is a communication officer aboard the Saber Claw, also the goddaughter of Captain Atilus. Her father and Mother are wealthy sheepherders and owners of several textile mills.

Sire (Vegus) Pompey head of the Pompey family and Father of Priscilla Pompey. He is wealthy Business Bear and an ex member of the Red Paw Fighter Squadron.

Sirena Pompey (Junia) is Priscilla's mother.

Deloris, Senator Maxumus personal assistant, had been the wife of a Tiberius Maxumus a cousin and childhood friend of Senator Maxumus. He was a member of the Golden Dragon Fighter Wing and was killed in action against the Arcrilians just days before their son was born. Also Angelina's cousin.

Tiberius Maxumus Jr. the son of Deloris and a member of the Bearilian Secret Service Intelligence and Investigative branch. Code name Scarecrow, also part of the Maxumus security team.

Other Bearilians:

Father Jacob Augustus the nephew of Angelina Maxumus and a Priest of the Creator of the Universe and His Word.

Johnathan Augustus the brother of Jacob and nephew of Angelina. He is an archaeologist and a historian.

Rebeca Maro, Angelina's receptionist and childhood friend and Protector.

Lt Commander Wu Fang the Chief Medical Officer BAF Saber Claw.

Lt Commander Tantous the Chief Engineering Officer BAF Saber Claw.

Lt Commander Vesuvius the Civil Engineering Officer BAF Saber Claw.

Marine Major Basil the head of ship Security BAF Saber Claw.

Sergeant Nighthunter, a Marine assigned to Saber Claw.

Sergeant Blackpaw, a Marine Assigned to Saber Claw.

Sergeant MacIntosh the Crew Chief of the Crimson Blade.

General Zantoran Chief of staff Fleet Marines.

Admiral Starpaw the head of Bearilian Fleet Security.

Coronal Rames the Commander of the 308th Knights Division assigned to Carnise Drift.

Major Tan Wu the Commander of the 308th Dagger Squadron.

Captain Northern Commander of the Green Dragon II Fighter Wing.

Commander Laki the Commander of the 248th Space Construction Battalion.

Lieutenant Bandar the Platoon Commander Black Ace 1rst Platoon 307th Division.

Sergeant Fisher, a Marine heavy weapons expert and part of Black Aces 1rst Platoon and his assistant Corporal Moon-Scar.

Dragons of Andreas Prime:

Gamey the Brave protector of the House of Maxumus

Widja the Wise protector of the House of Caesar

Grey Beard protector of the House of Augustus

Timothy, Dogon protector of the Pompey flock

Dragon Council:

Grey Talon, head of the Council.

Dawn Star, young member.

Red Fire is an ancient member on the Dragon council.

Armon is the Dogon representative to the Dragon Council and the Ambassador from the Southern Continent.

Antilleans:

Swarm Coronal Bantic, commander of the Antillean fighter wing, Death Swarm. He is also an old friend of Beary's family and Beary's God Uncle, who taught him to fly a skimmer at the age of 5.

Swarm Coronal Dantic, commander of the Antillean Fighter Wing Dark Swarm.

Captain Redantic the commander of the Antillean Destroyer Death Stinger.

Pro Council Granitic, Prime minister of the Antillean Council.

Terms

Time

Cycle is equal to the time it takes light to travel 1.079×10^9 KSMU

STU Standard Time unit equals the time it takes light to travel 1.798×10^7 KSMU

SUBSTU Sub Standard time unit equals the time it takes light to travel 3.0×10^5 KSMU.

Measurement

SUBSMU is one tenth of SMU.

SMU is a measurement equal to about one meter.

A click is equal to 250 SMU and is a military term.

KSMU is a measurement equal to one thousand SMU.

Main Groups

Arcrilian's—a group of space locust like creatures that invade planets to strip them of their natural resources.

Antilleans—are Ant like creatures that are farmers, and allies of the Bearilians.

Bearilian's—Races of Bears that belong to the Bearilian federation made up of several star systems.

Andreas Prime—Home of the Ursa Maxmimus Race and the Dragons and Dogons that served their families, Third planet in the Vandar system.